D0949356

Falling in Love

Falling in Love

Stories from Ming China

Translated by Patrick Hanan

University of Hawai'i Press
Honolulu

Library of Congress Cataloging-in-Publication Data
Falling in love : stories from Ming China / translated by
Patrick Hanan.
p. cm.
ISBN-13: 978-0-8248-2995-7 (pbk. : alk. paper)
ISBN-10: 0-8248-2995-6 (pbk. : alk. paper)
1. Chinese fiction—Ming dynasty, 1368–1644—Translations
into English. 2. Love in literature. I. Title: Stories from
Ming China. II. Hanan, Patrick.
PL2658.E8F38 2006
895.1'3460803543—dc22   2006000849

University of Hawai'i Press books are printed on acid-free
paper and meet the guidelines for permanence and durability
of the Council on Library Resources.

Designed by University of Hawai'i Press production department

Printed by Versa Press

Contents

Introduction

These seven outstanding vernacular stories are drawn from two Ming collections, *Xing shi hengyan* (Constant words to awaken the world), first published in 1627, and *Shi dian tou* (The rocks nod their heads), of approximately the same date. All seven stories deal with falling in love, and some with marriage as well.

Marriage in traditional China was decided by the family heads, while the details of the marriage contract were generally negotiated by a go-between. The process consisted of six steps (the "Six Rites"), the first three of which were preliminary: the overture by the boy's family, the request for the girl's horoscope, and the matching of horoscopes. The fourth step was the crucial one, the delivery of the agreed-upon betrothal settlement to the girl's family. It sealed the engagement; thereafter, although the girl lived at home until her wedding, she could almost be said to belong to the boy's family. In the fifth step his family proposed an auspicious date for the wedding, a date that, by convention, the girl's family accepted. In the sixth and final step the groom (or in some cases the go-between) escorted the bride with her trousseau to the groom's house, where they first worshiped heaven and earth, kowtowed to the groom's ancestral tablets, bowed to each other, and kowtowed to his parents. Soon afterward the bride's veil was removed, and she and her husband were able to look into each other's eyes for the first time. On the third day, the couple visited her parents and kowtowed to them, then returned to his family's compound to live. This system survived into the early years of the twentieth century.

In a significant variation, the groom married into the bride's family and lived in their household. This was most likely to occur when the girl's family had no sons to perform the ancestral sacrifices. The boy generally came from a poorer family with more than one son.

In broad outline, allowing for certain other differences due to time, place, and social class, these were the normal marriage procedures for Chinese families of some financial means, at least among the Han majority of the population, during most of the imperial period. The main difference concerned the bride's trousseau, which could sometimes take the form of a dowry as large as, or larger than, the betrothal settlement.[1] Needless to say, the size of such a dowry was also negotiated in advance.

Since marriage was primarily an alliance between two families in which social status and money were basic criteria, the choice of marriage partners was considered too important to be left to the individuals themselves. So far as possible, girls were segregated from boys at an early age and kept away from outsiders, at least until marriage. If they left the house at all, it was on some special occasion, such as a visit to a local temple to worship. Engagements were entered into early, so that the girl had a name to fix her thoughts on. Weddings were also held early, fourteen being an acceptable age for a bride. These measures were meant to ensure that on her wedding day she could be delivered to her fiancé as a virgin.

It was therefore highly unlikely that a girl and a boy could manage to see each other, fall in love,[2] consummate that love, and then either elope or else persuade their parents to let them marry. If the lovers were already engaged to other people, as they would probably have been, the cancellation of the engagements, with four sets of parents to placate and two settlements to return, would have been difficult, if not impossible. And weighing on everybody's minds the whole time would have been the fear of public ridicule.

Yet this highly unlikely chain of events becomes a reality in much Chinese fiction.[3] (At least, the falling in love becomes a reality; the romance sometimes turns tragic.) Popular song down through the ages had always been much concerned with clandestine assignations, but rarely dealt with the social consequences. The classic anecdotes of love leading to marriage were those concerning the poet Sima Xiangru of the second century, who fell in love with the young widow Zhuo Wangsun and eloped with her, and Han Shou of the following century, who fell in love with Jia Chong's daughter and consummated the affair in Jia's own house. Zhuo Wangsun's father eventually forgave the eloping couple, and Jia Chong decided to hush the matter up and marry his daughter to her lover. Both anecdotes involved only a parent of the girl, not the boy. The Tang dynasty tale "Yingying zhuan" (The tale of Yingying)[4] by Yuan Zhen (779–831), source of the famous play *Xixiangji* (The west chamber),[5] also involves only a parent of the girl. From that time on, an increasing number of classical tales (short fiction in literary Chinese) were written with the same kind of subject matter, as well as an increasing number of plays. In the landmark collections of vernacular stories made by Feng Menglong (1574–1646), of which *Constant Words to Awaken the World* was the third, and in the work of some of Feng's imitators, such as *The Rocks Nod Their Heads*, romantic love is one of the main themes.

This paradox—a prescribed practice of arranged marriage existing alongside an imaginative literature glorifying romantic love—was hardly peculiar to China; arranged marriages were the norm in most cultures until modern times, and romantic love was a staple literary theme in many of them. Of course, like most fiction, Chinese realistic fiction never tried to represent the commonplace as such, but rather to show an extraordinary event or series of events occurring against a *background* of the commonplace. Still, in China the difference between the prescribed practice and the extraordinary events of the romantic theme was singularly stark.

Lawrence Stone, in his study of marriage in England between 1500 and 1800, sets out a scheme of four "basic options" for the choice of marriage partners that is useful in considering the Chinese situation. The options may be restated as follows: parental choice without input from the children; parental choice with the children holding a veto; choice by the children with the parents holding a veto; and choice by the children with the parents informed but not consulted.[6] Almost all marriages in traditional China resulted from the first option: they were arranged by the parents without any input from their children. Only in the early decades of the twentieth century did the fourth option gradually become dominant. Of the motives for choice of partner cited by Stone (economic, social, or political interest; personal affection between the prospective bride and groom; physical attraction; and romantic love "as portrayed in fiction and on the stage"), only the first applied in traditional China. Yet the stories deal almost exclusively with the third and fourth motives, those of physical attraction and romantic love.

Since in principle there was little possibility of setting eyes on an eligible partner, let alone of meeting him or her, courtship was out of the question. Only with courtesans, by which I mean high-level prostitutes of particular beauty and talent, was courtship possible or indeed necessary; see the story translated as "The Oil Seller," of which courtship forms the main topic. In other romantic fiction access is the great problem, in contrast to comparable European literature. The Romeo and Juliet theme, for example, is often given as the classic literary case of young love thwarted by parents, but in Luigi da Porto's novella "Romeo and Giulietta," Romeo attends a masked ball given by Giulietta's father. She admires him and he joins her in a dance, and afterwards they exchange loving glances "at church and in windows."[7] He then makes a practice of sitting on the balcony outside her window until one night she discovers him there, and so forth. Similar opportunities abound in the version by Matteo Bandello[8] as well as in Shakespeare's play. But such a degree of access was unimaginable in Chinese fiction, let alone in Chinese life. A Chinese Romeo was unlikely to be able to see his Juliet, let alone to serenade her. And with regard to the masked ball, as late as 1904 the Chinese translation of a French novel happened to mention one, and the commentator promptly condemned it as a threat to Chinese morals.[9]

With almost no opportunity to meet, lovers had to resort to elaborate stratagems and risky escapades. (Part of the pleasure for the reader of these stories comes from the romantic adventure itself; a reader's interest in fiction is commonly driven by either fear or desire, and these stories provide both.) Young people fall in love at first sight, and if there is no way to consummate their love, they sometimes become physically ill. When they do meet, usually in tense situations, there is no time for the niceties of courtship; they make love immediately and then swear undying fidelity. The lovemaking is rapturous and the relationship unproblematic. The lovers are strikingly beautiful and talented, of course, and they often receive the special dispensation reserved for such paragons. The whole remarkable affair is set within a story of painstakingly realistic detail.

Although realistic romantic fiction—as distinct from the countless Chinese tales of love between young men and supernatural beings—goes back at least to the eighth century, there are reasons why it became particularly important in Feng Menglong's time. One strain of late Ming thought exalted the role of *qing* (the passions, especially passionate love). Feng himself inspired the compilation of an anthology titled *Qing shi leilüe* (The anatomy of love), a classified anthology of tales and anecdotes, many of which deal with romantic love. All seven of the stories in this volume are represented in the anthology in some fashion, either by analogues, reprinted sources, or simple references. The commentator on *Qing shi leilüe* takes a notably tolerant attitude toward behavior that was, by any contemporary definition, immoral. At the end of the reprinted source of "The Reckless Scholar," for example, he says nothing about the immorality of the elopement and merely notes what a risk the girl took in trusting her lover's word; he might well have been married already, and to a jealous wife at that.[10]

The evident sympathy of the authors for the romantic aspirations of their heroes and heroines stands in sharp contrast to mainstream ethical values. A copious literature of books and pamphlets existed in this period that condemned *all* fiction and drama, not because of their fictive nature, but because of the dubious moral examples that they chose to present.[11] As late as 1905, an article appeared in the influential journal *Xin xiaoshuo* (New fiction) deploring the influence on Chinese youth of the heroines of such popular translated novels as *La dame aux camélias* by Alexandre Dumas fils, *Joan Haste* by H. Rider Haggard, and *A Double Thread* by Ellen Thorneycroft Fowler. The writer expresses his concern that within a few decades such practices as kissing in public would become commonplace in

China.[12] And in 1906 the novelist Wu Jianren blamed *The West Chamber* and *The Story of the Stone* (*Shitou ji,* also known as *Honglou meng*), the most famous play and the most famous novel in the Chinese tradition, for misleading readers about the proper role of *qing*.[13]

But just because readers relished the romantic adventure in these stories, we cannot say that they subscribed to a romantic ethic of individualistic love. The desires of the imagination are not necessarily constrained by social values. However, the narrator in most of these vernacular stories still had to present himself as a custodian of traditional morality.[14] (Narrators in the classical tale, a fictional form that was directed at a more selective readership, seldom adopted such a role). Much as the vernacular writers sympathized with the desires of their young lovers, they also felt that the romantic theme had to be explained away or deplored.[15] If a love affair resulted in a successful marriage in defiance of moral values, they sometimes had their narrators resort to karmic myth, explaining the marriage as the consequence of a romantic liaison in a previous life, and as such, beyond the reach of moral law and custom.[16] If the love affair turned tragic, of course, the tragedy itself could be presented to readers as a salutary warning.

෴

All seven stories contain the theme of falling in love.[17] Each starts with an extraordinary situation and follows it up with ingenious plotting and an unexpected denouement. It is worth noting that most of the romantic heroes and heroines have no brothers or sisters; the purpose, I think, is to place the conflict between children and their parents, particularly their fathers, in the harshest possible light.

Two stories are at a certain remove from the others. "The Lovers' Tombs" is a homosexual love story of two students, both of whom are already engaged to young women. It is not the earliest fictional account of homosexual love in China, but it is the first in the vernacular and also the first to be worked out in terms of its social repercussions. "The Oil Seller" tells of a love affair between a young man and a courtesan. Prostitutes were the only women to whom a young man had ready access before his marriage—apart, perhaps, from the maids in his father's house. While dalliance with a prostitute was not regarded as a very serious matter in itself, marriage to a former prostitute meant allying the family with a person who, no matter how much fame and money she might have acquired, was not of respectable stock; in fact, until she married, she belonged to a separate, lower caste. The standard reference is "Li Wa zhuan" (The tale of Li Wa)[18] by Bai Xingjian (775–826), a classical tale that is briefly recounted in the prologue to "The Oil Seller." But the main story of "The Oil Seller" is very different. The hero's father has given up his son for adoption and gone off to serve in a monastery. The problem for the hero, gripped as he is by an obsessive desire to sleep with the famous courtesan, is that his social status as a humble oil seller is far below hers, even though as a prostitute she belongs to a lower caste.

Most vernacular stories of this period draw on much shorter accounts in literary Chinese.[19] At least two of the seven stories, "The Rainbow Slippers" and "The Reckless Scholar," were developed from full-blown classical tales (see the translations "Zhang Jin" and "The Provincial Graduate," in the appendix). The tales read almost like scenarios that the stories have filled out with detailed settings, incident, motivation, and commentary, and to which they have added an extra level of moral meaning.

We do not know the identity of the authors of the stories, but we can say something about their dates of composition. "Shengxian" was written much earlier than the others, probably as early as the fourteenth century. Readers will notice certain features that tend to set it apart. It is a great deal more terse. Its prologue (consisting of an introductory poem and some prose) is not a moral pronouncement; rather, it sets the scene for the meeting of hero and heroine. And as the romance progresses, warnings of dire consequences are issued at every step.

The other stories were all written much later, at about the time the collections were made, and probably *for* the collections. "Marriage Destinies Rearranged," "The Rainbow Slippers," and "Wu Yan" are almost certainly by a single author (who was not Feng Menglong).[20] "The Reckless Scholar" and "The Lovers' Tombs" are probably by a second author.[21]

The connections of "The Reckless Scholar" and "The Lovers' Tombs" to the work of Li Yu (1611–1680) are worth noting. Li Yu, who wrote stories as well as the novel *The Carnal Prayer Mat*,[22] was the great exponent of the comic erotic mode in Chinese fiction. "The Reckless Scholar," in particular, has a nexus of characters and events that we can discern, vastly transformed, in *The Carnal Prayer Mat*. Master Si, the flinty, scrupulously honest, parsimonious, unsociable retired official with the beautiful daughter almost certainly suggested to Li Yu the character Iron Door. Master Si's daughter, Ziying, is having an affair with someone hidden in her bedroom. To avoid discovery, they abscond together, taking with them Ziying's maid, whom her lover has also seduced. This resembles Quan's affair with Iron Door's daughter Jade Scent and her maid Ruyi in *The Carnal Prayer Mat*. Again, Master Si is so afraid to acknowledge the fact of the elopement that he fakes his daughter's funeral, just as in the novel. I also believe that the talented young rake who is the hero of this story supplied Li Yu with ideas for Vesperus (Weiyang Sheng) in *The Carnal Prayer Mat*. (Note how he patrols the temple in search of girls.) Unlike many other authors of vernacular fiction, Li Yu did not depend directly on literary sources in writing his fiction,[23] but he had close relations with previous literature, as these examples show.

Similarly, "The Lovers' Tombs" exerted some influence on Li Yu's stories of homosexual love, especially "The Male Mencius's Mother" in *Silent Operas* (Wusheng xi) and "House of Gathered Refinements" in *Twelve Lou* (Shi'er lou).[24] I mean particularly the stories' multiple voices on the subject of homosexuality: orthodox condemnation, vulgar raillery, romantic sympathy.

৯৯

The form of the stories also deserves attention. Each story begins with a prologue, which consists of a sententious poem followed by a short piece of prose. Some stories, such as "The Reckless Scholar," extend the prose into a brief essay that sets the theme within the Chinese tradition, while others add a short introductory story that prefigures in some fashion the theme of the main story.

Like the prologue, the main story is conventionally represented as told by a storyteller, who in these stories at least is a generic figure without any personal characteristics. Occasionally, the storytelling simulation is carried a step further, and a question is put to the storyteller by a member of the imaginary audience, as in "Wu Yan," when it becomes necessary to explain how the heroine managed to peep through the door at the hero despite her mother's presence in the room. The operations of narration—changes of focus or time, switches between scene and summary, explanations, projections into the future, and so forth—are all performed by the narrator with the use of well-established phrases. There is a pronounced element of commentary by the narrator, particularly on the moral significance of the action.

The commentary may be embodied in the couplets or short poems that are interspersed throughout the text and offer proverbial wisdom, moral judgment, or wry criticism. The couplets and poems come at key points, usually after significant plot developments. But originally they were at least partly designed to serve a purpose that is no longer relevant. The Chinese chapter was printed in one long paragraph—except for couplets, poems, and descriptive set pieces, all of which were indented—and thus these forms served to break up the text.

Descriptive set pieces are unrhymed compositions that make use of strict parallelism. They are generally euphuistic, using inflated language and classical allusion. In these stories they are used for describing such subjects as personal beauty or lovemaking.

Each story ends with a sententious epilogue poem reflecting on its meaning.

An interesting feature of two of the stories ("The Oil Seller" and "The Lovers' Tombs") is their use of popular song. In the sixteenth and seventeenth centuries, in particular, certain popular song forms captured the imagination of literary intellectuals, who collected existing songs and also wrote their own songs to the same tunes. Feng Menglong made two collections, including one of songs to the tune "Guazhi'er" (Hanging branch), which was popular in much of China and which was commonly composed in Mandarin. The tune could be used either for romantic expression or for satire. When the courtesan in "The Oil Seller" realizes that she is in love with the oil seller, she expresses her thoughts to herself in the form of a *Guazhi'er* song, and in both stories young men use the same tune for bawdy raillery.

ߝ

I am grateful to David Rolston for his detailed reading of the translation. I am also indebted, as ever, to Anneliese Hanan for her assistance.

NOTES

1. On dowries during the Song dynasty, see Patricia Buckley Ebrey, *The Inner Quarters, Marriage and the Lives of Chinese Women in the Sung Period* (Berkeley: University of California Press, 1993), pp. 99–113.

2. I am leaving the term "falling in love" undefined, without speculating whether—or rather, to what extent—the effect of love is produced by cultural or biochemical factors. Chinese thinking distinguished between love and mere sexual desire—*qing* and *se*, respectively. Falling in love at first sight was called *yi jian zhong qing*.

3. There is also a copious literature that glorifies heroic fidelity to an engagement, even though the engaged couple have never even met; an outstanding example is "The Unbreakable Marriage Bond of Chen Duoshou," the ninth story in *Constant Words to Awaken the World*. The vernacular fiction of the Qing dynasty, especially the so-called *caizi jiaren* novels (novels of the brilliant and beautiful, also known as scholar-beauty romances), show great ingenuity in exploiting certain aspects of the romance while claiming to adhere to the accepted morality.

4. See the translation by James R. Hightower in Victor H. Mair, ed., *The Columbia Anthology of Traditionial Chinese Literature* (New York: Columbia University Press, 1994), pp. 851–861, or that by Ste-

phen Owen in Owen, ed., *An Anthology of Chinese Literature* (New York: Norton, 1996), pp. 540–549.

5. See Stephen H. West and Wilt L. Idema, trans., *The Moon and the Zither* (Berkeley: University of California Press, 1991).

6. Lawrence Stone, *The Family, Sex and Marriage in England 1500–1800* (New York: Harper and Row, 1977), pp. 270–271.

7. Harry Levtow and Maurice Valency, *The Palace of Pleasure, An Anthology of the Novella* (New York: Capricorn Books, 1960), p. 132.

8. See William Painter, trans., *The Palace of Pleasure* (New York: Dover Publications, 1966), vol. 3, pp. 80–124.

9. See Zhou Guisheng's translation, titled *Du she quan*, of Fortuné du Boisgobey's *Margot la Balafrée*, *Xin xiaoshuo* 18:126. The commentator was the novelist Wu Jianren.

10. See "Mo Juren," *Qing shi leilüe, juan* 3 (Shenyang: Chunfeng wenyi chubanshe, 1986), 1: 82–83. The source story is translated in the appendix to this volume, under the title "The Provincial Graduate," together with the commentator's remarks.

11. See, for example, the sources excerpted in Wang Liqi, *Yuan Ming Qing sandai jinhui xiaoshuo xiqu shiliao*, rev. ed. (Shanghai: Shanghai guji chubanshe, 1981), pp. 167–430.

12. Jin Songcen, "Lun xieqing xiaoshuo yu xin shehui zhi guanxi" (On the relationship of romantic fiction to the new society), *Xin xiaoshuo* 17 (sixth month, 1905).

13. In the notes to his novel *Hen hai*. See Patrick Hanan, trans., *The Sea of Regret* (Honolulu: University of Hawai'i Press, 1995), introduction, pp. 4–5.

14. Note that the titles of both collections suggest a moral purpose. *The Rocks Nod Their Heads* title refers to the myth of a Buddhist priest in Hangzhou who preached his message so eloquently that the very rocks nodded their heads. Among the stories translated here, "Shengxian" is the exception; it contains several warnings, but not of the moral variety. It is significant that it is also much earlier than the rest of the stories.

15. On this subject, see C. T. Hsia, "Society and Self in the Chinese Short Story," included as an appendix to his *Classic Chinese Novel* (New York: Columbia University Press, 1968), pp. 299–321.

16. As in "Wu Yan" and, particularly, "The Reckless Scholar." Note that the source of the latter story, the classical tale "Mo Juren," does

not mention the karmic level at all; see the translation titled "The Provincial Graduate" in the appendix to this volume.

17. Some of them might be considered stories of seduction ending in mutual love.

18. See Glen Dudbridge, *The Tale of Li Wa, Study and Critical Edition of a Chinese Story from the Ninth Century* (London: Ithaca Press, 1983).

19. Sun Kaidi, in his *Xiaoshuo pangzheng* (Beijing: Renmin wenxue chubanshe, 2000), assembled the putative sources and analogues of the stories in both of these collections.

20. See my *Chinese Short Story: Studies in Dating, Authorship, and Composition* (Cambridge, MA: Harvard University Press, 1973), pp. 70–72. For a study of the genre of the vernacular story, see my *Chinese Vernacular Story* (Cambridge, MA: Harvard University Press, 1981).

21. There are distinct stylistic similarities—as well as significant differences—between twenty-odd *Xing shi hengyan* stories (including "Marriage Destinies Rearranged," "The Rainbow Slippers," and "Wu Yan") and the *Shi dian tou* stories. In *The Chinese Short Story* I argued that both sets of stories were probably by the same author, whom in *The Chinese Vernacular Story* I referred to as Langxian. However, the thesis of common authorship is far from proven, and I think it prudent here to consider the two sets of stories as by separate authors.

22. See my translation (Honolulu: University of Hawai'i Press, 1996). It should be distinguished from another translation that borrowed the title "Carnal Prayer Mat" from mine. (The latter is actually a reissue of an old and inadequate translation from the German.)

23. It should be noted that the story "I Want to Get Married" told by Aunt Flora in chapter 17 of *The Carnal Prayer Mat* comes from a tale of that name ("Nu yao jia"). It is found in *juan* 1 of the *Xuanxuan pian*, a Ming collection compiled by Xiaozhu Zhuren and edited by Deng Zhimo that is preserved in the Naikaku Bunko in Tokyo. As told by Aunt Flora, however, the story is somewhat changed and owes nothing textually to its source.

24. Gopal Sukhu and Patrick Hanan, trans., in Hanan, ed., *Silent Operas* (Hong Kong: Research Centre for Translation, Chinese University of Hong Kong, 1990), pp. 99–134; and Hanan, trans., in *A Tower for the Summer Heat* (New York: Columbia University Press, 1998), pp. 83–115.

Falling in Love

1

Shengxian

In times of peace the festive days stretch out
With music, song, and wine that's freely poured.
But once the royal carriage is on its way,
The people rub their eyes and await their lord.

*T*his verse sings the praises of the emperor's personal attendance at public festivals. Wherever an emperor established his capital, the outstanding people gathered there would complement the marvelous site, whose scenic beauty would enhance the enjoyment of all. The Tang dynasty, for example, had its Qujiang Pond and the Song dynasty its Jinming Pond,[1] each of which offered a glorious spectacle all year round. Young lords and ladies from the city, beautiful girls and brilliant youths, would go there to promenade and disport themselves. And from time to time the emperor himself would put in an appearance and take his pleasure among the people.

My story begins with an establishment called the Fan Tavern,[2] which was beside the Jinming Pond of the Eastern Capital.[3] It happened during the reign of Emperor Huizong of the Great Song Dynasty.[4] The tavern's owner was one Fan Dalang, who had an unmarried younger brother named Erlang.[5] Spring was just giving way to summer, and beside Jinming Pond the visitors were out enjoying themselves. Fan Erlang joined them

The full title is "A Passionate Zhou Shengxian Causes an Uproar in the Fan Tavern." It is no. 14 in *Constant Words to Awaken the World.*
   1. The former was outside the Tang capital of Chang'an, modern Xi'an; the latter was outside the Northern Song capital of Bianjing, modern Kaifeng.
   2. Fanlou, the name of an actual tavern or restaurant of that time.
   3. I.e., Bianjing, modern Kaifeng.
   4. R. 1100–1125.
   5. "Dalang" is a name given to the eldest son, "Erlang" to the second son.

there, and after observing the crowds of beautiful women and brilliant men, he called at a tea shop, where he noticed a girl who was just seventeen years old[6] and simply gorgeous. For a long time he stood rooted to the spot, gazing raptly at her.

> Alluring beauty!
> Alluring beauty!
> Easy to feel its spell,
> Hard to cast it aside.
> Ensconced in secret boudoirs,
> Hidden along willowed paths.
> On tiny feet she lightly goes,
> Her slender waist a virtual wisp,
> Soft cheeks reflecting the peach trees' red;
> Fragrant flesh gleaming a jade-like white.
> Alas, her grace stirs the reckless youngster,
> Her charm attracts the romantic stranger.
> Within the flowered screen the lovebirds are at play,
> Where would you go now to find the clouds and the rain?[7]

Now, romantic passion and sexual desire are both things beyond our control. The two young people in the tea shop gazed into each other's eyes and promptly fell in love. The girl's heart was filled with secret joy as she thought to herself, How marvelous if I could marry a young fellow like that! If I let this chance slip away, who knows when I'll get another? Then the thought struck her: How can I draw him into conversation and find out if he's married or not? Her young maid and her nurse,

---

6. Eighteen in Chinese. In these translations, ages have been lowered by a year to approximate to Western reckoning.

7. This is in the form of a pyramid poem *(jinzita shi)*, which is composed of pairs of lines of steadily increasing length, in this case from one syllable to seven. (The translation runs from five to twelve.) The pyramid poem was a form commonly used in literary games. This one starts off in exactly the same way as a pyramid poem in another early story, "Cui yanei bai yao zhao yao" (Master Cui courts disaster with his white falcon), no. 19 in *Jingshi tongyan*, a companion anthology. The latter story contains as many as nine pyramid poems; in fact, it may be described as built on pyramid poems. It is likely, therefore, if direct borrowing is involved, that the author of "Shengxian" borrowed it from there, rather than the other way around. "Clouds and rain" refers to sexual intercourse.

who had accompanied her to the tea shop, had no inkling of what was going through her mind.

By a remarkable coincidence, just at that point she heard a soft-drink vendor with his pails of drink outside the door. She wrinkled her brow in thought—and an idea occurred to her.

"Pour me some sweet water, would you?" she called to the vendor. He poured a cupful into a brass beaker and handed it to her, but she took one sip and threw the beaker into the air, crying, "Oh, no! What a dirty trick you've played on me! Just who do you think I am?"

I'd better listen to what she's saying, thought Fan Erlang.

"I'm the daughter of Zhou Dalang from Cao Gate. Miss Shengxian's my name, and I'm seventeen years old. I've never been tricked in all my life, and now *you* have to come along and try it on! And I'm not married, either!"

What she is saying sounds very odd, thought Fan. It must be for my benefit.

"Now look here, Miss!" said the vendor. "I wouldn't dream of tricking you!"

"But that's exactly what you did!" exclaimed the girl. "I found a blade of grass in my cup."

"Oh, that won't do you any harm."

"You were trying to scratch my throat. It's a pity my father's away. If he were home, he'd bring charges against you."

"Beastly man!" put in the nurse at her side, referring to the vendor.

A waiter heard the upraised voices in the tea shop and came over. "You can take your business outside," he said to the vendor.

From his position opposite the girl, Fan thought to himself, Since she's favoring me like this,[8] I'll have to respond. So he, too, called out to the vendor. "I'll have a cup of sweet water." The vendor poured him one. Fan took one mouthful, then threw the cup in the air, and cried, "Oh, no! You really *are* playing tricks on us! Just who do you think I am? I'm the brother of the Fan Dalang who owns the Fan Tavern. Fan Erlang's my name, I'm

---

8. In later editions, *guo xing* (showing extraordinary favor) was changed to *an di* (dropping hints).

eighteen, and I've never been tricked in my life. I'm a fair shot with a bow and a pretty good man with a bat. And I'm not married, either."

"*Are you out of your mind?*" cried the vendor. "What's the point of telling me all this? Do you expect me to play *matchmaker* for you? Go ahead and bring your charges—I sell drinks, I tell you, I'm not trying to trick anybody!"

"Of course you are! There was a blade of grass in my cup, too." The girl thrilled to hear these words.

The waiter came up and pushed the vendor out the door.

The girl got to her feet and said, "Come on, let's go home!" Then she glared at the vendor. "Don't you dare follow us," she said.

She clearly means me to follow her, thought the young man.

Because he did follow her, a crime occurred that defied solution.

> Save your words when you can;
> Halt your steps when it's right.

When the girl had had a chance to get some way off, Fan emerged from the tea shop and caught sight of her in the distance. He was thrilled to see her look back at him, and followed her all the way to her house. She went in, pushed aside the door curtains, and peered out, which gave him an even greater thrill. Then she went into the inner quarters, and Fan, like someone who had lost his mind, walked endlessly back and forth outside her door until evening, when he finally went home.

After returning that day, the girl refused to eat any food whatsoever, saying that she felt unwell.

"Did she have anything raw or cold to eat while she was out?" her anxious mother asked the maid who had accompanied her.

"No, ma'am, she didn't eat a thing."

When the girl had spent several days in bed, her mother came to her bedside and asked, "Well, what *is* the matter with you?"

"I feel sore all over, I have a headache, and also a slight cough."

Mrs. Zhou would have liked to call in a doctor to examine her, but with her husband away and no man in the house, she did not dare.

"Two doors away there's a Mrs. Wang," said her maid. "Why don't we get her to come over and look at the young mistress? She's known as Can-Do Wang—she delivers babies, does needlework, and arranges marriages, but she also knows how to read your pulse and tell if your illness is serious or not. Whenever the neighbors have the slightest complaint, they call her in." Mrs. Zhou sent the maid over to invite Mrs. Wang, who came in and paid her respects. Mrs. Zhou then explained that her daughter had been confined to bed ever since returning from a visit to the Jinming Pond.

"You needn't say another word, ma'am," said Mrs. Wang. "Let me just check her pulse."[9]

"Of course."

The maid showed Mrs. Wang into her daughter's room. As they entered, the girl, who had been asleep, opened her eyes and said, "Oh, I'm *so* sorry!"

"I don't mean to disturb you. I just want to read your pulse." The girl stretched out her arm.

"You're suffering from a headache, you're sore all over, and you're feeling run down and nauseous," Mrs. Wang declared, after checking her pulse.

"That's right," said the girl.

"But is that all?"

"Well, I do have a slight cough."

Had Mrs. Wang never heard these words, nothing would have happened.[10]

"This is a very strange illness," she commented. "How could anyone go on an outing and then come back with symptoms like these?" She turned to the maid and nurse. "Could you leave us alone for a moment? There's something I want to ask the young mistress."

9. Taking the pulse is the basic diagnostic method in Chinese traditional medicine.
10. This is a formula found mainly in early stories, highlighting the fact that some unspecified disaster is going to follow from this apparently trivial event.

"I know what you're suffering from," Mrs. Wang said, once the maid and nurse had left the room.

"How could you possibly know?"

"You have what's called an illness of the heart."

"How could that be?"

"Miss, before you came down with this illness, did you by any chance get a thrill from seeing someone at the pond? Could that be what happened?"

The girl hung her head and denied it.

"Look, miss, tell me the truth, and I'll find a way to save your life."

When she heard these welcome words, the girl told her all that had happened. "The young man's name is Fan Erlang," she concluded.

"You don't mean Fan Erlang from the Fan Tavern?"

"That's right."

"Then you can set your mind at rest. Anyone else I mightn't have known, but I happen to be well acquainted with Fan Erlang's brother and his wife, and fine people they are, too. And what a bright young fellow that Erlang is! His brother has asked me to look out for a wife for him. Now, let's just suppose I were to enable you to marry him, miss. Would you want that?"

"Oh, that would be marvelous," said the girl with a smile. "But I'm afraid my mother would never agree."

"Trust me, I know how to go about it. There's no need to worry."

"If you can do that for me, I'll see that you get a handsome reward."

Mrs. Wang returned to Mrs. Zhou and announced, "I know what your daughter's trouble is."

"Well, what is it?"

"Before I tell you, you'll have to pour me three cups of wine."

Mrs. Zhou called to the maid, "Bring some wine for Mrs. Wang." As she invited her to drink, she kept pressing for an answer. "And so what is she is suffering from?"

Mrs. Wang related everything that the girl had told her.

"Whatever am I going to do?" asked Mrs. Zhou.

"The only thing you can do is marry her to him," replied Mrs. Wang. "Unless you do, she won't recover."

"But I can't possibly do that with my husband away!"

"Look, ma'am, why not arrange the betrothal now but put off the wedding until your husband returns? You'd be saving your daughter's life—right here and now."

"Very well, then. But how do we set about it?"

"I'll go over and talk to them, then report back." Leaving the Zhou house, Mrs. Wang made her way to the Fan Tavern, where she found Fan Dalang behind the counter. After they had exchanged greetings, Dalang remarked, "Mrs. Wang, you've come just at the right time. I was on the point of sending for you."

"Why, may I ask?"

"Erlang went out a couple of days ago and wouldn't eat any supper after he came back. He said he didn't feel well. I asked him where he'd been, and he told me the Jinming Pond. Ever since then he's stayed in bed and not touched any food or drink. I was going to ask you to come and read his pulse."

Fan Dalang's wife came out and greeted Mrs. Wang. "Do come and look at my brother-in-law," she said.

"You are not to come in," Mrs. Wang said to Dalang. "I want to ask him myself how he came down with this illness."

"Very well," said Dalang. "You go in and see him alone. I'll stay out here."

Mrs. Wang found Erlang lying on his bed. "Erlang, it's me," she called out.

"Oh, Mrs. Wang," he replied, opening his eyes. "It's such a long time since I last saw you, and now I'm dying."

"What are you dying of?"

"I have a headache and a feeling of nausea, as well as a slight cough."

Mrs. Wang began to laugh.

"Here am I on my sickbed, and you're laughing at me!"

"I'm only laughing because I know the cause of your illness. What you're suffering from is Zhou Dalang's daughter from Cao Gate. Isn't that so?"

The moment she guessed his secret, Erlang leapt up in his bed. "How did you know?" he demanded.

"Her family sent me over to arrange a marriage to you."

Had Erlang never heard these words, nothing would have happened. As it was, he was ecstatic.

Receiving joyous news, our spirits soar;
Hearing welcome words, we feel a bond.

Following Mrs. Wang out of his bedroom, he greeted his brother and sister-in-law.

"You're getting up even though you're so ill?" asked his brother.

"I've completely recovered," he declared, to the great relief of his brother and sister-in-law.

"The Zhou family from Cao Gate have sent me to arrange a marriage to Erlang," said Mrs. Wang. Dalang was delighted to hear of the proposal.

Let me spare you the rest of the details. The two parties came to an agreement and the betrothal settlement was paid, all without incident. Fan Erlang, who used to spend very little time at home, now never went out, but helped his brother look after the tavern. And the girl, who normally did no needlework whatsoever, was now perfectly willing to sew. Both lovers were happy and contented as they looked forward to Zhou Dalang's return, when their wedding would take place.

The period of waiting lasted all the time from their engagement in the third month until the eleventh month of the same year, when Zhou Dalang finally came back. His return was celebrated by the neighbors and relatives with a party, which I won't dwell on.

The following day Mrs. Zhou told her husband what she had done.

"Has the settlement been paid?" he asked.

"Yes."

He glared at her, his eyes bulging, and began to abuse her. "You wicked old bag! Who gave *you* permission to arrange a marriage? The best that fellow can ever hope to be is the owner of a tavern. My daughter would certainly have gotten a husband from some rich and powerful family, but oh no, you had to go and promise her to him! You've cost us our whole position in society. We'll be a public laughingstock."

Just as he was abusing his wife, their maid called out. "Madam, come quickly and save the young mistress!"

"Why, what is it?"

"She was standing behind the screen, when for some reason she suddenly collapsed." Her mother, panic-stricken, raced to the scene, where she found the girl lying on the ground.

> Before you know if she's alive or dead,
> You see at once that her limbs are still.

Of all the multitude of physical disorders, those affecting our breathing are the most serious. From behind the screen the girl had heard her father shouting at her mother, refusing to let her marry Fan Erlang, and she suffered an occlusion of the breathing passages and sank to the ground. As Mrs. Zhou rushed to revive her daughter, however, Zhou Dalang caught her and held her back.

"You wicked old broad! If that little slut who disgraced our house is dying, then let her die! What's the point of saving her?"

Seeing her mistress held back by the master, the maid rushed forward herself to save the girl, only to receive a clout from the master that sent her reeling. At this point Mrs. Zhou herself collapsed, and the maid sprang to her mistress's side and managed to revive her. Mrs. Zhou then gave way to a hysterical sobbing, which brought the neighbors over to see what was the matter. All four of them, Mesdames Zhang, Bao, Mao, and Diao, came crowding into the room, for although Zhou Dalang was known to be an unreasonable man, his wife was always gentle and accommodating, and they were very fond of her.

Zhou Dalang took one look at the visitors and declared, "This is a private family matter. We don't need any advice." Hearing this tone of voice from him, the neighbors departed.

When Mrs. Zhou had a chance to examine her daughter, she found the body ice-cold, and cradling the girl in her arms, she began sobbing again. Her daughter had been alive, but had died because no one went to her rescue. Rounding on her husband, she accused him. "How could you be so *vicious?* I know why! Because you couldn't bear to part with the thirty or forty thousand cash needed for the trousseau. For that money you deliberately took my daughter's life!"

This accusation sent Zhou Dalang into a rage. "So you think I can't bear to part with thirty or forty thousand for a trousseau, do you? What an insult!" He stalked out.

Needless to say, Mrs. Zhou continued to seethe with anger. A daughter with the looks of a goddess, a daughter so clever, so skilled with her needle, a daughter perfect in every way—how could a mother be anything but furious at losing her?

Of course, Zhou Dalang bought her a coffin, which was borne into the house by eight men, a sight that caused Mrs. Zhou to sob as if her heart were breaking. "So you thought I couldn't bear to part with thirty or forty thousand for a trousseau, did you?" he said, glaring at his wife. "Well, take a look at your daughter's room. Every scrap of her jewelry is going into that coffin." Then and there he told the undertakers and their assistants to place the girl's body in the coffin and also sent orders to the grave keepers, Zhang Yilang and his brother, to dig a grave for her and line it with brick.

I will spare you the rest of the details. No sutras were read, and no religious service was held for the passage of her soul. Nor was any delay permitted with the funeral, which had to be held the very next day; Mrs. Zhou had asked that it be postponed a few days, but her husband was adamant. The funeral procession left early in the morning, and once the burial was over, the people went home.

> Alas, three feet of loveless earth
> Now lie above this loving girl!

Here the story divides, and I turn to a young man in his thirties named Zhu Zhen, a shady character who often assisted the undertakers in their work and was also employed as a grave digger. On this occasion he was hired to help lay the girl in the coffin and line the grave with brick. Returning home after the burial, he exclaimed to his mother, "The most tremendous piece of luck has come my way! Tomorrow I'll be rich."

"What luck are you talking about?" she asked.

"The funniest thing happened! The daughter of Zhou Dalang from Cao Gate died, and her parents got into a fight over it. Her mother accused her father of causing her death in a fit of rage, and he got so furious that he bundled her whole trousseau, worth thirty or forty thousand cash, into the coffin along with her. Riches like that—how can I help but go and pick them up?"

"But that's a really serious crime, not some misdemeanor for which you'd get off with a beating! What's more, your father's experience should be a warning to you. Twenty years ago he went out and dug up a grave. He had just gotten the lid open when the corpse started grinning at him. Your father never got over the shock—he died a few days after he came back. Son, don't go! It's a very serious crime."

"You can't change my mind, Mother." He pulled something out from under his bed and showed it to her.

"And don't take that, either!" she exclaimed. "Your father took it with him—he used it just that one time, and died."

"Everybody's fate is different. I've had my fortune told several times this year, and each time I was told I'd be rich. Don't try to stop me."

What do you suppose the object was that he pulled out? A leather bag containing a crowbar, an axe, a leather lamp, as well as an oilcan for the lamp. There was also a hemp raincoat.

"What's the coat for?" his mother asked.

"At midnight I'll need it."

It was the middle of the eleventh month, and the snow was falling heavily. He put the coat on and attached to the back of it a horizontal strip woven from a dozen bamboo skins. The strip was designed to smooth out the tracks that he made in the snow, so that no trace would be left behind.

At the second watch[11] that evening Zhu Zhen gave strict orders to his mother. "When I get back, I'll knock on the door. See that you open up for me."

Although the city itself was teeming with activity, in the broad, open spaces outside the walls all was quiet. Moreover, it was now the second watch and the snow was falling thickly. No one was about.

11. 9–11 p.m.

As Zhu Zhen left the house, he turned and looked back—no tracks were visible in the snow behind him. He made his way to the Zhou family tomb and stepped over the surrounding wall at its low point. Unfortunately, the grave keepers had a dog, and when it saw a stranger stepping over the wall, it came bounding out from its lair in the undergrowth and began to bark. However, Zhu Zhen had that day prepared a cake with poison in it, and when the dog barked, he tossed the cake in its direction. Seeing something thrown to it, the dog sniffed at the cake, liked the smell of it and gulped it down, then gave a single bark and fell over dead. Zhu Zhen approached the grave.

At this point one of the grave keepers, Zhang Erlang, called out to his brother, "Isn't that strange? The dog barked once and then didn't bark again. Perhaps there's a robber out there. Get up and take a look!"

"What have I got that anyone would want to steal?"

"But the dog gave one loud bark and nothing more. Perhaps there *is* a thief out there. If you won't get up and take a look, I will." He scrambled to his feet, threw on some clothes, grabbed his spear, and went out.

At the sound of the men's voices, Zhu Zhen had quietly taken off his raincoat and picked his way over to a willow tree, which was large and offered him perfect cover. With the rain hat covering his upper body he squatted down, his coat on the ground beside him. From that distance he saw the door of the cottage open and Zhang Erlang emerge into the bitter cold and shout at the dog, "You dumb critter, why were you barking just now?" He had been roused from a sound sleep, and the bitter cold came as a shock to him. Hastily shutting the door, he went back inside and called out to his brother: "You were right. There wasn't anyone." He quickly undressed and pulled the bedclothes up over his head. "It's freezing out there," he said.

"I told you there wasn't anyone."

It was about the third watch.[12] The brothers chatted for a while, after which no more was heard from them.

No gain without pain, thought Zhu Zhen to himself. He got to his feet, put on his hat and coat, and picked his way

12. 11 p.m.–1 a.m.

over to the grave, where he set about clearing away the snow with the crowbar. The masonry was his own handiwork from earlier that day. He drove the crowbar in and prized up the stone slabs, which he arranged on one side of him. Then, taking off his hat and coat and laying them beside him, he got two large nails from the leather bag, inserted them in the cracks between the bricks, and placed the leather lamp on top. From a bamboo tube he took out some embers and blew on them until they flared up. After adding some oil from the oilcan, he lit the lamp. With the crowbar he prized the nails out of the coffin, removed the lid, and placed it on one side, then addressed the corpse. "You'll have to forgive me, miss, but I do need to borrow a little of your jewelry. I will hold a service for you, though." He stripped off the jewelry that she wore on her head, which consisted of many gold and jade ornaments. Her clothes were harder to remove, but Zhu Zhen was nothing if not ingenious. He undid her sash, and looping one end around her neck and tying the other around his own, he stripped off all her clothes, even her underwear, leaving her naked. But then, at the sight of the girl's pale flesh, the loathsome creature was seized by an ungovernable lust and proceeded to violate her body, at which point, incredible as it may seem, she opened her eyes wide and embraced him! How is such a thing to be explained?

> This I read in the Book of Fate:[13]
> Nothing springs from the human will.

The truth is that the girl's mind had been fixed on Fan Erlang, and when she heard her father abusing her mother, she reacted with such fury that she expired. Now, however, on receiving this infusion of the yang force so soon after her death, she began slowly to revive. An astonished Zhu Zhen heard her cry out, "Who are *you?*"

He had his wits about him, however. "I've come on purpose to save you, miss," he replied.

She got to her feet—and understood what had happened. For one thing, she saw her clothes piled on one side, and for

13. *Qianding lu,* a short work by the Tang author Zhong Lu.

another, she saw the axe and crowbar lying nearby. How could she fail to understand?

Zhu Zhen would have killed her on the spot, except that he couldn't bear to give her up. "Brother," she said to him, "if you can help me get to see Fan Erlang in the Fan Tavern, I'll give you a handsome reward."

Zhu Zhen was thinking along these lines: Other people spend a lot of money getting a wife and still don't get one who's as good as this girl. If I take her home with me, no one will be any the wiser. "Now don't be scared," he said to her. "Let me take you home and I'll arrange for you to meet Fan Erlang."

"If I can see him again, I'll go with you."

Zhu Zhen gave her some of her own clothes to put on, then bundled up the valuables and the rest of her clothes, blew out the lamp, poured the oil back into the oilcan, gathered up his tools, and picked up his hat. He helped her out of the grave, then scrambled out himself. He replaced the stone slabs so that they fitted together exactly, then scooped up some handfuls of snow and spread it on top of the grave. He told the girl to climb onto his back, then put on the coat and, with the leather bag in one hand, the valuables in the other, and the hat on his head, made his way back to his own door, where he rapped three times. Realizing it was her son, his mother opened up, but as he came in she gave a gasp of surprise. "Why on earth did you bring the body back with you?"

"Keep your voice down, Mother." He deposited the articles he was carrying and took the girl into his bedroom. There he picked up a gleaming sword, pointed it at her, and said, "You and I need to have a little talk. If you go along with what I'm about to say, I'll take you to see Fan Erlang. But if you don't, well, do you see this sword? I'll cut you in two with it."

"What do you want me to do?" she cried in alarm.

"First, you're not to make a sound, and second, you're not to leave this room. If you do as I say, in a few days' time I'll have a word with Fan Erlang. But if you don't, I'll kill you!"

"I'll do as you say, I will."

Having issued his orders, Zhu Zhen went out and explained the situation to his mother.

Let me spare you the rest of the details. That night, needless to say, the girl had to sleep with Zhu Zhen. After a couple of days had passed, days in which she was not allowed to leave the room, she asked him, "Have you been to see Fan Erlang?"

"I've just come back from seeing him. He's confined to his bed because of you. As soon as he's better, he'll come and collect you."

This situation continued from the twentieth of the eleventh month until the fifteenth of the first month of the following year.[14] That evening Zhu Zhen said to his mother, "Every year I hear people saying what a great sight the lantern display is, but I've never been. This time I think I'll go. I should be back by about the fifth watch."[15] After issuing his instructions, he went into the city to see the display.

By an odd coincidence, at about the end of the fifth watch Zhu Zhen's mother heard cries of "Fire!" She rushed outside and found that a tavern four or five doors away was engulfed in flames. Panic-stricken, she rushed back inside to salvage her belongings. From her room the girl heard what was going on and thought, If I don't make a break for it now, I'll never get out. Standing in her doorway, she invited the old woman in to gather up anything she wanted from the room. The woman fell for the ruse and went in—and the girl escaped into the throng of people in the street outside.

Not knowing the way, she asked a passerby, "Where is Cao Gate?"

"Straight ahead," he replied, pointing.

She made her way through the gate, then asked someone else, "Can you tell me how to get to the Fan Tavern?"

"It's right ahead," he replied.

She was desperately afraid. If she ran into Zhu Zhen, she would be shown no mercy. She managed to make her way to the tavern, where she found a waiter standing in the doorway to greet customers. She gave a deep curtsy, to which he responded with a bow. "Anything I can do for you, miss?"

"Is this the Fan Tavern?"

"Yes."

14. The beginning of the Lantern Festival.
15. 3–5 a.m.

"Could you tell me where Fan Erlang is?"

The waiter thought to himself, That Erlang! He's lured this little charmer right to his door! "He's inside," he said.

She approached the counter and called out, "Greetings, Erlang!"

If Erlang had never heard those words, nothing would have happened. As it was, overcome by a sudden panic, he stepped down, went up close to get a good look at her, and received the most terrible shock. "Out! Out!" he began crying, over and over.

"Erlang, I'm not a ghost! I'm flesh and blood!" she protested.

There was no way he would believe it. Still shouting "Out! Out!" he steadied himself with one hand on the bench. As bad luck would have it, a number of cauldrons had been left on that bench, and in his blind panic he picked up one of them and hurled it at the girl's head. By a strange mischance it struck her on the temple, and with a great cry she slumped to the ground. The startled waiters rushed up to see what had happened, only to find a girl lying on the floor. Was she alive or dead?

> Last night in the garden the vicious eastern wind
> Stripped away the blossom and flung it on the ground.

The waiters found her lying dead in a pool of her own blood. Fan Erlang was still shouting "Out! Out!" Hearing all the commotion, his brother came rushing out to see what the matter was. He found Erlang shouting "Out! Out!" and demanded, "Why did you do it?" Eventually Fan Erlang came to his senses, and his brother repeated his question, "Why did you kill her?"

"She's a *ghost*, I tell you! She was the daughter of that seagoing merchant Zhou Dalang from Cao Gate."

"But if she *were* a ghost, there wouldn't be any blood! What on earth are we going to do?"

The incident had drawn a crowd of twenty or thirty onlookers to the front of the tavern, and before long the constables came in to arrest Fan Erlang.

"She's the daughter of Zhou Dalang from Cao Gate," Fan Dalang declared to the constables, "and she died back in the eleventh month of last year. Believing she was a ghost, my brother struck at her and killed her. I'm still not sure in my own mind whether she's a human being or a ghost, but before you arrest my brother, let me go and ask her father to come and identify the body."

"In that case, you'd better hurry up and get him over here."

Fan Dalang raced off to Zhou Dalang's house. He was met there by a nurse, who asked him his name.

"I'm Fan Dalang from the Fan Tavern, and I have urgent business with your master."

The nurse went in, and before long Zhou Dalang came out and greeted him. Fan Dalang explained what had happened, and ended by saying, "If I could persuade you to come and identify the body, I'd be eternally grateful."

Zhou was reluctant to give any credence to such a story, but Fan Dalang was not the sort of man to make things up. He accompanied him to the tavern, where, at sight of the girl's body, he was transfixed. "But she was dead! How could she have come back to life? It's just not possible!"

Without giving Fan Dalang a chance to explain, the constables took into custody all the people involved and next morning transferred them to the prefectural offices. Judge Bao[16] could make neither head nor tail of the case and remanded Fan Erlang to the prisons department pending judgment. After examining the corpse, he ordered the police department to investigate. The constables dispatched men to dig up the grave, but they found only an empty coffin. When questioned, the grave keepers said, "There was a snowfall one night last year in the eleventh month. We heard the dog bark, and then next morning when we went out to take a look, we found it lying dead in the snow. But that's the only piece of evidence we can think of."

A report was submitted to the judge, who flew into a rage and set a three-day limit for the apprehension of the grave robber, a deadline that was extended two or three times without any resolution of the case.

> Vanished like a golden vase down a well,
> Useless as an iron spear's needle tip.

16. A Song official who was transformed by popular myth into the most celebrated detective of Chinese literature.

Let me turn now to Fan Erlang in prison. It's just incomprehensible, he thought. She can't have been human—she was already dead! The undertakers who saw her body placed in the coffin and the people at the graveside can attest to that. But she can't have been a ghost either, or there wouldn't have been any blood when she was struck, nor would a body have been left behind or her coffin found empty. He turned these thoughts over and over in his mind, but still could not resolve the issue. Then another thought struck him: What a beautiful girl she was, just like a flower—it's *such* a pity! If she were a ghost, I could bear that. But if she was human, then I am the one who took her life, and for no reason whatsoever! He tossed and turned half the night, unable to sleep, throwing up idea after idea, only to cast doubt on each one.

Then the scene of their first meeting in the teahouse came back to his mind. How spellbound I was, he thought. We gazed deep into each other's eyes, but I had no chance to possess her. As to whether she's a ghost or a human, let me take my time and try to think it through. I was in such a panic at the time that I took her life—a horrible crime!—and now I'm locked up in here and still I can't understand it. How is all this going to end? But what's done is done—I can't change it. Thus a moment of remorse was followed by another idea, which in turn was followed by more remorse, and in this manner four more hours dragged by until finally he fell asleep.

In his dream he had a vision of Shengxian, now gorgeously dressed, coming toward him.

"So you're not dead, after all!" he exclaimed in astonishment.

"It was only a glancing blow that you gave me, and although I fainted, I didn't die from it. But that's twice now that I've *almost* died, and each time because of you! I heard today that you were in here, and I've specially sought you out to give you what your heart desires. Now, don't refuse me—this is all decreed by fate." Forgetting everything that had led up to that moment, Fan Erlang began making love to her, and in bed together their delight knew no bounds. When the lovemaking was over, they took a tender farewell of each other.

When Erlang awoke and realized it was only a dream, his

remorse and bewilderment were even greater than before. But next night the same thing happened again, and on the third night she came back once more and was more loving than ever. As she was leaving she said, "My allotted span of life was not over, and I was taken into the service of General Five Ways.[17] But I continued to love you with all my heart, and when I broke down and told the General what had happened, he took pity on me and gave me three days' leave. Now my time is up, and if I delay any longer, I'll be reprimanded, so I shall have to bid you an eternal farewell. But I've pleaded your case with the General. Just be patient, and in a month's time all your troubles will be over."

Fan Erlang was so overcome by anguish that he began to sob. When he awoke from his dream, he could remember everything she had said but was still unsure whether to believe it.

After precisely a month, the warden received an order from the judge to take Fan Erlang to the prisons department for interrogation. The reasons behind the judge's order were as follows: A certain Kaifeng street peddler named Dong Gui had that day taken a basket of his wares outside the city wall, and an old woman standing in front of her door had called him over and offered to sell him something. What was that something? A jasmine flower hair ornament made of pearls. On the night of the grave robbery, Zhu Zhen had dropped it on entering the house, and his mother had quietly picked it up. Not realizing its value, she now wanted to sell it for a string or two of cash in order to supplement her savings.

"How much do you want for it?" asked Dong Gui.

"Whatever you say."

"I'll give you two strings."

"All right."

After giving her the money, Dong Gui went straight to the inspector at the police department and told him what had happened. The inspector hurried over to Cao Gate and showed the ornament to Zhou Dalang and his wife, who identified it as one worn by their daughter at the time of her death.

Constables were dispatched to arrest the old woman. "My

17. A Daoist god in charge of matters of life and death.

son, Zhu Zhen, isn't in," she said. He was nowhere to be found, but later he was arrested by the constables down at the Sang-jiawa,[18] where he had gone to watch the shows. He was taken to the prefectural offices and sent by Judge Bao to the prisons department for interrogation. Unable to deny his guilt, he made a full confession.

Clerk Xue, who was in charge of the case, provisionally sentenced Zhu Zhen to execution as a grave robber. He did not sentence Fan Erlang to death, but to be branded and exiled to a prison camp. The sentences had still not been submitted to Judge Bao, when that same night Xue dreamt of a god resembling General Five Ways who angrily berated him. "What crime has Fan Erlang committed that you should sentence him to exile? Set him free at once!" Clerk Xue awoke in great alarm and altered the provisional sentence to read that Fan Erlang had struck a ghost, an action that did not qualify as homicide. The case fell into the category of paranormal phenomena, and the accused man should be released immediately. Judge Bao approved both decisions.

Fan Erlang returned home walking on air. Afterward, although he did eventually take a wife, he never forgot Shengxian's passionate love for him, and at seasonal festivals throughout the year he would visit the temple of General Five Ways and burn spirit money and offer sacrifices for her. There is a poem on the subject:

> Equally foolish were they in their passion;
> Strange was their love, and stranger still their tale.
> Were passion's presence weighed against its absence,
> Absence of passion would likely prevail.

18. The entertainment quarter of Bianjing, the Northern Song capital.

2
The Oil Seller

Though young men boast of their courtesan conquests,
Troubles arise like waves on the sea.
If you've money without looks, it's hard enough,
But with looks alone? Futility!
Even if you've looks as well as money,
You must weigh your approach most carefully.
For of all the fellows with grace and tact,
There's not a one who can equal me.

*T*his lyric to the tune "Moon over West River" sums up the
way the courtesan world operates. As the saying goes, the
girls favor looks, the madam favors money. So when a client
comes along who has the good looks of a Pan An and the riches
of a Deng Tong,[1] he will naturally be favored by both sides and
end up reigning supreme in the courtesan camp and presiding
over the feast of love. However, in addition to these consider-
ations of looks and money, there is also a two-syllable mantra,
bangchen—*bang* as in the support of a shoe and *chen* as in the
lining of a garment.[2] If a courtesan has just one good feature
and a man treats her with *bangchen*, she will be transformed
into a paragon of beauty, for he will go out of his way to hide
whatever shortcomings she may have. In addition, if he is meek
and mild in his approach and does everything in his power to
help, catering to all her likes and dislikes and empathizing with

---

The full title is "The Oil Seller Takes Sole Possession of the Queen of Flowers."
The story is no. 3 in *Constant Words to Awaken the World*.
  1. Icons of male beauty and great wealth, respectively. Pan An (Pan Yue)
lived in the fourth century. Deng Tong was the favorite of Emperor Wu of the
Han.
  2. The term *"bangchen"* is common in Ming and Qing dynasty songs, many
of which are in a courtesan's voice.

her every desire, how can she fail to love him? That is what the word *bangchen* means. In the world of the courtesan, he who can *bangchen* will come off best, regardless of whether he has looks or money.

Take the case of Zheng Yuanhe[3] when he was living in the beggars' hostel. He was utterly destitute, and his looks were no longer what they had been. Then Li Yaxian came upon him in the midst of a snowstorm and was overwhelmed with pity. She wrapped him in an embroidered cloak, fed him with the choicest of gourmet food, and even made him her husband—and she did all of this not because she coveted his money or admired his looks, but because Zheng had behaved considerately and tactfully toward her, showing himself so adept at *bangchen* that she could not bear to be without him. Just imagine! That time when she felt unwell and had a sudden craving for horsemeat soup, he went out and slaughtered his own piebald stallion and made the tripe into broth for her! Because of that act alone, she would never have been able to forget his love. He went on to win first place in the metropolitan examination, while she was ennobled as Lady Qianguo. The beggars' songs led to an immortal disquisition, while the beggars' hostel gave way to a magnificent palace. The mantle of success covers up all things, and in the courtesan world theirs became an exemplary tale.

> When fortune wanes, even gold will lose its glitter;
> When fortune waxes, even iron will cast a glow.

My story tells how Emperor Taizu, after founding the great Song dynasty, was succeeded by Emperor Taizong and then by six other emperors, each of whom favored civil over military affairs, as a result of which the nation was at peace and the people were contented. But the eighth emperor, Huizong, the Daoist Lord, put his faith in the likes of Cai Jing, Gao Qiu, Yang

---

3. Zheng Yuanhe and Li Yaxian (Li Wa) are the hero and heroine of the famous classical tale "Li Wa zhuan" by Bai Xingjian (775–826). See Glen Dudbridge, *The Tale of Li Wa, Study and Critical Edition of a Chinese Story from the Ninth Century* (London: Ithaca Press, 1983).

Jian, and Zhu Mian;[4] built great imperial parks; and gave himself over to the pursuit of pleasure instead of attending to the affairs of state. As a result the people seethed with discontent, and the Jurchen[5] enemy seized this moment to launch an attack that tore to shreds the rich tapestry of that entire world.

Not until two emperors had been taken prisoner and the future Emperor Gaozong had crossed the river on a clay horse[6] and resigned himself to ruling over a mere corner of a divided empire did the fighting cease. Meanwhile, for several decades the people had been subjected to innumerable hardships.

> We live among the arms of war,
> We make our homes amid the strife,
> Where killing seems like idle sport,
> And plunder is a way of life.

Let me single out a resident of Bliss Village on the outskirts of the city of Bianliang,[7] a man named Xin Shan, whose wife came from the Ruan family. Together they ran a food store from which they made a comfortable living. Rice was their main item, but they were well stocked also with wheat, beans, tea, wine, salt, and other provisions. Although both were in their forties, they had only one child, a daughter named Yaoqin, who was a pretty little thing and as bright as a button. At the age of six, she was sent to the village school, where every day she learned to recite a thousand words. By the age of nine she could write poetry, and in fact a poem of hers titled "A Maiden's Thoughts" was widely quoted at the time:

> As she removes the curtain's golden hook,
> Quiet is the incense burner, cold the room.

4. Minister, favorite, eunuch, and favorite, respectively, of Emperor Huizong (r. 1100–1125). Their influence over the emperor was generally blamed for the loss of north China to the Jurchen.

5. A people from the northeast of China who in 1126 defeated the Song and set up the Jin dynasty in north China.

6. According to myth, after the emperor and the former emperor had been captured by the Jurchen, Prince Kang, the future Emperor Gaozong, escaped the Jurchen armies by riding a miraculous clay horse over the Yangzi River.

7. Capital of the Northern Song, the modern Kaifeng.

> Fearing to disturb the pillow's lovebirds,
> She trims the lamp and sighs—a double bloom.[8]

By the age of eleven, she had mastered the arts of lute playing and chess, as well as those of painting and calligraphy. As for needlework, her speed was such that it astonished everyone who saw it. And these were all natural talents of hers, not skills that she could have been taught. Having no son of his own, Xin Shan wanted to find a son-in-law who would join his household and look after him and his wife in their old age, but it was hard to find anyone to match his daughter's multifaceted talents, and so although he received numerous proposals, he did not accept any of them. Then, in a catastrophic turn of events, the Jurchen enemy ran amuck and laid siege to the city of Bianliang. Although there were plenty of troops available to come to the emperor's rescue, the prime minister held to his policy of appeasement and forbade them to attack, with the result that the enemy grew even stronger and, after smashing their way into the capital, abducted both the current and the former emperors. By that time all the people living on the outskirts of the city had fled in panic, taking their old and their young with them.

Xin Shan took his wife and eleven-year-old daughter and joined the refugees in their flight, carrying all their valuables on their backs.

> Nervous as a dog that has lost its master,
> Frantic as a fish that has escaped the net,
> Hunger, thirst, and toil their lot,
> As far from home they flee.
> To Heaven, to Earth, to their ancestors they pray
> That they may not run into the Jurchen foe.
> How true!
> It's better to be a dog in time of peace
> Than a human being in time of war.

8. The shape of a double flower formed by the burnt wick of the lamp, signifying a pair of lovers.

As it turned out, it was not the Jurchen they ran into, but a beaten remnant of the Song imperial army. At sight of the refugees, most of whom were carrying their belongings on their backs, the soldiers set up a false cry. "The Jurchen are coming!" and lit a fire by the side of the road. It was getting dark, and the people became so terrified that they fled helter-skelter, trying desperately to save themselves. The soldiers then seized their chance to rob them. Anyone who refused to hand over his belongings was killed on the spot. In this manner one chaos generated another, and a second layer of misery was heaped upon the first.

Under the mutineers' onslaught, Yaoqin stumbled and fell, and by the time she had scrambled to her feet again, her parents were nowhere to be seen. She didn't dare call out, but hid all night among some old tombs by the roadside. When she emerged at dawn to look around, she found herself in the midst of a sandstorm, with corpses strewn all over the road. Her fellow refugees of the day before had vanished, she didn't know where. Missing her parents, she cried and cried, but since she was unsure which direction to take in order to find them, she could only press on to the south, crying every lingering step of the way. She had not gone more than a mile when, heartbroken and hungry, she spotted an adobe shack. There must be somebody living there, she thought; I'll beg a little broth from them. But when she reached the shack, she found it tumbledown and deserted—the residents had fled. At the base of the wall she sat down and burst into sobs.

As the old adage puts it, without coincidences there'd be no stories. By a very strange coincidence indeed someone came by that wall she was sitting under, a neighbor of theirs, Bu Qiao by name. Known generally as Master Bu, he was an idler, a disreputable character who made a habit of sponging off other people.

Master Bu had also been separated from the other refugees by the mutineers' charge, and he was walking along on his own when he heard a girl sobbing and went over to investigate. Yaoqin had known him since she was a little girl, and now, in these dire circumstances, with her parents nowhere in sight, to come upon such a neighbor was like finding a member of her own family. She stopped crying, got to her feet, and greeted him with the cry, "Uncle Bu, have you seen my father and mother?"

Bu Qiao made a quick calculation: Those soldiers took everything I had—I've no money left. This is a gift from Heaven, a rare treasure that I must lay up for the future. He told her a lie. "When your father and mother couldn't find you, they were heartbroken. They've gone on ahead, but before they did so, they told me, 'If you should see our daughter, bring her back to us at all costs.' They promised me a handsome reward."

Astute as Yaoqin was, she found herself in desperate straits, and in any case, an honorable person is gullible simply by virtue of being honorable. She took Bu at his word and went along with him.

> She knew it wasn't proper company,
> But at a pinch she thought it best to go.

Bu Qiao shared with her a little of the dry rations he had on him. He also gave her instructions. "Your parents set off last night. If we can't catch them on the road, we'll cross the river, go directly to Jiankang,[9] and meet up with them there. While we're traveling, I'll treat you as my daughter and you must address me as father. Otherwise, people are going to think I've taken some lost child under my wing, which could be very embarrassing."

Yaoqin promised to do so, and they set off, traveling together on foot or by boat, addressing each other as father and daughter. By the time they reached Jiankang, they had heard rumors that Prince Wuzhu[10] of the Jurchen was leading an army across the river, which meant that Jiankang would not be safe. At the same time they heard that Prince Kang[11] had ascended the throne and set up his temporary capital in Hangzhou, whose name he had changed to Lin'an. And so they took

9. Modern Nanjing.
10. I.e., Wanyan Zongbi (d. 1148), fourth son of the Jurchen emperor Aguda.
11. He became Emperor Gaozong.

a boat as far as Runzhou, and then made their way through Suzhou, Changzhou, Jiaxing, and Huzhou as far as Lin'an, where they put up at an inn. Thanks to Bu Qiao, Yaoqin had been brought from Bianliang to Lin'an, a distance of over a thousand miles, but by now the small amount of money he had on him was completely gone—he even had to sell his overcoat to pay their bill at the inn. All that was left to him was this one piece of human merchandise, Yaoqin herself, whom he now proposed to sell. Learning that Wang Jiuma's brothel on the West Lake was looking for a girl to adopt, he invited Wang over to the inn to appraise his merchandise. Wang saw how beautiful Yaoqin was and negotiated a price of fifty taels.[12] After receiving payment, Bu took Yaoqin to the Wang establishment. In speaking to Wang, he was shrewd enough to say only, "Yaoqin's my own daughter, and it's a pity she has to go into your line of business. In training her, you must treat her gently, and naturally she'll be obedient and cooperative. Just don't get impatient with her." To Yaoqin, however, he said, "Jiuma is a close relative of mine. I'm leaving you with her for the present, while I take the time to look for your parents. As soon as I've found them, I'll come back for you." That was why Yaoqin was quite happy to go to Wang's.

> Pity this brilliant girl
> Caught in a web of vice.

After Wang Jiuma had acquired Yaoqin, she gave her a complete set of new clothes and hid her away in a secluded room at the back of the building. Every day she tried to nurse the girl back to health by offering her good food and drink. She also tried to win her affection by lavishing endearments upon her. As for Yaoqin, she felt that since she was there, she might as well make the best of it. But when several days had gone by and no word had come from Bu Qiao, she began to pine for her parents and asked Wang, with tears in her eyes, "Why hasn't Uncle Bu been to see me?"

"What Uncle Bu?"

12. A tael was an ounce of silver.

"The Master Bu who brought me here!"

"He told me he was your father."

"His surname is Bu, mine is Xin." She went on to relate in detail how she had fled Bianliang and been separated from her parents, how she had run into Bu Qiao and been brought to Lin'an, and how he had talked her into coming here.

"I see," said Wang. "So you're an orphan—utterly helpless. Well, there's something I'd better explain to you. That fellow Bu sold you to us for fifty taels. We're a bordello, and we rely on our girls for a living. I have three or four adopted daughters, but none of them is truly outstanding. I adored your looks the moment I saw you, and I've treated you like my own daughter. When you grow up, I promise you that you'll live well and never want for anything."

At last Yaoqin realized the trick that Bu Qiao had played on her and she burst into sobs. Wang tried to console her, but it was a long time before the girl would stop crying.

Wang changed her name from Yaoqin to Wang Mei, and everyone in the house called her Miss Mei. Wang also taught her music and dancing, in both of which she excelled. By the age of thirteen she possessed a rare kind of delicate beauty, and the sons of the rich and powerful families of Lin'an all admired her looks and offered handsome presents just to meet her. And there were also men of more refined interests, who had heard of her literary talent and besieged the house every day asking for her poems or calligraphy. She gained a vast reputation and became known not simply as Miss Mei, but as the Queen of Flowers.[13] The young rakes of the West Lake even composed a song to the "Hanging Branch" tune[14] about her qualities:

> Where among the courtesans
> Would you find a girl so fair?
> With music, painting, poetry
> And other arts to spare.

13. Prostitutes were known as flowers.
14. A popular song tune from the middle of the sixteenth century, one much imitated by writers. It was employed for both romantic and satirical purposes.

Even she who's likened to the lake[15]–
Even she could not compare.
The lucky devil who gets to her
Will risk his life without a care.

Because of her great reputation, she had no sooner turned thirteen than men started to make offers for her first night. But Mei refused, and Wang, who regarded her daughter as wealth incarnate, looked on her refusal as an imperial decree and did not dream of violating it.

Another year went by, and Mei was now fourteen. The general rule in brothels is that twelve is too early for a first night. It is known as Trying Out the Flower, and it occurs when the madam is more concerned with profits than the girl's suffering. The clients who go in for it earn themselves a hollow reputation, because they fail to derive the full pleasure from the act. Thirteen is known as Opening the Flower, and by this time the girl has reached puberty and is able to receive the man, so this is held to be the right age. At fourteen, a first night is known as Plucking the Flower. While in ordinary households fourteen is still considered young, in brothels it is held to be too late. By fourteen Mei had not been deflowered, and the young rakes composed yet another song, this time to the "Hanging Pearl" tune:

A flowering quince,[16] that's our Wang Mei—
All for show.
Fourteen years and still not done;
What good's a name without the real thing?
Unless she lacks an opening,
She must be a two-in-one.[17]
For if she had a real pudendum,
She'd have yielded to it long ago.

15. I.e., Xishi, the icon of female beauty, who was associated with the West Lake at Hangzhou.
16. *Mugua*, i.e., good only to look at.
17. I.e., a hermaphrodite. The previous line refers to a *shi nü,* or stone maiden, a woman with an undeveloped (hypoplastic) vagina.

When Wang got wind of this satire, she feared for the reputation of her house and tried to persuade the girl to start taking clients, but Mei was adamant. "I can take clients only after I've seen my parents and been given their approval."

Vexed though she was, Wang could not bear to put any pressure on her. She waited for some time, until a certain very rich man, Master Jin, happened to offer as much as three hundred taels. With such a huge sum in prospect, Wang devised a plan that she confided to Jin: if he wanted to sleep with Mei, he would need to do such-and-such.

On the fifteenth of the eighth month, Jin announced that he was inviting Mei on an excursion to the lake to see the tidal bore.[18] When she arrived at the boat, she found three or four hangers-on, past masters at this sort of thing, who engaged her in games of guess-fingers and wine forfeits[19] and by one means or another managed to ply her with enough wine to get her hopelessly drunk. They then helped her back to the upstairs apartment at Wang's and laid her unconscious on the bed. It was warm at the time, and she was thinly clad. Wang attended to her personally, stripping her stark naked and turning her over to Jin for his ministrations. Jin's penis was nothing out of the ordinary. Gently parting her thighs, he applied some spit and thrust his way in. By the time Mei felt the pain and began to awaken from her dream, he had already had his way with her. She tried to struggle, but there was no strength left in her limbs and she had to endure his abuse a while longer. Not until the leaves went dark and all the blossoms fell did the clouds and rain finally cease.[20]

> The buds beneath the rain are newly opened;
> Her brows in the mirror are not as they were.

At the fifth watch, she awoke from a drunken stupor and realized that she had been robbed of her virginity by the

---

18. The famous surge of the tide up the Qiantang River near Hangzhou.

19. Drinking games in which the loser, not the winner, has to drink up.

20. The loss of virginity is symbolized by a storm stripping the blossom from the trees.

madam's trick. She wept for herself as yet another pretty face condemned to a sorry fate, the victim of violent abuse. After getting up to relieve herself, she dressed and then lay down on a bamboo couch beside the bed, crying softly as she faced the wall. When Jin approached her and made an overture, he received a swipe across the face that left him with several bright red scratches. Greatly put out, he waited until dawn, then told the madam, "I'm leaving." She tried to persuade him to stay, but he was already out the door. Now, it is customary after a first night for a madam to come in the next morning and offer her congratulations, after which the rest of the staff does the same. The festivities go on for several days, and the client stays in the brothel at least half a month and sometimes as long as two months. Jin's departure early the next morning was unparalleled in brothel history.

Uttering cries of shock and dismay, Wang threw on some clothes and dashed upstairs, where she found Mei sprawled on the couch, her eyes brimful of tears. In hopes of persuading her to take up the role of courtesan, Wang readily admitted the wrong she had done, but Mei still said nothing, and Wang was forced to retreat downstairs. All that day Mei continued to weep and would touch neither food nor drink. Pleading illness, she refused from then on to go downstairs or even to see any clients.

Wang lost all patience with her, but knowing the girl's violent temper, she was loath to resort to any harsh measures lest Mei be alienated forever. On the other hand, the primary aim was to have the girl earn money, and if she took no clients, she would be no use even if she lived to be a hundred. For several days Wang dithered, unable to come up with a solution. Then she thought of a sworn sister of hers, Liu Sima, someone whom she saw frequently. Liu was highly skilled at persuasive discourse, and she was also on good terms with Mei. Why not invite her over and let her try out her powers of persuasion? If she could get Mei to change her mind, they'd celebrate the new business prospects in grand style. She told her servant to invite Liu into the front parlor, where she confided what was troubling her.

"Well, you see before you the female Sui He, the distaff Lu

Jia,"[21] declared Mrs. Liu. "I can talk an arhat into falling in love or the moon goddess into wanting to marry.[22] You just leave it to me."

"If you can bring this off, I'm ready to get down on my knees and kowtow to you. But do have another cup of tea before you start, in case your mouth runs dry."

"I owe this mighty mouth of mine to Heaven itself. If I go on talking until tomorrow, it'll never run dry."

After a few cups of tea, she made her way to the back apartment, where she found the door shut tight. She rapped lightly and called out, "Niece, are you there?" At the sound of her voice, Mei opened the door, and they exchanged greetings. Liu then took a seat at the bottom of the table, with Mei beside her.[23] On the table Liu noticed a sheet of fine white silk depicting just the sketch of a beauty's face—the coloring had yet to be added. She began praising it. "Such *beautiful* work! What talent you have! I don't know how Jiuma had the luck to meet up with such a smart girl, a fine person and a fine artist too. If we had several thousand taels at our disposal and searched through the whole city, I doubt that we could find anyone to equal you."

"Stop making fun of me. Anyway, what brings you here today?"

"I've been meaning to come and see you for ages, but so much has been going on at home that I haven't had the time. However, when I heard that you'd celebrated your first night, I simply made the time to come over, particularly to congratulate Jiuma."

At mention of the first night, Mei flushed, hung her head, and said nothing. Liu realized that she was overcome with embarrassment. She moved her chair closer and took Mei's hand in hers. "Look, child, our girls aren't namby-pambies, you know.

21. Sui He and Lu Jia, both of the early Han dynasty, were classic persuaders, i.e., strategists with special oral gifts. In fiction and drama, go-betweens and panders were often compared to them. Here Liu lauds herself in grandiloquent terms, in the manner of the stock go-betweens of Chinese drama.

22. An arhat is a Buddhist saint. Chang'e stole the elixir of immortality from her husband and fled to the moon.

23. To show exaggerated deference, Liu, who is actually the guest, leaves the place of honor to Mei.

Why are *you* behaving like one? If you're going to be this bashful, how are you ever going to make any big money?"

"What would I want to make money for?"

"Child, even if you don't want money, your mother will surely expect her investment to pay off now that you've grown up. As the proverb says, live by the mountain, make your living off the mountain; live by the sea, make your living off the sea. She has several girls in her house, but none of them comes close to you. You're the only good melon in her melon patch, and she treats you differently from the others. You're a clever girl, but you need to understand about the things that really matter. I hear that after your first night you've refused to see any clients. What do you mean by that? If everybody did as you want to do, the house would be like a batch of silkworms with no one to feed them any mulberry leaves. Your mother has shown you special favor, and it's up to you to do her credit—not have the other girls making nasty cracks about you."

"Let them! I don't care!"

"Dear, oh dear! That may be a small matter, but do you really understand the way things work in the brothels?"

"What about it?"

"In our business we depend on our girls for food, clothes, and other necessities, and if by some stroke of luck we manage to get a presentable one, we're like a landowner who has just bought a choice piece of fertile land. While she's still a child, you can't wait for the girl to grow up, but after the first night the crops are ripe and ready for harvest, and you wait anxiously every day for the profits to roll in. A new client is welcomed at the front door while the last one is being shown out the back. Master Zhang presents you with this; Master Li with that. There's a constant hustle and bustle of activity, which is what makes for a famous house."

"But how *shameful!* I would never do anything like that."

Liu put one hand over her mouth and gave a little snort of laughter. "But is it up to *you* to make that decision? The madam is the one in charge of the house. If a girl doesn't do as she's told, she gets whipped for the slightest misdemeanor, whipped until she's more dead than alive. At that point you'll do as you're told, all right. Look, Jiuma has never been hard on you. She took pity on you because of your intelligence, your good looks, and your genteel upbringing, and she wanted to safeguard your integrity and preserve your self-respect. But just now she told me a great many things about you. She said that you don't know when something is done for your own good and that you have no sense of what really matters in life. She's very disappointed in you. She's asked me to try and persuade you to change your ways. If you continue to hold out like this, you'll only get her back up and then she'll show you a very different face. She'll scream at you and beat you until you're more than ready for the next world! As with everything else in life, beginnings are what you have most to fear. Once she starts beating you, she'll follow up with another beating every morning and evening until you can't stand the pain any longer. You'll be forced to see clients all the same—except that the fabulous reputation you now enjoy will be drastically diminished. What's more, you'll become the butt of the other girls' jokes. In my opinion, she has you under her thumb and you can't wriggle out. Far better to count your blessings, throw yourself into her arms, and secure your own happiness."

"But I'm the daughter of good, honest folk, and it's no fault of mine that I've fallen into prostitution. If you would only recommend to her that I marry, that would be a nobler thing than building a whole nine-story pagoda! But as for standing in the doorway and smiling at strangers, receiving an endless succession of men, no, I'd rather die! I absolutely refuse."

"Child, marriage is a fine aspiration for a prostitute, of course—I would never advise anyone otherwise. But there are several different kinds of marriage."[24]

"How do you mean, different?"

"There's true marriage and false marriage, wretched marriage and happy marriage, opportune marriage and necessary marriage, close-out marriage and incomplete marriage. You'll

24. The expression translated as "marriage" in this story is *cong liang*, which means escaping through marriage from the base *(jian)* caste to which prostitutes (and people of certain other occupational categories) belonged into respectable *(liang)* society.

have to be patient with me while I explain. What do I mean by true marriage? Well, in order to form the ideal couple, a brilliant youth needs a beautiful girl, just as a beautiful girl needs a brilliant youth. But the road to happiness is never smooth, and they often fail to find each other. If by some lucky chance they do happen to meet, it's a matter of instant attraction, after which they're inseparable. Each is as willing as the other to marry, and like a pair of silk moths they won't part even in death. That's what's known as true marriage.

"What do I mean by false marriage? Well, there's a type of client who falls for a prostitute even though she doesn't care for him. In fact, she's not really interested in marrying him at all. She's just using the prospect of marriage as a way of getting him excited enough to loosen his purse strings, and when it gets close to the wedding, she finds some excuse for not going through with it. There's also a type of infatuated client who knows perfectly well that the prostitute doesn't care for him but insists on marrying her anyway. By putting up a large sum of money he arouses the madam's enthusiasm, after which there is no question of the prostitute turning him down. But after she's been forced to join his household, she feels resentful and sets out to break all the rules, doing everything from throwing tantrums to publicly taking a lover. It's impossible for him to keep her, and sooner or later, after six months or a year perhaps, she's sent back to resume her old trade. Marriage has been used as a pretext for making money. That's what's I mean by false marriage.

"What do I mean by a wretched marriage? As in the last case, the client is in love with a prostitute who doesn't love him. He throws his weight about, and the madam is so afraid of him that she agrees to the marriage. The girl herself, who has no choice in the matter, departs from the brothel in tears. But once she enters his mansion, there's no escape, and the discipline is so strict that she can scarcely hold her head up. As something between a concubine and a maid, she has to endure a life that seems worse than death. That's what I mean by a wretched marriage.

"Now, what about a happy marriage? When a prostitute is ready to make her choice, she happens to meet a client with a gentle disposition who is wealthy and whose wife is kind and considerate but has no children. The prostitute looks forward to marrying the man and bearing his child, after which she'll share the wife's position. And so she marries him in order to enjoy a comfortable life before the birth of a child and a new status after it. That's what's called a happy marriage.

"What about an opportune marriage? When the prostitute has had her fill of the romantic life, she capitalizes on her fame and her multitude of suitors to choose one who thoroughly pleases her. In this way, she goes out on top, changing her way of life in time to avoid the indignities that await her. That's what's known as an opportune marriage.

"What about a necessary marriage? In this case the prostitute has no intention of marrying, but she feels resentful, either because of official coercion, or because she's been cheated by some local bully, or because her debts have mounted so high that she can't repay them, and so she takes the first available chance, good or bad, to buy some peace and quiet and find a safe refuge. That's what's known as a necessary marriage.

"What about a close-out marriage? When a prostitute reaches middle age and has been through all the stresses and strains of this business, if she happens to meet a mature patron whose interests match hers, she winds up her career and spends the rest of her life with him. That's what's known as a close-out marriage.

"And what do I mean by an incomplete marriage? In general, when two people fall for each other and start a red-hot affair, it's just a fleeting passion with no thought for the long term. Either his parents won't accept her, or his wife turns out to be jealous and throws one fit after another, and so the prostitute is returned to the brothel and the client demands his money back. There are other cases in which the man loses his money and cannot support the woman. Then when she can no longer stand the misery, she goes out and hustles again. That is what's known as incomplete marriage."

"But since I do want to get married," said Mei, "what's the best way of going about it?"

"Child, I have the perfect solution for you."

"I would be eternally grateful for any advice you can give me."

"So far as marriage is concerned, a girl becomes clean only when she crosses the threshold.[25] What's more, in your case, since you've already been trifled with, even if you were going to be married tonight, you could hardly call yourself a virgin. You should never have ended up in this kind of place, but such was your fate. Your mother has gone to a great deal of trouble on your behalf, and if you don't help her out for a few years and make a thousand or more taels for her, she'll never agree to let you leave. And there's a further point to consider. Even if you insist on marrying, you still have to choose a good man. You surely wouldn't go off with any of this stinking lot, would you? But since you're not receiving any clients now, how would you even know who's worth marrying and who isn't? If you persist in refusing to receive anyone, your mother will be forced to find someone willing to put up the money and then sell you to him as a concubine. That's another kind of marriage altogether! He may be old or ugly or a vulgar lout, and your whole life will have been wasted! You might as well be tossed in the river—at least you'd make a splash and the people watching would cry out in sympathy. In my opinion, you'd be better off if you did what people want and accepted the clients your mother finds for you. No ordinary person would dare aspire to meet a girl with looks and talent like yours. You'll have the sons of the nobility as well as distinguished and powerful men for your clients, the sort of people who won't disgrace you for the rest of your life. First, you'll have all the pleasures of romance, which you should enjoy while you're young. Second, you should help your mother build up her business. Third, you should force yourself to save up some money of your own, so that in the future you won't have to ask other people for anything. In five or ten years' time, if you should meet some understanding person with whom you

25. This sentence, which reads like a quotation, states that lower-caste girls become "clean," i.e., become accepted into respectable (liang) society, only through marriage. An additional difficulty for Mei in finding a good husband is that she is no longer a virgin, as the next sentence points out.

get along well, I'll personally act as your go-between and arrange a splendid marriage for you, and by then your mother will be in a position to let you go. That way, you'll both benefit."

Mei gave a faint smile, but said nothing. Liu knew she was weakening. "Everything I've said is sincerely meant," she added. "If you do as I suggest, one day you'll thank me." She got up to leave.

Every word she uttered had been overheard by Wang, who was crouching down outside the door. As Mei showed Liu out, she came face to face with Wang and promptly shrank back into her room, flushing with embarrassment.

Wang accompanied Liu back to the parlor. "At first she was as hard as iron," said Liu, "but after I had talked my head off, she melted. Find a follow-up client for her as soon as you can; I'm quite sure she'll take him. When that happens, I'll come back and offer my congratulations." Wang thanked her effusively and invited her to stay to dinner. By the time they parted, both women were quite drunk.

Later, the young rakes of the West Lake made up another "Hanging Branch" song on the subject of Liu's powers of persuasion:

> Liu Sima, oh, Liu Sima,
> How powerful, your tongue!
> No female Sui or distaff Lu would show such skill.
> You say your piece and always overcome.
> With a drunk, you talk him sober;
> With a clever man, you talk him dumb.
> You spoke to a girl of iron will
> And forced her to succumb.

On thinking over the advice she had been given, Mei concluded that it made sense, and from that day forward, whenever anyone came to see her, she received him warmly. Once the second night was over, clients swarmed to the brothel in endless succession, leaving her no time to herself, while her reputation grew by leaps and bounds. For one night with her the client had to pay ten taels of silver, and even at that price the competition was fierce. Wang made a good deal of money, to her infinite delight, but as for Mei, although she kept her eyes open for a man who met her requirements, he was not to be found—for the moment at least.

> Easier to find a priceless gem
> Than it is to get a loving man.

At this point my story breaks off to tell how inside Qingbo Gate in Lin'an there lived the owner of an oil shop named Zhu Shilao. Three years before he had adopted a boy named Qin Zhong,[26] who was another refugee from Bianliang. Qin Zhong's mother had died long before, and his father, Qin Liang, had sold his son to Zhu Shilao at the age of twelve and gone off to become an acolyte at the Upper India Temple. Zhu Shilao, who had recently lost his wife and had no children of his own, treated the boy as his son, changing his name to Zhu Zhong and setting him to learn the retail oil business. At first father and son managed well in the shop, but later Zhu Shilao began to suffer lumbar pains and had to spend most of his time sitting down or in bed. Work became too much for him, and so he took on another clerk, Xing Quan, to help out in the shop.

Four years flew by, and Zhu Zhong, who was now sixteen, had developed into a handsome youth. Although he had come of age, he was still single. In Zhu Shilao's household there was a maid named Orchid, now over twenty, who fancied young Zhu and had several times baited her hook in hopes of catching him. But Zhu Zhong was a well-behaved young fellow, and anyway the maid was ugly and did not appeal to him, so her passion went unrequited. Unsuccessful in her attempts at seducing him, she turned her attentions elsewhere and tried her wiles on the new clerk. Xing Quan, nearing forty and still unmarried, was easy prey, and on more than one occasion the pair held secret trysts. But because they felt inhibited by Zhu Zhong's presence in the shop, they looked for a reason to get him thrown out.

Coordinating their efforts—she inside the household and

26. The name Qin Zhong is a near-homonym of *qingzhong,* meaning a sentimental lover.

he outside—they put their scheme into operation. Affecting an air of injured innocence, Orchid complained to Zhu Shilao, "Several times the young master has tried to take liberties with me. He's been behaving very badly." Zhu Shilao, who used to dally with Orchid himself, felt a twinge of jealousy on hearing this. For his part, Xing Quan hid some money that had come in from sales and reported to Zhu Zhilao, "The young master's been out gambling. His behavior's gone from bad to worse. Several times we've had a shortfall in cash, and it's always because he took it."

At first Zhu Shilao did not credit the accusations, but he heard them over and over again, and in his muddle-headed old age, not knowing what else to do, he called Zhu Zhong in and berated him. Now, Zhu Zhong was a perceptive youth, and he was well aware of the plot that Xing Quan and Orchid had hatched against him, but he also knew that if he tried to defend himself, he would only stir up a tremendous quarrel, and if by some chance the old man did not believe him, he would be unjustly condemned as a villain. An idea came to him. "Business is slow these days," he told Zhu Shilao, "and we really don't need two people in the shop. Why not let Xing Quan run it on his own? I'd be more than willing to take out a load of oil and try to sell it, bringing back whatever I made each day. Why, it would mean adding another line of business!"

Zhu Shilao was inclined to agree, but Xing Quan dissuaded him. "*He* doesn't want to go out selling oil! For several years now he's been pilfering cash to add to his private savings and now he reckons that he has more than enough. He also resents the fact that you haven't arranged a marriage for him. He's not concerned with helping us out; it's *his* future he's interested in—taking a wife and setting up a household of his own."

Zhu Shilao sighed. After I've treated him as a son, he thought, to think that he would harbor such a wicked idea! May Heaven withhold its blessings! But enough of all this! He's not my own flesh and blood, and if we can't stay close, then let him go! Handing Zhu Zhong three taels, he sent him on his way. But he also let him take his clothes and bedding with him—an instance of the man's kindness. Zhu Zhong, who had anticipated that he would be dismissed, bowed four times and left the premises choking back his sobs.

> Because of slander Xiao Ji lost his life;[27]
> Shen Sheng too, when somebody smeared his name.[28]
> Small wonder then, if real sons are treated thus,
> That an adopted son should get the blame.

Let me explain at this point that when Qin Liang went to serve in the temple, he never told his son.

After he had left Zhu Shilao's house, Zhu Zhong rented a tiny room beside Zhongan Bridge, deposited his bedding and other belongings, locked the door with a newly bought padlock, and then scoured the streets and lanes in search of his father. Only when several days of searching had failed to turn up any information did he call a halt. During his four years with Zhu Shilao, he had been scrupulously loyal and honest and had never put aside a penny in private savings. All he possessed were the three taels he had been given on his departure—hardly enough to start a business. He wondered what trade he could practice and, after casting about in his mind, came to the conclusion that the oil business was the only one he was familiar with. He was known at the oil mills, and selling door-to-door was a secure way to make a living. And so he bought a carrying pole as well as other equipment and handed over the rest of his money to a mill for the purchase of oil. The people there knew him as a good, honest man. They knew, too, that although he had worked in the shop from boyhood, he was going off to peddle oil only because Xing Quan had stirred up trouble and forced him out, and they felt a keen sense of injustice on his behalf and were predisposed to help. So they selected only the finest grade of clarified oil and also gave him a break on quan-

---

27. The filial son of an emperor of the Shang dynasty. After his mother died, the emperor listened to slander from his second wife and drove his son out. The son died of melancholia.

28. Son of a duke of the Spring and Autumn period. His father wanted to install his favorite's son in his place. He drove Shen Sheng out, forcing him eventually to kill himself.

tity. With these advantages, Zhu Zhong was able to be a little more liberal in his pricing, and his oil proved easier to move than that of his competitors. Every day brought in a little profit. He lived frugally, reserving the money he saved for daily necessities, clothes, and so forth, and never indulged in any lavish expenditure. There was just one unfinished task that preyed on his mind—finding his father. I've been known as Zhu Zhong for the longest time, he thought, and nobody is aware that my real name is Qin! Even if my father came looking for me, he'd have nothing to go by. So he changed his name back to Qin.

Storyteller, if someone from the upper classes, someone with a splendid career, corrects his name by petitioning the court or by notifying institutions such as the Ministry of Rites, the Imperial Academy, or the National Academy, the registers will be brought up to date and everyone will be aware of the change. But who is to know when a mere oil seller tries to correct his name?[29]

Zhu Zhong, however, had a solution. He wrote a large "Qin" on one of the buckets of oil that he carried and a "Bianliang" on the other, so that his buckets showed the change and people could tell his identity at a glance. In this manner, the people in the center of Lin'an learned his original name and began to call him Oil Seller Qin.

One mild day in the second month, he heard that the priests of Zhaoqing Temple were about to hold a service lasting nine days and nights, and knowing that a great deal of oil would be required, he took a load there. The priests had heard of Oil Seller Qin, and they had also heard that his oil was of finer quality and also cheaper than that of his competitors, so they gave him their exclusive custom. On each of the nine days of the service he delivered oil to the temple.

> A mean and grasping streak will bring no gain,
> A fair and honest heart incur no loss.

On the ninth day, Qin Zhong had disposed of his oil and was leaving the temple with his carrying pole. The weather was

29. This paragraph is a question asked by an imaginary member of the audience.

fine, and the grounds were swarming with visitors. He walked along the river, gazing at the vivid red of the peach blossom and the pale green of the willows on Ten Prospects Embankment, and he also watched the pleasure boats on the lake as they plied their way back and forth with music playing. The view held him entranced. He walked on a bit and then, feeling rather tired, turned back to the other side of the temple and gazed at the broad expanse in front of him. Laying down his pole, he sat on a rock to rest his feet. Close by on one side was a house overlooking the lake. It had a bamboo gate, painted gold, and a clump of fine bamboos inside a vermilion trellis. From the understated elegance of the exterior, you could well imagine what the house itself was like. At that moment three or four men emerged who were dressed as scholars or officials, as well as a girl who was seeing them off. At the door they bowed to each other, and after a polite exchange the girl went inside again. Qin Zhong observed all of this with fascination. He had never set eyes on anyone of such delicate beauty as this girl or with such a soft, voluptuous figure, and for some time he remained transfixed while a feeling of sensual languor swept over him. A somewhat naïve youth, he knew nothing about courtesan behavior and was genuinely puzzled as to what sort of house this might be. Still rapt in thought, he noticed a middle-aged woman come out accompanied by a young girl with braided hair. The woman leaned against the doorpost and looked idly about, then spotted his carrying pole and buckets and exclaimed, "Look at that! We were just going off to buy some oil, and here's oil right in front of us. Let's get some from him." The maid brought out the oil vessel and took it over to Qin Zong and called out to him.

Realizing what she wanted, he replied, "I'm right out of oil, I'm afraid, but if your mistress needs some, I'll bring it tomorrow." The maid, who possessed an elementary reading knowledge, noticed the "Qin" on the buckets and reported to the woman, "The oil seller's name is Qin." The woman had heard of a certain Oil Seller Qin who had a reputation for being fair and honest in his dealings, so she told him, "We need oil every day. If you're prepared to deliver, you can have our custom."

"Thank you, ma'am, for your support. I'll see that the oil is delivered without fail."

The woman and the maid went in again, leaving Qin Zhong to his thoughts. I wonder what the relationship is between this woman and that girl I saw before. When I'm delivering oil here every day, how marvelous it would be if I could feast my eyes on the girl, not to mention picking up a tidy profit.

He was just about to set off when he noticed two bearers carrying a sedan chair with a black silk screen racing toward him, followed by two pages. In front of the door, the bearers set the chair down, and the pages entered the house. That's very odd, thought Qin Zhong; I wonder who they've come for. After a short while two maids came out, one carrying a band-box of crimson felt, the other a visiting-card case of speckled bamboo with flowers painted on it. They handed the articles to the bearers, who tucked them away beneath the seat. Then the pages came out. One was clutching a zither case, the other several hand scrolls, while a green jade flute dangled from one of his wrists. They were escorting the girl that Qin Zhong had seen before. She stepped into the chair, and the bearers lifted it up and bore it back the way they had come, with the maids and pages following on foot. For a second time Qin Zhong was deeply affected by the sight of this girl. Now more mystified than ever, he picked up his pole and walked slowly away.

He had gone only a little distance before he noticed a tavern beside the river. As a rule he never drank, but today, after seeing this girl, he was swept by alternate feelings of ecstasy and depression. Putting down his carrying pole, he stepped inside and found himself a table. A waiter approached. "Will you be meeting any guests here, sir, or are you on your own?"

"I'll have three cups of your premium wine for myself. Also a dish or two of fresh fruit. No meat dishes, though."

As the waiter poured the wine, Qin Zhong asked, "Whose is that house with the gilded bamboo gate?"

"That? Oh, that's Master Qi's garden house. Wang Jiuma is living there at present."

"Just now I saw a young woman getting into a sedan chair. Who was she?"

"That's the famous prostitute Wang Mei, commonly known as the Queen of Flowers. She came down from Bianliang and then got stranded here. Music and singing, dancing, the other arts—she's good at the whole lot of 'em. The people she goes with are all bigwigs who need ten ounces of the shiny stuff just to spend a night with her. As you might imagine, the average man doesn't get a look in. She used to live outside Yongjin Gate, but the place was too cramped, and about six months ago Master Qi—he's a friend of hers—lent her his garden house."

The fact that she was from Bianliang triggered Qin Zhong's homesickness and redoubled his longing for her. After drinking a few cups of wine, he paid the bill, shouldered his pole, and left. All the way back this thought was running through his mind: What a terrible shame such a beautiful girl should fall into prostitution! Then he laughed at himself. If she hadn't, as an oil seller I could never even have set eyes on her! He thought about her a little longer and ended up even more infatuated. The days of man are as grass, he thought. If I could hold such a beautiful creature in my arms for a single night, I'd die content. Then another thought struck him: What nonsense! I carry my loads about all day long for a mere pittance. How could I even dream about anyone so far above me? I'm like the toad in the ditch lusting after swan's flesh! Then another thought: The people she goes with are all sons of noblemen. As an oil seller, even if I had the money, I doubt that she'd agree to see me. And still another thought: They say madams are interested in nothing but money. She'd agree to see a beggar if he had the money, so surely she'd see a businessman like me with a spotless reputation. So long as I have the money, she'll see me, all right. But where am I going to get it? These thoughts whirled through his mind as he walked along talking to himself.

Could you have ever imagined such an infatuated fool as this man? Here he was, a petty tradesman with a working capital of only three taels, and he would need ten to go and spend a night with the famous courtesan! What a pipe dream! However, as the saying goes, where there's a will, there's a way. After puzzling over the problem from every angle, he finally came up with a plan of action: Every day from tomorrow on I'll put aside my working capital and save all the rest. If I manage to save one *fen*[30] a day, by the end of the year I'll have three ounces six

30. One hundredth of an ounce.

qian,[31] and in only three years I'll have reached my goal. If I can save two *fen* a day, it'll take me only a year and a half. And if I can do a little better still, a year should be almost enough.

These thoughts were racing through his mind as he arrived home and let himself in. The whole way he had been preoccupied with such ideas, but when he took a look at his bed, he began to feel depressed. He turned in, having lost his appetite, but all night long, with the beautiful courtesan on his mind, he tossed and turned and couldn't sleep.

> A face like a flower
> Kindled sexual desire.

When morning came at last, he scrambled to his feet, loaded up with oil, cooked and ate his breakfast, locked his door, hastily shouldered his carrying pole, and went straight to Wang's house. He entered the gate, but did not dare go into the house; instead, he craned his neck and peered in. Wang had just gotten out of bed, and her hair was still uncombed. She was telling the maid to buy some food when Qin Zhong recognized her voice and called out her name. She looked out, saw it was Oil Seller Qin, and smiled. "What an honest fellow! You're as good as your word." She told him to bring his load inside, where she measured out one full vessel of oil, over five catties in weight, and offered him a fair price for it. Qin Zhong did not try to haggle, which pleased her greatly. "This will do us for only two days," she said. "If you'll deliver here every second day, we won't deal with anyone else." Qin Zhong agreed and went off with his pole.

His one regret was that he had not met the Queen of Flowers. The good thing is that I've won their patronage, he thought. If I don't see her this time, I'm bound to see her the next, and if I don't see her then, I'll see her the time after that. But there's just one problem: it isn't economical to bring oil all this way just for Wang Jiuma. Zhaoqing Temple is on my way here, and although the priests aren't holding any services just now, they must surely need oil at other times as well. I'll take

31. One tenth of an ounce.

this load over there and ask them. If I can get the patronage of the monks' cells, I'll be able to dispose of my whole load on this Qiantang Gate route. He went over to the temple to ask, and it turned out that the priests already had him in mind as a supplier. He had come just at the right time and, in varying amounts, they bought the rest of his oil. He arranged with the cells to make a delivery every other day. Since this was an even-numbered date, on odd-numbered dates he would work a different route. On the even-numbered dates, he would leave the city by the Qiantang Gate and go first to Wang's, ostensibly to sell oil but actually to see the Queen of Flowers. One day he might see her, another day he might not. If he didn't, the time he had spent longing for her would be wasted, but even if he did see her, that fact would only increase his longing.

> Heaven and Earth will end
> Before this passion dies.

He visited Wang's many times, until everyone in the house, from the highest to the lowest, knew who Oil Seller Qin was. Time flew by, and before he knew it a year or more had passed. Day in and day out he had put aside varying amounts of money, choosing always the finest silver. Sometimes it might be three *fen*, at other times two, but always at least one. When he had accumulated a few *qian*, he would convert them into a larger piece. As the days and months passed, he acquired a sizeable package of bits and pieces. Even he did not know how much they were worth.

On one of the odd-numbered days it happened to be raining heavily, and Qin Zhong stayed home instead of going on his rounds. On looking at the package of silver, he felt rather pleased with himself. I'll use this day off work to go and weigh it and see what it comes to, he thought. Holding an umbrella, he crossed the street to the silversmith's, where he asked to borrow the big scales in order to weigh his silver. The silversmith did not take him seriously, thinking to himself, how much would an oil peddler have, that I'd need to set up the big scales for him? I'll give him the five-ounce balance instead. I doubt he'll need the number 1 lifting cord, either.

Qin Zhong opened the package, which was full of bits and pieces, mostly small, with just a few ingots among them. The silversmith was a callow creature who, when he saw this amount of money, underwent a complete change of attitude. A man can't be judged by his looks, or the ocean measured with a pint pot, he reflected. Hastily setting up the big scales, he brought out a number of weights of varying sizes. Qin Zhong weighed all the silver together, and it came to exactly sixteen ounces, a full catty. After deducting my three ounces of working capital, he thought, the rest will do for a night with the courtesan and still leave something over. Then another thought struck him: I can't go offering all this loose change to people! They'd only look down their noses at me. Why don't I have it converted into full ingots while I'm here at the silversmith's? That would make a much better impression. He weighed out ten ounces and had the silversmith cast them into a standard-quality ingot, then had another one ounce eight *qian* cast into a small ingot of low-quality silver. That left four ounces two *qian*. He combined that into a single small piece that he used to pay the casting fee and buy new shoes with bound edges as well as new socks. He also had a cruciform turban made.[32] Returning home, he thoroughly laundered and starched his clothes, and bought several sticks of benzoin to scent them with. He then chose a fine day and early in the morning dressed up in his new clothes.

> No rich or noble client was he,
> But a dashing fellow nonetheless.

Smartly dressed, he tucked some money in his sleeve, locked his door, and made straight for Wang's house. Until the moment he arrived he was full of joyous anticipation, but at the gate a feeling of shame suddenly asserted itself. All the other times I've been here it was to deliver oil, he thought. Now all of a sudden I'm showing up as a client. How can I even open my mouth? As he hesitated in front of the gate, it creaked open and Wang emerged. At the sight of Qin Zhong, she exclaimed, "Mas-

---

32. I.e., with a Buddhist swastika design.

ter Qin, why aren't you at work? And you're so smartly dressed! Where are you off to?"

At this point, Qin Zhong could only put on a bold front, step forward, and bow to her, a greeting she had to return. "I've come specially to visit you, ma'am," he said.

Wang was an old hand, shrewd enough to deduce what was going on. Seeing him decked out like this and hearing him talk of a visit, she thought to herself, He must have taken a fancy to one of our girls, and now he wants to spend a night with her, or perhaps just have a short time. He may not be the Buddha almighty, but we can't pick and choose our clients—we have to take what we get. And his money pays for the groceries just like anyone else's. Beaming from ear to ear, she replied, "If you've come to visit me, I'm sure it will be to my advantage."

"There's something highly improper that I wanted to ask you, but I'm too embarrassed to say the words."

"Don't worry, go ahead and ask. But let's move into the parlor first."

Although Qin Zhong had been to Wang's house as an oil seller a hundred times, the armchairs in the parlor had never made the acquaintance of his bottom; today they were introduced for the first time. Wang naturally sat Qin Zhong in the guest's place and called for tea to be served. Before long the maid brought in a tea tray, but seeing Oil Seller Qin in the guest's place and not understanding why her mistress would treat him like that, she hung her head and dissolved into giggles.

"What's so funny?" Wang snapped. "Such manners in front of a guest!"

The maid stifled her giggles, collected the teacups, and left the room. Only then did Wang open the conversation. "Well, Master Qin, what was it you were going to ask me?"

"Just that I wanted to invite a young lady from your household to share some wine with me."

"I don't suppose for a moment that you mean *only* wine. Surely you want to sleep with her, too? But you're such a steady young fellow. When did you get these romantic notions?"

"It's been my earnest desire for some time now."

"Well, you know all the young ladies in the house. Which one do you fancy?"

"Only the Queen of Flowers, nobody else. I'd like to spend a night with her."

Wang assumed he was mocking her, and she turned on him. "Now you're going too far! You're trying to make fun of me, I suppose?"

"I'm an honest person. I'd never deceive you."

"Go on! Even a slops bucket has a pair of lugs on it![33] Surely you've heard what her fee is? Why, you could sell up your whole business and still not have enough for half the night! You'd better pick someone you can afford and enjoy yourself with her."

Qin Zhong pulled back his head and shot out his tongue as if awestruck. "What a *promotion!* I hardly dare ask how many thousand taels I would need for a night with the Queen."

At his bantering tone, Wang's mood changed. "You wouldn't need *that* much," she conceded with a smile. "No more than ten of the best. Dinners and sundries extra."

"I see," said Qin Zhong. "Well, that's no great problem." From his sleeve he brought out a single shiny ingot of fine silver and handed it to her. "This weighs ten ounces. It's full weight and standard quality. Please keep it for me."

He also took out a small ingot and gave it to her. "This little one weighs two ounces. Please take it and use it to pay for a modest dinner. If you help me succeed in this, I shan't forget, and after it's all over I'll have another present for you."

Wang looked at the large ingot. She couldn't bear to let it out of her hands, but she was also afraid that Qin Zhong's action might be the result of some sudden impulse; one day he might regret the loss of capital. She felt she ought to sound him out.

"It can't have been easy for a tradesman like you to save up all this money. You ought to think twice before going ahead."

"My mind is made up. Don't you worry about me, ma'am."

Wang tucked the ingot away in her sleeve. "That's all very well, but we still have many obstacles ahead of us."

"But you're the head of the household. What obstacles could there be?"

"Our Mei consorts only with the sons of the nobility and

33. Handles in the shape of ears.

with rich and powerful men. You can truly say of her that 'She talks and laughs with the greatest minds; her friends include no unlettered man.'[34] She'll surely recognize you as Qin the tradesman and refuse to see you."

"Then it all depends on your trying every possible approach, doesn't it? If you succeed, I shall never forget your kindness!"

Wang saw that he was absolutely determined. She knitted her brow in thought, and an idea occurred to her. "I do have a plan, but its success will depend on your good fortune," she said with a broad smile. "If it works, you mustn't congratulate me, but if it fails, you mustn't blame me either. Yesterday Mei went to a party at Academician Li's from which she has yet to come back. Today she's down for an outing on the lake with Master Huang. Tomorrow Zhang the Recluse and his literary group have asked her to attend their poetry club. As for the day after tomorrow, the son of Minister Han gave us money several days ago to hold a party here. Come along the day after that, and we'll see how matters stand. I have a word of advice for you, though. Don't come here selling oil for the next few days. Try to maintain a little dignity in advance of the meeting. And there's one other thing. In those cotton clothes you don't look at all like one of our upper-class clients. Change into a silk gown before you come next time, so that the maids won't recognize you. It'll also be easier for me to make up a story about you."

"I understand perfectly," said Qin Zhong, as he took his leave. For the next three days he did no business and never went out selling oil. Instead he bought a secondhand silk gown at a pawnshop and strolled about the streets in it, practicing the deportment of a cultivated gentleman.

> While still unversed in brothel conduct,
> He studies Confucian etiquette.

Let me pass over the next three days. On the fourth day he rose early and went to Wang's, but he was too early—the gate

34. Originally from the prose piece "Loushi ming" by Liu Yuxi (772–842).

was still shut. At first he thought of taking a turn about the grounds, but in the strange garb he was wearing he couldn't risk going to Zhaoqing Temple, lest the priests comment on it. So he walked over to Ten Prospects Embankment and strolled about for a long time before returning. The gate was now open, but a sedan chair and a horse were waiting in front, while inside a number of servants were sitting idly about. Qin Zhong may have been naïve, but he had his wits about him. Instead of going in, he quietly beckoned to the groom. "Who do the chair and horse belong to?"

"They've been sent over from the Han compound to fetch the young master," said the groom. Qin Zhong realized that young Han had stayed the night and was still there. He turned and went back to a restaurant, where he ate a set meal and waited a while before going back to check for news. This time the sedan chair and the horse were gone, but Wang met him inside the gate. "I'm terribly sorry, but she has no time today, either," she said. "Young Han has taken her off to his eastern estate to enjoy the early plum blossom. He's a client of long standing, and I couldn't very well object. I understand that tomorrow she's going to Lingyin Temple to call on a chess master and play a game with him. Master Qi has also been here two or three times hoping to arrange something. He's our landlord, someone we can't say no to, and whenever he visits, he'll stay for three or four days—I'm never sure myself how long. Master Qin, if you really want to sleep with her, you'll just have to be patient and wait a few more days. If you can't wait, well, that gift that you left here the other day has not been touched, and you are free to take it back."

"All I'm concerned about is that I can count on your help. For me, it's better late than never. I'm willing to wait for her, even if it takes a thousand years."

"In that case, I'll see to it personally."

As he was taking his leave, she added, "Master Qin, there's one more thing. When you come to ask for news, don't come too early. By three or four in the afternoon I ought to know for certain whether she has any engagements that evening. In fact, the later you come, the better; that's when I can pull it off. Please don't take offense."

"Oh no, not at all."

That day he did not attend to any business. Beginning the next morning, he loaded up and took a different route, not the one that led through Qiantang Gate. Every evening after work he dressed up and went over to Wang's to see if there was any news, but the Queen was never free. This pattern of fruitless visits continued for over a month.

On the fifteenth of the twelfth month, a heavy snowfall finally cleared, and the west wind turned the snow to ice. It was bitterly cold, but fortunately the ground was dry underfoot. Qin Zhong put in half a day's work, then dressed up as before and went off to inquire. This time Wang was beaming as she welcomed him. "Today's your lucky day! It's ninety-nine percent certain."

"Why not a hundred percent?"

"A hundred percent? Well, the key person hasn't shown up yet."

"She *is* coming, though?"

"Today she was invited by Marshal Yu to go and enjoy the snow, and a banquet was arranged on a boat on the lake. The marshal is an old gentleman of seventy who no longer goes in for the romantic side of things, and he did say he would bring her back this evening. Why not go into the bridal chamber and warm yourself up with a cup of wine while you wait?"

"Please show me the way."

She led him on a circuitous route past many rooms until they came to a residence that was a small bungalow, not an upstairs apartment. It was extremely airy and spacious. The room on the left was a spare maid's room and furnished in the usual manner with bed, table, and chairs, but prepared for general use. The room on the right, which was locked, was the Queen's bedroom. It had small rooms on each side of it. The one in the middle was a sitting room. A landscape by a well-known artist hung on the wall; a rare bronze censer stood on a table burning a cake of ambergris and on either side of it there were desks with antiques placed on them. Many handwritten poems were stuck on the walls, but Qin Zhong, who was embarrassed by his lack of literary cultivation, did not presume to go and inspect them. If the outer rooms are as elegant as this, he thought, her bedroom must be magnificent. If I'm able to enjoy myself to the full tonight, ten taels will not be too high a price to pay.

Wang showed him to a chair in the sitting room, where she played the host. Soon a maid arrived with a lamp, and then a square table was carried in. Six dishes of fresh fruit and a hamper of delicacies were placed on the table, as well as a fine wine whose bouquet pervaded the room.

A cup of wine in her hand, Wang urged him to drink. "All of our girls are busy with their clients tonight, so it's fallen to me to keep you company. Come on, you can drink to your heart's content." Qin Zhong had no great capacity for wine, and he was too preoccupied, anyway, with more serious matters, so he drank only half a cup, and then declined to drink any more.

"I expect you're hungry," said Wang. "Eat a little food, and then try some more wine." A maid brought in two bowls of glistening white rice and placed them in front of him, as well as a bowl of blended soup. Wang, who had a strong capacity for drink, did not eat anything, but kept him company with the wine.

After Qin Zhong had finished one bowl, he laid down his chopsticks. "You have a long night ahead of you," urged Wang. "Do have a little more." Qin Zhong ate another half bowl. Then a maid came in with a lantern and announced, "Your bath is ready, sir. Please come with me."

Qin Zhong, who had already had one bath, did not dare refuse, but went to the bathroom, where he found soap and scented water waiting for him. He washed himself, then dressed again and returned. Wang ordered the food hamper taken away and had the wine put in a chafing dish. The early part of the evening was now over, and the bells of Zhaoqing Temple had finished their tolling, but the courtesan had still not returned.

> Where is Beauty making merry?
> Her lover strains his eyes to see.

As the saying goes, waiting makes the heart grow anxious. When the courtesan failed to return, Qin Zhong became extremely worried, while the madam at his side kept up a stream of incoherent, bawdy remarks urging him to drink up. Two more hours passed before he heard a commotion outside—the Queen of Flowers was back! A maid came in to report her arrival, and Wang scrambled up and went off to welcome her. Qin Zhong also got to his feet. Mei appeared to be in a terribly drunken state. The maidservants helped her as far as the doorway, where with bleary eyes she took in the bright lights and the dirty dishes, and stopped. "Who's been drinking in here?" she asked.

"Child, it's that young Master Qin that I spoke about the other day. He's a great admirer of yours, and he's been sending you presents for ages. You've had no time for him, so he's been kept waiting for more than a month. Fortunately you're free today, so I've invited him over to keep you company."

"I've never heard of any Master Qin in Lin'an. I shan't see him."

She turned and began to walk off, but Wang put up her hands and barred the way. "He's a good, sincere man. I would never deceive you." Mei had to turn back. Stepping into the room, she raised her head and looked at him. He seemed somewhat familiar, but in her drunken state she could not recall his name.

"Mother, I know this man," she said, "and he's not anyone important. I'll only be laughed at if I receive him."

"Child, this is the Master Qin who owns the silk shop inside Yongjin Gate. I expect you met him when we used to live near the gate, and that's why he looks familiar. You mustn't confuse him with anyone else. I was impressed by the sincerity of his intentions and made him a promise that I would hate to have to break. For my sake, do let him stay over for the night. I shouldn't have arranged this, I know, and tomorrow I'll make up for it." As she said this, she pushed her forward. Mei was unable to defy her and had to enter the room and greet Qin Zhong.

> The old bawd's tongue is hard to flee,
> Her hand is harder still.
> Better not challenge either one,
> But simply do her will.

Qin Zhong caught every word of this exchange but pretended he hadn't. Mei curtsied and took a seat to one side of him while she studied his face, still unconvinced of his identity. She sat there without a word, the picture of dejection, then ordered her maid to bring some heated wine and filled a large cup with it. Wang assumed she was going to offer it to her guest, but instead Mei downed it herself in a single draft.

"You're drunk already, my dear," said Wang. "You really oughtn't to have any more."

Mei took no notice, insisting, "I'm *not* drunk!" She proceeded to down a dozen more cups in quick succession. This was wine coming on top of wine, and it made her so drunk that she became unsteady on her feet. She told a maid to open the bedroom door and light her lamp and then, without taking off her jewelry or undoing her sash, she kicked off her shoes and flopped down on her bed fully clothed.

Wang was full of apologies for Mei's behavior. "She's badly spoiled, and all too apt to lose her temper. She's out of sorts today for some reason that has nothing whatever to do with you, so please don't take offense!"

"Not at all."

Wang urged Qin Zhong to drink some more wine, but he steadily refused. Ushering him into the bedroom, she whispered in his ear, "She's drunk. Be gentle with her." Calling to the girl, she said, "Come on, child, up you get. Take your clothes off and go to bed properly." But Mei was already sound asleep and made no response. Wang had to withdraw.

The maid cleared away the wine things, wiped the table, and called out, "I'll say goodnight now, Master Qin."

"If you have any hot tea, I'd like a pot of it," he replied. She made a flask of strong tea and brought it in, then went off to sleep in one of the side rooms, closing the bedroom door behind her.

Qin Zhong saw that Mei was sound asleep with her face to the wall. She was lying on top of the embroidered coverlet, and he worried that in her drunken state she might be susceptible to cold, but he did not dare awaken her. On the railing of the bed he noticed a satin coverlet, which he gently took down and spread over her. Then he trimmed the lamp until it shone brightly, picked up the flask of tea, took off his shoes and lay down beside her, his left hand holding the flask to his chest, his right hand resting on her body. Not for a moment did he dare to shut his eyes.

> Though lacking consummation,
> This counts as making love.

Mei slept until midnight, when she awoke and began to feel the overpowering effects of the wine—an acute congestion inside her chest. Scrambling up, she squatted among the bedclothes with her head between her knees, racked by one dry heave after another. Qin Zhong sat up at once, and realizing she was about to vomit, put down the flask and began stroking her back. After some time, she lost control and, in less time than it takes to say it, her throat opened up and she began vomiting. To prevent the bedding from getting soiled, Qin Zhong spread out the sleeve of his gown and covered her mouth. Despite herself, Mei now began vomiting in earnest, and when she had finished, with her eyes still shut, she asked for some tea to rinse out her mouth.[35] The flask was still warm to the touch, and Qin Zhong poured out a cup of strong, sweet-smelling tea and handed it to her. She drank two cups in quick succession, but although she now felt somewhat more comfortable, she was still exhausted, and she lay down again, turned her face to the wall, and went back to sleep. Qin Zhong took off his gown, rolled up the sleeve that held her vomit, and placed the gown beside the bed. He then returned and held her as before. She slept on until dawn, when she turned over and found a man lying beside her. "Who are *you?*" she demanded.

"My name is Qin."

Mei tried to recall the events of the previous night, but her memory was too hazy and she could not be sure.

35. His rolling up of the soiled gown is described twice, evidently by mistake. The first description, which comes at this point, has been omitted in the translation.

"I must have been really drunk last night!"

"Not so very drunk."

"Did I vomit?"

"No."

"Oh, that's not so bad, then." She thought for a moment. "But I distinctly remember vomiting and then having some tea to drink. Surely I didn't dream all of that?"

"No, you did vomit," admitted Qin Zhong. "I saw you had had a drink too many, and so I kept a flask of tea warm against my chest just in case. After you vomited, you asked for tea, and I poured you some. You were gracious enough to drink two cups of it."

She was aghast. "But how *revolting!* Where did I throw up?"

"I was afraid you might soil the bedding, so I caught it in my sleeve."

"Where is it now?"

"Rolled up in my gown. It's over there, out of sight."

"But what a shame. Your gown will be *ruined!*"

"It was fortunate to be blessed by you."

Has there ever been such a tactful person, she asked herself, more than a little pleased with him.

By now it was broad daylight, and she got up to relieve herself. Then, glancing at Qin Zhong, she suddenly remembered who he was—Oil Seller Qin. "Now tell me the truth: What sort of person are you? And what were you doing here last night?"

"When the Queen of Flowers does me the honor of asking me something, I wouldn't dare tell a lie. I am the Qin Zhong who comes here all the time delivering oil." He went on to tell her in detail how he had first seen her saying goodbye to visitors and then seen her stepping into a sedan chair; how he had felt an intense love and admiration for her; and how he had saved up his money to spend a night with her. "To be able to be close to you all last night—why, it was the high point of my life, and now I'm perfectly content," he concluded.

This made Mei feel even more sorry for him. "But I was drunk last night and unable to entertain you. You've spent a great deal of money—all for nothing. Don't you regret it?"

"With a heavenly being like you, my only fear was that I

might not serve you properly. To me the great blessing is that I haven't displeased you. I would never dare to hope for anything so far beyond me!"

"But as a tradesman, after you'd saved up a little money, why didn't you use it to support your own family? This isn't the sort of place you should be visiting."

"I live by myself. I don't have a wife."

She paused a moment before continuing. "Will you be coming back again after you leave here today?"

"Being close to you all last night—that thought will console me for the rest of my life. I wouldn't dare indulge in any more wishful thinking."

There are precious few men in the world as good as this one, she thought. He's kind, honest, generous, considerate, tactful, and he appreciates the good in me and overlooks the bad—why, he's one in a million! It's such a pity he belongs to the tradesman class! If he were a gentleman, I'd gladly give myself to him in marriage.

As she turned these thoughts over in her mind, the maid brought in the water for their morning wash, as well as two cups of ginger soup. Qin Zhong washed his face, but because he had never removed his turban during the night, he did not need to dress his hair. He took a few sips of ginger soup, then got up to take his leave.

"Why not stay a little longer? There's something else I want to say to you."

"I admire you so much that I value every moment I can be with you, but a man has to take stock of himself. In spending the night here I took too great a liberty, and if the story ever gets out, I'm afraid it will harm your reputation. The sooner I leave, the better."

She nodded and sent the maid out of the room, then quickly opened her vanity case and took out twenty taels, which she handed to Qin Zhong. "I put you to a lot of trouble last night. Don't tell anyone about it, but this is meant as a contribution to your business." When Qin Zhong refused to accept it, she continued, "Look, my money is easily come by. This is to repay you for a night's affection. Now, don't be stubborn. If you need more, there'll be other opportunities to help you. As for the soiled clothing, I'll have the maid wash it out and return it to you."

"My poor clothes aren't worthy of your concern; I can wash them myself. But it's not right to accept your gift."

"What nonsense!" She stuffed the money in his sleeve and turned him around until he faced the other way. He concluded that it would be impossible to refuse and, after bowing deeply, left with the soiled gown rolled up in a bundle. As he passed by the madam's door, the maid noticed and cried, "Mother! Master Qin is leaving." Wang, who was on the commode at the time, called out, "Master Qin, why are you leaving so early?"

"I have some business I need to see to. I'll be back another day to thank you for all your help."

Let me turn to Mei. She had done nothing with Qin Zhong, and when she considered the genuine affection he had shown her, she began to feel remorseful after he left. Because she was suffering from a severe hangover, she canceled all her engagements and stayed home, but all day long her thoughts were of Qin Zhong rather than of her countless other clients. A "Hanging Branch" song depicts her mood:

> Oh, my handsome love!
> You're not one to haunt the houses of ill fame;
> You depend on your honest tradesman's name.
> I never dreamt you'd be so sensitive
> As to feel my joy and pain.
> I doubt you'll ever lose your temper
> Or play a double game.
> I tried to put you out of my mind,
> But you popped right in again.

My story now turns to Xing Quan in Zhu Shilao's household. He was involved in an intense affair with Orchid, and when he found that Zhu was disabled and bedridden, he cast aside whatever scruples he had had. On several occasions Zhu Shilao raged at the two lovers, and so they decided to take action. In the dead of night they gathered up all the money in the shop and absconded with it; no one knew where. Not until early the next morning did Zhu Shilao learn of the theft.

He appealed to the neighbors for help, drew up a list of the stolen property, and had a search conducted that went on for days without success. He now deeply regretted falling for Xing Quan's lies and driving Zhu Zhong out of the house; at last, after all this time, he realized the latter's true worth. Hearing that he was renting a room near Zhongan Bridge and peddling oil for a living, Zhu Shilao thought it best to bring him back again; that way he would have someone to depend on in his old age. His one concern was that the young man might hold a grudge against him, so he asked the neighbors to do their best to persuade him to return, urging him to remember the good times rather than the bad. No sooner had Qin Zhong heard the news than he packed up his belongings and moved back into the Zhu household, where his reunion with Zhu Shilao was the occasion of many tears. Shilao entrusted all of his capital to Qin Zhong, who also had more than twenty taels of his own. He rebuilt the shop and sold oil again from behind the counter. Now that he was back in the Zhu household, he called himself Zhu Zhong once more instead of Qin Zhong.

Within a month Zhu Shilao's illness had taken a critical turn and, when medical treatment proved ineffective, he died. Zhu Zhong beat his breast and cried his heart out, just as if the dead man were his own father. He saw to the laying-in, wore mourning dress, and held seven services, one on every seventh day following the death. The ancestral tomb lay outside Qingbo Gate, and Zhu Zhong saw to it that the funeral was conducted with such scrupulous concern for the proprieties that all the neighbors praised his virtue.

When these matters had been taken care of, Zhu Zhong reopened the shop. It was an old establishment that had always done good business, but because of Xing Quan's ruthless, grasping ways, it had lost many of its customers. Now that Zhu Zhong was back in charge, they rallied around and the business thrived as never before, to the point at which he urgently needed an experienced assistant. One day a professional middleman named Jin Zhong brought in a candidate in his fifties. As it happens, the man was none other than the Xin Shan who had once lived in Bliss Village on the outskirts of Bianliang. In the flight south he and his wife had been separated from their daughter by the soldiers' onslaught. Rushing from one place to another in great distress, they had somehow managed to survive the next few years. Recently they had heard that Lin'an was a thriving center in which most of the northern refugees had settled, and suspecting that their daughter might have drifted there, they had come searching for her, so far without success. By now, however, all their money had run out; in fact, they owed money for food and were regularly chased away from the stores. They were at the end of their tether when they happened to hear Jin Zhong mention that the Zhu oil shop was looking for a sales assistant. Since Xin had run a general store himself and had experience selling oil, and since Zhu Zhong was, like himself, a former resident of Bianliang, Xin had asked Jin to recommend him.

When Zhu Zhong questioned Xin Shan about his background and found that they were fellow citizens of Bianliang, he was deeply moved. "Since you and your wife have nowhere else to go, you must come and live with me, like fellow townsmen staying with one another. In due course, when you hear news of your daughter, you can make other arrangements." He gave Xin Shan two strings of cash with which to settle his food bills, and Xin Shan brought his wife along to meet Zhu Zhong. A spare room was made ready for them, and they did their utmost to be of help, both inside and outside the household. Zhu Zhong was very pleased with them.

A year or more flew by. Many fathers, noting that Zhu Zhong was unmarried despite his relatively mature years and also that he was well-to-do, honest, and dependable, offered to marry their daughters to him without a betrothal settlement. But Zhu Zhong, having seen the Queen of Flowers' superb beauty, had set his heart on finding an outstanding girl and would not even consider an ordinary one. And so more time went by, and the issue was continually put off.

> When once you've seen the sea, no mere lake will do;
> Your only clouds will be those atop Mt. Wu.[36]

36. A reference to the "Gaotang Rhapsody" by Song Yu. It tells of King Xiang's dream of his meeting with the goddess of Mt. Wu, an archetypal sexual

Let me turn to Mei in Wang's establishment. Because of her fame, she was caught up in a ceaseless round of revelry by day and night, so that, as the saying goes, she was "sated with delicacies, weary of silk and satin." However, when something happened to displease her, such as when a client lost his temper or acted jealous or jilted her, or when she herself felt unwell or had a hangover, and at midnight there was no one beside her to offer any tender affection, she would start thinking of Master Qin's sterling qualities and regret that fate had not brought them together again.

As it happens, her own fate as a courtesan was about to change. A year later, trouble arose.

In the city of Lin'an there lived a young gentleman who was the eighth son of Wu Yue, the prefect of Fuzhou. Master Wu had recently returned to Lin'an from his father's post lavishly supplied with money, and he liked to spend his time gambling, drinking, and frequenting the brothels. He had heard of the Queen of Flowers' reputation, but had not met her. On a number of occasions he had sent people over to arrange a meeting, hoping to spend the night with her, but Mei had been told that he had a nasty temper, and so she was reluctant to take up with him and had put him off with one excuse after another. Wu had also visited the brothel several times himself with his henchmen, but with no better success.

It happened during the Qingming Festival, when families were tending their ancestral graves and people everywhere were going on spring outings. Mei was worn out from the daily excursions. Moreover, she had promised people many paintings and poems that she had not yet completed, so she told the staff, "If any clients call, just say I'm not at home." She shut her door, lit a fine incense, set out her writing things, and was just about to start when she heard an uproar outside—it was Wu with a dozen of his henchmen who had come to invite her to an outing on the lake. Because he had been rebuffed by the madam on previous occasions, he began by roughhousing in the parlor, vandalizing the furniture, and then continued in the

---

encounter that supplies much Chinese erotic imagery. The lines are from the poem "Li si" by Yuan Zhen (779–831).

same manner right to Mei's door, which he found to be locked. Now, brothels have a way of deterring clients. The prostitute will hide in her room with the door locked from the outside, and the client will be fobbed off with the excuse that she is out. A naïve client would have been taken in, but Wu was far too sophisticated to fall for a trick of this sort. He ordered his men to wrench off the lock and then kicked the door open, leaving Mei with no time to escape. Wu spotted her, and without giving her a chance to protest, had two of his men seize her hands and drag her out of the room, while he kept up a stream of curses. Wang was about to come forward and apologize in hopes of appeasing him, but at this nasty turn of events she had no choice but to keep out of sight. In fact the entire staff vanished without a trace. Wu's men dragged Mei out the front gate and hurried her down the street with no concern for the tiny, narrow slippers she was wearing, while Wu himself swaggered along behind. At Lake Inlet, his men pushed her into a boat and finally released her. Ever since joining the Wang household at the age of eleven, she had been raised in luxury and treated like some priceless jewel; never before had she been subjected to such humiliation. Facing the bow of the boat, she put her head in her hands and gave way to sobs. Scowling at the sight—wrathful as Guan Yu at the Single Sword Meeting[37]— Wu turned his chair away and sat there, his men at his side. As he gave the order to cast off, he put on a prize exhibition of nonstop ranting and raving. "Little slut, little whore, you don't appreciate the favor I'm doing you! Any more of your tears, and you'll get a good hiding!" Mei continued to cry, undaunted by his threats.

As soon as they reached Mid-Lake,[38] Wu ordered the picnic hamper placed in the pavilion. He himself went ahead, telling his men, "Get that little slut to join me." But Mei clung to the rail, refusing to go and bawling loudly. Wu felt frustrated. After

37. The reference is to a famous adventure of Guan Yu, one of the heroes of the Three Kingdoms saga; see the novel *Sanguo yanyi*, chapter 66. It is also the subject of numerous plays. Guan Yu was invited to a feast where his hosts planned to assassinate him, but he managed to intimidate them.
38. A tiny island in the middle of the West Lake. It is barely big enough to accommodate the pavilion built on it.

drinking a few cheerless cups of wine, he returned to the boat and tried his hand at pulling her off the rail, but she lashed out with both feet and sobbed more loudly than ever. Wu flew into a rage and told his men to strip off all her hairpins and earrings. With her hair in wild disarray, she made a dash for the bow and was just about to throw herself into the water when Wu's servants caught her.

"You can act up all you like, you won't scare me," said Wu. "Even if you die, it'll only cost me a few taels—nothing worth worrying about. Still, it would be a pity if you did die. If you'll stop your crying, I'll let you go home without any further hassle."

At these words, Mei did stop crying. Wu directed the boat to an isolated spot beyond Qingbo Gate, where he had her shoes and foot bindings removed, exposing her tiny feet, which looked like nothing so much as a pair of tender bamboo shoots. Telling his men to help her ashore, he snarled, "You little slut! Since you're so clever, you can get yourself home. I can't spare anyone to take you back." So saying, he pushed off with the pole and headed back to the middle of the lake.

> How often are the finer things destroyed!
> How rarely is tender beauty cherished!

In her bare feet Mei could scarcely walk. I have both beauty and talent, she thought to herself, and it's only because I've fallen into prostitution that I have to endure this sort of abuse. Making friends with all those young noblemen didn't do me any good, either; in a pinch I couldn't turn to them for help but still had to suffer this humiliation. Even if I do get back, how am I ever going to hold my head up again? Death—that's the best option! But to die in obscurity—that would mean throwing away all the fame I've acquired. At this stage of my life even some village woman is better off than I am. It's all the fault of that smooth-talking Liu Sima, who lured me into her trap and brought me to this state! A pretty face spells a sorry fate, as the old saying goes, but it doesn't have to be *this* sorry! The more she thought about it, the more miserable she felt, until finally she burst out crying.

By an odd coincidence, that same day Zhu Zhong had been visiting Zhu Shilao's grave outside Qingbo Gate. After the ceremony he sent the sacrificial vessels back by boat and came home himself on foot, passing by this very spot. On hearing a woman cry, he went over to see what was the matter. Despite her wild hair and grimy face, there was no mistaking Wang Mei's beauty. "Queen of Flowers, how did you get into such a state?" he exclaimed.

Through her sobs she heard a familiar voice, stopped crying and looked up, and there in front of her stood the ever sensitive and tactful Master Qin. At such a time it was like seeing a member of her own family, and all her woes poured spontaneously forth. Zhu Zhong felt real anguish for her and shed tears himself. From his sleeve he pulled a white silk sash about five feet in length and tore it into two strips which he gave her to bind up her feet with, while he himself wiped away her tears and drew up her hair, comforting her the whole time with kind words. When she had gotten over her crying, he hurried away to call a curtained sedan chair, which he invited her to step into. He then escorted the chair on foot all the way back to Wang Jiuma's establishment.

All this time Wang had had no news of her daughter. After inquiring everywhere, she was in a state of near panic when suddenly she saw Master Qin bringing her back, returning her like some brilliant lost jewel, and of course she was overjoyed. What's more, she had not seen Qin delivering oil in a long time, but she had often heard that he had inherited the Zhu business and was now both well off and highly respected, and naturally she saw him in a different light. She also noticed the state her daughter was in, and when she learned of the suffering the girl had endured and of the debt they owed to Zhu Zhong, she bowed deeply in gratitude and invited him in for some wine. It was getting late, and after a few cups he got up to go, but Mei would have none of it.

"Ever since we first met I've been drawn to you," she said, "and I was dying to see you again. This time I absolutely refuse to let you leave here with nothing." Wang added her voice to Mei's. As for Zhu Zhong, he was overjoyed.

For his benefit Mei played music and sang songs and

danced with all her consummate artistry. Zhu Zhong might have been in the midst of some romantic dream he was so enraptured—in fact, he almost danced for joy himself. And in the dead of night, when they had drunk their fill, they went hand-in-hand into the bedroom, where the ecstasy of their lovemaking can be left to the imagination.

> He a young man in his lusty prime,
> She a woman well versed in love.
> He spoke of three years' longing
> And dream after anguished dream,
> She of a year of yearning
> And her joy in lying cheek to cheek.
> He felt indebted to his earlier *bangchen*,
> Which led to favor piled on favor.
> She was glad she had arranged this night,
> With much more love than before.
> The courtesan tipped the perfume from her sachet,
> Staining the silk beneath;
> The oil seller spilt the oil from his vessel,
> Soaking the bedding below.
> "What vulgar louts they were, who spent their money to no
> purpose,
> But enabled me to play the game of love!"

When they had finished their lovemaking, Mei said, "I want to ask you something that's very dear to my heart, and you mustn't put me off with any excuses."

"I'd go through fire and flood if you needed me to. I'd never try to make excuses."

"I want to marry you."

Zhu Zhong laughed. "If you wanted to marry ten thousand men, you still wouldn't get as far as me. Stop making fun of me—you'll only shorten my days on earth."[39]

"What do you mean, 'making fun of you'? I'm absolutely serious. Ever since I was thirteen and Mother got me drunk and

---

39. A conventional expression. The notion behind it is that too much joy will exhaust one's lifetime ration of happiness.

I lost my virginity, I've wanted to get married.[40] The only trouble was that I had never been close to anyone and couldn't tell a good man from a bad, and I was afraid I might make a mistake in this, the most important decision of my life. Later, although I went with many men, they were all grandees or plutocrats, drunkards or lechers, men who knew only how to buy their pleasures and had no real desire for love. I've looked everywhere, and you're the only honest and true gentleman I've come across. Moreover, I understand that you're single. Unless you reject me because I'm a prostitute, I'm willing to marry you and serve you all the days of my life. If you should reject me, I shall take a strip of white silk and strangle myself before your very eyes, to demonstrate my utter sincerity. That would at least be better than dying at the hands of that vulgar lout yesterday, dying an ignominious death, the butt of everybody's jokes." She burst into loud, racking sobs.

"Please don't distress yourself. To receive your love—why, it's more than I could ever have hoped for, since you're so far above me. I would never dream of making any excuses, but you're a priceless treasure, and I'm quite poor. How could I ever afford it? Much as I'd love to, I simply can't."

"That's no problem. To tell you the truth, when I was thinking ahead about marriage, I saved up some money and valuables and sent them out of the house for safekeeping. It won't cost you a penny to buy me out."

"But even if you buy yourself out, you're used to great mansions, gorgeous dresses, superb cuisine. . . . How will you get by in my house?"

" 'Live the simple life and die without regret.' "

"But even though you may be willing, I'm afraid your mother won't agree."

"I know how to handle her." She explained how she would do so.[41]

They went on talking until dawn.

40. *Cong liang.* Used of a prostitute, it means to join respectable society by marrying.
41. The Chinese uses a formula to indicate that what she said is being withheld from the reader.

Mei had deposited trunks full of valuables with each of three friends, the sons of Academician Huang, Minister Han, and Marshal Qi. Explaining that she needed the trunks, she now had them transported one after the other to a secret location, then arranged for Zhu Zhong to pick them up and hold them for her at his house. Next she took a sedan chair to Liu Sima's and told her of her plan to marry.

"Well, I did mention marriage to you before, but you're still rather young, you know. Anyway, who is this man you want to marry?"

"Never mind who he is, Aunt. Of course, I took your advice to heart and am planning for a true, happy, and close-out marriage, not a false, wretched, or incomplete affair. Provided you're prepared to speak up for me, I'm quite sure Mother will agree. All I have as a gift for you is ten taels, enough for a few hairpins only, but you have to help us with Mother. If we succeed, the go-between's fee will be yours as well."

At the sight of the money, Liu smiled so broadly that her eyes practically disappeared. "You're a member of the family, and this is a blessed event we're talking about, so what would I want with your money? I'll just keep it for the time being, as if I were holding it in trust. You can leave this business entirely to me. The only problem is that your mother looks on you as a money tree and will not let you go so easily. I expect she'll want at least a thousand. Is that client of yours willing to part with that kind of money? I really ought to meet him to discuss it."

"Aunt, that's no concern of yours. Just assume that I'm buying myself out."

"Does your mother know that you've come to see me?"

"No."

"Then stay here and have a bite to eat while I go over and discuss it with her. When we've worked things out, I'll come back and report."

After taking a sedan chair to Wang's house, Liu began by asking about the incident with Master Wu. On hearing the whole story, she said, "In our business, if we bring up a halfway decent girl, we can make some money and also feel safe and secure at the same time. The girl will take on any client and earn something for us every day. But my niece's reputation is so great that she's like a piece of dried fish dropped on the ground—every bug wants to get a piece of it. It's a thriving business, no doubt, but hardly a comfortable one. The money that comes in each night sounds like a lot, but that's only an illusion. Whenever a young nobleman visits, he brings with him a few hangers-on who stay until dawn and cause no end of trouble. And there are always a good many retainers, each of whom you have to dance attendance on. If there's anything not quite to their satisfaction, they curse you up hill and down dale as well as smash up your furniture. And you can't very well complain to their master, either, and so you end up with a case of acute depression. In addition, there are the literary men, the poetry societies, the chess clubs, and the official functions several days each month. And among the rich and powerful young men there's always a rivalry going on. If you please one, you offend another; if this one's happy, that one's angry. Take this quarrel with young Wu, for instance. How terrifying it must have been! One false move would have cost you your business. And you can't go bringing suit against a member of an official's family—you just have to grin and bear it. You've been blessed by good fortune, and things are peaceful now; the storm has passed you by. But if some unfortunate incident does occur, it'll be too late to do anything about it. I've heard that Wu is in a foul mood and means to come back and make more trouble for you. And my niece isn't in the best frame of mind either, refusing to cater to anyone. That's your main problem right there. It's a disaster in the making."

"I worry about it all the time. Even this Wu is a man of some importance, not a mere nobody, yet the wench absolutely refused to receive him. That's what put him in such a bad mood. There was a time, when she was young, that she would do as she was told. But she has this phony reputation now, and because our rich and powerful clients keep on praising her, she's become spoiled and arrogant and has to have her own way in every little thing. When a client arrives, if she wants to receive him, she will, but if she doesn't want to, once she's made her decision, a whole team of oxen couldn't pull her out of it."

"All our girls act like that once they've made a bit of a name for themselves."

"Let me ask you your opinion about this possibility. Suppose I did have a man who was willing to put up the money. I'd be tempted to sell her off and be free of the constant anxiety once and for all."

"Great idea! Sell her, and you can buy five or six others for the same money. If you're lucky and get them cheap enough, you might end up with as many as a dozen. A bargain like that— why not snap it up?"

"I have given it some thought, but our powerful clients wouldn't be willing to come up with the money; all they want to do is exploit us. And she'd refuse anyone who *would* put up the money, running him down and giving herself all kinds of airs. If you happen to hear of a good prospect, *please* do act as go-between and arrange a match. If the wench refuses, try to persuade her. She won't listen to a word I say—you're the only one who has her confidence and can talk her around."

Liu burst out laughing. "You know, I came here today for precisely that purpose, to act as her go-between. But how much would you need to let her go?"

"You're a reasonable person. In our business we believe in buying cheap but not in selling cheap. What's more, for several years she's been the toast of Lin'an—everyone knows her as the Queen of Flowers. I hope you don't think I'd let her go for three or four hundred? I'd want at least a thousand."

"Let me talk it over with him. If he's prepared to put up that much, I'll come back and let you know. Otherwise, I won't be back."

As she left, she asked, disingenuously, "And where is my niece now?"

"Don't ask! Ever since she was ill-treated by Master Wu, she's been afraid he'll come back in a bad temper, so she takes a sedan chair and goes out visiting all day to air her grievances. The day before yesterday she was at Marshal Qi's; yesterday she was at Academician Huang's; today I don't know where she is."

"Well, you're the one in charge, and once you've made your decision, she'll just have to fall into line. If by some chance she does refuse, I should be able to talk her around. Mind you, once I've found the right man, you're not to go pleading ignorance!"

"I've given you my word, and that's that."

Wang saw her to the gate, where Liu said goodbye and left in her sedan chair.

> A female Lu Jia who'd talk your head off,
> A distaff Sui He with few words—or a lot,
> If you had a mouth on you like this old bawd,
> You could start a tidal wave in a pint pot.

Once home, Liu spoke to Mei. "Well, I've told your mother, and she has agreed. Provided the money is forthcoming, it's as good as done."

"The money has already been seen to. But be absolutely sure you're at our place tomorrow to complete the arrangements. You mustn't leave us in the lurch, or I'll have to trouble you all over again."

"Everything is set, so of course I'll be there."

Mei took leave of Liu and went home, where she said nothing about what had happened.

At noon next day, Liu arrived at the brothel.

"How did everything go?" asked Wang.

"It's practically settled—except that I haven't spoken to my niece yet." She went into Mei's room, where the two women greeted each other and held a brief discussion.

"Has your man arrived?" asked Liu. "And where are the goods?"

Wang Mei pointed to the head of the bed. "In those trunks there." She opened five or six leather trunks and produced thirteen or fourteen packages of fifty taels each as well as some precious gems, the total value of which came to a thousand. Liu's eyes popped out at the sight, and she fairly drooled. So young, but with such foresight! she thought. I can't imagine how she managed to save up all this! The girls in my house receive clients just as she does, but they don't begin to compare with her! They can't make her kind of money, of course, but even the few cash they do have in their purses they spend on melon seeds or candy, and then when their foot bindings wear out, they expect *me* to buy them the cloth for new ones! Wang Jiuma had all the luck when she got this girl. She's made a lot of money in her time here, and she's about to hand over this big sum as she leaves. What's more, the money is right here on the premises, with no extra effort required to get it. Liu kept these thoughts to herself rather than expressing them to Mei, who noticed that she was plunged in thought and assumed she was concerned about her compensation. She quickly brought out four rolls of Luzhou silk, two jeweled *chai* hairpins, and a pair of phoenix-head jade *zan* hairpins[42] and laid them on the table. "These are for you, Aunt, as the go-between's fee."

Liu was in high good humor as she reported to Wang. "My niece is prepared to buy herself out at the same price, not a penny less. That's even better than having a client buy her out, because it avoids any mediation by outsiders and saves you the expense of all those parties as well as a ten or twenty percent commission."

When Wang learned that her daughter had so much saved up in her trunks, she was visibly chagrined. Why was that, do you suppose? Well, madams are the most ruthless people in the world; if a prostitute manages to earn something, the madam is happy only if it ends up with her. Some prostitutes keep their private savings in their boxes, and if the madam gets wind of it, she waits until the girl goes out, then breaks the lock and cleans out the box. But because Mei enjoyed a great reputation and had important people for her friends, and because she made good money for her mother—and also because of her own rather peculiar temperament—Wang would not have dared offend her without some very good reason. That was why she had never intruded into the girl's bedroom and was unaware that she had so much money.

Liu noticed the grim expression on Wang's face and guessed the reason. She hastily added, "Now, don't you go having any second thoughts. All this money was saved up by your daughter herself; none of it belongs to you. If she'd wanted to spend it, she would have done so. If she had been irresponsible enough to keep a paramour, you would never even have known about it. This is the happy outcome of her own frugality. Moreover, if she had no money at all and was about to get married, you wouldn't turn her out into the world stark naked, would you?

42. Among other differences, *chai* hairpins have two prongs, *zan* one.

She'd need to be smartly dressed from top to bottom in order to hold up her head in the new household. But now that she has managed to come up with all these things by her own efforts, you won't have to worry about providing a stitch of clothing for her—in fact, you get to gorge yourself on every last penny of the money. And even though she's buying herself out, that doesn't mean she'll cease to be your daughter. If she manages to do well, she'll surely bring you presents at festivals. Even after she marries, she won't have any parents of her own, and you can be grandmother to her children. There really are benefits to this."

This speech cheered Wang up, and she gave her consent. Liu brought out the money, weighed each package, and handed it over. She also gave Wang the gems, appraising each one in turn. "I've deliberately valued these on the low side. If you decide to sell them, you ought to be able to make a few dozen taels extra." Although Wang was also a madam, she was actually quite a simple soul and believed everything that Liu told her.

After Wang had taken possession of the money and gems, Liu had her steward draw up a marriage contract, which she handed to Mei. "While you're here, Aunt," said Mei, "could I ask a favor of you? Once I've taken leave of Father and Mother, could I stay with you for a couple of days until the wedding?"

Liu had received many presents from Mei, and she was mortally afraid that Wang would renege on the agreement, so she was anxious to have the girl out of the house and see the affair settled as soon as possible. "Yes, that's what we should do," she said.

Mei packed up her dressing table and her card case, the trunks, the bedding, and so forth that she had in her bedroom. Whatever belonged to the house she left where it was. Her packing done, she accompanied Liu out of her room, took leave of her foster parents, and said goodbye to the other women. Like the others, Wang shed a few tears. Mei told the servants to carry her luggage, and stepping gaily into the sedan chair, accompanied Liu to her house. There she was given a pleasant, secluded room, in which her luggage was deposited. The girls in the house came along and congratulated her.

That evening Zhu Zhong sent Xin Shan over to inquire and learned that Mei had bought herself out. After choosing a lucky day for the wedding, he sent a bridal chair with musical accompaniment to fetch his bride. As chief matchmaker, Liu then escorted Mei to the groom's house. That night in the bridal chamber Zhu Zhong and the Queen of Flowers took an unbounded delight in each other.

> Although they had made love once before,
> It was as if they were newly wed.

The next day Xin Shan and his wife asked leave to pay their respects. Both they and the bride felt the shock of recognition, and when they heard what each had been through, they wept openly in one another's arms. As soon as Zhu Zhong realized that Xin Shan and his wife were actually his father-in-law and mother-in-law, he asked them to be seated while he and his wife bowed to them again. The neighbors were astounded, and that day they held a feast to celebrate the double reunion, a feast that was enjoyed by all. On the fourth day after the wedding, Mei asked her husband to prepare some generous presents and send them to her friends in gratitude for safeguarding her belongings—and also as a way of announcing her marriage. This was typical of the way she followed through on her obligations. She also took presents to Wang and Liu, presents that they appreciated.

When the first month was over, Mei opened her trunks, which were full of gold and silver and also of at least a hundred rolls of silks and satins, to a total value of over three thousand taels. She gave the keys to her husband, so that over time he could buy up real estate and restore the family fortunes. The oil business he left to his father-in-law to run. In less than a year Zhu Zhong had achieved a spectacular success, and he and his family, attended by a full complement of servants and maids, lived in grand style.

So grateful was Zhu Zhong for the succor he had received from the spirits of Heaven and Earth that he vowed to present the local temples with a full set of incense and candles as well as a three months' supply of oil for their colored glaze lamps. He fasted and bathed himself, then set off to burn incense and give thanks. Beginning at Zhaoqing Temple, he visited Lingyin, Faxiang, Jingci, and the India temples. These last were shrines to the bodhisattva Guanyin and consisted of Upper, Middle, and Lower India, all of them popular. They could be reached only by road, however, not by boat, so Zhu Zhong had his men carry one load of incense and candles and three loads of clarified oil, while he traveled by sedan chair.

He went first to Upper India, where the priests welcomed him into the main hall. An elderly acolyte named Qin lit the candles and added the incense.

Zhu Zhong's prosperous circumstances had brought changes in his physique and temperament. He now cut an imposing figure, far different from the way he had looked as a boy, and the elder Qin had no idea that the visitor was his own son. But he was intrigued by the fact that the oil buckets bore a large "Qin" as well as a "Bianliang" on their sides. (By a remarkable coincidence, when Zhu Zhong visited the Upper India temple, he happened to be using those two buckets.)

After Zhu Zhong had finished his prayers, the elder Qin brought out a tray, and the abbot offered Zhu Zhong some tea. "I wonder, honored benefactor, if I might ask how your buckets came to have those two words on them?" asked the elder Qin.

Zhu Zhong noticed the questioner's Bianliang accent and responded with another question: "Why do you ask, venerable sir? Might you be from Bianliang too?"

"Yes, I am."

"Then let me ask you your name, and how you came to be a priest in this temple, and how long you have served here."

The elder Qin gave his full name and place of birth, and continued, "In the year ____ I came here to escape the soldiers, and since I had no way of making a living I gave up my twelve-year-old son Qin Zhong for adoption by the Zhu family. That was eight years ago, but because I'm getting on in years and have long been plagued by ill health, I have never left the temple to seek news of him."

Zhu Zhong threw his arms around his father, sobbing, "*I

am your son, Qin Zhong! I used to deliver oil for the Zhu shop, and because I was hoping to find you, I wrote those words on my buckets to show who I was. I never dreamt we would meet here! It must be Heaven's will!"

The other priests exclaimed in astonishment at the sight of a father and son being reunited after eight years. That night Zhu Zhong stayed with his father at Upper India, and each man related what had happened to him during the intervening years.

Next day Zhu Zhong took out the prayers he had written for the Middle and Lower India temples and changed the "Zhu" of his surname to "Qin," thus reverting to his original name. After offering the prayers, he returned to Upper India and implored his father to return home with him and be looked after in peace and comfort. But the elder Qin had been a priest for too long and adhered to a strict diet, and he was reluctant to go and live with his son.

"Father, we've been apart for eight years, and I've never been able to serve you as a son. Moreover, I've recently taken a wife, and she needs to pay her respects to her father-in-law."

His father had no choice but to consent. Qin Zhong had his father ride in the sedan chair, while he walked behind. At his house, he brought out new clothes for his father to change into, then asked him to take a seat in the ceremonial hall while he and his wife bowed low before him. Then the wife's parents came out and paid their respects. A grand celebration was held in which the elder Qin joined, although he kept to vegetarian food and soft drink. The next day the neighbors came with presents they had jointly bought and congratulated them on four counts: the wedding, the reunion of wife and parents, the reunion of husband and father, and Qin Zhong's reversion to his original name. The celebration went on for days.

The elder Qin did not wish to stay; he longed for the quiet of the religious life in Upper India, and Qin Zhong did not dare oppose his father's wishes. He contributed two hundred taels to the temple to construct separate quarters for his father to live in, and every month he paid his father's living expenses. He made a personal visit to his father every ten days, and he and his wife visited at the seasonal festivals. His father lived on into his eighties and died sitting upright in the meditating position. By his own wish, he was buried in the temple grounds. But all of this lay in the future.

Qin Zhong and his wife lived together into their old age. They had two sons, each of whom studied and made a name for himself. And to this day, in the jargon of the brothels, if people want to praise someone as particularly good at *bangchen*, they will call him a "Master Qin" or an "oil seller." There is a poem that makes the point:

> Spring, and with fresh flowers everywhere
> Bees and butterflies seek the flower's heart.
> Why did young lords lose to an oil seller?
> None could compete in the romantic art.

3
Marriage Destinies Rearranged

Marriage destinies are fixed by Heaven;
They're not the fruit of any human scheme.
If you're blessed, you'll marry though far apart;
If not, though near at hand, you'll never mate.
From paradise the peach-tree blossom flows;[1]
Red leaves from palace ladies float downstream.[2]
If the book of destiny mentions love,
Who needs a go-between to mediate?

*T*his lyric to the tune "Moon over West River" means that in general our marriages are determined by our past lives—they cannot be brought about through our own efforts. But listen while I relate a story of marriages that could not possibly have been foretold, a story titled "Prefect Qiao Freely Amends the Book of Marriage Destinies."

When and where did this story originate, you ask. It took place in the Jingyou period[3] of the great Song dynasty, when

---

The full title is "Prefect Qiao Freely Amends the Book of Marriage Destinies."

1. A reference to the legend of two young men, Liu Chen and Ruan Zhao, who wandered as far as a Peach Blossom Spring, where they met two female immortals. The legend appeared first in the *Youming lu* compiled by Liu Yiqing (403–444), but it later absorbed motifs from the famous Peach Blossom Spring described by the poet Tao Yuanming. See, for example, the early Ming play by Wang Ziyi, *Liu Chen Ruan Zhao wu ru taoyuan*.

2. A Tang story. Lu Wo happened to pick up a red leaf with a poem on it from the palace moat. When later the emperor released the women in his palace, Lu Wo happened to choose the one who had written the poem. Similar stories are told of other figures. The most elaborate version is "Liu hong ji," in the Song collection of tales called *Qing suo gao yi*.

3. 1034–1037.

there lived in the city of Hangzhou a man by the name of Liu Bingyi, a doctor by profession. He and his wife, Mistress Dan, had a son and a daughter. The son, named Liu Pu, was a strikingly handsome youth who had already come of age, and he was engaged to Zhuyi, daughter of a certain Widow Sun. From childhood on, he had thrown himself into his studies and done well, but when he turned fifteen, his father had wanted him to give up his academic work and train to be a doctor. Liu Pu, however, had set his heart on success in the civil service and declined to change careers.

His sister, Huiniang, was fourteen and engaged to the son of the neighboring herbalist, Pei Jiulao. She was a radiantly beautiful girl with an enchanting presence. What did she look like?

> Her brows delicately arched;
> Her eyes brimful of tenderness.
> Her form as lithe as a willow wand in a breeze;
> Her face as lovely as a petal on a stream.
> Light and graceful in her movements,
> Rivaling Feiyan of the Han palace.[4]
> Sweet and romantic in her disposition,
> Matching Xishi of the state of Wu.[5]
> A Daoist immortal sent down from Heaven,[6]
> The moon goddess descended to Earth.[7]

Let me leave the subject of Huiniang's beauty and tell how after Liu Pu had grown up his father spoke to his mother about the wedding. He was just about to send the matchmaker over to the Sun family to propose an early date when another matchmaker arrived from the Peis requesting an early date for *their* son's wedding. "Please convey our thanks to Mr. Pei," Mr. Liu instructed that matchmaker, "but our daughter is still very young

---

4. Zhao Feiyan, a favorite of Emperor Wudi of the Han dynasty, who became his empress. She was a classic beauty, noted for her slenderness.
5. The classic beauty of the Spring and Autumn period.
6. An immortal from the Ruizhu Palace, a dwelling place of Daoist immortals.
7. Chang'e, another iconic beauty, who stole her husband's elixir of immortality and fled with it to the moon.

and we haven't assembled her trousseau yet. We'll need to wait a little longer, until our son's wedding is over and done with, before we turn to our daughter's. At present it is quite impossible to do as Mr. Pei asks."

The matchmaker reported back to that effect. Now, Mr. Pei, who had had his son late in life, doted on the boy and could not wait for him to grow up, get married, and provide him with grandchildren. He was most unhappy with Mr. Liu's excuses,[8] and sent the matchmaker back again with the following message: "Your daughter is now fourteen, which can hardly be considered too young. If she joins our household, she will be treated just like any daughter of ours; we certainly won't be hard on her. As to the size of the trousseau, that's entirely up to you; it's of no concern to us. I hope very much that you will see your way to agreeing with me." But Mr. Liu was determined to see his son married before he turned to his daughter, and although the matchmaker made several visits, he still refused. Mr. Pei had to curb his impatience.

If Mr. Liu had agreed at that stage, he would have saved himself a great deal of trouble. Instead, his stubborn refusal resulted in a remarkable event, the story of which has been told and retold ever since.

> Just one false move in chess,
> And the whole game is lost.

After rejecting the Pei proposal, Mr. Liu sent Mrs. Zhang, the matchmaker, over to the Suns' to propose a date for his son's wedding. Widow Sun, whose maiden name was Hu, had married Sun Heng, a scion of one of the oldest Hangzhou families, at the age of fifteen. At sixteen she gave birth to a daughter, Zhuyi, and barely a year later to a son, Sun Run, whose style was Yulang. However, her husband died while the children were still in their infancy. As a woman of principle, she refused to remarry, but raised the children herself with the help of a nursemaid, a decision that earned her the name Widow Sun.

---

8. Not without a certain amount of justification. It was customary for the girl's father to accept the wedding date as proposed by the boy's father.

Time flew by, and in due course the children grew up. Zhuyi became engaged to the Lius' son, while Yulang was betrothed in childhood to Wenge, daughter of the artist Xu Ya. Both Zhuyi and Yulang were equally good-looking, with creamy, jade-like complexions, and both were blessed with a natural cleverness, Yulang at his studies, Zhuyi with her needle. What is more, they behaved admirably to their mother as well as to each other.

Mrs. Zhang duly delivered Mr. Liu's message about a date for the wedding. Widow Sun was very close to both her children, and she would have been perfectly content to wait a little longer. But when she reflected that marriage was the critical event in young people's lives, she felt obliged to accept. "Please inform the master and mistress that our family is headed by a widow and cannot provide an elaborate trousseau, just everyday clothes," she said. "They mustn't think too badly of us."

When Mrs. Zhang reported back to Mr. Liu, he prepared eight boxes of delicacies and sent them to the Suns together with a proposed wedding date. Now that the date was settled, Widow Sun went to work feverishly to prepare the trousseau. As the day approached, both mother and daughter found the thought of parting harder and harder to bear and spent much of their time crying and sobbing together.

Unfortunately, Liu Pu caught a chill and began sweating so profusely that the chill developed into ague, he lost consciousness, and lay close to death. Medicine had no more effect on him than water splashed on a rock, and prayers and divinations were equally useless. Scared out of their wits, his parents stifled their sobs and kept a silent vigil at his bedside. "His condition is so critical," said Mr. Liu to his wife, "that he surely won't be able to go through with the wedding. We'd better tell the Suns that we'll need to choose another date once he's better."

"Look here, old fellow," retorted his wife. "Do you mean to tell me that at your age you *still* don't understand how these things work? For people in desperate straits the joy of a wedding breaks the curse of the illness.[9] If we hadn't arranged a

9. *Chong xi,* a folk belief that the joy of a wedding will overcome the evil fortune responsible for the illness.

wedding for him already, we would want to do so now, but since it's all settled, why on earth would we want to put it off?"

"As I see it, his condition is very dangerous indeed. If he marries and the wedding breaks the curse, of course that would be wonderful. But if it doesn't, we'll have done serious harm to this girl, who'll have to bear the stigma of remarriage."

"Look, old fellow, you're always more concerned about other people than you are about yourself. You and I have put a lot of effort into arranging this match. Unfortunately, our boy's ill fate has condemned him to this sickness on the eve of his marriage. If we put off the Suns and he recovers, all well and good. But if the worst happens, what leverage will we have with them? If they were to return just *half* of the betrothal settlement, that would be considered more than generous. We'd have lost our son *and* the money!"

"What do you suggest, then?"

"In my opinion, you should tell Mrs. Zhang not to mention our son's illness but to bring the girl to our house, where she'll be something like a child wife.[10] If our boy recovers, we'll choose another day to celebrate the wedding. But if he doesn't, and the time comes for her to remarry, we'll see that we get back the settlement and all of our other expenses before we let her out of the house. It's the ideal arrangement."

Mr. Liu, who was of a meek and tractable disposition, did as his wife said and went off to warn Mrs. Zhang against letting out the secret. But as the old adage says,

> If you don't want it known,
> You'd better not do it.

Mr. Liu may have deceived the Suns, but he had a next-door neighbor named Li Rong, who had once managed a pawnshop and whom everyone called Manager Li. He was an extremely sly character who loved nothing better than ferreting out people's secrets and then gossiping about them. Because he had made

---

10. *Yang xifu,* a daughter-in-law who lives with her in-laws before she is old enough to marry.

money in shady dealings while working in the pawnshop, he was now well off. His house adjoined the Lius', and he wanted to force them to sell their property to him. When Mr. Liu refused, relations soured between the neighbors, and Li longed for the Lius to suffer some mishap so that he could gloat over their misfortune. On learning that Yulang was gravely ill, he exulted—and promptly informed the Suns. Widow Sun worried that the illness might be harmful to her daughter's future, so she sent the nursemaid to fetch Mrs. Zhang.

Mrs. Zhang was in a quandary: if she denied that Yulang was ill and he happened to die, she was afraid that Widow Sun would hold it against her, but if she confirmed the illness, she was equally afraid that the Lius would resent it. In the end, she hesitated to say anything at all. Noting her hesitation, Widow Sun pressed even harder for an answer, until Mrs. Zhang finally gave way and admitted that, yes, he had caught a chill but it was nothing really serious, and she fully expected him to recover by the time of the wedding.

"But I heard that he was critically ill! How can you make so light of it? This is a serious matter, you know. I've been through all kinds of trouble raising my children. They're my pride and joy, and I give you fair warning: if you deceive my daughter by fudging the truth, you'll have me to reckon with!" She went on, "Go back to the Lius and tell them this: If their son is seriously ill, why don't we wait until he's better and then choose another date for the wedding? Anyway, their son and my daughter are both still young, so where's the need for all the haste? When you have their answer, come back at once and tell me."

Mrs. Zhang did as she was told. As she was going out the door, Widow Sun called her back again, "I know you won't tell me the truth. I'm going to send our nursemaid with you, so that I'll know what's really going on."

"There's no need for that at all!" said Mrs. Zhang in an anxious tone. "No matter what, I'd never do anything to harm you." But Widow Sun was adamant; after giving the nursemaid instructions, she sent her off with Mrs. Zhang.

Mrs. Zhang could hardly shake the nursemaid off; she was forced to take her to the Lius'. As they approached the house,

Mr. Liu was just coming out, and Mrs. Zhang took advantage of the fact that the nursemaid didn't know who he was. "Just wait here a moment," she said. "I need to ask someone a question." She rushed ahead and, pulling Mr. Liu aside, reported what Widow Sun had told her. "She's so worried about it," Mrs. Zhang added, "that she's sent her nursemaid here with me to find out the truth. What are we going to tell her?"

Liu was disconcerted to hear of the nursemaid's presence. "Why didn't you stop her?" he grumbled.

"I tried to, several times, but Widow Sun took no notice, and I had no choice but to bring her. Why don't you invite her inside and let her sit down while you and the mistress take the time to think out what to say. Just see that you don't involve *me* in any trouble."

Before she had finished speaking, the nursemaid came up. "This is Mr. Liu," Mrs. Zhang said. The nursemaid gave a deep curtsy, and Mr. Liu bowed in response. "Please come inside and sit down, miss," he said.

They entered the gate and went into the parlor, where Mr. Liu said, "Mrs. Zhang, could I ask you to keep the young lady company while I call my wife?"

"Of course."

He rushed inside and related everything to his wife. "That nursemaid is in the house right now," he added. "What are we going to say to her? If she wants to come in and see our son, how are we going to cover things up? We'd better postpone the wedding."

"Oh, what a useless creature you are! They've accepted our betrothal settlement, so she belongs to us. What is there to be afraid of? Just don't panic. We'll find a way." She instructed her daughter: "Go and tidy up the bridal chamber and then invite that woman from the Suns in for some tea." As Huiniang left, Mrs. Liu went into the parlor and greeted the nursemaid. "Well, miss, what message have you brought from your mistress?"

"My mistress was so worried on hearing that the young master was ill that she sent me to ask after him. She also wanted me to give you and the master this message: If the young master is only in the early stages of recovery, she is afraid he may not be fit enough to go through with the wedding. In that case it would be better to wait until he is completely restored to health and then choose another day."

"I'm ever so grateful for your mistress's concern, but although the young master has been a little under the weather, it's nothing serious, just a chill that he happened to catch. As for choosing another date, that's quite out of the question, I'm afraid. In our modest line of business, we've had to skimp and scrape in order to afford the wedding. If we let this date go by, all that expenditure will be wasted. Besides, sick people need the joy of a wedding to break the curse—it speeds up their recovery. I've heard of many cases in which, to save themselves trouble, people have actually taken illness as the *reason* for holding a wedding. In our case we agreed on the wedding date days ago and have already invited all our relatives to the wedding feast. If we suddenly change the date now, it won't occur to any of them that *you're* the unwilling party; they're bound to think *we* can't afford a daughter-in-law. Once that story gets around, we'll be laughed to scorn by everybody, and our name will be mud. Please go back and tell your mistress she shouldn't worry. We'll take full responsibility."

"Quite right, ma'am," replied the nursemaid, "but may I ask where the young master is? After I've given him the mistress's best wishes, I'll be able to report back and set her mind at rest."

"He's just taken some medicine to make him sweat and is sleeping soundly. Let me convey your good wishes for you. And now I think we've covered everything we needed to talk about."

"I *told* your mistress that he caught a chill and it was nothing serious," said Mrs. Zhang. "But she wouldn't believe me and insisted that you come along too. You see now that I wasn't telling any lies."

"Well, I'll take my leave, then," said the nursemaid, getting to her feet.

"Oh, but you can't go yet!" said Mrs. Liu. "We've been so busy talking, we've forgotten to drink our tea." She invited the nursemaid inside. "My own room's in a mess, so let's go into the bridal chamber," she said, leading the way.

Looking around her, the nursemaid noted how perfectly

everything was arranged. "As you see, we've got everything just so," said Mrs. Liu. "How could we possibly agree to change the date? Even if the young master should wish to go on sleeping in my room after the wedding, he'll join the bride in here just as soon as he's better." The nursemaid noted the elaborate preparations and believed what she was told.

Mrs. Liu had a maid serve tea and cakes, and asked Huiniang to keep the nursemaid company. Our Zhuyi is awfully pretty, thought the nursemaid, but this girl is simply stunning. As she and Mrs. Zhang took their leave, Mrs. Liu gave strict instructions to the latter: "See that you come back and tell me what happened."

The nursemaid went back with Mrs. Zhang and told her mistress everything, which left the widow in a quandary. If I agree, she thought, I'm afraid he may be seriously ill, and if the worst comes to the worst, my daughter will be the one to suffer. But if I don't agree and it's only a minor illness from which he is already on the road to recovery, I'll have held up the wedding. She was unable to decide the issue and finally said to Mrs. Zhang, "Let me think this over. Come back tomorrow morning and I'll give you my answer."

"Very well. Take your time, by all means. I'll see you in the morning."

Widow Sun then talked the matter over with her son, Yulang. "What are we going to do about this?"

"It looks as if his illness is serious, and that's why they wouldn't let the nursemaid see him. We'll just have to tell them to change the date, and they'll have no choice but to call off the wedding. However, that'll mean a waste of money for them, and we'll appear inconsiderate, and if their son does get better, relations are bound to be awfully strained between us. But if we agree and he does take a turn for the worse, we'll be in a real bind—it'll be too late then to do anything at all. Actually, I have the perfect solution, if you'd care to hear it. It's one that would protect us against both dangers."

"And just what is this perfect solution?"

"When Mrs. Zhang comes tomorrow morning, tell her that you'll keep the wedding date, but that the bride will not be bringing any of her trousseau with her. On the third day after the wedding,[11] she's to come home and stay here until he's better, at which point she goes back *with* her trousseau. Under this plan, even if the worst comes to the worst, she won't be under their control. Now, doesn't that protect us against both dangers?"

"But that's so *infantile!* What if they take her under false pretences and then on the third day refuse to let her come home?"

"Well, yes . . . er, what do we do about that?"

His mother thought for awhile before replying. "When Mrs. Zhang comes tomorrow, we'll have to do as you suggest, but we'll keep your sister out of sight and dress you up and send you over instead. As a precaution, you'll need to pack a gown as well as shoes and socks. On the third day, if they let you come back, fine. If they don't, you should stay on for a while to see what's happening. If anything goes wrong, you just put on your gown and come straight home. No one will be able to stop you!"

"That's the *last* thing in the world I'd ever do! If anyone got to know about it, I'd never be able to hold my head up again!"

At her son's refusal, Widow Sun lost her temper. "*So what* if people get to know? It's only a joke! Where's the great harm in that?"

Yulang was a devoted son, and when his mother flared up, he quickly added, "I'll do it. The only problem is that I wouldn't know how to dress my hair. What about that?"

"I'll send the nursemaid along to attend on you."

And so their plans were laid. The next morning, when Mrs. Zhang came for the answer, Widow Sun told her what she had agreed with her son, adding, "If they accept, the wedding will take place. If not, let's set another date."

Mrs. Zhang took the proposal back to the Lius, who agreed to both conditions. Can you think why? Because Liu Pu's illness had taken an even more serious turn, and if the worst happened, so long as the Lius had managed to inveigle the girl into their household, they'd be in business. And so they made the

11. Traditionally, the bride paid a visit home on the third day after the wedding.

best of a bad deal and refrained from haggling over the details. Little did they realize that Widow Sun had seen through their scheme and was about to send them a fake instead of the genuine article. Mrs. Liu would end up emulating General Zhou:[12]

> One whose strategic skills were world renowned,
> But who lost the lady as well as his men.

Let me spare you the rest of the details. On the wedding day, Widow Sun dressed Yulang up until he looked so much like her daughter that she herself could hardly tell the difference. She also taught him something about women's etiquette. Everything went perfectly, except for two features that were hard to disguise and might give him away, she feared. What features were they, you ask? Well, first there was the problem of his feet, which differed from those of a girl. A girl's feet are arched and pointed; as she minces along, her phoenix slippers peep out from beneath her skirt like flowers shimmering in the breeze. But Yulang was a male, and his feet were three or four times the size of a woman's. Although they were covered by a floor-length skirt and although Yulang was instructed to walk slowly and take tiny steps, his feet still looked a little odd. But at least they were down below, and provided no one lifted his skirt and looked, they might still pass unnoticed. The other problem had to do with earrings. Earrings are regularly worn by girls, who prefer them tiny and exquisite and insist on a lilac shape. Girls from even the poorest families will buy themselves a pair of earrings, if not of gold or silver, then of copper or tin. Yulang was dressed up as a bride, his head covered in jewels, and he would hardly look right without earrings. His left ear had been pierced in childhood as a precaution.[13] His right ear, however, was not pierced, so how could he wear an earring on it? Widow

---

12. Zhou Yu, a general of the state of Wu in Three Kingdoms time. He arranged the marriage of the sister of Sun Quan (ruler of Wu) to Liu Bei (ruler of Shu) in hopes of gaining a key stronghold. In the end, Zhou gained nothing; he merely lost heavily in battle.

13. If a fortune-teller predicted mortal danger for a child, one remedy was to pierce the child's earlobes. Cf. story no. 28 in the companion anthology compiled by Feng Menglong, *Gujin xiaoshuo*.

Sun racked her brains before coming up with an answer. Can you guess what it was? She sent the nursemaid to fetch a tiny plaster, which she stuck on his right earlobe. If anyone asked, he was to say that he had a sore on the hole that made it impossible to wear an earring. His pierced left ear should be kept plainly visible so as to mislead people.

When all the preparations had been made, they hid Huiniang in one of the other rooms and waited for the welcoming party from the bridegroom's house.

Toward evening the sound of drums filled the air—the bridal sedan chair had arrived. Mrs. Zhang was the first to enter. She was delighted at the sight of the bride, who was adorned like a goddess, but she missed Yulang. "Why isn't the young master here?" she asked.

"He came down with a slight indisposition this morning. He's resting at present and can't get up." The matchmaker had no inkling of what was afoot and did not pursue the matter. Widow Sun regaled the visitors with wine and delicacies, after which the master of ceremonies chanted a nuptial poem and invited the bride to enter the sedan chair.[14] Yulang donned the bridal veil and took leave of his mother. Widow Sun escorted him out the door, all the while pretending to cry. The bride stepped into the chair, where the nursemaid joined her without any trousseau save for a single leather case. Widow Sun gave strict instructions to Mrs. Zhang. "As agreed between us, she is to come back here on the third day. See that you keep your word, now." Mrs. Zhang repeated her promise.

Let me turn to the welcoming party, who escorted the sedan chair all the way to the Lius' door, their flutes and pipes grating on the ear, their lanterns dazzling the eye. The master of ceremonies went in and said, "The bride is about to leave the sedan chair, but there is no groom here to welcome her. You surely don't expect her to perform the wedding ritual on her own?"

"Of course not. We'll do without it," said Mr. Liu.

14. In a traditional wedding, the master of ceremonies chanted a nuptial poem at the bride's house. She then traveled in a decorated sedan chair to the bridegroom's house, where the master of ceremonies chanted another poem, after which the bride stepped out of the sedan chair.

"I know," said his wife. "Let's have our daughter do it instead." She told Huiniang to come out and welcome the bride. The master of ceremonies intoned another nuptial poem and invited the bride to step out of the sedan chair. The nursemaid and Mrs. Zhang supported her, one on each side. After Huiniang had greeted her, they entered the ceremonial hall, where they first kowtowed to Heaven and Earth, and then to their parents, in-laws, and relatives. At the sight of two girls kowtowing, the servants could hardly suppress their giggles. Afterward, the sisters-in-law bowed to each other.

"Let's go to my room and try to break the curse for my son," said Mrs. Liu. The musicians struck up a tune as she led the bride to Liu Pu's bed. Pulling aside the bed curtain, Mrs. Liu called out, "My boy, your bride has come to cure your illness. Try to pull yourself together, now." She repeated this several times, but no sound came from the bed, and when Mr. Liu shone the lantern on his son, he found him unconscious, his head lolling to one side. In his weakened state, he had been driven into a coma by the pounding of the drums. His parents sprang into action, pinching the pressure point below his nose and calling for hot water, of which they forced a few mouthfuls down his throat. He broke into a cold sweat and at last regained his senses.

Telling her husband to see to their son, Mrs. Liu led the bride into the nuptial chamber, where she lifted the girl's veil and looked at her—as pretty as a picture. The relatives present all exclaimed in admiration, but Mrs. Liu was mortified. Our daughter-in-law is so beautiful, she thought, that she's a perfect match for our son. If we had both of them to care for us in our old age, my lifetime of hard work would have been well worthwhile. But he had the misfortune to get this serious illness on the eve of his wedding and has little chance of surviving. If the worst should happen, she'll certainly marry again, and that's nothing to rejoice over.

But let me leave Mrs. Liu's concerns and turn to Yulang. Among the many relatives present, he was most struck by his sister-in-law's beauty. What a stunning girl, he thought. It's such a pity I'm engaged! If I'd known how splendid this girl was, I'd certainly have tried to get her as my wife.

Strangely enough, while he was admiring her, she was pursuing a similar line of thought about him. Mrs. Zhang always said she was beautiful, she thought. *I didn't believe her, but it's true. The only pity is that my brother lacks the good fortune to enjoy her company, and tonight she'll have to sleep alone. If *my* husband were to be as good-looking as this girl is, he'd be just ideal, but that's too much to hope for.*

Let me leave them to their mutual admiration and return to Mrs. Liu. She invited the relatives to the wedding feast, after which they went off to their own rooms to sleep. The master of ceremonies and the musicians had already been sent off. Since there was nowhere for Mrs. Zhang to sleep, she went home.

Yulang was in the bridal chamber, where the nursemaid helped him off with his jewelry. He sat down, a candle in his hand, not daring to go to bed.

Meanwhile Mrs. Liu was discussing the matter with her husband. "She's only just arrived in the house, and we can't expect her to sleep on her own. Let's get our daughter to keep her company."

"That might not be so suitable. Why not let her sleep on her own?"

Mrs. Liu ignored him and turned to her daughter. "Tonight you'll keep your sister-in-law company in the bridal chamber, so she won't feel lonely." Since Huiniang was strongly drawn to her sister-in-law, this arrangement suited her perfectly. Her mother took her into the chamber and said to the bride, "Since your husband is indisposed and can't join you in the chamber tonight, I've told my daughter to sleep with you instead."

Yulang was terrified that his secret would be revealed. "I feel awfully shy with strangers," he replied. "It's *really* not necessary."

"Oh, pish! You two are much the same age, and you look as if you could be sisters. It's only right that you should spend some time together. What is there to be shy about? If you feel uncomfortable, why don't each of you sleep in your own bedclothes?" To Huiniang, she said, "Go and fetch yours."

Yulang felt both alarm and joy. Joy, because he was genuinely attracted by this girl's beauty, and Heaven was actually lending him a helping hand. Now that Mrs. Liu had told the girl to join him in bed, he thought he had a fair chance of success with her. But alarm also, because he was afraid she might not consent, and if she started screaming, all would be lost. Then he had a further thought: If I let this opportunity slip, when will I ever get another? She looks as if she's the right age; I expect she's beyond puberty. I'll need all my finesse to gradually arouse her, but she'll be caught, never fear.

As these thoughts passed through his mind, Huiniang was telling the maid to carry her bedding into the chamber and lay it on the bed. Mrs. Liu then got to her feet and left with the maid. Shutting the door, Huiniang went up to Yulang and, smiling broadly, said to him, "Sister-in-law, I noticed you had nothing to eat. Aren't you hungry?"

"No, no, I'm not hungry."

"Well, if you do want anything, just let me know and I'll get it for you. Speak up, now, don't be shy."

Yulang was touched by her courteous concern. "Thank you, you're most kind."

Huiniang noticed a large piece of burnt wick on the lamp. "Sister-in-law, what a fine lamp bloom that is![15] And it's pointing straight at you. That means there's joy in your future."

"Now you're making fun of me. It means joy for you, not me."

"You're teasing," said Huiniang, as they bantered together. "It's getting late," she said. "Do go to bed."

"After you."

"How can I possibly go first? I'm the host, you're the guest."

"Ah, but in this chamber you are the guest."

"Then I'll lead the way." She undressed and lay down.

Overhearing this give-and-take, the nursemaid sensed that Yulang's intentions were none too honorable, and she went and whispered in his ear, "Master, think very carefully about what you're doing. This is a serious matter. If the mistress got to hear of it, even I would be in trouble."

"You don't need to tell me, I know that perfectly well. Now go off to sleep."

---

15. The shape of a flower formed by the burnt wick of a lamp, signifying love.

The nursemaid made up a pallet for herself on the other side of the room and lay down. Lamp in hand, Yulang went to the bed, pulled aside the bed curtain, and shone the lamp inside. Huiniang lay beside the wall in her rolled-up bedding. At sight of Yulang with the lamp, she giggled. "Come to bed, sister-in-law. What are you shining that lamp on me for?"

Yulang smiled. "I just wanted to see where you were sleeping before I got into bed." He set the lamp on a small table beside the bed, then undressed and came back inside the bed curtain. "Why don't we both sleep the same way around? It's more fun like that, should we want to talk."

"Fine."

Yulang wriggled inside his bedclothes, stripping off the clothes from his upper body but leaving his underwear on. "How old are you?" he asked.

"Fourteen."

"Who are you engaged to?"

She was too bashful to reply. Yulang brought his face close to her pillow and murmured in her ear, "There's no need to be so bashful. We're both girls, after all."

This brought a reply from her. "He's the son of the Pei family who own the herbalist's shop."

"May I ask when the happy day is going to be?"

"They've sent a matchmaker over several times recently to set a date," she whispered, "but my father told them I was still too young and they should wait a bit longer."

Yulang laughed. "That must have *really* upset you!"

Huiniang pushed his face away from her pillow. "You're not nice! You wheedled that out of me, and now you're teasing me about it. Anyway, if *I'm* upset, I can't imagine how *you* must be feeling."

Yulang brought his face back to the pillow. "Tell me, just what would I be upset about?"

"This is your wedding night, but you're on your own. How can you help being upset?"

"But I have you with me, so I'm not on my own. Why should I be upset?"

Huiniang laughed. "In that case, you're my wife."

"But I'm older than you, so I'm the husband."

"But I performed the wedding ritual in place of my brother, so I'm like him. I should be the husband."

"Let's not quarrel about it. Let's just be a female married couple."

In the course of their suggestive banter, they had grown more and more intimate with each other. Yulang saw no difficulties ahead of him. "Since we're a married couple, why don't we share the same bedclothes?" As he said this, he opened her bedding and lay down beside her, stroking her body, which was soft and smooth to the touch. She still had her underwear on, however.

By now Huiniang's passions were so inflamed by Yulang that she entirely forgot herself and let him stroke her, offering no resistance at all. When he came to her chest, he found a pair of small, upstanding breasts, soft as cotton floss, with nipples like water lily seeds—truly delightful. Huiniang also felt Yulang's body and remarked, "How soft and smooth you are, sister-in-law!" But when she came to his chest and found two tiny nipples and nothing more, she wondered, She's older than I am, so why are her breasts so small?

After stroking her for some time, Yulang embraced her, bringing his mouth against hers and slipping his tongue inside. She thought that her sister-in-law was just playing games with her, and she, too, clasped him in both arms. After holding his tongue in her mouth for a while, she then inserted her tongue into his mouth. He held it there, then sucked hard, which made her whole body dissolve in a sensual languor.

"We're not acting like a female married couple; we're like a real one," she said.

Yulang realized that her passions were aroused. "If you want to play that game, why don't we take off our underwear and be really intimate?"

"But that would be so *embarrassing!* I wouldn't feel right."

"It's only fun, after all. What is there to be embarrassed about?" He undid her drawers and removed them, then felt her private parts. At once she brought both hands down to cover them.

"Sister-in-law, stop fooling around!"

Yulang cupped her face in his hands and planted a kiss on her lips. "Why not? You can feel me."

She undid his drawers and felt inside, but what she found was a penis standing stiffly erect. With a gasp of surprise she whipped her hand away. "Who *are* you? Coming here pretending to be my sister-in-law!"

"I'm your husband. What else do you need to know?" Raising himself above her, he tried to part her thighs with his hand, but Huiniang pushed him off.

"If you don't tell me the truth, I'll start screaming, and then you'll be in trouble!"

Her threat alarmed Yulang, who quickly interjected, "Now, don't do anything rash. Let me explain. I'm Yulang, your sister-in-law's brother. When we heard that your brother was seriously ill, we didn't know what to expect, and my mother couldn't bear to let my sister marry under those conditions, but she also worried about canceling the wedding your family had arranged, so she dressed me up as the bride. When your brother recovers, she'll send my sister over. I never dreamt that Heaven would grant me this blessed union, and that I would become your husband. But remember, this is a secret between the two of us. No one else must know." He turned over again to face her.

Huiniang had been strongly attracted to him from the first, when she thought he was a woman, and now that she knew he was a man, her delight knew no bounds. Moreover, she had been brought by Yulang to a pitch of passionate feeling. Apprehensive but also ecstatic at the same time, she put up only a half-hearted resistance. "You're such a *deceiver*," she murmured.

Yulang was in no mood to argue. Clasping her in a tight embrace, he gave free rein to his passion.

> One was a lad in the springtime of his youth, tasting the fruits of bliss.
> The other was a girlish virgin, sampling the sweets of passion.
> One said, "Tonight the wedding candles will seal our destiny."

The other said, "Between the sheets we'll try our married
love."
One said, "It is our destiny; we need no go-between."
The other said, "Let's never forget, but swear eternal vows."
Each burns with a fiery passion; neither thinks of family
ties;
Pursuing the ecstasy of the moment, ignoring their duty to
those they'll wed.
Two by two the butterflies dance among the flowers;
Pair by pair the mandarin ducks play amid the waters.

After they had made love, they slept tightly clasped in each
other's arms.

Meanwhile the nursemaid had been terrified that Yulang
would get himself into trouble. She lay on her pallet at the side
of the room, unable to close her eyes. First she heard an exchange of banter, then a knocking of the bedposts accompanied
by much panting and sighing, and she knew that the deed was
done. She gave a silent cry of anguish.

The next morning, after Huiniang had gone back to her
mother's room to wash and the nursemaid was doing Yulang's
hair, she whispered, "Sir, you told me last night you wouldn't
do it, but you broke your word. You *did* do it! What if they find
out?"

"I didn't go looking for her—her mother brought her here.
How could I possibly turn her away?"

"You should have stuck to what you said you'd do."

"But just think of it! A gorgeous girl like that in the same bed
as me! Why, a man of iron couldn't have stood it—how could *I*
be expected to? So long as you don't let the secret out, no one
will ever know."

Once Yulang was dressed, he went into Mrs. Liu's room to
pay his respects. "Child, you've forgotten to put on your earrings," she remarked.

"No, I didn't forget. I have a sore on the hole in my right ear,
and I can't wear an earring. I have a plaster on it."

"Yes, I see."

Yulang returned to the chamber, where the female relatives
visited him. Mrs. Zhang was also there. Once Huiniang was

dressed, she came in too, and she and Yulang exchanged smiles as they greeted each other. That day Mr. Liu invited all the relatives on both his and his wife's sides of the family to a feast with musical entertainment, and the drinking went on until evening, when the relatives went home. Once more Huiniang came to keep Yulang company for the night.

Their lovemaking and pledges of eternal fidelity were twice as ardent as the night before. In this manner the third day passed with the two sisters-in-law inseparable. However, the nursemaid, who was on tenterhooks the whole time, kept urging Yulang to leave. "We're past the third day now. You should say something to Mrs. Liu about it. Let's go home."

But Yulang and Huiniang were both on fire, and he was not in the least inclined to go home. "How can *I* bring up the subject of going home?" he asked disingenuously. "My mother will have to send Mrs. Zhang over with a request."

"You're right," said the nursemaid, and promptly left for home.

After Widow Sun had sent her son off disguised as a bride, she was constantly on edge. When Mrs. Zhang did not come back at once to report, she waited anxiously until the nursemaid's return on the fourth day. In response to her questions, she received a detailed account of how the son was suffering from a grave illness, how his sister had kept Yulang company, and how the two of them had slept in the same bed and made love together.

Widow Sun stamped her feet and moaned aloud, "That *would* have to happen! Quick, go and get Mrs. Zhang."

Before long Mrs. Zhang arrived.

"The other day you promised that my daughter would be back on the third day, which has come and gone," said Widow Sun. "I'd be much obliged if you'd take this up with them, and bring her home without any further delay."

Mrs. Zhang took this message to the Lius, accompanied again by the nursemaid. Mrs. Liu happened to be idly chatting in Yulang's chamber when they arrived and gave her the message. Yulang and Huiniang, who were unable to face the thought of parting, silently hoped that Mrs. Liu would not agree.

As it turned out, she did not agree. "Mrs. Zhang, you've had long experience as a matchmaker—surely you know about these things? Has there ever been a rule that said daughters-in-law had to return on the third day? At first, Widow Sun wasn't prepared to let her daughter marry, and nothing could be done about that, but now that the girl's here, she belongs to us. We can't go on trying to please her mother! I've been to all kinds of trouble to get this daughter-in-law, and it would not have been right to send her back on the third day. If Widow Sun finds it so hard to part with the girl, she shouldn't have married her off in the first place. She has a son too, and no doubt she'll expect him to bring a daughter-in-law into the home. We'll see then whether she agrees to let *her* daughter-in-law go home on the third day. I've heard she knows a lot about correct behavior. Well, let her try and explain that!"

Mrs. Zhang was left speechless by this outburst, which she didn't dare report to Widow Sun. For her part, the nursemaid was so afraid someone might burst into the chamber and catch the young couple in the act that she kept a close watch on the door and did not dare go home again.

Ever since the wedding night, when Liu Pu broke out into a cold sweat from shock, he had been slowly on the mend. He was delighted to learn that his fiancée was now his wife and also that she was exceptionally beautiful, and as a result his recovery went even faster. Within a few days he could sit up, and after that he spent only half his time lying down. Each day he grew a little stronger, until he could even dress himself, at which point he wanted to go to the bridal chamber and see his wife. Since he was still in the early stages of recovery, Mrs. Liu was afraid he couldn't walk on his own, so she had a maid help him, while she followed behind. In this manner they made their way step by step to the chamber. The nursemaid was sitting in the doorway. When the maid said, "Please let the young master in," the nursemaid stood up and bellowed at the top of her lungs, "The young master's coming in!"

Yulang had his arms around Huiniang and was joking and laughing with her, but when he heard that someone was coming in, he broke away at once. Liu Pu pulled aside the door curtain and entered the room. Huiniang exclaimed, "It's such a treat to see you up and about again, brother, but you shouldn't overdo it."

"That's all right, I'm just taking a little walk. I'll go and lie down afterwards." He bowed to Yulang, who turned his back on him and curtsied.

"Careful when you bow!" Mrs. Liu warned her son. Then she noticed that Yulang was standing with his back to them. "Here's your husband," she said. "He's better now, and he's come specially to see you. Why have you got your back to us?" She went up to Yulang and pulled him beside her son. "My boy, you and she make the perfect couple."

Liu Pu was delighted with his wife's extraordinary beauty. It is indeed true that when people undergo a happy experience their spirits soar, and as a result his illness receded a little further.

"Son, you'd better go and lie down," said Mrs. Liu. "You mustn't strain yourself." She had the maid help him back again. Huiniang also went in.

Yulang observed that although Liu Pu looked ill, he still cut a handsome figure. It would be no disgrace for my sister to marry a man like that, he thought. Then a further thought struck him: Now that he's better, if he wants to come and sleep with me, our secret will be out. I'd better go home at once.

That night he mentioned this concern to Huiniang. "Now that your brother is better, I can't stay here anymore. If you can persuade your mother to send me home again, my sister will come here in my place, and no one will be any the wiser. If I stay any longer, it will all come out."

"*You* can go home easily enough, but what's to become of *me?*"

"I've given that a lot of thought, but you're engaged to someone else and so am I, and there's no way to change that. What *can* we do?"

"If you can't think of any way we can marry, I'll join you as a spirit, I swear. I would *never* be so shameless as to marry anyone else!" She burst out sobbing.

"Don't distress yourself," said Yulang, wiping away her tears. "Let me try to think of something." But then they began clinging to each other once more, and the subject of Yulang's return was set aside.

One day after lunch, when the nursemaid was at the back of the house, Yulang and Huiniang shut the door and began discussing their problem from every angle, but they still could not come up with a solution. Surrendering to despair, they wept silently in each other's arms.

Let me turn to Mrs. Liu. Ever since her daughter-in-law had arrived in the house, she and her own daughter had been inseparable. As soon as it grew dark, they would shut their door and go to bed, where they would remain until late in the morning. Mrs. Liu was distinctly unhappy about it. At first she thought it was just because they loved each other dearly, and put it out of her mind, but later, when the pattern repeated itself day after day, she became extremely suspicious. However, she still put it down to youthful lethargy, and was several times on the point of remarking on it when she reflected that her daughter-in-law had only just arrived and was still a guest, having never shared a bed with her son. She had to be patient.

Then, inevitably, disaster struck. Mrs. Liu happened to be going past the bridal chamber when she heard the sound of crying from inside. Peeping through a crack in the wall, she saw her daughter and daughter-in-law locked in each other's arms and weeping softly. Finding this behavior more than a little strange, she was about to explode when it occurred to her that her son had only just recovered and was sure to fly into a rage if he learned of it, and so for the moment she curbed her impatience. Pulling aside the door curtain, she was about to enter when she found the door locked. "Open this door at once!" she shouted. The couple inside heard her voice, wiped away their tears, and rushed to open up.

Marching in, Mrs. Liu demanded, "What were you doing, weeping in each other's arms in broad daylight behind a locked door?" Their faces flushed with alarm, but they had no reply, which only confirmed Mrs. Liu in her suspicions. In a cold fury, she laid hold of Huiniang. "A fine thing you've been up to! You come along with me, my girl. There's something I want to say to you." She pulled the girl into a spare room at the back of the house. The maid, who had no idea why she was doing it, scampered out of the way.

Mrs. Liu bolted the door, while the maid crouched down outside, peeping through a crack. She saw her mistress hunting for a stick, then screaming at her daughter, "You little slut! Tell me the truth this minute if you want to escape a thrashing! Any fudging, and I'll beat your tail off!"

At first Huiniang held out. Her mother went on, "Little slut! Just tell me this. Why, when she's been here such a short time, are you two so much in love that you can't bear to part, but lock your door and weep in each other's arms?"

Huiniang had no answer. Her mother picked up the stick meaning to beat her, but she hadn't the heart to do it. Meanwhile Huiniang felt she couldn't conceal the affair any longer. Now that things have come to this state, she thought, I might as well make a clean breast of it. I'll beg Father and Mother to cancel the engagement with the Peis and marry me to Yulang instead. If they won't agree, I'll just have to take my own life.

"The other day when the Suns heard that my brother was ill," she told her mother, "they were concerned for their daughter's future and wanted to know what would happen, so they called on you and Father to postpone the wedding. When you refused, they dressed up their son Yulang as the bride. They never expected that you would tell me to keep him company, which is how we became husband and wife. Now we love each other so much that we've vowed to spend the rest of our lives together. When my brother recovered, Yulang was afraid our secret would get out, and he wanted to go back home and send his sister here in his place. But I believe that a woman should never take a second husband, and I told Yulang to find some way for us to marry. He couldn't think of any possible way, and since we can't bear the thought of parting, we started to cry, and that's when you found us. This is the truth that I'm telling you!"

Seized by an ungovernable rage, Mrs. Liu threw the stick away and stamped her feet in a frenzy, screaming, "I never thought that old bag would be so deceitful as to trick me by dressing up her son! No wonder she wanted him back on the third day. But now that he's ruined my daughter, I'll *never* forgive him! I'm going to finish that scoundrel off if it's the last thing I do!"

She opened the door and rushed out. Huiniang, alarmed that she was about to beat Yulang, threw modesty to the winds and tried to grab hold of her, but found herself pushed away and left sprawling on the floor. By the time she had scrambled to her feet, her mother was already outside. She gave chase, followed by the maid.

Meanwhile, the moment Yulang saw Mrs. Liu drag Huiniang off, he realized that their secret was out. He was already in a panic when the nursemaid came in and said, "You'd better watch out, sir! You're in big trouble! I was at the back and heard a furious row going on in the spare room. I peeped in and saw the mistress beating Miss Liu with a stick, trying to force the truth out of her."

The thought of Huiniang being beaten was like a knife twisting in Yulang's heart. It brought tears to his eyes, but he didn't know what to do. "If you don't leave now, something awful is going to happen to you very soon," warned the nursemaid. Yulang pulled off his hairpins, drew up his hair, and took the gown and the shoes and socks from his case and put them on. Then he left the room, pulling the door to behind him, and half ran, half stumbled all the way home.

> Its jeweled cage destroyed, the phoenix flies;
> Its golden shackles loosed, the dragon flees.

Widow Sun felt a mixture of emotions when she saw her son returning in a panic. "Why are you in such a state?" she asked. When the nursemaid told her what had happened, Widow Sun rounded on her son. "I sent you there as a temporary measure. How could you *do* such a wicked thing? And if you'd come back on the third day, what you did would have stayed secret and we wouldn't be in this mess. What a detestable old bag that Mrs. Zhang is! She never came back to report after leaving here that day. And, Nursemaid, you never came back again either, and it gave me fits! What are we going to do, now that my son has gotten us into trouble and ruined that girl?

You, you worthless boy, what good are you?" Yulang was visibly shaken by his mother's tirade.

"The young master wanted to come back, but Mrs. Liu wouldn't let him," said the nursemaid. "And I was so afraid that the pair of them would get themselves into trouble that every day I kept watch outside the door and didn't dare come home, either. Today I was in the back of the house for just a moment, and that's when she caught them. Luckily the young master managed to rush home and hasn't suffered any harm. He should lie low for the next few days. It would be wonderful if they decided to hush it all up!" Widow Sun told her son to hide out until they heard what was happening at the Lius'.

Meanwhile Mrs. Liu had rushed to the chamber and found the door locked. Assuming that Yulang was still there, she stood outside, screaming, "Damned scoundrel! What do you take me for, that you have the gall to come here with your fancy tricks and ruin my daughter! Well, today you've got me to reckon with, and you'll soon see what I'm capable of. Out you come, and be quick about it! If you don't open up, I'll beat the door down!" At that moment Huiniang arrived and tried to pull her mother away from the door. Her mother rounded on her. "You little slut, have you no shame at all? Trying to stop me, indeed!" But in shaking the girl off, she was too violent, and the door gave way and sent both of them sprawling in a heap on the floor inside. "Damned scoundrel! You made me fall!" she said, but when she scrambled up to go after Yulang, he was nowhere to be seen. She searched, but couldn't find him. "Oh, you're a clever one, you are!" she said. "You've escaped, all right, but even if you've escaped to Heaven itself, I'll go up there and pull you down again."

She turned to Huiniang. "Now that you've done this disgraceful thing, what if the Peis get to hear of it? How will you ever be able to hold your head up again?"

"It was just a moment's slip," said Huiniang through her tears. "I'm begging you, Mother, *please* take pity on me. Persuade Father to find a way to cancel the engagement to the Peis and marry me to Yulang instead, so that I can make up for my mistake. If you won't agree, I shall just have to take my own life." She fell weeping to the floor.

"That's easy for you to say! They've sent us the betrothal settlement and arranged to receive a daughter-in-law. If we ask them to cancel the engagement without giving a reason, they'll never agree! When they ask why we want to cancel, what do you expect your father to say? That his daughter has found a man all by herself?"

Huiniang flushed with shame under her mother's sarcasm and hid her face in her sleeve, crying bitterly. Mrs. Liu had an instinctive love for her daughter, and seeing her so distraught, she began to worry about the girl's health. "Child, it isn't your fault. It's all because of the evil trick that old bag played on us, sending that scoundrel here dressed up as a bride. In my ignorance I told you to keep him company, and you fell right into his trap. But at least nobody knows about it. Put it out of your mind and try to preserve your dignity—that's the only solution in the long term. But as for canceling the Peis and marrying that scoundrel, it's out of the question."

Huiniang wept and wailed even more over her mother's refusal, but sympathetic though she was, Mrs. Liu also felt furious with her daughter. She was at her wits' end as to what to do.

In the midst of the uproar, Mr. Liu returned from his doctor's rounds. As he walked past the door, he heard the sound of crying and recognized his daughter's voice, then heard his wife saying something. He didn't know quite why, but he felt distinctly uneasy. At last, losing patience, he pulled aside the door curtain and asked, "Why are you two in such a state?"

When Mrs. Liu had explained in detail, he was speechless with fury. Then something came to his mind and he began blaming his wife. "It's all your fault, you old bag; you've ruined our daughter. When our boy got seriously ill, I wanted to postpone the wedding, but you went on and on insisting on that date. Then, when the Suns sent their nursemaid over to suggest postponing the wedding, I was willing enough, but once again you had to jabber away and deceive them. And when the bride arrived, I told you we ought to let her sleep on her own, but oh no, you had to pressure our daughter into keeping her company. *Some company!*"

Because Yulang had escaped her, and because she couldn't bear to take her feelings out on her daughter, Mrs. Liu was chock-full of suppressed anger, and when she heard her husband's litany of accusations, she exploded. "You old cuckold! According to you, we should have let our son be cheated by that scoundrel!" She rammed her head into his midriff, and Mr. Liu, unable to contain his own fury, grabbed her and began hitting her. When Huiniang tried to intercede, all three ended up in a tangled heap on the floor.

The maid flew to Liu Pu's room. "Sir, come quick! The master and mistress are fighting in the bridal chamber!"

Liu Pu scrambled out of bed, made his way to the chamber, and tried to intercede. At sight of their son urging them to stop, the Lius finally did stop fighting—they were worried that, having so recently recovered from his illness, he might strain himself—but they continued abusing each other as "old cuckold" and "old bag."

Liu Pu persuaded his father to leave the chamber, then asked his sister why they were fighting and where his wife was. Huiniang was too frightened and ashamed to reply; she hid her face in her sleeve and wept silently. Liu Pu grew impatient. "Come on, tell me what this is all about!" Finally his mother explained it to him.

He went white with anger and for some time said nothing. "Family scandals should never be aired in public," he said at last. "If this gets out, we'll be laughed to scorn. But since we're already in this situation, let's decide what to do about it." Mrs. Liu held her tongue and left the chamber. Despite Huiniang's struggles, her mother seized her by one arm and dragged her to her room, which she padlocked before going back to her own room. Overcome by her shame, Huiniang sat weeping in a corner.

> All the waters of the great River Xiang
> Would not suffice to wash away that shame.

When Manager Li heard the commotion next door, he crouched down and put his ear to the wall, but although he caught the gist of it, he did not learn the details. The next morning, when the Lius' maid came out, he beckoned her into his house and asked her about it. At first she wouldn't say, but then he produced forty or fifty cash and held them out to her. "If you tell me, you can have this to buy goodies with," he said. At sight of the money, the maid's face lit up. She tucked it away and proceeded to tell him the whole story from start to finish.

He fairly hugged himself with delight. I'll tell the Peis about the scandal and egg them on to make a scene with Liu, he thought. He'll be far too ashamed to stay here, and the house will be mine! He raced over to the Peis and told them everything, adding a few touches here and there to incite them even more.

Pei Jiulao and his wife were already irritated with the Lius for rejecting their suggestion of a wedding date, and when they heard of the disgraceful behavior of their prospective daughter-in-law, they were predictably furious. Pei went straight to the Lius', called Mr. Liu outside, and began haranguing him. "When I sent a matchmaker over to suggest that we hold the wedding, you strongly objected, claiming that your daughter was too young. Instead you kept her safe at home, where she found herself a lover! If you'd listened to me, that wouldn't have happened. We're good, honest folk in my family, and we certainly don't want such a disreputable creature as that. Return the betrothal settlement immediately and get yourself another son-in-law. Don't try to ruin my boy's life."

At these accusations Mr. Liu's face turned red, then white. How does he know what happened only last night, he wondered. This is *very* strange! But he could hardly acknowledge the truth of the accusations—he had to deny them. "Kinsman, tell me, what is all this about? You're just making it up to smear my family! If other people heard what you're saying, they might think it was true, and then both of us would lose face."

"Damned wretch! You really are an old cuckold! Everyone knows the disgraceful things your daughter's been up to, and yet in front of me you try to cover it up with all this poppycock." He dashed forward and pressed his hand against the other man's cheek.[16] "You old cuckold! Not an ounce of shame in you! I'll send you a mask to wear in public."

These insults were too much for Mr. Liu, and he retorted in

16. A gesture of contempt.

kind. "You old scoundrel! Why are you insulting me in front of my own door!" He butted Mr. Pei, knocking him to the ground, and they began to fight. When Mrs. Liu and Liu Pu heard the commotion, they came out to see what it was and found the two men struggling with each other. They rushed forward to pull them apart.

Mr. Pei jabbed his finger at Mr. Liu and roared, "Oh, well done, old cuckold! I'll have something to say to you in court!" He went off, still cursing.

"Why did Pei come here and pick a quarrel so early in the morning?" Liu Pu asked his father.

Mr. Liu repeated what Pei had said.

"But how did he get to know? This is all very strange." Then he added, "Well, now that it's public knowledge, what are we going to do about it?"

Recalling the insults Pei had heaped on him, Mr. Liu grew even more angry and stamped his feet. "It's all the fault of that old bag in the Sun household. She ruined our family and blackened our reputation, exposing us to this kind of nastiness! Unless I take her to court, I'll never have a moment's peace." Liu Pu tried to dissuade him, but without success. After getting someone to draw up the accusation for him, Mr. Liu headed straight to court.

Prefect Qiao was receiving accusations at his morning session. Although he hailed from Guanxi,[17] he was upright and honest as well as clever, and he showed sympathy for talented individuals and love for the common people. His judgments were rendered with god-like skill, and throughout the prefecture he was known as Clear Skies.

When Mr. Liu arrived at court, he ran slap into Mr. Pei, who noticed the accusation in the other man's hand and assumed he was the target of it. "You old cuckold! You allow your daughter to do shameful things and then come and accuse me! I'm going with you to see His Honor." He stepped forward and tried to hold Liu back. They began scuffling again, and in the process

17. Shaanxi province, in the west of China. The point may be that he was a shrewd judge who hailed from a frontier area better known for producing warriors.

both accusations were lost. The two men arrived in the courtroom locked together.

Prefect Qiao ordered them to kneel down on opposite sides of the room. "What are your names? And why were you brawling?" he asked. They both began shouting at once. "Wait your turn!" ordered the prefect. "You there, old fellow! Come forward and present your case first."

Mr. Pei came forward on his knees and testified. "My name is Pei Jiulao. I have a son, Pei Zheng, who has been engaged since childhood to Huiniang, the daughter of that man over there, Liu Bingyi. This year they both turned fourteen, and being elderly myself and devoted to my son, I wanted to see them married as soon as possible. Several times I sent a matchmaker over to suggest holding the wedding, but Liu Bingyi kept raising difficulties, claiming that his daughter was too young. Meanwhile, believe it or not, he allowed his own daughter to prostitute herself! She was in love with Sun Yulang, and she secretly invited him into her house, hoping to back out of the engagement. This morning I went over there to talk about it, but I got assaulted and abused for my pains. In desperation, I came here to seek Your Honor's protection, but again he pursued and attacked me. I beseech Your Honor to give a ruling in the case and save my life!"

"You can step down now," said the prefect, after hearing the testimony. Calling on Liu Bingyi to come forward, he asked him, "And what do you have to say?"

"I have a son and a daughter," Mr. Liu began. "My son, Liu Pu, is engaged to Zhuyi, the daughter of Widow Sun, and my daughter is engaged to Pei's son. Some time ago, when Pei wanted to set a date for the wedding, I disagreed, for two reasons: first, my daughter was still very young and we hadn't assembled her trousseau, and second, I was just then arranging my son's wedding. Unfortunately, on the eve of the wedding, my son came down with a sudden illness, and we didn't dare let him sleep with the bride. Instead we told our daughter to keep her company. But Widow Sun had deceitfully kept her daughter out of sight and instead sent us her son, Sun Yulang, disguised as the bride, and he proceeded to rape my daughter. I was about to come and lodge an accusation when this fellow Pei got wind of it and came to my house and started a fight. I lost my temper and shouted at him. It's just not true that I was trying to back out of the engagement."

The prefect was greatly intrigued by this story of a man dressed up as a woman. "But a man dressed up as a woman will naturally look different. Do you mean to say you couldn't tell?" he asked.

"We are used to weddings, but there's no point in a man dressing up as a woman, so no one ever checks. Moreover, Sun Yulang has a beautiful complexion, just like a girl's. My wife and I were delighted when we saw him and not in the least suspicious."

"Since the Suns had betrothed their daughter to your son, why would they dress up their son and send him instead? There must be a reason." After a moment's thought, he added, "Is Sun Yulang still in your house?"

"No, he escaped back home."

The prefect sent runners to arrest Widow Sun and her two children and other runners to summon Liu Pu and his sister Huiniang. Before long, they had all been brought in.

When the prefect looked up at Yulang and his sister, he noticed that they were indeed equally beautiful, with identical looks. Liu Pu was also very handsome, while his sister Huiniang was gorgeous. The prefect marveled to himself: What fine-looking young couples! Then and there he formed the intention of helping them realize their desires. "Why did you dress your son up as your daughter, deceiving the Lius and ruining their daughter?" he asked Widow Sun.

She explained that the Lius' son fell gravely ill, but that Liu Bingyi refused to postpone the wedding. Fearing that her daughter would suffer for the rest of her life, she sent her son in disguise, to help break the curse of the illness and then return on the third day. It was just a temporary measure; she never imagined that Liu Bingyi would tell his daughter to join her son in bed, leading to this result!

"I see," said the prefect. He turned to Mr. Liu. "Since your son was gravely ill, of course you should have postponed the wedding. What were you thinking of when you stubbornly refused? If you had done as the Suns wanted, your daughter would not have incurred this disgrace. Your actions provoked this incident, which has come to involve your own daughter."

"I shouldn't have listened to what my wife said, but it's too late now."

"What utter nonsense! You're the head of the family. Why should you do what your wife says?" He then called Yulang and Huiniang forward. "Sun Yulang," he said, "you dressed up as a girl, which was wrong to begin with, but then you went and seduced a virgin. Now, what would be the proper punishment for that?"

Yulang kowtowed. "I have done wrong, I know, but it was not my intention to try to sleep with her. It was Mrs. Liu who sent her to keep me company."

"She didn't realize you were a man, so she told her daughter to keep you company. She meant well. Why didn't you object?"

"I did object, strenuously, but she insisted."

"According to the law, I should have you beaten, but I shall take into account your youth and also the fact that both sets of parents are to blame, so I'm letting you off this time." A weeping Yulang kowtowed and thanked the prefect through his tears.

The prefect then turned to Huiniang. "You did wrong, but there's no need to go into that. Tell me this: do you wish to marry Pei or Sun? I want the truth, now."

"I did have an illicit affair, and my conduct was at fault, but I can never change husbands," she said, weeping. "Moreover, I feel a strong affection for Sun Yulang and have vowed never to marry anyone else. If Your Honor insists that we part, I shall have to take my own life. I would not have the gall to try and eke out a dishonorable life as the object of public scorn." As she finished speaking, she burst into loud sobs.

The prefect noted that her testimony came from the heart and he was filled with sympathy for her. Ordering her to step aside, he called on Pei and gave him this order: "I would have found that Huiniang should marry into your family, but she has lost her virginity to Sun Yulang, and her conduct has been at fault. If you were to accept her as a daughter-in-law, your own family's reputation would be impaired and you would become an object of ridicule, while she would bear the stigma of taking a second husband. You would never be at peace with each other. And so I am ordering that she marry Sun Yulang to restore her honor. I am also ordering the Suns to return the betrothal settlement. Your own son should choose another wife."

"She behaved disgracefully," said Pei, "and naturally I don't want her. But Sun Yulang destroyed the marriage we had arranged, and giving her to him would mean rewarding the guilty parties, which is something I cannot accept. I'd rather do without the betrothal settlement, if only you would order her to marry some other person. That would relieve some of my anger."

"Since you don't want her in your family, why are you being so vindictive?"

Mr. Liu also entered a plea. "Your Honor, Sun Yulang already has a fiancée. My daughter can hardly become his *concubine!*"

The prefect had assumed that Sun Yulang was not engaged and had settled the case accordingly. Confronted with this new information, he said, "Well, what shall we do about this?" Addressing Sun Yulang, he continued, "Since you already had a fiancée, ruining a girl's virtue was even worse! Where is she now?"

When Yulang did not dare respond, the prefect went on, "Who is she? You're not *married,* are you?"

"She's the daughter of Xu Ya, and no, we are not married," said Yulang.

"That makes it easy to settle," said the prefect. He called on Pei. "Sun Yulang was already engaged. Since he's now going to marry your son's fiancée, in order to relieve your feelings I am awarding his fiancée to your son."

"I would never dare object to Your Honor's enlightened decision," said Pei, "but I'm afraid Xu Ya may refuse."

"I have made my decision, and no one will dare refuse. Go home at once and fetch your son. I'll send a runner for Xu Ya and his daughter, and we'll match them up in court." Pei Jiulao quickly returned home and fetched his son, Pei Zheng. Xu Ya also arrived with his daughter. The prefect noted their regular good looks and concluded that they made a suitable match. "Sun Yulang seduced Liu Bingyi's daughter, and I've ordered them to become husband and wife," he said to Xu Ya. "I've made the decision that your daughter should marry Pei Jiulao's son, Pei Zheng. I expect to receive a report that all the weddings have taken place today. If anyone refuses to comply, he will be severely punished." When Xu Ya saw that the prefect had made his decision, he did not dare object. The others were also willing to comply.

The prefect then took up his brush and wrote out his decision as follows:

> A brother took his sister's place at her wedding, and two sisters-in-law slept together. The love of parents for their children is human nature, but pairing a male with a female led to a surprising result. Put dry tinder near a naked flame, and it's no wonder it catches fire. The finest jade was paired with the brightest pearl; they happened to make a perfect match. The Sun boy gained a wife through his sister; he had no need to find a lover by clandestine means. The Liu girl got a husband through her sister-in-law; she longed for a fine suitor, and she was not disappointed.[18]
>
> People love one another and marry; rituals arise from what is right. But the friendship between the families was lost, and an expedient was in order. I have instructed Xu Ya to accept Pei Zheng as his son-in-law, allowing him to marry the fiancée of Sun Yulang. The latter had taken another's fiancée, and now his fiancée is taken by another. Thus the enmity between the two families has been put to rest.
>
> Pleasure is best when shared,[19] and now each of these three couples is as happy as fish in water. The principals may have changed, but sixteen ounces still make a pound. If engagements unite families, then the couples were not mismatched from their previous lives. Naturally the parents are the matchmakers in forming loving relationships, but I in my official capacity play the matchmaker for lovers who are not engaged. And now my decision has been rendered. Let all of you enjoy your wedded bliss.

18. Based on a quotation from the *Poetry Classic* (Mao 33). Several other classical quotations are woven into the prefect's decision.
19. A quotation from *Mencius* 1B.1.

When he had finished writing, Prefect Qiao called the clerk in to read the decision in court to all those involved. Everyone accepted its provisions, kowtowing and thanking the prefect. He ordered the treasury to provide them with six lengths of red silk, which he told the couples to drape over themselves. He called in three groups of musicians and ordered three gaily decorated sedan chairs for the brides. The grooms and their parents followed on foot.

The affair caused a sensation in Hangzhou, where people remarked on what a fine, considerate judge the prefect had proved to be and praised both his virtue and his wisdom.

Following the young couples' weddings, nothing more needs to be said about them. Manager Li, however, had hoped to draw Widow Sun and Pei Jiulao into a quarrel with Liu Bingyi and then, when "the snipe and the oyster were locked in battle," he, as the fisherman, would come along and scoop up the spoils.[20] He never expected that the prefect would not punish the couple, but actually facilitate their marriage. In the neighborhood it was regarded as a wonderful story, not in the least disgraceful, a fact that made Li very resentful. When, before a year was out, Prefect Qiao chose Liu Pu and Sun Yulang as licentiates and sent them off to the provincial examination, Li felt too ashamed to go on living in Hangzhou and secluded himself in the country. Later both Liu Pu and Sun Yulang passed the metropolitan examination in the same year and received posts in the capital, where they served with distinction and also helped Pei Zheng obtain an official post. Their families enjoyed great honors and wealth. Liu Pu rose to be grand secretary of the Longtu Pavilion. And even Manager Li's house fell into the possession of the Lius.

What advantage did the sly little schemer gain? Someone in later times wrote a poem about his unscrupulous nature, as a warning to others:

---

20. A reference to an ancient fable (see the *Zhanguo ce* [Intrigues of the Warring States], *Yance* [Intrigues of Yan] 2, "Zhao qie fa Yan"). A snipe was trying to peck at an oyster when the oyster closed its shell and caught the snipe's beak. Neither would give way until a fisherman came by and caught them both.

Since kindness is the basis of virtue,
Why bother to be sly to this degree?
Never did the ancients, choosing a house,
Try to buy up their neighbors' property.

There is also a poem praising the prefect's decision:

A lovers' mismatch it was, based on fate,
Put right by a judge romantic and wise.
(The mantle of success covers all things.)
Not for nothing was he known as Clear Skies.

4
The Rainbow Slippers

He loves to get the better of fellow men,
And otherwise a secret grudge he'll nurse.
But who can grasp the contrary ways of Heaven?
He who gets the better will come off worse.

*N*ot long ago there was a man named Qiang who loved to take advantage of others and bully those weaker than himself. The residents of the neighborhood were all intimidated by him and gave him the nickname Upper Hand. One day he was walking down the street when he saw a stranger ahead of him stop and pick up a money belt. The belt looked heavy, and Qiang assumed that there was something in it. He rushed up and blocked the other man's way. "Kindly give me back my money belt. It slipped off just now."

"But I was in *front* of you," said the stranger. "How could it have slipped off *you*? That doesn't make sense."

When the man refused, Qiang shot out his hand to grab the belt and managed to seize one of the straps. A tug-of-war ensued. When the neighbors came crowding around and asked what the quarrel was about, each man insisted that the money belt was his. The neighbors could not decide who was telling the truth, but one older man had a suggestion. "Neither of you has any proof. Just tell us what's inside, and the belt will go to the one who gets it right."

"Oh, I can't be bothered with your little guessing games," said Qiang. "I know my own belt when I see it. Give it back to me, and you'll hear no more about it. If you don't, I'll fight you to the death."

The full title is "Lu Wuhan Refuses to Give up the Rainbow Slippers."

These remarks as good as told the bystanders that the money belt did not belong to Qiang, but many of them were afraid of him, and in hopes of currying favor, they came forward and tried to soothe the stranger's feelings. "Sir, don't you realize who this Mr. Qiang is? He's a great figure in these parts. You picked up the belt, so presumably it doesn't belong to you. The obvious thing would be to use it to get into his good graces."

But the stranger was in no mood to be soothed. "I agree it wasn't mine, but money ought to be gotten by honorable means, not by force. Since you gentlemen have been kind enough to try and mediate, I'm perfectly prepared to open it up and see what's inside. If there really is a windfall in there, let's split it three ways. Mr. Qiang and I will each take a third, and the other third will go to you gentlemen in appreciation of your services, so that you can hold a celebration in the tavern."

"Very good," said the older man. "Let go, Mr. Qiang. I'll take it." Opening the belt, he found a large cloth wrapper containing two ingots of gleaming, snow-white silver with several layers of paper around them. Each of the ingots weighed ten ounces.

Qiang's heart was set on having the ingots, so he tried to hoodwink the others. "It would be a great pity to ruin these two ingots by cutting them up into three shares," he said. "I have a few ounces of loose silver on me that I was going to buy a horse with. Let me give them to this man and keep the ingots for myself." He produced three or four packets of odd pieces of silver that together weighed no more than four ounces. Even the cost of the bystanders' celebration would have to come out of it.

When the stranger refused to accept the silver, the two men resumed their quarrel, until one of the bystanders offered the former some advice. "This Mr. Qiang is not someone you want to tangle with, you know. You'd do well to get what you can and go on your way."

The older man offered similar advice. "We'll let you have the whole four ounces—we don't want a share of it. We get to drink all the time, and to please you two we'll do without the celebration." As he was saying this, Qiang whipped the two ingots out of his hand, and the stranger had no choice but to accept the four ounces.

"I have no loose cash left," said Qiang, "but the owner of

that tavern up ahead is a cousin of mine. I've taken up a lot of your time, I know, but you really must join me there for a drink."

"In that case, this man should come along too," said the bystanders with a laugh. "From now on, you two will be on good terms." All fourteen or fifteen of them trooped into Zhu Sanlang's tavern and took seats upstairs. Qiang was in a high good humor over getting the ingots for next to nothing, but he could not help feeling a certain discomfort—he was indebted to the bystanders for their help, but in beating out the stranger he had deprived them of their share of the money. Moreover, the owner of the tavern was his cousin, and he dearly wanted to show off. So he ordered nothing but the best wine and food, and they all ate and drank freely, until they were quite drunk and could eat no more. The bill came to over three taels, which Qiang put on his own account. The guests then said goodbye and went their separate ways. The stranger, who had obtained four ounces of silver free and clear, went home.

Two days later, Qiang was about to buy the horse, but the tavern needed to be paid and there was no money left in the house. He had to take the two snow-white ingots to a silversmith to have them assayed, hoping to make a little extra on the quality of the silver. The silversmith turned the ingots over and examined them, then weighed them in his hands a few times. "Where did you get these?" he asked.

"In the course of business."

"Then you've been had. These are fakes—they have a core of iron. The outside may be silver, the thinnest possible layer of it, but inside they're all iron and lead."

Qiang refused to believe him and insisted that he chisel them open. "Don't blame me if it spoils them," said the silversmith. He set to work chipping a hole in one ingot, and the layer of silver split off, revealing the forgery. Qiang still could not believe his eyes. Never in his life had he found himself on the losing end of a deal, and he'd gone into this one of his own free will—nobody was to blame but himself. He sat beside the counter in the silversmith's office staring blankly at the ingots. By this time the news had drawn a large number of people there. They came in, inspected the fakes, and began airing their opinions, which only made Qiang more furious than ever. He was just looking for some excuse to make a scene when two constables walked in, barked out an order, and without giving him a chance to explain, put a chain collar around his neck and took him and the fake ingots away.

As it happens, the county treasury had received several fake ingots in its tax revenue, and the magistrate had secretly sent the constables out to find and arrest the forgers. The mold used in casting the ingots in this money belt, whoever may have dropped it, matched that of the fake silver in the treasury, which was why the constables had arrested him and taken him to court. As soon as the magistrate saw the shape of the ingots, he concluded that Qiang was the criminal who had forged them, and without giving him a chance to defend himself ordered him to be given thirty strokes with the heavy bamboo, to be held in prison, and to make good the value of the ingots, for which he set a three-day deadline. Qiang was forced to sell off all his property and transfer the proceeds to the treasury. He then begged a favor of someone, who explained to the magistrate's office how the ingots had been obtained. The magistrate accepted the explanation, pardoned him, and set him free, but Qiang's total loss came to over a hundred taels. His modest property had been wiped out. The people in the neighborhood made up a jingle about him that circulated as a joke.

> Upper Hand, oh, Upper Hand,
> Your affairs have gone to pot!
> You obtained two ingots made of iron;
> You had a hundred taels and lost the lot;
> Whacked in court with the heavy bamboo,
> On the hook for drinks—disastrous upshot!
> You lost this time, but you shouldn't get mad.
> And as for your nickname, it's best forgot.
> Try not to bully your neighbors again—
> Too weak you'd be to suck up your own snot.

This prologue story is called "Upper Hand Qiang Loses a Windfall through His Own Greed," and it illustrates the maxim

"He who gets the better will come off worse." I shall now tell another story, one titled "Lu Wuhan Refuses to Give up the Rainbow Slippers." Like the last one, it tells how someone who tried to take advantage of another person brought catastrophe upon himself.

> Too many treats ruin the digestion,
> Excess of pleasure spells disaster.

In the Hongzhi reign[1] of the present dynasty, there lived in the city of Hangzhou in the province of Zhejiang a young man by the name of Zhang Jin, who came from a family that had been extremely wealthy for many generations. As a child he worked hard at his studies, but when both of his parents died at an early age, there was no one left to restrain him, and he cast his education aside and spent all his time with a group of frivolous young rakes. In so doing, he learned a great deal about popular music and football, and grew accustomed to flaunting himself in the brothels and making a close study of the courtesan world. Because he was handsome and dashing as well as amorous and sensitive—and also because he had money to spend—many of the girls fell in love with him. This was enough to turn his head completely, and he ceased to pay any attention to his own family. Although his wife reproached him constantly, she had to let him go his own way.

It happened one day in spring when the peach trees on the West Lake were in full bloom. The night before, Zhang Jin had issued an invitation to two celebrated courtesans, Jiaojiao and Qianqian, as well as to several young men. A boat had been ordered for an excursion on the West Lake. Dressing for the occasion, Zhang wore a fashionable crepe-silk turban and a pale rose gown of patterned Wu silk with an embroidered white damask jacket, as well as damask stockings and crimson shoes. He carried a fan decorated with a painting and calligraphy, and he was accompanied by a pretty boy called Qingqin, his catamite, who carried a cape over his left arm and held with his right hand a viol and a flute, both with covers of Sichuan

1. 1488–1505.

brocade. After leaving his house, Zhang was swaggering along Chessmen Lane in the direction of Qiantang Gate when suddenly he looked up and saw a girl opening the upstairs blind in a house overlooking the street. She was about to empty the morning slops. This girl possessed an extraordinarily delicate kind of beauty. What did she look like? There is a Qingjiang Air that describes her:

> So gorgeous is she! Whose daughter is this,
> Surpassing the paragon[2] in beauty?
> Her face a perfect oval, powder-white,
> Her locks? Dark clouds they seem to be.
> If I could just get close to her,
> I'd lose the souls within me![3]

One look at her, and the strength ebbed from Zhang's limbs. He stood rooted to the spot, reluctant to turn away. Then he gave a cough. After tipping out the slops, the girl was about to close the blind when she heard the cough and looked down. A handsome young man, a dashing figure in brilliant clothes, was staring right up at her. Their eyes met, and they gazed at each other. She found herself giving him a faint smile, which made him even more delirious. The only problem was that they were too far apart to communicate. As they gazed, the front door opened and a middle-aged woman came out. Zhang Jin hurriedly turned away to avoid her. When the woman was some way off, he came back and looked for the girl, but in the meantime she had let down the blind. He stood there for some time, but saw nothing. He told Qingqin to note the address so that tomorrow he could make inquiries about her, and as he left he looked back several times.

The West Lake was a favorite haunt of his, but after seeing this girl, he dragged himself along, as weary as if he were on a hundred-mile trek through the mountains. Emerging from the Qiantang Gate, he arrived at the boat he had ordered. By this time the two courtesans and the young rakes were already on

2. A reference to the classic beauty Xishi.
3. In other words, my souls (plural) would melt with joy.

board, and when they saw Zhang Jin, they came out on the bow to greet him. He went aboard, and Qingqin set down the cape and the flute. The boatman cast off and headed for the middle of the lake. It was a fine, clear day, and along the embankments the peach blossom and the new willow leaves basked in the sunshine, while swarms of young men and women enjoying a spring outing strolled back and forth, wine cups in their hands. A poem sets the scene:

> Hills beyond hills, towers beyond towers,
> How long will the music and dancing last?
> Drunk on the scented breeze, the revelers
> Take the present capital for the past.[4]

The young rakes in the boat began showing off their skills at music and song. Zhang Jin, however, whose mind was fixed on the girl he had seen, was in no mood to enjoy himself. He sat there idly musing, his chin cupped in his hands, as if lamenting the passing of autumn rather than enjoying the arrival of spring. "You're usually not at all like this," said the others. "Why so gloomy today? There must be a reason." Zhang Jin gave only a noncommittal reply.

"Come on, don't be so down in the mouth," they went on. "Cheer up and have some wine. If there's anything bothering you, we'll soon put it right." They turned to the courtesans. "He probably thinks you two aren't making enough fuss of him, and that's why he's cross. Hurry up and give him a glass of wine." The two women duly poured out a cup and offered it to him. Badgered by his companions, Zhang did make an effort to join their drinking games, but his heart was not in it. Well before evening he got ready to leave, and the others did not try very hard to dissuade him. He returned the same way he had come, through the Qiantang Gate and along Chessmen Lane. At the girl's door he gave another cough, but saw no movement upstairs. At the end of the lane, he doubled back again, a course he repeated several times without any response. "Let's come back

---

4. I.e., they take Lin'an (Hangzhou), capital of the Southern Song, for Bianjing, capital of the Northern Song.

again tomorrow, sir," said Qingqin. "If we keep going back and forth like this, it will only make people suspicious." Zhang had to agree.

The next day he made inquiries in the neighborhood about the family the girl belonged to. This is what he was told: "Her father, Pan Yong, is known as Evil Star. He and his wife have this one girl, now fifteen, called Shou'er. Pan Yong has some slight connection to an official's family, and he trades on that to extort money and hospitality from people. There's no one in the district who's not afraid of him—and no one who doesn't hate him, either. He's a shameless, cunning scoundrel."

Zhang Jin filed these remarks away in his mind. When next he strolled past her door, it so happened that the girl had opened the blind and was gazing off into the distance, and the two saw each other again. Loving glances passed between them, more loving than before. From then on, Zhang was constantly back and forth beneath her window to look for her, signaling his presence with a cough. Sometimes he saw her, sometimes he didn't. Whenever he did, they made eyes at each other, expressing a deeply felt passion. The only problem was that there was no way for him to get upstairs.

On the fifteenth of the second month the moonlight was as bright as day. Zhang was too restless to settle down at home, so after supper he walked alone in the moonlight to the Pans' door. No one else was about. He saw the girl roll up the blind, lean out of the window, and gaze at the moon. He looked up at her and gave a faint cough. She understood, and shared a smile with him. He brought out a red damask sash from his sleeve, and after slipping a folded message inside, rolled it into a ball and threw it up to her. She held out both hands, and it fell right into them. After studying the message in the moonlight, she tucked it away in her sleeve, then took off one of her slippers and tossed it down. Zhang caught it in both hands, and saw that it was a rainbow-colored slipper no longer than the distance from his thumb to his index finger. He wrapped it inside a sash and put it in his sleeve, then gave an extravagant bow, to which the girl responded. But just at the height of their excitement, she was called away by her parents and had to close the window and go downstairs.

Zhang plodded dejectedly home and spent the rest of the night in his study. Unwrapping the slipper, he examined it by lamplight. It was truly a golden lotus petal,[5] made with the finest needlework. What did it look like? There is another Qingjiang Air that describes it:

> Look at this tiny slipper
> Of silk that is soft indeed.
> It vies with a lotus bloom.
> Adorning it with flowers,
> How little thread you would need!
> No wonder it's fragrant, undefiled—
> It's never been worn outside her room.

Zhang looked at the slipper for a while, then wrapped it up again. I must find someone to take her a message, he thought. How can I find a way to get up there? If we just go on ogling each other like this, it may be a feast for the eyes, but not for anything else. What would be the point of it? He thought and thought, and concluded there was only one course that offered any hope of success.

The next day about noon he put some money in his pocket and went off to the Pans' house. Looking up, he could not see his beloved, so he sat down in a house some distance off to see who called there. He was in luck, because before long he noticed a saleswoman go in carrying a small box. After a couple of hours, she came out again and retraced her steps, still carrying the box. Zhang hurried after her and found that she was none other than the Mrs. Lu who made a habit of visiting the great houses to sell artificial flowers and face powder to the women. She actually had a house herself at the end of Chessmen Lane. Although she called herself a seller of flowers and cosmetics, her true specialties were those of the matchmaker, the bail bondswoman, and the procuress, and for that reason her place was a hive of activity. From the front part of it, her son, Lu Wuhan, ran a shop selling pork and wine. A violent man given to hard drink and wild behavior, he would often adminis-

5. A tiny bound foot was described as a golden lotus petal.

ter a few blows even to his own mother, and she, for fear of his fists, did his bidding in everything without raising the slightest objection.

When Zhang called out her name, she turned and saw who it was. "Oh, Mr. Zhang, where did you spring from? I haven't seen you in days."

"I went to look up a friend, but he was out, and I came back this way. Why haven't you been to visit us? Those wenches of mine are looking forward to seeing your flowers."

"I've been meaning to visit your good lady, but I've been tied up with all kinds of trivial business."

As she said this, they arrived at her front door. Lu Wuhan was extremely busy in his shop selling pork and wine. Mrs. Lu turned to Zhang. "I can offer you a cup of tea, but it's very cramped inside, and I wouldn't want to inconvenience you."

"I can do without the tea, but I would like to take a walk with you and have a little chat."

"Just a moment, then." She quickly went inside and deposited the box before re-emerging. "What was it you wanted me to do for you, sir?"

"This is no place to talk. Come with me." He led her to a tavern, where he chose a private room. The waiter set out cups and chopsticks, and asked, "Are you expecting anyone else?"

"No, it's just the two of us. We'll have two bottles of your best wine warmed up and some fresh fruit to go with it. Bring the hors d'oeuvres first. Three or four of your best varieties will do." The waiter soon returned with the order, set it down, and poured the wine, of which they drank a few cups each. Zhang then sent the waiter off, shut the door, and said to Mrs. Lu, "There's something I want to ask you to do, although I'm afraid it may be more than you can handle."

She laughed. "Far be it from me to boast, but the biggest problems in the world get solved when I take them on. Whatever it is, you just tell me, and I'll settle it for you, I guarantee."

"Excellent!" He set both arms on the table, bent forward, and said in a low voice, "There's a girl who wants to have an affair with me, but we have no one to carry messages back and forth, so it's impossible to bring it off. I happen to know that you're on familiar terms with the family, and I'm here to beg you to take her a message. If by your good offices we're able to meet, I'll certainly show my appreciation. Here are ten taels of the shiny stuff as an advance payment, just to get you started. If you can pull it off, there's another ten taels in it for you." He took two large ingots from his sleeve and set them down on the table.

"The money is my least concern. But tell me, whose little dolly are we talking about?"

"Shou'er, of the Pan family on Chessmen Lane. You know the family well, I take it?"

"So it's that little monkey, is it? She always looks so demure, a proper little virgin, not at all as if she were tempted to stray. But how did she fall into your hands?" Zhang gave a detailed account of their chance meeting and the gift of her slipper the previous night.

"You know, there are serious problems with this," she said.

"What problems?"

"The old man is very strict, and they don't have a single servant. It's just the three of them, and they're always together. Moreover, they're very strict about their doors, closing up early in the evening and opening late in the morning. How would you ever get in? I'm afraid I can't take it on."

"Look, a moment ago you said that the biggest problem in the world would get solved if you took it on. You can't use trivial things like these as an excuse for begging off. I suppose you think I offered you too little, and so you're deliberately raising difficulties. Well, I don't care about the cost, and I do need you to take this on. What if I add another ten taels, plus two bolts of satin for your burial garments?" Mrs. Lu's eyes were already sparkling at the sight of the snow-white ingots, and now, thinking of the reward she would reap later, she couldn't bear to pass up the chance.

"Well, sir, since you're so determined," she said after a moment's thought, "I daresay you'd think I wasn't showing you the proper respect if I declined. Let me see what I can do to come up with a plan—subject to your and her destinies, of course. If I pull it off, it'll be your good luck. But if I can't, I'll have done my best, and you're not to go blaming me. You keep the money for the present. When I have some positive leads, I'll come and collect it. But you'd better let me have that slipper she gave you—I'll need it to break the ice."

"I won't have any peace of mind unless you take the money."

"Then I will take it, but I'll return it if things don't work out," she said, tucking the silver away in her sleeve. Zhang took out the sash, unwrapped the rainbow slipper, and handed it to her. She examined it. "Nice workmanship!" she exclaimed, as she hid it away. They ate and drank some more and then went downstairs, where Zhang paid the bill. After they had left the tavern and were about to part, Mrs. Lu said, "It'll take time to arrange this, sir. You mustn't be too impatient. If you're going to set a deadline for me, I'm afraid I won't be able to take it on."

"All I'm asking is that you do your best. A few days here or there won't matter. If you have any good news to report, come straight to my place." With that they parted.

> He had to entertain a procuress
> To seal a lifelong bond of happiness.

Ever since she saw Zhang Jin, Shou'er's mind was in a daze, and she lost all interest in food and drink. If I could only marry him, my life would be worthwhile, she thought. I wish I knew where he lives and what his name is! If only on that moonlit night she could have grown a pair of wings and flown down and gone off with him! The crimson sash he gave her she treated as if it were her lover, hugging it to her as she lay in bed. She slept until almost noon the next morning, and when she awoke she was still in a state of blind infatuation. Not until her mother came and called her did she get up.

Two days later, when her father had left the house after breakfast, Shou'er, who was upstairs, began fondling the sash again. Then she heard voices downstairs followed by the sound of someone coming up. Hastily she hid the sash and went to the head of the stairs, where she found the Mrs. Lu who sold artificial flowers and face powder coming up accompanied by her mother. Mrs. Lu had a small box with her.

"Shou'er," said Mrs. Lu, "yesterday I got in some very nice

flowers in a new style and I've brought them over to show you."
She opened the box and took out a flower. "Now, what do you
think of this? Doesn't it look just like the real thing?"

"It's certainly beautifully made," said Shou'er, taking it in
her hand. Mrs. Lu brought out another flower and handed it to
Mrs. Pan.

"Just look at this one, ma'am," she said. "I don't suppose you
ever saw this sort of design when you were growing up?"

"You're perfectly right. When I was a girl, we had only those
crude things, nothing as exquisite as this."

"And these are merely the medium quality. They go all the
way up to super-excellent. A glance at one of them will give the
blind back their sight and the elderly their youth—as well as
adding a few years to their lives."

"Do show us some of those," said the girl.

"I'm just afraid you may not be able to appreciate them. I
can't show you anything as expensive as that."

"But even if we can't afford them, surely we can still admire them?"

"I was only joking," said Mrs. Lu with a laugh. "Don't take
me so seriously, Shou'er. Even if you wanted the whole lot,
it wouldn't amount to so very much. Let me bring them out
and show you. You can choose the ones you like best." She
brought out several flowers that were even more exquisite.
Shou'er picked out a few of the best ones.

"How much do you want for these?"

"Come now! When have I ever haggled with you, that you
should even ask me that question? They cost whatever you say
they do." She added to Mrs. Pan, "Ma'am, if you have any hot
tea, I'd love a cup."

"Oh, I got so carried away looking at these flowers that I
forgot all about the tea. Since you'd like it hot, I'll go and boil
up some more." She went downstairs.

Once she had left, Mrs. Lu rearranged the flowers in the box
and brought out a red silk package from her sleeve and set it
among them.

"What's in the package?" asked Shou'er.

"A certain very important item that is not meant for your
eyes."

"Why ever not? I insist on seeing it." She went to pick it up.

"It's definitely not for you to see!" said Mrs. Lu, at the same time allowing Shou'er a chance to pick it up. "Oh dear!" she exclaimed over and over, after the girl had done so. She made a pretense of trying to snatch it back, but Shou'er whipped it away. On opening it, she found the rainbow slipper she had given to the young man two nights before and flushed crimson.

Mrs. Lu snatched it back. "Grabbing other people's things — the very idea!"

"What can this slipper be worth, that you value it so highly? You wrap it up in silk, and you won't let anyone see it."

"You say it's not worth anything?" said Mrs. Lu with a smile. "I'll have you know that a certain gentleman considers this slipper as precious as life itself. He told me to conduct a search for the matching one."

Shou'er was well aware that Mrs. Lu had been sent to convey a message, and she was thrilled. She took up the slipper again. "You know, Mrs. Lu," she said with a smile, "I have a slipper that's a perfect match for this."

"Well then, now that we've matched the slippers, how are you going to respond to the young gentleman?"

"You know all about it," said Shou'er in a low voice, "so there's no need for me to pretend. I might as well ask you what I want to know. What kind of person is he? What is his name? And what's he like?"

"His name is Zhang Jin. He's fabulously wealthy, and he has a tender, loving nature. He's been in agony day and night for love of you — unable to eat or sleep. When he learned that I knew your family, he begged me to find out from you whether there was some way you could let him into the house."

"You know how strict my father is! He's ever so vigilant about our doors. At night he waits until I've blown out my lamp and gone to bed, then takes a lantern and shines it on me before he goes to bed himself. How could *I* ever come up with a way for us to meet? But Mrs. Lu, if *you* have some scheme to bring us together, I'll be ever so grateful."

Mrs. Lu gave her an appraising look. "That's no problem," she said. "I do have a plan."

"What is it?" asked Shou'er eagerly.

"You go to bed a little earlier than usual and stay there until your parents have checked on you with the lantern. When you hear a cough down on the street, you take four strips of cloth,[6] knot them together, and hang them out your window so that he can use them to climb up. Early the next morning he goes down the same way. Even if you see each other for a hundred years, no one will ever know. You'll be able to enjoy yourselves to your hearts' content. What do you say to that?"

Shou'er was thrilled. "Thank you *so* much for all your help! But when can he come?"

"It's too late for tonight. I'll call on him first thing in the morning and arrange it for tomorrow night. But I shall need some kind of token to give him, to show that I've done my part."

"Here, take him both slippers as a token. He can bring them back when he visits me tomorrow night." She had not finished speaking when her mother came in with the tea. Mrs. Lu hurriedly stuffed the slippers inside her sleeve and drank two cups of tea.

"Mrs. Lu, it's a little awkward to find the money for the flowers today," said Shou'er. "May I pay you later?"

"A few days won't matter. I'm not one to fuss about such things." She picked up her box and took her leave. Mrs. Pan and Shou'er saw her to the door.

"If you have any time tomorrow, I hope you'll come back for a chat," said Shou'er, as she was leaving.

"I know," said Mrs. Lu. Mrs. Pan had no idea what this exchange implied.

> Rake and beauty send each other loving glances;
> Hell-bent on sex, yet still he needs a go-between
> Who's glib and crafty, full of schemes for secret trysts.
> How many upright households has this old bawd misled?
> Fearing neither Heaven nor Earth nor casual slurs,
> Deceiving the parents, she sets the lovers' scene.
> Mad with love, they'd gaze but never meet each other
> Except by fate. So vent your anger, strike her dead!

6. Possibly the strips of cloth used for foot binding.

Mrs. Lu did not go home. Instead she went straight to Zhang's, telling his wife that she had come to sell flowers. When she asked after Zhang, she was told he was not at home. His womenfolk snapped up all of her flowers, some paying cash, others buying on credit. She spent a little time with the women, and then, when Zhang had still not returned, took her leave. Early the next morning, she put the slippers in her sleeve and went back to Zhang's, but was told that he hadn't returned from the night before and that no one knew where he was. Back she went to her house, where she found Lu Wuhan fuming; he wanted to kill a pig but his assistant had left. Seeing his mother, he exclaimed, "You're here in the nick of time. Come and help me tie up a pig."

Mrs. Lu, who went in fear of her son, didn't dare say no. "Wait a moment while I change," she said, going inside. Lu Wuhan followed her in and saw a red silk package fall from her jacket as she took it off. He assumed that the package was full of money and picked it up, then took it outside and opened it, only to find a pair of rainbow-colored slippers inside.

What girl has feet this small, he marveled. He examined the slippers for a while, then said to himself, Someone with feet like this simply has to be pretty. One night with her in my arms would make my whole life worthwhile! Then he was struck by another thought: How did these slippers come into Mother's possession? What's more, they're well worn, yet so valuable that they're wrapped up in silk—there must be a reason for it! I'll wait until she starts looking for them and then give her a good scare—that'll get the truth out of her. He wrapped the slippers up again and tucked the package away.

When Mrs. Lu had taken off her outer clothes, she helped her son tie up the pig for slaughter, then washed her hands, dressed again, and went in search of Zhang. As she was going out the door, she felt inside her sleeve—the slippers were not there! Hastily she turned back and started looking for them, but they were nowhere to be found. She cried out to high Heaven in her panic.

Lu Wuhan, who was watching his mother's panic with a calculating eye, let her continue with her searching until she sighed in frustration, then asked, "Have you lost something? You seem so upset!"

"It's very important, but it's not anything I can talk about."

"Perhaps your eyesight isn't what it was. If you'll give me just a hint, I'll help you look. But if you can't talk about it, you'll just have to go on looking by yourself. It'll be none of my concern."

Something about her son's tone struck Mrs. Lu as suspicious. "If you picked it up, give it to me. A lot of money hangs on this, enough to set you up in business."

At the mention of money, Lu Wuhan thrilled with excitement. "I did pick up something," he said. "But you'll have to tell me what it's all about before I give it to you." Calling him inside, his mother told him in detail, from start to finish. Although Lu Wuhan was delighted with what he heard, he pretended to be shocked. "It's a good thing you told me. Otherwise, you might have gotten us into serious trouble."

"But why?"

"The old saying is perfectly true: If you don't want anyone to know about something, don't do it. This sort of affair can never be kept secret. Moreover, that old bandit Pan Yong—is he someone you can afford to rile? If this gets out, and he learns that you were given money to play the pander, not only will I be unable to set myself up in business, even my stock-in-trade will wind up in his hands. And he won't stop at that, either."

Frightened by her son's warning, Mrs. Lu exclaimed, "You're absolutely right! I'll return the money and the slippers and tell him it wasn't feasible. I won't be involved in any way."

"Just where *is* the money?" asked Lu Wuhan with a smile. She brought it out and showed it to him.

He put it in his sleeve. "Mother, I'll take charge of the money and the slippers. If those people get into some other kind of trouble and you are dragged in, we'll use this as evidence in your defense. And if that doesn't happen, the money will come in very handy. Surely he'd never dare to claim it back?"

"But what am I going to tell Mr. Zhang when he asks for her reply?"

"Just say that her doors are too closely guarded and nothing is possible at present. If you see an opportunity, you'll go and tell him. Put him off a few times, and he'll stop coming."

Now that her son had taken both the money and the slippers, Mrs. Lu didn't dare ask for them back—she had no hold over him, and anyway, she was fearful of the trouble he might cause. Nor did she dare go and arrange the assignation for Zhang Jin.

Lu Wuhan used the money to buy splendid clothes and a crepe-silk turban. That same day he waited until his mother had gone to bed and then late in the evening he dressed up in the new clothes, tucked the slippers in his sleeve, locked the front door, and headed for the Pans' house. The sky was overcast and the moon by no means bright. Fortunately it was late and there was no one about. He gave a faint cough underneath the eaves, and on the upper floor Shou'er heard it and unlatched the window, which creaked as it began to open. Lest it awaken her parents, she picked up the teapot from the table and poured some tea on the hinges, and when she opened the window further it made no sound. She tied one end of the cloths around an upright and let the other end hang down. At sight of the cloths Lu Wuhan exulted. Gathering up his gown, he sprang forward, gripped them with both hands, planted his feet against the wall, and gradually hauled himself up. On reaching the window, he stepped lightly over the sill. Shou'er pulled up the cloths and shut the window.

Lu Wuhan at once took her in his arms and kissed her on the lips, and she slipped her tongue into his mouth. Both of them were ablaze with desire, and anyway, it was pitch dark and impossible to tell that he was an imposter. They embraced, then stripped and went to bed. Wuhan parted her thighs and reared himself above her, while she arched her body to meet his thrusts. It was a case of mutual passion, and Wuhan gave free rein to his desires.

> Nutmeg bud[7] by withered vines ensnarled;
> Haitang blossom by sudden squall destroyed.

7. Symbolizing a virgin.

The owl commandeers the oriole's nest;
The phoenix mates with the common crow.
"Oh, my heart and liver!" he cries, lapsing into butcher's
    language;
Oh, my darling, my dear! she thinks, taking him for the one
    she loves.
Hongniang arranged a tryst—and got Zheng Heng![8]
Guo Su copied Wang Xuan—and charmed Xishi![9]
Oh, pity this gorgeous, exquisite gem,
So lightly given to a vulgar lout!

Only when the lovemaking was over did they begin to talk about themselves. Wuhan produced the slippers and expressed his love for her, while Shou'er told how she had longed for him. Then, with their passions still not satisfied, they made love again, this time with more tenderness than before. At three in the morning she got up, opened the window, and lowered the cloths again, and he climbed down and raced home. She pulled the cloths up and stowed them away, then gently closed the window and went back to bed. Over the next six months, unless it was raining or the moon was shining too brightly, Lu Wuhan came every night, and the pair enjoyed a close and loving relationship.

Little by little Shou'er's appearance and mode of expression underwent a change, which made her parents suspicious, but although they questioned her several times, she kept mum and gave nothing away. But one night when Wuhan was visiting her, she said to him, "I don't know quite how, but my parents must have noticed something, because lately they've been asking me questions all the time. I've denied everything time and again,

8. In the play *The West Chamber (Xixiangji)*, the maid Hongniang arranges a tryst between her mistress Yingying and Zhang Hong. Here the writer imagines that she mistakenly arranged it for Zhang's nasty rival, Zheng Heng.

9. In an anecdote titled "Zhuluo yu" found in Fan Shu's *Yunxi youyi* (*juan* 1), the Tang poet Wang Xuan visited the supposed site where Xishi, a beautiful village girl, was once "discovered" by a passing gentleman. Wang composed a series of poems in Xishi's honor, and the gesture so captivated Xishi's spirit that she appeared and made love to him. Then another man, Guo Su, heard of Wang Xuan's good fortune and tried unsuccessfully to emulate him, ending up as an object of ridicule. Here the writer imagines that Guo Su had succeeded in captivating Xishi's spirit.

but the last couple of nights they've been more watchful than ever. If they ever find out, we'll both be in trouble. From now on you'd better stop coming. Let's wait until they ease up before we have another night together."

"You're right," said Wuhan, although in his heart he felt quite differently. At three o'clock he departed once more. That night Pan Yong, drowsy with sleep, thought he heard people murmuring upstairs. He listened intently, hoping to hear what they were saying before going up and catching them in the act, but after a while he fell asleep again and did not awaken until dawn.

"That little slut of ours is up to no good, and that's a fact, but she always denies it," he said to his wife. "Last night I clearly heard voices upstairs. I meant to listen a bit longer, then go up and catch them, but I fell asleep."

"I've had my suspicions, too. But there's simply no way for anyone to get upstairs from the outside. You don't suppose it could be some ghost or spirit that comes and goes without a trace, do you?"

"We'll just have to give her a good hiding and beat the truth out of her."

"No, no, don't do that! As they say, you shouldn't wash your dirty linen in public. One stroke of the cane and the neighbors will know all about it, and then the news will spread and nobody will want to marry her. Whether or not there's anything going on, let's move her downstairs to sleep. We'll lock her door before we go to bed at night, and all our worries will be over. You and I will move upstairs to her room and find out just what's been going on."

"You're right," said her husband. After supper that night, he told his daughter. "From now on you're to sleep in our bedroom. We'll move upstairs and sleep in yours." Shou'er knew perfectly well what this implied, but she didn't dare disobey, just silently bemoaned her fate.

That night, when they exchanged bedrooms, Pan Yong locked the girl's door and said to his wife, "If someone comes upstairs tonight, once I've caught him I'll treat him as a common burglar and do him in—that should relieve my feelings." Leaving the window unlatched, he lay in wait for the intruder.

Let me turn back to Lu Wuhan. He had not been at all pleased to hear Shou'er insist that he should wait a while before renewing his visits, but he managed to get through the next few nights without visiting her. After a dozen nights, however, his lustful desires were raging out of control, and he wanted to go and enjoy himself with her again. Lest Pan Yong catch him in the act, he took with him for his own protection a sharp knife of the kind used for slaughtering pigs. Locking the front door, he went straight to the Pan house and gave his usual cough. But although he waited a while, there was no sign of any movement upstairs. She can't have heard me, he thought, and coughed twice more, again without any response. He wondered if she had gone to sleep. He repeated the procedure three or four more times, until it was three o'clock and his plan was no longer feasible, at which point he had to return. But, he reflected, she knew I hadn't been for a good many nights, so why would she be expecting me tonight? I can hardly blame her for that.

The next night he went again, and once more there was no response from upstairs. This time he grew impatient, and also somewhat angry. On the third night he got a little drunk, then waited until midnight and took a ladder with him as he went over to the Pans'. He gave no signal, just climbed up the ladder and tugged gently at the window, which creaked open. Stepping inside, he pulled the ladder up after him, shut the window, and felt his way to the bed.

> Keen to induce the dream of sex,
> He flies to the bower of bliss.

For the first night or two after they moved upstairs, Pan Yong and his wife had been intent on finding out what was going on and did not dare to sleep too soundly. But after a dozen nights of utter silence in which not so much as a mouse could be heard, they began to suspect that their daughter had not been up to anything after all, and relaxed their vigilance. By an odd coincidence, that very night the catch on Shou'er's door had broken off, and the room could not be locked. "Just lock up the front and back doors," said Mrs. Pan to her husband. "You can seal her bedroom door with a strip of paper. I don't imagine we'll have any problem tonight." He did as she suggested.

That night they drank a few cups of wine, climbed into bed together in a mellow mood, and did certain unmentionable things together that left them both exhausted. Locked in each other's arms, they fell into a sound sleep, which is why they were completely unaware that Wuhan had climbed up the ladder and opened and then closed their window.

Feeling his way to the edge of the bed, Wuhan was about to undress and get in, when he heard the sound of two people snoring. He was gripped with fury. No wonder she pretended to be asleep and took no notice when I coughed those times, he thought. The little slut has hooked somebody else, and she made up that excuse about her parents questioning her so that I wouldn't come anymore. It's obvious—she wanted to break up with me! The ungrateful little slut, what good is she? He pulled out his knife, felt for the throats of the two people in bed, and deftly slipped it into one of them and gave a sudden slash. He killed Mrs. Pan first, then, fearing that her windpipe might not be severed, he twisted the knife three or four times until she could not possibly have survived. He then turned the knife over and killed Pan Yong. Wiping the blood off his hands, he tucked the knife away, pushed the window open, and let down the ladder. Once outside, he shut the window after him, climbed quietly down, hoisted the ladder onto his shoulder, and raced home.

When Shou'er first changed bedrooms, she was scared that her lover would come and give his signal, revealing their secret. Only when her parents made no mention of any such thing the next morning did she begin to feel at ease. When a dozen nights had gone by without incident, she relaxed completely. On this particular morning she awoke and waited until nine o'clock, surprised that she had not heard her parents coming downstairs. She knew there was a seal on her door, and she didn't dare break it, so she tried calling from inside her bedroom. "Father, Mother, get up! It's late! Why are you still in bed?" She called for a long time, with no response. There was nothing for it but to open the door and go upstairs herself.

On pulling aside the bed curtain, she found a pool of blood covering the bed and two corpses lying in the middle of it. She fell to the ground in shock, then after some time regained her senses and, with one hand resting on the bed, burst out sobbing. Who could have killed them, she wondered. After she had wept for a while, another thought struck her: This is a capital crime. If I don't tell the neighbors, I'll be involved myself. She took the key and opened the front door. Overcome by bashfulness, she stood inside the door as she shouted, "Help! Neighbors, help! My father and mother have been killed! Please come and tell me what to do!"

She repeated this several times, and the neighbors and passersby came surging into the house, forcing her back.

"Where were your parents sleeping?" they demanded.

"They were perfectly all right when they went upstairs to bed last night, and this morning the front and back doors were still locked. I have no idea who could have killed them."

The people rushed upstairs and, opening the curtain, found the couple murdered in their bed. Looking around, they noticed that the room faced the street, but although there was a window, the first-floor eaves were recessed, providing no foothold for anyone to use in climbing up. Shou'er added that the doors had been securely locked and only just now reopened. No one else had been in the house. "This is a very strange business—dreadful!" said the people present. They reported it to the head constable of the precinct, and he escorted the next-door neighbors and Shou'er to court.

Poor Shou'er! She had never been out of the house before, but today she had no choice. Wearing a veil that came up to her eyes, she locked the front door and accompanied the others to the prefectural court.

The incident caused a sensation throughout much of Hangzhou. As the news spread, Lu Wuhan realized that he had killed the wrong people, but there was nothing he could do about it. Driven half out of his mind, he remained at home in a quarrelsome mood. Mrs. Lu, who knew something of her son's movements, felt sure that he was involved in the murder, but she did not dare ask him. She was on tenterhooks and did not venture outside the house, either.

If you're in the right, you'll face a thousand;
If your conscience is bad, you won't leave home.

The prefect was in court as the group arrived. They reported as follows: "Last night, at Pan Yong's house on Chessmen Lane, Mr. Pan and his wife were murdered. The doors had not been forced open. We've come here with their daughter, Shou'er, to report the crime."

The prefect called on Shou'er to come forward. "Give me a detailed account of when your parents went to bed and where they were sleeping," he said.

"Last night at dusk, after they'd had their supper, they locked the doors and went upstairs together. This morning, when they hadn't risen by nine o'clock, I went upstairs to see what was the matter and found them lying inside their bedclothes, murdered. The upstairs window was still shut, and the doors downstairs had not been tampered with—both were still locked."

"Was anything taken?"

"No, everything was still there."

"How can people be murdered when the doors haven't been opened? And when there's nothing missing? This is very odd." He thought for a moment. "Who else do you have in your family?" he added.

"Just my father, my mother, and me. No one else."

"Did your father have any enemies?"

"No, none."

"How very strange!" He pondered for some time—and then it suddenly dawned on him what must have happened. He told Shou'er to lift her head and saw a veil covering half her face. Ordering his men to take it off, he saw that the girl was extraordinarily beautiful.

"How old are you?" he asked.

"Sixteen."

"Are you engaged?"

"No," she murmured.

"Where were you sleeping?"

"Downstairs."

"Why were you downstairs and your parents upstairs?"

"I used to sleep upstairs, but half a month ago we exchanged bedrooms."

"Why?"

She was unable to answer. "My parents wanted to change, I don't know why," she said.

The prefect roared at her, "It was *you* who murdered your parents!"

Visibly shaken, Shou'er burst into tears. "Your Honor! My own father and mother! How could I ever *do* such a thing?"

"I know you didn't murder them yourself, but I'm positive your lover did. Come on, out with his name and be quick about it!"

Unnerved though she was, she denied having a lover. "I don't even set foot outside the house. How could I do such a thing! If I did, the neighbors would certainly know about it. Ask them, Your Honor. They'll tell you what kind of person I am."

"They didn't know about the murders," said the prefect with a laugh. "How would they know about something like this? Obviously, you were having an affair with someone. Your parents found out and made you sleep downstairs to cut off the man's access. Then he murdered them in a fit of rage. Why else would your parents move you downstairs?"

As the saying goes, guilty parties give themselves away. As each accusation hit home, Shou'er first flushed, then blanched, and finally began to stammer, unable to get a word out properly. Observing the state she was in, the prefect felt even more certain of his conclusion, and ordered that the finger press be applied. The attendants sprang forward and pulled out Shou'er's jade-white hands, which were far too delicate to endure such harsh treatment. No sooner was the finger press in place than the pain became unbearable, and she quickly confessed. "It's true, Your Honor! It's true! I do have a lover."

"What is his name?"

"Zhang Jin."

"How did he get up to your room?"

"He used to wait until my parents were asleep and then give a cough to signal his arrival in the street below. I would tie up one end of some cloths that I had knotted together and let the other end hang down so that he could use it for climbing up. Before dawn he would go down the same way. This went on for about six months. Then my parents got some inkling of it and questioned me several times, but I always denied it. I told Zhang Jin he shouldn't come any more, lest our secret be exposed, and he agreed. Afterward my parents moved me downstairs to sleep and locked the doors. To cover up my wrongdoing, I was perfectly prepared to sleep downstairs and break off with him. This is the truth that I am telling you. As for my parents' murder, I honestly don't know why it happened."

After her confession the prefect ordered the finger press removed, then issued a warrant and sent four constables rushing off to arrest Zhang Jin.

> You may stay at home and close your doors,
> And disaster will strike from the sky.

After parting company with Mrs. Lu at the tavern, Zhang Jin had spent three days in a brothel, then returned home to hear that she had twice come looking for him. He rushed off to get her news. But because Mrs. Lu was frightened by what her son had said, and also because she no longer had the slippers, she chose to deceive him. "Shou'er has them," she said. "She asked me to convey her regards and tell you that her father is so terribly strict these days, and keeps such a close watch on both doors, that there's no chance of your getting in. Before long, however, he'll be going on a trip lasting about six months, and once he has left, you'll be able to visit her freely again." Zhang Jin believed what she said and regularly asked her if there was any news. Later on he caught sight of Shou'er on a few occasions, and they exchanged smiles, but each was under a misapprehension. She thought he was her nocturnal visitor and gave him a joyous smile, while Zhang thought he had still to seduce her and put himself out to be charming. But when days passed without any definite news, Zhang's yearning gradually gave way to an illness, and he stayed at home to recover from it.

On the day I spoke of he was brooding in his study when a servant announced that there were four constables outside who wanted to ask him some questions. He was alarmed, thinking their questions must have something to do with the brothel he had visited, but he still had to go out and ask the men why they had come.

"We understand it has something to do with taxes or the corvée," they told him. "You'll find out when you get to court."

Zhang ceased worrying, changed his clothes, and after distributing some money to the constables, accompanied them to court. A number of his servants followed behind. On the way they heard the news that Pan Shou'er and a lover had murdered both of her parents. Zhang was shocked. Could that wench really have been responsible for something like that, he wondered. It's a good thing I never had an affair with her! She's nothing but trash, and she almost got me involved in a scandal.

Soon they arrived at court. The prefect saw that Zhang was a handsome youth who did not look at all like a murderer, and he began to have doubts about his conclusion.

"Zhang Jin," he said, "why did you seduce the daughter of Pan Yong and then kill her parents?"

Zhang Jin was a stylish young rake whose knowledge of the world was limited to the brothel quarter and whose long suit lay in philandering and adultery; he had never faced the majesty of the law. He had been quaking inwardly when first brought into court, but when he heard that the murders of Pan Shou-er's parents were being blamed on him, he felt as if he had been struck by a thunderbolt—he was scared speechless. Only after a long struggle did he manage to come out with a response. "She and I intended to have sexual relations, but we never did. I never even went upstairs in her house, let alone killed her parents."

"Pan Shou'er has already confessed that you had an illicit affair with her over a period of six months. How dare you deny it!" roared the prefect.

Zhang Jin turned to Pan Shou'er. "We *never* had an affair! Why are you trying to destroy me?"

Up to this point Shou'er had not believed Zhang Jin responsible for her parents' deaths, but when he denied having an affair with her, she began to suspect that even the accusation of murder might be true. Weeping and sobbing, she stuck to her charge, and Zhang Jin was unable to come up with a convincing rebuttal. The prefect gave the order to place him in the foot press. Shouting in unison, the attendants surged forward and seized him by the arms and legs.

Poor Zhang Jin! He had been raised in the lap of luxury, so that even the slightest burl in the garment next to his skin was too much for him to bear; how could he possibly endure such torture as this? No sooner was the press clamped on his feet than he began squealing like a slaughtered pig. Kowtowing again and again, he cried, "I confess! I confess!"

The prefect had his men release the press and told Zhang to write his deposition. "I don't know the facts, so what do you expect me to write?" he said between sobs. He turned to Shou'er again. "Somebody seduced you and now you're dragging me in to take the blame. But it's no use my saying anything. I might as well confess to whatever it was you testified to."

"You brought this on yourself," she said. "Of course you'll confess! Are you trying to say that you didn't flirt with me from down in the street? Or that you didn't throw a sash up to me? Or that you didn't receive any rainbow slippers from me?"

"All those things are true. But I never did join you upstairs."

"If one fact checks out, the rest will too," roared the prefect. "Come on, no more talk! Hurry up and write your confession!"

Zhang Jin bowed his head and wrote out the deposition to Pan Shou'er's dictation—and in that perfunctory manner pled guilty to a capital crime. After he had signed the deposition, it was handed to the prefect, who read it and sentenced him to death. As for Shou'er, although she knew nothing of the murder, her lascivious conduct had been responsible for the murder of her parents, and she was given the same sentence. After each had received thirty strokes with the flat bamboo, Zhang was held on death row, and Shou'er in the women's prison. And there we shall leave her.

Luckily for Zhang Jin, the constables knew that he was rich and pulled their blows as they beat him, with the result that he did not suffer any serious harm. He was brought to prison still protesting his innocence, but there was no way for him to appeal. As for the jailers, they were as elated as if they had just had a load of silver arrive at their prison, and they fawned all over him. "Mr. Zhang, how could you do such a thing?" they asked.

"Brothers, let me be frank with you," said Zhang Jin. "I really did see that girl, and we meant to sleep together, but we never actually met. Somebody, I don't know who, deceived her, and now she's accusing me instead of him! Tell me, do you really think that someone like me is capable of murder?"

"Then why did you confess?"

"How could I have withstood the torture—me, with my delicate physique? Moreover, I've been ill for days and have only just got out of bed—it would have meant suffering one shock on top of another. If I confessed, I'd get a few more days of life. If I didn't, I'd die tonight. This is karmic retribution, needless to say. Still, Pan Shou'er gave such a vivid and detailed account that there must be *something* behind it. I'd gladly offer you gentlemen ten taels as drinking money if you'd only take me over to see her. If I can find out the truth, I'll die content."

"There's no problem in seeing her," said one of the head jailers. "But ten taels isn't enough."

"Five more, then?"

"Look, there are a great many of us, and the money doesn't go very far when it's divided up. We'll need at least twenty."

Zhang Jin agreed to pay it. With two jailers gripping him under the arms, he was taken as far as the palisade gate of the women's cells. Pan Shou'er was in a cell, crying bitterly. When the jailers brought her to the gate and she caught sight of Zhang, she began screaming at him through her tears. "You false-hearted beast! I was taken in by you, and you seduced me. But what harm did I ever do to you, that you should be so vicious as to kill my parents and destroy my life?"

"Don't shout. Let me explain in detail what happened so that you can check it carefully. When I first saw you, you sent me loving glances, and we were both attracted to each other. Then on that moonlit night I gave you my sash and you responded by giving me your rainbow slipper. There was no way I could meet you, so when I found out that Mrs. Lu the flower seller used to visit your house, I gave her ten taels to take the slipper to you and find out how things stood. She reported that you had taken the slipper back, but that your father was terribly strict and the doors were closely watched. However, he would soon be going on a trip lasting several months, and once he left she would arrange a meeting for us. Then days passed, ever so many days, and after six months there was still no definite news. When I saw you from time to time, you always gave me a smile. I agonized day and night over you, until I developed a case of lovesickness and had to stay at home to recover. I never did go to your room, and yet you keep on making these false accusations about me!"

"Heartless beast!" sobbed Shou'er, "You're *still* denying it! That day you told Mrs. Lu to bring the slipper back and arrange a meeting. Her plan was that I would wait until my parents were asleep and then, as soon as I heard a cough from down on the street, I would let down some cloths for you to climb up on. The next night you gave a cough and, as arranged, I let down the cloths for you. You produced the slippers as a sign of good faith. From then on you came every night. But my parents noticed something and questioned me several times, so I told you not to come any more, in case our secret got out and we were both disgraced. I asked you to wait until my parents had relaxed their vigilance before renewing your visits. But you, you vicious beast, were full of hatred for my parents, and last night you somehow or other got upstairs and killed them both. And you're still denying it. In fact, you won't even admit what happened before then."

Zhang Jin thought for a moment. "Since you had an affair with me for six months, you must be very familiar with my body and my voice. Now take a good look at me. Don't you see any difference?"

"Good point, sir!" said the jailers. "If there really is no difference, you're a monster. Mere execution would be too good for you. Death by slicing wouldn't be too much."

Shou'er hesitated for some time, then looked hard at him, studying him closely.

"Well?" asked Zhang Jin. "Am I the one or not? Tell me. Don't dither."

"His voice was very different from yours, and he seemed bigger, too. We were always in the dark, so I could never examine you closely. All I remember is that you had a protruding scar on your left side the size of a copper coin. That's the only distinguishing mark."

"That's easy enough to check," said the jailers. "Master Zhang, please take your clothes off and let's see. If you don't have a scar, we'll appeal to His Honor tomorrow, offering ourselves as witnesses, and you'll be cleared."

"I'm greatly indebted to you," said a much relieved Zhang Jin, quickly stripping off. When the jailers examined him, they found a body as white as jade and free of any scar. Shou'er looked on, too, and was struck dumb.

"Well, miss, *now* do you believe it wasn't me?"

"Of course it's a clear case of injustice," said the jailers. "To-morrow we'll lodge an appeal." They helped him back to a cell, where he spent the night.

Next morning, when the prefect ascended his tribunal, the jailers knelt before him and told him of the firsthand evidence provided by Zhang Jin and Pan Shou'er during the night. He was astounded and had both of them brought out for further questioning. First he ordered Zhang Jin to approach and tell his story in detail from start to finish.

"You gave the slipper to Mrs. Lu, and she never gave it back to you. Is that right?" asked the prefect.

"Yes."

The prefect then called Shou'er, who gave her detailed account of events.

"Is it true that you gave the slipper to Mrs. Lu and then Zhang Jin gave both slippers back to you when he visited you the following night?"

"Yes."

The prefect nodded. "In that case, Mrs. Lu double-crossed Zhang Jin and gave the slippers to someone who impersonated him and seduced you." He sent constables to arrest Mrs. Lu.

When she was brought in, the prefect ordered that she be given forty strokes before he even began questioning her. "At first, Zhang Jin asked you to take a message to Pan Shou'er. After arranging a meeting for the following night, why did you trick him into not going and give the slippers to someone else so that he could impersonate Zhang and seduce the girl? Tell the truth, and your life will be spared, but say just one word that isn't true, and I'll have you beaten to death on the spot."

Mrs. Lu's skin had been broken and bruised by the forty strokes, and she didn't dare say anything but the truth. She told in great detail how she had used her flowers as a pretext for calling; how she had worked out a plan and set a time for the meeting; how she had visited Zhang Jin several times but that he was always out; and how she had returned on the last occasion and helped her son to kill a pig. She also told how she had dropped the slippers; how her son had scared her; how Zhang Jin had later come to find out the news; and how, with no slippers to give him, she had fobbed him off with an excuse. About the seduction of the girl and the murder of her parents, she knew nothing whatever.

Noting that her testimony tallied with that of the two defendants, the prefect realized that Lu Wuhan was the culprit and sent constables to arrest him.

"Lu Wuhan, you seduced a girl from a respectable family and killed her parents," he began. "What do you have to say for yourself?"

Lu Wuhan denied both charges. "Your Honor, I'm only a simple tradesman; I would never do any such thing. It was Zhang Jin who got my mother to take messages back and forth, and then seduced the Pan girl and killed her parents. He can't pin it on me!"

Before he had even finished testifying, Shou'er started shouting, "That's the voice of the man who seduced me! Your Honor, check to see if he has a protruding scar on his left side." The constables were ordered to strip him, and the scar was found just where she said it would be.

At that point, Lu Wuhan capitulated and declared over and over again that he was willing to pay with his life. He confessed to seducing the girl and then killing her parents by mistake. The prefect ordered that he be given sixty strokes and sentenced him to death. The murder weapon was found and sent to the treasury. Shou'er's death sentence was to stand. Mrs. Lu, who had corrupted a girl from a respectable family, was sentenced to exile in accordance with the law. Zhang Jin had wrongfully planned to seduce the girl, and although he had not in fact done so, he was the real source of the catastrophe. He, too, was given a sentence of exile, commutable to a fine as guaranteed by a bondsman. The sentences were passed in open court one after the other. The prefect then prepared the documents for submission to higher authority.

Meanwhile the following thoughts were running through Pan Shou'er's mind: I was seduced by Lu Wuhan and I'm responsible for the deaths of my parents. What disgrace I've brought upon myself! But it's too late to do anything about it now, and I'm too ashamed to go on living. She stood up, rushed forward, and dashed her head against the granite facing of the court steps. Her brains spilled out, and she died.

> Pity this flower-like girl in love with sex,
> Transformed into a wronged and bloody spirit!

The sight of the girl dashing her brains out was too much for the prefect, who ordered Lu Wuhan to be given another forty strokes, making a hundred in all, and then had him locked in a cell on death row. He was to be executed after the autumn equinox, once the sentence had been approved. The prefect also summoned the neighbors to carry Shou'er's body out and to sell off Pan Yong's property. The proceeds were to be used to buy coffins for the three dead family members as well as plots for their burial. Any money left over was to be deposited in the treasury.

When Zhang Jin saw Shou'er dash her head against the steps, he was overwhelmed with pity. It was all because of me that three people lost their lives and a whole family was destroyed, he thought. He returned home, rewarded the constables and jailers with gifts of money, and paid the fine in lieu of exile. After recovering his health, he had services held in Buddhist and Daoist temples for the passage of the souls of Shou'er and her parents. He also undertook a year-long vegetarian fast and vowed never again to seduce any women or even to visit any brothels. He led a quiet, carefree life at home, and lived to the age of seventy. Someone at the time wrote a poem reflecting on these sad events:

> "Gambling tends to theft, lechery to murder"—
> What the ancients once said is true indeed.
> If you can stay untouched by either vice,
> It's a quiet and peaceful life you'll lead.

5
Wu Yan

The lecher's every thought is plucking blooms,
Which drains his vigor, and his virtue too.
Do not, I pray you, pluck so wantonly,
For lust is Buddha's number one taboo.

The story goes that during the Southern Song dynasty there was a licentiate named Pan Yu living in Jiangzhou. His father, Pan Lang, had served as prefect of Changsha but had now retired. After winning first place in the provincials, Pan Yu was preparing to take leave of his father and embark for Lin'an to compete in the metropolitan examinations. The night before his departure, his father had a dream of a First Scholar's nameplate being brought with great fanfare to his house—and the name on it was none other than that of Pan Yu! Early the next morning he called his son in and told him the news. Pan Yu was delighted because he assumed it meant certain success in the examinations next spring. On his way to the capital, he made merry and indulged himself to the full. In due course he arrived in Lin'an and went looking for lodgings. On coming to a certain small inn, he was welcomed by the owner, who asked, "Is your name Pan, by any chance?"

"Yes, but how did you know?"

"I had a dream last night in which the Earth God[1] appeared and told me that this time the First Scholar would have the surname Pan and that he would arrive here at noon the following day. I was to take care to give him a warm welcome. Now,

The full title is "Master Wu Has an Assignation on the Neighboring Boat."
    1. The local guardian spirit.

150

you happen to fit the god's prediction perfectly, so if you don't find us too rough and ready, I hope you'll consider staying here with us."

"If the prediction comes true, of course I'll be glad to pay double the rate," said Pan Yu. Telling his servant to fetch his baggage, he settled in.

The landlord had a very pretty daughter who was just fifteen years old. When she heard her father talking about the god's prediction, she assumed that Pan Yu was destined to become First Scholar and peeped at him through the window. At sight of a handsome, elegant young man, she felt strongly attracted to him but had no way of communicating her feelings.

One day Pan Yu needed some water to mix with his ink. The boy who worked in the inn happened to be out, and Pan Yu went himself to the kitchen, where he happened to come upon the landlord's daughter. As she slipped away to avoid him, she gave him a smile. Pan Yu was utterly captivated; he handed the boy two gold rings and a hairpin to give to her and told him to find an opportunity to convey his greetings and request an assignation. She accepted the gifts with pleasure and, taking off a silk purse that she wore at her waist, she sent it to him in return, promising to come to his room when next her father left the house.

Several days went by without an opportunity, and Pan Yu had almost given up hope, but when the examinations were over, the landlord gave a party to help the candidate unwind. The drinking went on until late at night, by which time the host was hopelessly drunk. Pan Yu was just about to turn in when he heard a tap on his door. He opened it, and there stood this girl. Without a word, he led her into his room, where they made love, taking great delight in each other. He promised to make her his concubine after his triumph in the examinations.

That night his father back home had a second dream about the welcoming party bearing the First Scholar's nameplate and accompanied by great fanfare. This time, however, it continued on past his house. In his dream he shouted after it, "This is the place where it belongs!"

"Not so," said the official charged with delivering it. When

Pan Lang caught up with the party, he found that the First Scholar's name was indeed that of someone else.

"The First Scholar should have been your son," added the official, "but because he has done something discreditable, the Emperor of Heaven has ordered his future prospects curtailed and chosen another in his place."

Pan Lang awoke with a start, unsure whether to believe what he had dreamt, but before long the results came out, and when he read the official list, he found that the First Scholar was indeed the man whose name he had seen on the nameplate. His own son had failed.

When Pan Yu returned home, his father questioned him and the son had to admit what he had done. Again and again father and son sighed with regret over what might have been.

A year or more passed, and the son, who still hankered after the girl in Lin'an, sent off a servant with a betrothal settlement, but it turned out that in the meantime she had married someone else. Pan Yu was filled with remorse. In later years, although he took the examination several times, he failed each time and died a broken man.[2]

> For a moment's pleasure
> A great career was lost.

Storyteller, according to you, history shows innumerable cases of brilliant youths and beautiful girls who have had clandestine affairs and then gone on to win fame and glory—and also to provide us with admirable examples. How could the Great Abacus in the hands of the Lord of Heaven have miscalculated so badly in such cases?[3]

Gentle reader, there is something you ought to know. Philandering and adultery destroy a person's lifelong integrity, which is a grievous sin. But if the couple was fated to marry because of some attachment formed in a past life, and if the

---

2. There are numerous such cautionary tales about the behavior of examination candidates.

3. A simulated intervention by a member of the imaginary audience.

Heavenly Matchmaker has already tied their feet with his red thread, then the marriage was predestined and did not result from their present behavior, whether or not they engaged in a clandestine affair. But listen while I tell you another story.

Like the last one, this story also took place in the Song dynasty, during the reign of the Emperor Shenzong. A certain official from Bianjing, Wu Du by name, succeeded in the metropolitan examination and was appointed subprefect of Changsha. He and his wife, Mistress Lin, had a son, Wu Yan, who was now fifteen, a handsome lad with a dashing, romantic air about him. He had been studying since childhood, had read widely in the classics and histories, and was an accomplished poet, but he also had a distinct peculiarity. Can you guess what it might be? This handsome young fellow had to have three quarts of rice and two or three pounds of meat every day, plus over a gallon of wine, not to mention other refreshments. And these quantities were all upper limits laid down by his father after careful consideration to avoid damage to his son's digestion. As far as Wu Yan was concerned, he was still quite hungry after such meals; he was never able to satisfy himself fully.

In the third month of the year, Subprefect Wu completed his term in Changsha and was appointed prefect of Yangzhou. The local officials came all the way to Changsha with a large boat to welcome their new prefect. That day Wu Du packed up his belongings, said goodbye to his Changsha colleagues, and set off. Blessed by a following wind and smooth sailing, he came in due course to Jiangzhou, the place where Bai Juyi once gave a merchant's wife his "Song of the Lute," the poem that contains the line "The Jiangzhou marshal's blue shirt was wet with tears."[4] Prefect Wu's boat, under a full spread of sail, was making steady progress in midstream when a sudden squall sprang up. The angry, tumultuous waves almost capsized the boat, and the sailors turned pale with fright, to say nothing of Prefect Wu and his wife. The sailors rushed to lower the sails and head for shore, but the mile or two of water that they had

4. This is the last line of Bai Juyi's (772–846) poem "Pipa yin." The marshal was the author.

to cross still took them a good four hours of hard work. When they looked back at the other boats on the river, they saw that they, too, were scrambling frantically for safety.

"If we get to shore, we'll give everlasting thanks to Heaven!" exclaimed Prefect Wu. He told the sailors to row harder, and finally they reached shore, cast anchor, and tied up. Another official's boat was moored a hundred or two feet away, and its hatch door was open and the bamboo blind rolled halfway up. Beneath it stood a middle-aged woman and a beautiful girl, with three or four maids behind them. Wu Yan had already observed them through the bamboo blind in his own boat and had noted that the girl was simply stunning. What was her beauty like? Here is a poem that describes it:

> Eyes like autumn water, bones of jade;
> Her face a flower, brows like the willow.
> Surely a goddess [5] come down from the moon!
> How could such beauty on this earth grow?

Wu Yan was delirious with excitement. He would have liked nothing better than to fly to the girl's side and fold her in his arms, but the distance between the boats was too great, and he could not even get a perfect view of her. Then he had an idea. "Father, why don't we get the sailors to move us alongside that other boat," he said. "We'd be safer over there." His father followed his suggestion and asked for the boat to be moved. Under direct orders from the prefect, the sailors were not about to disobey. They weighed anchor, cast off, and moved close to the other boat.

Wu Yan had been hoping he would be able to feast his eyes on the girl after they drew alongside, but they had barely arrived when the hatch door shut—and his feverish excitement turned to ice.

Do you know who the official in the next boat was? His name was He Zhang, and he came from Nanjing. He, too, was a graduate of the metropolitan examination. After serving as

5. Chang'e, who stole her husband's elixir of immortality and fled to the moon.

assistant magistrate of Qiantang,[6] he had been appointed treasurer of Jingzhou and was traveling there with his family when he was held up by the same storm and also put in at Jiangzhou. The local subprefect happened to be a graduate of the same year, and He Zhang had taken this opportunity to go into town and pay him a visit, which was why his womenfolk were passing the time looking out the door. The middle-aged woman was his wife, Mistress Jin, and the beautiful young girl was their daughter, Xiu'e. He Zhang had no son, only this daughter, who was now fourteen. In addition to her heart-stopping beauty, she had a natural talent for fine needlework. Furthermore, when she was a child her father had brought in a tutor to teach her how to read and write, and her compositions were of a high order. Because she was their only child, Treasurer He and his wife doted on her more than anything in the world and wanted to marry her to a promising son-in-law who would live with them, but it was hard to find the right person, and she was still not engaged. She and her mother were watching the panic on the other boats when they noticed Prefect Wu's boat drawing alongside, and her mother told a maid to let down the blind and shut the hatch door. As a fellow member of the bureaucracy, Prefect Wu was curious about the other man and sent a servant to inquire what post he held. Before long the servant came back and reported, "He's He Zhang, the treasurer of Jingzhou, and he's on his way there to take up office."

"I got to know He Zhang quite well when I went up to take the examination," Prefect Wu explained to his wife. "He was appointed assistant magistrate in Qiantang. I hadn't heard about this promotion. Since we've run into each other here, I really ought to go and pay my respects." He told a servant to take his visiting card over and then report back.

"The people on the boat say Master He has gone into town to pay a visit," said the servant on his return. Just at that moment someone in the bow called out, "He's back."

Prefect Wu had his official robes brought out and watched from inside the cabin as Treasurer He arrived in a four-man sedan chair with a large retinue. The treasurer had been to call

6. Part of Hangzhou prefecture.

on the subprefect of Jiangzhou only to find that he had lost his parents just a few days before, hence the speedy return. As he stepped out of his sedan chair, he noticed another boat beside his and wondered what official it might belong to. Boarding his boat, he was just about to ask his servants when Prefect Wu's card was handed to him. At once he sent over an invitation. The hatch doors being directly opposite each other, it was necessary for the prefect only to step across. The two men bowed to each other, exchanged some conversation and drank some tea, then Prefect Wu took his leave.

Before long, the treasurer paid a return visit, and the prefect insisted that he stay for drinks. He called his son out to be introduced, and told him to join them. The treasurer, who had no son of his own, noted Wu Yan's outstanding good looks and refined manner, and was already disposed in his favor. But then when he asked the boy some questions about ancient and modern texts and Wu Yan gave fluent answers, he was even more impressed and praised him again and again. With his talent and knowledge, he thought, this youth is really quite admirable. He'd be the ideal match for my daughter, except that his home is in Bianjing and ours is in Nanjing. It's such a pity we're so far apart—a marriage would be very hard to arrange. Such were the treasurer's thoughts, which he had to keep to himself.

"How many sons do you have?" asked Prefect Wu.

"Actually I don't have any sons, only a daughter."

That beautiful girl I saw must be the daughter, thought Wu Yan. She looks about the same age as I am. If only I could marry her, my life would be complete. But he has only this one daughter, and I doubt that he would let her marry someone from such a long way off. There's no point in even bringing up the subject. Then another thought struck him: At present I can't even see her, let alone try to get her as a wife. How could I be so foolish!

When the prefect heard the treasurer say he had no sons, he commented, "So you don't have a son yet? You really do need one, of course. You ought to take a concubine, to increase the chances."

"Thank you for the advice. I am thinking of doing just that."

They continued their conversation until suddenly they realized how late it was. As they parted, the prefect said, "If the wind dies down during the night, we'll be off in the morning. I'm afraid there may be not be any time for goodbyes."

"We haven't seen each other in such ages," said the treasurer, "and there's no knowing when we'll meet again. I do hope we'll be able to spend another day together."

Returning to his own boat, the treasurer found his wife and daughter still up and waiting with candles for his return. More than a little tipsy, he began telling his wife what a gracious host the prefect had been. He also praised Wu Yan in extravagant terms, describing his youthful good looks, his broad learning, and his many fine qualities, and predicted a great future for him. He would invite both father and son over the following day, he added. Because his daughter was present, he didn't care to mention his interest in Wu Yan as a son-in-law, but the daughter, on hearing his account, had already conceived a deep admiration for the youth.

Next day the storm was raging more fiercely than ever. In the distance, water and mist merged together, and the waves towered a good twenty feet high—the roar they made drowned out all other sounds. Not a single boat was out on the river to show that sailing was even possible, and the prefect resigned himself to staying an extra day.

Early in the morning the treasurer sent over an invitation to both father and son. With thoughts of Xiu'e weighing on his mind, Wu Yan had spent a restless night, and he leapt at the chance; he couldn't wait to set foot on her boat in hopes of gaining another look at her. But his father failed to cooperate; he thought that if they both attended, it would be too much trouble for their host. And so he wrote a note excusing his son and went over alone in the afternoon. For all his resentment, Wu Yan was in no position to object to this arrangement. Fortunately, the treasurer would not hear of his excusing himself and several times sent a servant to press him to come. Wu Yan would not have dared accept without his father's permission, but eventually he received it. After changing his clothes, he went over, paid his respects, and joined the men in their drinking.

From the rear cabin Xiu'e was agog at his presence. She tiptoed forward and peeped through a crack in the door that led to the main cabin, noting that he was elegantly dressed and even more charming and debonair than before. Just what did he look like? Here is a poem describing him:

> Lovely as He[7] with his powder-white face,
> Dashing as Xun[8] with his natural scent;
> If Wu Yan were riding downtown with Pan,[9]
> I wonder for whom the fruit would be meant.

When Xiu'e saw how handsome he was, her desires flared up. He really does look dashing and elegant, she thought. If I were able to marry a man like that, all my hopes would be fulfilled. But how could I even bring up the subject with my parents? His family would have to ask for my hand. But he doesn't even know how I feel about him. I'd try to arrange a meeting, but my parents are always around, and there are so many pairs of eyes and ears on our two boats that there's nowhere we could even be alone. It's obviously impossible. I might as well forget it!

While these thoughts whirled through her mind, her eyes remained riveted on Wu Yan. Now, when someone's mind is full of loving thoughts, even if the object of her affection has extremely ugly features, she will still find them attractive. In the case of Wu Yan, who was handsome to begin with, she naturally directed her gaze to his good looks and found them more charming than ever. Then the thought occurred to her: If I let this man get away, even if I should marry someone from a great family, there's no guarantee that he'll have Wu Yan's combination of talent and looks. She thought and thought, racking her brains, but still could not think of a way to meet him. In her frustration, she walked off and sat down. But no sooner had she done so than she felt as if she were being pushed up again, and her feet carried her back to her observation post at the door. She peeped for a while, then turned and went back and sat

---

7. He Yan, a beautiful youth of the Three Kingdoms period who had a particularly pale complexion.

8. Xun Yu, another icon of male beauty. His clothes gave off a scent.

9. As Pan An went through the streets of Luoyang, female admirers lined up to throw fruit into his carriage as a gesture of admiration.

down. Then after a short while she was at the door again. Like the horses circling a merry-go-round lantern, she was back and forth and back again every few moments. If only she could have taken a few extra steps to join him and declare her love!

Storyteller, let me ask you a question. She wasn't the only one in that rear cabin; her mother and the maids must have been there too. Are you seriously suggesting that they never noticed any telltale signs of her love-struck behavior?

Gentle reader, there's a perfectly good reason for it. Her mother had a chronic ailment that required her to take a nap at noontime. At this moment, sleeping soundly, she had no opportunity to see what was going on. And as for the maids, they couldn't wait for their mistresses to stop ordering them about to sneak off and enjoy themselves—*they* weren't about to bother their heads over things that didn't concern them! That was why no one was aware of what the girl was doing. Before long, however, her mother awoke, and Xiu'e had to subdue her feet and remain glumly in her chair.

> When will she meet the one she loves?
> Just now it seems a hopeless cause.

Meanwhile, although Wu Yan was physically present at the party, his thoughts were concentrated on the rear cabin. He stole glance after glance in that direction and, noting that the door was tightly shut and that there was no response from inside, he sighed under his breath, Miss He, I came here especially for your sake, and the fact that I can't see you shows how weak the destined bond between us must be! Plunged in gloom, he was in no mood to drink. When it grew dark and the party broke up, he went despondently back to his cabin and collapsed onto his bed without undressing.

After escorting his guests back, the treasurer invited his wife and daughter into the main cabin for a late supper. Xiu'e's mind was full of thoughts of Wu Yan, and she sat at her parents' side as if in a drunken stupor, saying nothing and touching none of her wine and food. Noticing her behavior, her mother asked, "Child, why aren't you eating anything? You're sitting there in a daze."

She had to ask several times before she got a response from her daughter. "I'm not feeling very well. I can't eat a thing."

"If you're feeling out of sorts, perhaps you'd better go to bed," said her father. Her mother got up, and telling one of the maids to bring a lamp, saw Xiu'e to her bed. A little later she came back to check on the girl. She told the maid, as soon as she had had her supper, to make up a pallet beside Xiu'e's bed and keep her company.

Inside the bed curtain, Xiu'e tossed and turned, unable to sleep. Then suddenly she heard someone outside chanting a poem. She listened intently—it was Wu Yan's voice! The poem went as follows:

> If we can dream from worlds away,
> Why no bond when we're feet apart?
> Let our pleasures not be fleeting!
> For I still hope to pledge my heart.

She was thrilled. I've spent the whole day trying to think of a way to meet him, she thought, and here he is chanting a poem right outside my window! Heaven must be helping our romance! It's the middle of the night and I doubt that anyone's awake—the perfect time to meet. Then she began worrying that the maids might still be awake, and she called out several times without getting any response. Satisfied that they were sound asleep, she threw on a robe, trimmed the lamp so that it shone brightly, and gently eased the window[10] open.

Wu Yan must have been waiting just outside, because when the window opened, he slipped in and clasped her in his arms. Both apprehensive and thrilled at the same time, she had no chance to tell him of all the loving thoughts she had devoted to him that day. Without even shutting the window, they embraced, undressed, and went to bed, where they made love.

At the very height of their rapture, one of the maids got up to relieve herself and began screaming, "Help! The window's

10. There is an error in the original edition that has been copied into the modern editions. In several cases, beginning here, *chuangmen* (window sash) is written as *cangmen* (hatch door).

open. There must be a thief on board!" Her screams aroused everyone on the boat, and they rushed to the doorway. The treasurer and his wife came in and told the maids to light some lanterns and conduct a search.

Wu Yan was petrified. "What am I going to do?" he cried out to Xiu'e.

"Don't panic," she said. "Hide in the bed. I doubt that they'll look in there. Once I've got rid of them, I'll see you back to your boat." He had just left her and was getting into her bed when a maid noticed one of his shoes and called out, "Here's the thief's shoe! He must be hiding in the bed!"

The treasurer and his wife came in to search. Their daughter tried to fend them off, insisting over and over again that there was no one there, but they took no notice of her. Wu Yan was discovered and dragged out, with Xiu'e exclaiming, "Oh, no! Oh, no! How horrible!"

"Damned scoundrel!" said the treasurer. "Why did you have to come in here and defile my household?"

"String him up and beat him," suggested his wife.

"No, don't beat him," said the treasurer. "Let's just throw him in the river." He ordered two sailors to carry him out on their shoulders, one taking the head, the other the feet, while Wu Yan kept pleading for his life.

Xiu'e tried to hold them back. "Father! Mother! It was all *my* fault! It had nothing to do with him!" Her father did not reply, but simply gave her a push that sent her sprawling, and the men heaved Wu Yan into the water with a great splash. At this point Xiu'e, casting aside all modesty, stamped her feet, beat her breast, and cried out, "Master Wu, I am the one who cost you your life!" Then a thought struck her: Since he died for my sake, I'd be too ashamed to go on living without him! She rushed out of the cabin door and leapt into the river.

> Oh! Pity this delicate girl,
> Transformed into a water sprite!

No sooner had she leapt into the water than she awoke with a start—it was all a bad dream! She was lying in her own bed, and beside her the maid was shouting, "Miss! Wake up!" She opened her eyes and found that it was broad daylight and the maids were up and about. Outside the storm was still raging.

"What were you dreaming about, miss?" asked her maid. "You were crying so hard I couldn't wake you up." Xiu'e gave her some vague explanation, but to herself she thought, Perhaps I don't share any bond with Wu Yan, as this horrible dream indicates. Then another thought occurred to her: If I really made love with him as in that dream, I'd die content. By this time that experience was causing such turbulence inside her that she became even more infatuated. Lying in bed was too boring, so she pushed away her pillow and got up. The maids were nowhere to be seen. She shut her door, then looked at the window and said to herself, Last night Master Wu came through that very window as large as life and took me in his arms and brought me to bed. I simply don't believe that it was only a dream. Then another thought struck her: If I had such good fortune in my dream, I must surely share a bond with him in my waking life! With this thought running through her mind, she opened the window and peeped out. The window of Prefect Wu's boat was wide open, and there sat Wu Yan staring blankly at her boat. His and Xiu'e's beds were both in the rear cabins, opposite each other and only five or six feet apart; if the two windows had been removed, they'd have shared the same room. Wu Yan had been enthralled with thoughts of her all night long, and at dawn he had risen, opened his window, and started gazing at the treasurer's boat—filled with a hopeless desire, like the toad that lusted after swan's flesh. However, the two of them did share a destined bond, because as fate would have it, at that very same moment she opened her window, and they came face to face, looking straight into each other's eyes, to the astonished delight of both. They smiled as if they already knew each other. Xiu'e was tempted to say something in the hope that he would arrange a meeting, but she was afraid she might be overheard. Instead she picked out a sheet of peach-blossom letter paper, ground up her ink, dipped in her brush, and wrote out a poem, which she folded into a tiny package. She then drew a lace handkerchief from her sleeve, placed the package inside and rolled it into a ball, which she tossed over to the other boat. Wu Yan caught it in both hands and gave an extravagant bow, to which she responded. He then opened the handkerchief and read the poem:

> Golden words on flowered paper,
> A tender heart inside the lace.
> Should you follow King Xiang's example,
> This room will be our trysting place.[11]

Beside the poem there was a column of tiny characters: "Tonight I shall trim the lamp and await you. A pair of scissors clattering on the table will be the signal. Be sure to come."

Wu Yan was ecstatic. I never expected her to have such a brilliant talent, he marveled. She's truly remarkable! Singing her praises, he reached for a sheet of gilt notepaper and wrote a poem of his own, then took off a brocade sash that he wore at his waist, rolled it into a ball with the poem inside, and tossed it over to the other boat.

When Xiu'e read it, she was even more amazed, for it was the very poem she had heard Wu Yan chanting in her dream! How is it, she thought to herself, that the poem he has just composed is the one I've already heard in my dream? It seems as if he and I are destined to become man and wife and I was given that dream as a sign. A column of tiny characters followed the poem: "After receiving your most precious love, I would never dare to disobey." She tucked the message away in her sleeve. When the maid knocked on her door with the wash basin, she was still in a state of dreamy infatuation. Gently she closed the window and dismissed the maid. Next her mother came in to see how she was, but when she saw her daughter already up, she ceased to worry.

This time it was the prefect's turn to play host. Before noon the treasurer was at the other boat, and his wife was taking her midday nap. Xiu'e brought out Wu Yan's poem, and savored it again and again. She exulted at the prospect before her and could hardly wait till evening. But what an extraordinary thing! Normally, her days passed in the blink of an eye,

11. The reference is to the erotic encounter between King Xiang and the goddess that is told in the "Gaotang Rhapsody."

but on this day of all days it seemed as if the sun were tethered by a rope and could never set. How nervous she became! But slowly the daylight turned to dusk, when the thought struck her that the maids would be in the way, making things very awkward; she would have to do something about them. At dinner she presented her private maids with a large jug of wine and two dishes of food. The two girls flew at the wine like thirsty dragons at the sight of water, draining it to the last drop. Soon afterward, Treasurer He returned from the banquet completely drunk. Xiu'e began to fear that Wu Yan might be drunk, too, and unable to come to her. Her anxiety mounted. She went to the rear cabin and shut the door, telling the maids to scent her pillow and coverlet. "I have some needlework to do," she told them. "You two can go off to bed." The wine was starting to have its effect on them. Their faces and ears were flushed, their limbs felt weak, and their heads reeled. They were longing to go to bed but hadn't liked to ask, and now that they were told to do what they desperately wanted, they hastened to arrange their bedding and go to sleep. No sooner had their heads touched the pillow than they began snoring like a pair of steam bellows.

Xiu'e waited a good two hours, listening carefully for any voices from either of the boats. When all was quiet, she concluded it was safe and let her scissors clatter on the table.

Wu Yan heard the signal. With this assignation on his mind, he had not dared to drink much wine. After the treasurer left, he had gone to his cabin and listened intently. He waited for two hours, and still nothing happened. Then just as he was beginning to have doubts, he heard the sound of scissors clattering on a table. Thrilled, he got up, tiptoed over and gently eased the window open, then stepped outside and pushed it shut. Leaping onto the other boat, he tapped three times at her window. Xiu'e opened it, he slipped inside, and she pulled the window shut behind him. Once more they formally greeted each other. In the lamplight Wu Yan looked closely at her and found her infinitely desirable. But by now their passions were aflame — neither had time for any conversation. Wu Yan held her, undid her buttons, and undressed her, after which they went to bed, her soft breast pressed against his chest, her jade-white body held lightly in his arms. Their lovemaking was rapturous:

A tap on the window, the sash opens;
As in a dream she watches him come near.
All the love in the world will not suffice.
"The maids are sound asleep, so never fear."

Their lovemaking was soon over, and they began to express their feelings for each other. Xiu'e told Wu Yan that the poem she had heard in her dream was the same as the one he had given her. "What an amazing thing!" exclaimed Wu Yan. "The dream I had last night was exactly the same as yours. It was because I thought it so strange that I was sitting there in a daze. I never expected Heaven to cause you to open your window and peep out, which made it possible to fulfill our love. It seems as if we were destined for each other from a previous life, and that prompted our dreaming souls to inform us in advance. Tomorrow I'll beg my father to propose marriage so that we can spend our lives together."

"Exactly what I was longing for!"

At this moment of high passion, they began making love again, and this time their love was even deeper than before. Afterwards they fell asleep.

Unfortunately, at about midnight the storm subsided, and by the fifth watch the boats began to depart. The treasurer's and the prefect's boats readied their sails and cast off. As the men hoisted sail, they broke into their rhythmic chanting, which caused Wu Yan and Xiu'e to awaken with a start. They overheard one of them saying, "With this sort of following wind, we ought to make it as far as Qizhou!"

Wu Yan moaned in horror. "What are we going to do?" he asked.

"Keep your voice down!" she said. "If one of the maids hears us, we'll be in real trouble. Now that we're in this spot, there's no use doing anything hasty. Settle down, and let's think what to do."

"I hope that dream the night before last isn't going to come true!" His remark reminded Xiu'e that in her dream it was a maid noticing his shoe that led to the discovery. She reached out, felt for his silk shoes, and hid them safely away. Then she thought long and hard about their problem from every angle and finally came up with an idea. "I know what to do," she declared.

"And what is that?"

"In the daytime you'll hide under the bed, and I'll just say I'm ill. I won't leave the cabin for meals with my parents, but will have all my food brought in here. When we get to Jingzhou, I'll give you some money, and you can escape in all the confusion while people are going ashore. Take the first available boat for Yangzhou, and once there ask your father to write a letter proposing marriage. If my parents accept it, fine. If they don't, I'll just have to tell them the truth. They love me dearly, and if we get to that point, I think they'll have to agree. Then we can be husband and wife again!"

"That would be marvelous!"

At dawn, when the maids had risen and left the cabin, both Wu Yan and Xiu'e got up. Hastily he dove under the bed and lay there curled in a ball, screened by boxes on both sides and the bed curtain in front. Miss He planted herself on the edge of the bed and did not stir. She had her morning wash but did not comb her hair. Instead, she purposely slumped across the table.

Her mother found her like that and exclaimed, "Goodness! Why haven't you done your hair? And why do you have your head down on the table?"

"I don't feel well. And I can't bear to have my hair done."

"I expect you got up too early and caught a chill. Why don't you go back to bed and try to get some more sleep?"

"I can't sleep properly. That's why I'm sitting here."

"Well, if you're going to sit there, at least put some more clothes on. Don't get cold, or you'll only make matters worse." She told the maids to find her a cape to put on.

Xiu'e had been sitting there for some time when a maid came in to say that breakfast was served. "My dear, don't try to eat any breakfast when you're not feeling yourself," said her mother. "Have the maids make you up some nice gruel. It'll be better for you."

"I don't care for gruel; I'd rather have rice. But the fact is I don't feel up to going out. Tell them to bring it in here."

"In that case, I'll stay and keep you company."

"Mother, the maids will only act up if you're not there to keep an eye on them. You'd better go."

"You're quite right." She left, telling the maids to take the food into the cabin and place it on the table.

"Off you go," said Xiu'e to the maids. "I'll call you when I'm ready." She put the latch on the door and beckoned to Wu Yan to come out from under the bed and have some breakfast. He scrambled out, stood up, and stretched, then glanced at the food on the table—two meat dishes, one vegetable dish, and two bowls of rice. Xiu'e had a small appetite, and two bowls were her regular amount. But try to imagine, if you will, how those two bowls were going to satisfy Wu Yan, with his three-quarts-of-rice appetite! He gave a faint grin, picked up the chopsticks, and in just a few mouthfuls had polished off both bowls. He didn't care to say anything, however, just braced himself against the pangs of hunger and dove back under the bed. Xiu'e opened the door, called in the maids, and ordered two more bowls of rice.

The two maids discussed her order between themselves. "She's always needed only two bowls before. Why is she eating twice as much now that she is supposed to be ill? Weird!"

These remarks were overheard by her mother, who called on her daughter. "My dear, why are you eating so much when you're not feeling well?"

"It's all right. I just wasn't full." It was the same that day with all three meals. The treasurer and his wife put it down to the fact that their daughter needed more nourishment now that she had grown up. Little did they realize that there was some-one on board who was eating for her, someone who even so felt weak with hunger.

> To carry on their secret love
> She told a monumental lie.

After supper that evening Xiu'e told Wu Yan to get into bed, then undressed and followed him. When her mother came in to check, she found her daughter already in bed and merely asked how she was feeling. After shutting the door, the maid also went to bed.

Wu Yan, who felt unbearably hungry, remarked to Xiu'e, "This is going well, except for one thing."

"And what is that?"

"Well, to be frank, I do have rather a large appetite. The three meals I had today wouldn't equal one of mine. If I have to put up with this sort of hunger, I don't know if I can last until we get to Jingzhou."

"Why didn't you say so? Tomorrow I'll simply ask for more."

"But if you ask for a lot more, won't they get suspicious?"

"Don't worry, I know how to handle it. But just how much do you need?"

"There's no way you could possibly satisfy me! I can easily go through a dozen bowls at a sitting."

Next morning, he again hid under the bed. She pretended to be ill and lay there groaning with pain. In their distress, her parents wanted to call a doctor in to treat her, but that was impossible—they were in the middle of the river. For her part, Xiu'e didn't want to see any doctor; she just kept on crying out that she felt terribly hungry. Her mother sent in a stream of food, but her daughter still complained that it was too little. Altogether she managed to get a dozen bowls, which alarmed her mother, but when she urged her daughter to eat less, Xiu'e threw a tantrum. "Oh, take it away then! I don't want anything anymore. You might as well let me *die* of starvation!"

Her mother doted on her daughter, and she responded to the display of temper with a smile. "Why get upset, dear? I was only trying to help. If you can eat more, by all means do. Just don't force yourself." She even handed her the bowl and chopsticks.

"I can't eat with you watching me, Mother. Please leave, all of you, and let me take my time. Otherwise I'm not sure that I'll be able to finish." Her mother did as she asked and also told the maids to leave. Xiu'e threw on the cape, got down from the bed, and shut the door. Wu Yan wriggled out. He was starving from the night before, and at sight of the food, without deferring to Xiu'e for an instant, he shot through the dozen bowls like a meteor through the sky, not pausing even to raise his head. When only a little over one bowl was left, he stopped.

Xiu'e was watching open-mouthed. "Is that *still* not enough?" she whispered.

"It'll have to do. I'm too embarrassed to eat any more." He rinsed his mouth out with a cup of tea and scrambled back under the bed. Xiu'e finished off the rest of the food, then opened the door and lay down again.

The maids were waiting outside for her to open the door. Rushing in, they found that every scrap of food had been eaten. After gathering up the dishes, they joked on their way to the galley. "An eating disorder—that's what she has!"

They told her mother, who shook her head over the news. "How could she possibly eat all that food? This is a most peculiar disease!" She informed her husband at once and urged him to call a doctor and consult a diviner. Even her husband couldn't believe it, and gave orders that his daughter was not to be given her way at lunchtime, lest her eating habits do irreparable damage to her internal organs. But well before noon Xiu'e began moaning with hunger. When her mother tried gently to dissuade her, the girl burst out sobbing, and her mother was forced to give in. It was the same in the evening. Her parents concluded that she had contracted some strange disease and were thoroughly alarmed.

That evening they docked at Qizhou and told the sailors they would not be leaving the following day. Early next morning they sent a servant into town to call on a well-known doctor. At the same time, they prayed to the gods and had divinations made.

Before long a doctor arrived.[12] He was splendidly dressed and had a dignified bearing. The treasurer invited him into the main cabin, where they exchanged greetings and sat down. Because he was dealing with an official, the doctor was particularly respectful. After drinking two cups of tea, he asked about the cause of the illness, then went to the rear cabin to examine the patient's pulse. Afterwards, he came back and took his seat again.

12. Incompetent but supremely self-confident doctors were a standard comic feature of Chinese drama and fiction.

"Well, doctor, may I ask what it is that my daughter is suffering from?"

The doctor gave a cough and replied, "Your daughter has a case of infantile dyspepsia."

"But you're mistaken, surely? Infantile dyspepsia is a childhood disease, and my daughter is fourteen.[13] How could she get that at this stage?"

The doctor smiled. "You are acquainted with some of the facts, sir, but not all. Although your daughter is fourteen, we are still at the beginning of the year, so she is really only thirteen. In fact, if she was born toward the end of the year, she'd be only a little over twelve. Just think, sir. Surely a twelve-year-old can be considered an infant? Generally this illness originates in a maladjustment of the eating and drinking patterns, combined with a failure to adapt to changes in climate. Dyspepsia in the lower abdomen results in a sluggish digestion, which leads to a high temperature that rises to the chest and causes the patient to feel hungry. When she takes food or drink, it merely increases her temperature. That is why the condition grows more serious by the day. In her case, if it is allowed to go untreated for another month, it will be incurable."

The treasurer perceived a certain logic in the doctor's explanation. "Your diagnosis is eminently reasonable," he said, "but how is the illness to be treated?"

"First I shall treat the sluggish digestion, which will eliminate the wind-heat. Once the high temperature has been halted, the eating and drinking will naturally decrease, and she will return to normal."

"If you can produce such marvelous results, of course I shall reward you handsomely."

The doctor got up and took his leave. The treasurer sealed an envelope with the payment for the medicine, and had a servant go and fetch it. It was quickly decocted and offered to Xiu'e. She, however, was intent on getting to Jingzhou as soon as possible and had not the least desire to take any medicine. When first she saw her parents calling in doctors, she tried to stop them, but she couldn't very well tell them the truth, and so

13. The doctor would not have seen the patient's face, only her arm.

she had to leave them with their burden of anxiety. When she learned what the doctor had said, she laughed to herself. The medicine they gave her she poured in the commode—after first sending the maids out of the room. Of the diviners her parents consulted, some held that the alignment of the stars was unfavorable and had offended the Crane Spirit; Buddhist priests would need to be called in to offer sacrifices, after which everything would of course be all right. Others maintained that in the countryside Xiu'e had encountered some lonely spirit or hungry ghost, and if only a Daoist requiem could be held, she would be cured. The treasurer and his wife duly filled each prescription, but the remedies had no effect whatever, and Xiu'e continued to eat as heartily as before.

Then they called in a second doctor, a more exalted version of the last, who arrived in a sedan chair with a retinue of four servants. After an exchange of greetings, he launched into a high-flown disquisition, then asked about the cause of the illness, and finally checked the patient's pulse.

"Has anyone examined her, sir?" he asked the treasurer.

"Yes, the other day we called a doctor in."

"And what was his diagnosis?"

"He said it was infantile dyspepsia."

This doctor roared with laughter. "It's *consumption!* How could anyone say it was infantile dyspepsia?"

"But she's still very young. How could she have consumption?"

"Your daughter's case does not result from any overexertion of the emotional or sensory faculties, but from a congenital weakness. It's what we call juvenile consumption."

"But the abnormal appetite—what's the reason for that?"

"When the hot and cold factors come into conflict, the fever that results from the congenital weakness extends upward, which tends to promote feelings of hunger."

From behind the screen the girl's mother heard this remark and sent word that her daughter was not running a fever. "Ah, but this is a case of internal heat and external cold," responded the doctor. "It's a thermolysis of the bones. That's why she's not aware of it." He asked to see the prescription written by his predecessor and commented, "Medicine as powerful as this will only weaken her constitution. A few more doses, and she'd be beyond hope. Let me decoct some medicine to cure her fever, bring her organs into harmony, and reduce her hunger. At that point, if she is gradually treated with pills to nourish the yin element and strengthen the blood, she will be cured."

"We are greatly indebted to you for your marvelous skill," said the treasurer, as the doctor took his leave.

Before long, a servant was sent to invite a third doctor. He was an old man with white hair and sideburns, who hobbled slowly along. No sooner had he taken a seat than he began boasting of his ability to diagnose the most difficult cases. "A certain official is indebted to me for saving his life and a certain lady for prescribing a very effective medicine," he announced. He continued with a long self-serving screed, then asked the details of the patient's condition, and finally went to examine her pulse.

The treasurer was taken in by the doctor's bombast, which he found fascinating. He reflected, As the proverb says, it's best to choose an old doctor but a young diviner. Perhaps this man will have some success.

After examining the girl's pulse, the doctor remarked to the treasurer, "You are indeed fortunate, my dear sir, in meeting up with me. I am the only person capable of diagnosing your daughter's illness."

"What illness is it, may I ask?"

"It goes by the name of dysphagia."

"But with dysphagia it's difficult to *swallow!* She's eating several times her normal amount of food, so how could it possibly be that?"

"Ah, but there are several forms of dysphagia. The form your daughter has is what is commonly known as rodent dysphagia. In private the patient eats an unlimited amount of food, but in the presence of other people, she finds it hard even to swallow. Eventually the overeating leads to bloat, which turns into parasitic tympanites. When the two illnesses join forces, they are extremely difficult to treat. Fortunately, your daughter's case is in its early stages and is still treatable. I'll guarantee to cure it once and for all."

He rose to his feet, and the treasurer saw him off. By this

time the whole family believed that the girl was suffering from rodent dysphagia as they nervously consulted doctors and diviners. They had no idea that Xiu'e was consigning all the medicine she received to the bowels of the commode and laughing at them behind their backs. The treasurer had spent several days in Qizhou and could not prolong his stay indefinitely. After discussing the matter with his wife, he asked the doctor for a prescription and bought an extra supply of medicine for his daughter to take on the journey. Other doctors would be consulted when they reached Jingzhou. For writing the prescription, the old doctor actually cheated them out of a good deal of money, which was a great stroke of luck for him. There is a poem on the subject:

> Perhaps he wasn't master of his trade;
> Improvisation was his special skill.
> He found an illness where there wasn't one,
> And left the treasurer to foot the bill.

As the saying goes, when it comes to sexual passion, young men and women are evenly matched. At first Xiu'e, who was still a virgin, tended to shrink back during intercourse, and for his part Wu Yan was timid and nervous and hesitated to let himself go. As a result, neither experienced the full rapture. But after two or three days they found themselves gradually entering the realm of bliss and began to throw themselves into their pleasures heedless of everything else. One night a maid awoke around midnight and was astonished to hear murmuring from the bed and a rhythmic knocking of the bedposts, followed a little later by much panting and sighing. Next morning she told her mistress who, because of her daughter's flushed and radiant face, so unlike that of an invalid, had already formed her own suspicions. Now that she had supporting evidence, she did not go and tell her husband, but went to the back cabin to see for herself. No tell-tale signs were visible, however. When she studied her daughter's face closely, she found it twice as lovely as usual, but she didn't care to ask outright about it, and she didn't know what else she could do. She sat there a while and then left. After breakfast, still as anxious as ever, she went back again to observe her daughter, and this time she began probing for information. But Xiu'e noticed how strange the questions were and gave nothing away.

Then all of a sudden the sound of snoring was heard. Wu Yan had done extra duty the night before and gotten no sleep, and now, having eaten well, he was sound asleep under the bed. There was nothing Xiu'e could do to hide the fact. As soon as her mother heard the snoring, she sent the maids out of the cabin, put the latch on the door, and peered under the bed. Against the wall she found a youth curled up and sleeping comfortably. She moaned to herself in silent anguish. "So this is what you were up to while you pretended to be ill and nearly scared your father and me to death!" she said to her daughter. "You've behaved so disgracefully I wonder how you can still hold your head up! And as for this abomination—where did *he* come from?"

Xiu'e flushed with shame. "It's my fault. I made a mistake, but I hope you'll cover it up for me, Mother. He's Prefect Wu's son."

"But you never even met him!" exclaimed her mother in astonishment. "What's more, that day when your father visited them, he was there too, and the party didn't break up until late. Then very early the next morning we set sail, so how did he get here?"

Xiu'e explained truthfully and at length how she had been impressed by her father's praise of Wu Yan; how the next day she had peeped at him from behind the screen; how that night she had dreamt of him; how the next morning she had opened her window and arranged to meet him; and how the boat had set sail while they were both still asleep. She added, "Your unworthy daughter was carried away by her foolish passion and has lost her good name and brought dishonor to you and Father. For that I cannot escape the blame. But the fact that two people who live a thousand miles apart were thrown together because of a storm—that must mean that ours is a predestined union, one devised by Heaven, not by man. Master Wu and I have vowed to live and die together, and neither of us will break that vow. Mother, I hope that you will try to persuade Father to somehow accept the situation. There's still time to make good the wrong that I did. If Father doesn't agree, I shall take my own life; I absolutely refuse to eke out a dishonorable existence. Well, Mother, I've told you everything now—to my shame—and the decision is up to you." She dissolved into tears. The whole time they were talking, Wu Yan kept up his thunderous snoring from beneath the bed.

Her mother was both angry and exasperated. She would have treated her daughter harshly, save for two things: she was used to indulging her and could not bear to be without her, and she was afraid the maids would overhear what she said and start tattling. So she bit her tongue, pulled the door open, and walked out.

Xiu'e waited until her mother had left, then scrambled down from the bed, put the latch back on the door, and awakened Wu Yan. "If you were going to snore, you could at least have done it more quietly!" she scolded. "You alerted my mother, and now our secret is out." This news so terrified Wu Yan that he broke into a cold sweat and his teeth chattered together so badly that he couldn't get a single word out.

"Pull yourself together!" urged Xiu'e. "I've just had a talk with my mother and asked her to try to persuade my father.[14] If he agrees, well and good. If he doesn't, I shall sacrifice myself as I did at the end of that dream. I definitely won't let you suffer the consequences alone." Tears streamed down her cheeks.

Meanwhile her mother had hastily summoned the treasurer and sent the maids out of the cabin. Before she could say a word, however, her tears started trickling down her cheeks. Her husband assumed she was grieving over her daughter's condition and tried to console her. "According to that doctor, we can expect to see some results in a few days' time. There's no need to take on like this."

"Did you hear what that silver-tongued old rascal said? Rodent dysphagia indeed! A doctor like that wouldn't be able to diagnose anything in a thousand years, let alone get results in a few days."

"Just what are you saying?"

14. The Chinese uses a formula here to avoid repeating what the reader already knows.

She gave a detailed account of all that had happened. The treasurer was so furious at the news that he almost fainted.

"That's it! Enough! A shameless hussy like that, who does such a disgraceful thing, blackening our family name—what earthly good is she? Let's do away with her tonight and be rid of this disgrace once and for all."

These words so startled his wife that the color drained from her cheeks as she tried to dissuade him. "You and I are middle-aged, and we have just this one child. If we lose her, what do we have left? Come to think of it, Master Wu comes from a fine family, he's good-looking and talented, and he would have made an excellent match for our daughter. By all means blame him for taking part in this clandestine behavior instead of asking for her hand, but this is the situation we find ourselves in, and there's nothing we can do about it. Let's make the best of things. Get a servant to take him home on the quiet with a letter for Prefect Wu. The prefect should then send someone back here with the betrothal settlement, after which a wedding can be held that will satisfy both parties. But if we make the affair public, we'll only be giving ourselves a bad name." After pondering the matter, the treasurer concluded that the only course was to do as she suggested. He went out and asked the sailors, "Where are we now?"

"That's Wuchang up ahead."

The treasurer gave orders for a short stop at Wuchang so that he could send one of his servants home. He wrote a letter, then called in a trusted servant and gave him instructions. Soon they reached Wuchang, and the servant went ashore and hired another boat, which tied up alongside the treasurer's.

The treasurer and his wife then visited the rear cabin. Xiu'e was so ashamed upon seeing her father that she hid her face in the bedclothes. The treasurer said nothing to her except "A fine thing you've been up to!" He then called Wu Yan out from under the bed. Uncertain of what the treasurer and his wife had in mind for him, Wu Yan crawled out trembling with fear and prostrated himself on the floor, declaring that he deserved to die.

Keeping his voice down, the treasurer berated him, "You impressed me as being young and well educated, and I thought you had a great future. I never imagined you would be so lacking in principle as to disgrace my household like this! By rights I ought to vent my feelings by throwing you in the river. However, out of consideration for your father, I am going to spare your life and send you home. If you can succeed in the examination, I shall marry my unworthy daughter to you, but if you lack the necessary ambition and drive, you can give up all hope of her." Again and again Wu Yan kowtowed his acceptance. The treasurer then told him to hide under the bed again.

Late that night when no one was about, the treasurer had his servant smuggle Wu Yan aboard the other boat. Not even the maids were allowed to catch a glimpse of him.

As they parted, both lovers feared the treasurer might have some evil intention in mind, but heartbroken though they were, they didn't dare burst out crying. Xiu'e pulled her mother aside. "I don't know what Father means to do, but to set my mind at rest you must get our servant to bring me back a letter from Master Wu." Her mother gave instructions to the servant.

Early next morning Wu Yan's boat sailed back, while the treasurer's boat went on to Jingzhou. Xiu'e was genuinely afraid that Wu Yan might meet with disaster on the way home and she became so anxious that she literally worried herself sick.

> Their sudden parting was as cold as ice;
> Their ardent longing was as hot as fire.
> Of all the three hundred and sixty ills,
> That of love is easily the most dire.

Let me turn now to Prefect Wu, who had departed from Jiangzhou in the small hours of the morning. After they had sailed a dozen miles, it was time for breakfast, and when Wu Yan did not appear, his father simply assumed that he had drunk too much the night before. At noon, however, when there was still no sign of his son, the prefect was puzzled. The boy's mother went to call him, but there was no response, and they became alarmed. The prefect then told a servant to open up the bed curtain and see how he was—and the bed was empty! Frightened half to death, his parents lamented to high Heaven.

They could not understand how he might have disappeared. The people on the boat all said the same thing: "It's simply beyond belief! There was never more than that one boat there, so where *could* he have gone? He must have fallen into the river." The prefect had the boat anchored and found workmen to drag the river. From Jiangzhou to where the boat was anchored, a distance of over thirty miles, the men dragged the riverbed thoroughly, but failed to find a body. Sacrifices were then held for the soul of the deceased, and his mother cried herself close to death. Having lost his son, the prefect also lost any interest in serving, and his staff had to exhort him again and again before he would proceed to his seat of office.

Then a few days later the treasurer's servant arrived with Wu Yan. The prefect's reaction on seeing his son was a mixture of joy and astonishment. From the treasurer's letter he learned what had happened and delivered a stern lecture to his son. For several days he hosted the treasurer's servant, and then, after preparing the betrothal settlement, he wrote a response to the treasurer's letter and told one of his own servants to accompany the man back to Jingzhou and ask for Xiu'e's hand in marriage. Wu Yan took the opportunity to include a personal letter for Xiu'e.

The two servants took their leave of Prefect Wu and went straight to Jingzhou, where they presented themselves to the treasurer. He accepted the settlement, wrote a reply, and sent the prefect's servant home again.

When Xiu'e read Wu Yan's letter, she began to make a gradual recovery.

As for Wu Yan, he studied day and night. At examination time he traveled to the capital and succeeded at his first try in graduating as a metropolitan scholar. By an odd coincidence he was appointed magistrate of Xiangtan county in the prefecture of Jingzhou. At news of his son's success, the prefect resigned his own position and moved with his son to the latter's seat of office, where he chose an auspicious day for the wedding. His colleagues all came to offer their congratulations.

> Beneath the candles a pair of newlyweds,
> But under the quilt a couple of old friends.

After her marriage, Xiu'e served her parents-in-law in exemplary fashion and proved a gentle and understanding wife to her husband, gaining a considerable reputation for virtue. Later, the treasurer, who missed his daughter greatly, moved his family to the capital and spent the rest of his life there. Wu Yan rose to the position of grand secretary of the Longtu Pavilion. He had two sons, both of whom succeeded in the examinations.

This story is titled "Master Wu Has an Assignation on the Neighboring Boat." A poem runs as follows:

> Matched in beauty and in talent,
> Each in secret composed a rhyme.
> A destined love was realized[15]
> That poets will hymn for all of time.

15. The Chinese attaches the sardonic phrase "under the bed."

6
The Reckless Scholar

A harvest moon and a blossoming spring
Have ever been the cause of secret grief.
Why dream of lines exchanged beside a wall,[1]
Or give your heart to poems on a leaf?[2]
A cracked spittoon is not a lovely sight;
No blemished jade has ever been held dear.
And what of him who'd risk his life for sex?
Gallant—but only if you wish to jeer.

This poem by an anonymous author urges men to control their libidos and restrain their licentious behavior, which ruin a woman's virtue and deplete the man's moral credit.[3] We are endowed, you must understand, with a set of emotions that are realized in many situations ranging from the joy of reunion to the sadness of parting, but on this occasion I shall put aside the negative emotions and tell you of a few heartwarming things instead.

If other men are well stocked with food and fuel and laden with riches, if they have more silk and satin than they can possibly wear and more delicacies than they can possibly consume, and if I, by contrast, am short of food and fuel, half-starved, and shivering with cold, I will find it impossible to be happy. On the

---

The full title is "The Reckless Scholar Gains a Wife by Force."

1. A reference to the *West Chamber*. In Act 1, Zhang Junrui chants a poem beside the wall and Cui Yingying responds with a matching poem.

2. In a Tang story, Lu Wo happened to pick up a red leaf with a poem on it from the palace moat. Later, when the emperor married off his palace women, Lu Wo happened to choose the one who had written the poem. There are several other versions of the story, the most elaborate being "Liu hong ji" in the Song collection of tales *Qing suo gao yi*.

3. An age-old belief that by good deeds one accumulates unseen moral credit, which then influences one's own or one's family's fortunes.

other hand, there have indeed been men of integrity and high ideals who loved the moral way despite their poverty, men such as Yan Hui[4] with his meager food and drink and his humble dwelling-place, and Zixia[5] with his patched and tattered clothing. These men kept up their spirits and remained as happy as ever despite their abject condition.

Let us now consider another case, that of the civil official who rises to ministerial rank or the military official who is promoted to commander-in-chief. Each man has his entourage as well as splendid robes and accoutrements. Think of the grandeur, the glory of it all! If I, by contrast, have never achieved any success in life and have fallen behind my contemporaries, how can I possibly be happy? However, there have indeed been men of great talent and learning, men of vast plans and ambitions, who achieved neither fame nor success but led happy lives owing to their own self-satisfaction and feeling of superiority.

Thus there are men who are not enamored of either wealth or rank. In the case of sexual desire, however, men are like bees or butterflies ravishing the blossoms; they drill their way into the flowers' hearts and never give up until, like moths flying into a lamp, they drown in the lamp's oil.

The one person in history who was not addicted to sexual desire was the Man of Lu.[6] He was living on his own when one night a storm sprang up that damaged the house next door. The widow who lived there rushed over to join him, but he barred the door and would not let her in. Another such case was that of the licentiate Dou Yi.[7] He was studying by moonlight

4. One of the disciples of Confucius. See *Analects*, 6.11. D. C. Lau, trans., *Confucius, The Analects* (London: Penguin Books, 1979), p. 82: "The Master said: 'How admirable Hui is! Living in a mean dwelling on a bowlful of rice and a ladleful of water is a hardship most men would find intolerable, but Hui does not allow this to affect his joy. How admirable Hui is!'"

5. Another disciple of Confucius.

6. Lu Nanzi. For the anecdote, see a commentary to the "Xiangbo" poem of the *Poetry Classic* (Mao 200). Kong Yingda's commentary tells how the widow outside the door pleads with her neighbor, citing the example of Liuxia Hui, who remained unmoved while a girl was sitting on his knee. He replies (through the door) that that was all very well for Liuxia Hui; he himself was not capable of it.

7. Probably Dou Yi (914–966), compiler of the *Xing tong*, a manual on

when a girl came up and tried to seduce him, but he turned her away with some high-minded advice. However, from the time of Pangu[8] down to the present, these are the only two cases of men who have not strayed when presented with the opportunity for sex. (It is impossible to vouch for the story of Liuxia Hui,[9] who is said to have retained his composure with a girl sitting on his knee.) By contrast, over the years untold numbers of secret assignations and covert affairs have taken place.

As the saying goes, men who wish to seduce women are faced with a gigantic barrier, whereas for women who are out to seduce men the barrier is paper-thin. If a woman leaves no opening, if she makes no slip, a man, no matter how hard he plots and schemes, will end up with nothing more than a spring dream. True, there have been two dashing, handsome men whose illicit affairs did lead to marriage—Sima Xiangru[10] and Han Shou.[11] But in Han's case, if Jia Chong's daughter had not peeped at him through the lattice window, he would never, for all his light-footed agility, have dared leap over the northeast corner of the wall and consummate the affair (which resulted in the girl's theft of the precious perfume). And as for Sima, for all his dashing elegance and brilliant clothes, if Zhuo Wangsun's daughter had not come and listened to him playing the "Phoenix Seeks a Mate" tune, he would never have been able to elope with her and consummate the affair (which led to their running a tavern together). Hence both cases of elopement and illicit relations were the work of women. However, if we continue to place the blame on women, that certainly does not mean that men are in the clear! Otherwise, how would we explain that expression used of them: "risking life itself for the sake of sex"? The truth is that a man has philandering and seduction on the brain, and given the slightest hint of acquiescence on the part of the woman, he will start winking and making eyes at her,

---

criminal law, who appears in anecdotal literature and in fiction (see the *Feilong quanzhuan*) as a stickler for propriety both in the home and at court.

8. In Chinese mythology, the creator of the universe.

9. He is mentioned as a paragon in the *Analects* and in *Mencius*. See also n. 6 above.

10. See his biography in the *Shi ji* (Historical records).

11. See *Shishuo xinyu* (A new account of tales of the world), chap. 35.

slipping a suggestive word or two into their conversation, or insinuating some dubious proposition into a riddle. He will then set to work thinking up countless schemes, which he will try out one after the other until eventually he succeeds and has an affair with her. The possibility that this behavior could result in the loss of his good name, or even of his life, hardly concerns him, which is why he is described as "risking life itself for the sake of sex." No man is willing to turn away from lust and honor virtue, as this poem implies:

> By sex and beauty we're easily misled;
> How many are they who can resist their draw?
> Even if Hui did stay calm with girl on knee,
> Try to emulate the man who locked his door.[12]

My story tells of a provincial graduate named Mo Ke, whose style was Shuihe. He lived in Lingui county of Guilin prefecture of Guangxi province during the Yongle period[13] of the present dynasty, and he came from one of the oldest families in the district. His father, Mo Kao, after taking the preparatory examination all of his life, was still looking forward to draping himself in a licentiate's gown when along came this Shuihe, who had no sooner taken the preparatory examination than he was chosen for study in the prefectural school—all at the tender age of eleven! At that point a local rich man named Wang offered a substantial settlement and arranged a betrothal between young Shuihe and his daughter. Now, it is a general truth that youths of the greatest natural intelligence are also the most precocious. By the age of nine, Shuihe, an exceptionally clever and ingenious boy, was fully acquainted with the facts of life. From school age on, whenever an opening presented itself with a young maid, he would grab her and take advantage of her by kissing her on the lips and fondling her breasts. By the time he was fifteen, he was well past puberty and began to frequent the brothel quarter with his friends. The prostitutes loved him for his boyish good looks and romantic sensibility and were

12. A reference to the story of Liuxia Hui and the Man of Lu.
13. 1403–1424.

even willing to forgo payment in order to consort with him, and as time went by he developed into a full-blown rake. His debauchery greatly distressed his parents, and their anguish developed into an illness that led to both their deaths.

One of Shuihe's relatives encouraged him to marry even though he was still in mourning, but as the wedding day approached his fiancée succumbed to a sudden illness. Distraught as Shuihe was at the news of her death, when he attended the laying-in and noticed how ugly she was, he congratulated himself on a lucky escape. Then and there he determined to rely on his own observation in choosing a wife. As a result, one potential match after another fell through, and he ended up spending his time in the brothels.

Then, surprisingly enough, at the age of eighteen he won a place in an examination for overlooked talent and came in a very creditable second. The great and wealthy families of the district now vied with one another to obtain him as a son-in-law. However, Shuihe was so pleased with himself that he set his sights even higher than before. Believing that success in the forthcoming metropolitan examination was a certainty, he replied to all the marriage overtures with unblushing conceit. "Let's wait for the honor roll before thinking of nuptials."

Having shelved the question of marriage, he hastily prepared for the journey to the capital to take the examination. Leaving his family affairs in the hands of the relative I have mentioned, Shuihe arranged to travel in the company of a group of classmates.[14] It was winter, and all along the way they were met by rain, snow, and bitter cold. Ever since his success in the examination, he had indulged himself with wine and women, and his health was already in a weakened state, which left him vulnerable to chills. He fell ill on the journey but managed to reach Yangzhou, where he took to his bed at an inn. His classmates called in doctors to treat him and delayed their journey for several days, but although his illness showed some signs of improvement, Shuihe realized he would need time to recover and could hardly attend the examinations. His companions, intent on their own hopes of success, had no choice but to leave

14. I.e., graduates of the same year.

him behind. Instructing his servant Laiyuan to take good care of him, they continued on their way to the capital.

> Without any further ado,
> They went their separate ways.

Shuihe's illness lasted over a month, but by the middle of the first month of the new year he had fully recovered. He still didn't dare exert himself, however, but stayed in his lodgings to rest. During his illness he had dreamt of the bodhisattva Guanyin[15] sprinkling his brow with life-restoring dew, after which his fever had subsided, his illness departed, and he began a slow recovery. When the innkeeper heard about the dream, he said, "The Guanyin in the Jade Flower Temple[16] has always been the most effective, often helping people in trouble. It was probably she who manifested herself." In his gratitude for the divine assistance, Shuihe pledged to go to the temple and give thanks, and settled on the first of the second month for his visit.

That day he bought joss sticks, paper money, and the like and, giving them to Laiyuan to carry, left the inn and sauntered along in the direction of the temple. The brilliant clothing and insignia on display in the city center were a splendid sight. In addition, merchants had flocked to Yangzhou from all parts of the country, resulting in a confused press of horses and carriages trying to weave their way back and forth—the very picture of a thriving prosperity. As he walked along, Shuihe surveyed the scene and felt a surge of joy, even of exhilaration. He reflected how true the poet's line was: "For a gorgeous spring, go ye down to Yangzhou."[17]

Arriving at the temple, he went first to the Guanyin Shrine to fulfill his pledge, and then on to the other shrines to worship. In the culture of Guangxi, great reverence has always been shown to the supernatural, and Shuihe was particularly devout. Afterward he went to see the relics of the jade flowers.

---

15. The goddess of mercy.
16. *Qionghua guan*, formerly known as Fanlici, which was in the Houtuci (Earth Spirit Shrine).
17. From Li Bai's poem "Huanghelou song Meng Haoran zhi Guangling."

These flowers, which once grew in the Earth Spirit Shrine, were planted during the Tang dynasty. How shall I describe their beauty? A poet of earlier times[18] has written the following:

> Many are the blooms in this world below,
> But even in Heaven this flower is rare.
> It first took root in the holiest shrine,
> So firmly it could not be moved from there.
> Its buds were supreme among other blooms;
> From a single plant a myriad branches grew.
> Its scent it shared with the cassia flower;
> Its color it took from the lilac's hue.
> Bedewed, it was frozen talcum powder;
> It looked like rouge while the sunlight played.
> The goddess of the moon danced in the breeze,
> And beneath the gentle rain naiads swayed.
> Its quiet beauty woven of misty threads,
> Its broken shadows filtered moonlight.
> One day it cast aside the commonplace
> And rose to Heaven from our worldly blight.
> And now its lingering scent is all for naught—
> It merely serves as stimulus for thought.

There was just one plant of jade flowers in existence, and it grew in Yangzhou, but in the transition from the Song dynasty to the Yuan it suddenly withered and died, and jade flowers became extinct in the world. Later, Eight Immortals flowers were planted in their place, but they were not the same. The temple was originally named Great Blessings,[19] but apparently because the flowers were so famous, its name was changed to Jade Flower. Poets who visited the site through the ages all wrote poems about it.

After enjoying the scene, Shuihe returned to his lodgings.

---

18. The jade flowers were a favorite topic for poets passing through Yang-zhou. The first six lines are taken almost verbatim from a poem by Xianyu Shen (1018–1087). See Li Tan et al., eds., *Yangzhou lidai shici* (Beijing: Renmin wen-xue chubanshe, 1998), 1.177. It appears that the author of this story, writing after the unique plant became extinct, was responsible for the rest of the poem.

19. Fanli.

Two days later he visited the site of the labyrinth[20] of the Sui dynasty palace and then toured all the scenic wonders of Yangzhou. By this time he was in a joyous, carefree mood, fully restored to health and spirits, which served only to revive his amorous instincts. Back he went to the brothel quarter to seek his pleasure among the courtesans.

Soon it was the middle of the second month, the midpoint of spring, when the young ladies and gentlemen of Yangzhou were accustomed to make their way to the Jade Flower Temple to burn incense and pray for good fortune—and also to take the opportunity of a spring outing. Hearing of this custom, Shuihe visited the temple daily after breakfast and strolled about everywhere, hoping for a romantic encounter. But after several days of this routine, he had still found no one who interested him in the slightest. Why was that, do you suppose? Well, if the womenfolk of great families went out to worship, they were always escorted in their sedan chairs by a bevy of maids and menservants. Once they arrived at the temple gate, they would wait inside their chairs until their servants had cleared away all the sightseers, and while they were worshipping their servants would be clustered behind them. No matter how gorgeous the women were, you could not get a glimpse of them, let alone try to seduce them. Even middle-class women with some claim to beauty were hard to find, because in order to avoid harassment they often confined their visits to the early morning hours before any sightseers had gathered. As for the crowds of women who were pushed here and there in the crush of people, they came either from poor families or from the surrounding villages, where you would not expect to find any outstanding talent. That was why Shuihe found no one to interest him.

The nineteenth of that month commemorated Guanyin's becoming a bodhisattva, and on that day the number of worshippers increased severalfold. The temple was packed with visitors until noon, when they dispersed. Feeling somewhat listless, Shuihe strolled over to Zitong Hall[21] and sat down. Although the Jade Flower was composed of many buildings, the

20. The Milou, built by the last emperor of the Sui dynasty, Yangdi.
21. Zitong, i.e., Wen Chang, god of literature.

main shrine was the one devoted to Zhen Wu, god of happiness and ruler of the world, while the other most popular places of worship were those of the bodhisattva Guanyin, savior of those in distress, and His Sacred Majesty Guan Yu,[22] revered by Chinese and foreigners alike. Zitong Hall was concerned only with literature, and of all three hundred and sixty professions and trades, that of writer and scholar has the fewest practitioners; hence before the throne of the God of Literature no incense was to be seen—the place was deserted. After sitting there a while, Shuihe went downstairs. He had gone out the door of the temple and was on the point of returning to his lodgings when he noticed a beautiful girl followed by her maid coming in to worship. One glance was enough to make him lose his head. I've been searching for days, and now at long last I've found a stunning girl, he said to himself. What a piece of luck!

Who do you suppose the girl was? She was the daughter of a man with the double-barreled surname Xiesi who had once served as secretary in one of the ministries. He was descended from foreigners[23] who had settled in Jiangdu, and since the surname Xiesi was rather awkward, they had discarded the "Xie" and called themselves simply Si. This Master Si was a somewhat stiff-necked person who was unable to get along with his colleagues, had lost his official position, and was now living in retirement at home. The girl, Ziying, was his only child.[24] His wife, Mistress Ping, had fallen ill three years before, and Ziying, in the course of praying for her mother's recovery, had pledged a pair of embroidered silk pennants to the bodhisattva Guanyin. Unfortunately, her mother had reached the end of her allotted span and failed to recover, but despite her death the pledge still had to be fulfilled. Ziying had finished embroidering the pennants and informed her father that she wished to visit the temple and donate them on the day commemorating Guanyin's buddhahood. Her father, who also venerated the bodhisattva, allowed his daughter to go, reflecting that at fourteen

22. A hero of the Three Kingdoms epic *Sanguo yanyi*. He was later deified.
23. The term used implies that his ancestors had arrived in the previous Yuan dynasty, when China was ruled by the Mongols.
24. The Ming edition has a gap of a few characters at this point.

she was still a child. He told her not to go early, however, in the belief that in the morning the temple would be swarming with people. There was just one problem. Because he had tried to be scrupulously honest during his official career, his savings were extremely meager, and after his retirement, because he never intervened in other people's business,[25] his door was as quiet as the grave. He had once had several capable servants, but this high-minded poverty was too much for them to bear, and they had all decamped for more exciting positions. All that remained were a few less mobile villagers who worked for him as men-servants and maids. He told two of the maids to accompany his daughter to the temple. They dressed up for the occasion, but to Ziying's eyes they looked like a couple of witches, and she was extremely upset. "If they're allowed to come," she told her father, "people will only laugh at us!" So her father told her private maid, Lianfang, to accompany her instead, together with two village men to escort the sedan chair.

At the temple the escorts attended on Ziying as she donated the pennants, and then as she worshipped at the shrine of Guan Yu in the main hall, but as she came to Zitong Hall, since it was deserted, with nobody in sight, they took themselves off to find their own amusement.

Now that Ziying had come within Shuihe's field of vision, he would have liked nothing better than to rush up and declare his love, but he saw from her demeanor that she had an imperious air about her and didn't dare approach for fear of stirring up trouble for himself. He recalled that the Dong Zhongshu[26] Study Terrace behind Zitong Hall was always deserted, and thought this girl might conceivably visit it. Why not lie in wait below the terrace and get a good view of her? Since Shuihe had spent his time roaming about the temple, he knew all of its bypaths, and so he turned back and hid below the terrace.

Now, this Dong Zhongshu had once been the chief minister of the Prince of Jiangdu. The prince had an overbearing, aggressive personality that Dong Zhongshu tried to correct by in-

<hr />

25. I.e., he did not peddle his influence in lawsuits.
26. The scholar, philosopher, and adviser to Emperor Wu of the Han. For his service in Yangzhou, see his biography in the *Han History*.

structing him in the rites. The prince duly reformed his conduct and did good works, and for that reason the city built this terrace, commissioned a statue of Dong Zhongshu, and named the terrace the Dong Zhongshu Study Terrace. The average person was unlikely to know these things, so no one ever went there. Nonetheless, it was about to provide Shuihe with the romantic encounter that he was seeking.

When Ziying arrived at Zitong Hall to worship, she noticed that the censer had gone out, and in her imperious way she ordered her maid to get the escorts to bring something to relight it with. Lianfang went down the steps to call the men, but they were nowhere to be seen. As she wondered anxiously what to do, she felt an urgent desire to relieve herself and looked about for a suitable place. She walked to the back of the hall and then along a narrow path that brought her to a secluded spot where the bamboos and trees enhanced each other's beauty and there were several ornamental rocks from Lake Tai that were both massive and also wonderfully intricate. Beside one of the rocks grew a large winter-sweet. Even our garden at home doesn't have as many great rocks, or a winter-sweet as big as this, she thought. Then, squatting down beside the rocks, she began to relieve herself. Long ago Grand Secretary Tao Gu composed a poem that could have been written about this maid:[27]

> A girlish beauty soft and sweet
> Beside a rock in a quiet glade;
> The pomegranate opens up,
> And down the precious pearls cascade.

Once she had finished, she hastily turned back and went upstairs to report. Ziying complained impatiently about the amount of time she had taken. "I couldn't find either of the men," said Lianfang, "and even the bearers have taken off. Miss, why not make do with things as they are?"

While Ziying inserted the joss stick in the cold censer and

27. Tao Gu (903–970) was a poet and high official. I do not know where the writer found this poem. The pomegranate refers to the maid's drawers.

prostrated herself in prayer before it, Lianfang kept thinking of the scenery at the back of the building, which she would have liked to revisit. Approaching Ziying, she said, "Miss, there's a spot behind this building with rocks and trees. It's perfectly quiet and delightful, just the place for us to enjoy ourselves. Why not go and have a look?"

"How did you happen to see it?"

"I needed to relieve myself, and I found my way there."

"Wretched creature! If someone had come along and seen you, you'd have died of shame!"

"But it's ever so quiet, and there's no one around. Further on you can see a high terrace, and I expect there's also something worth seeing on top of that."

Ziying was still a child, and when she heard how pleasant it was and that there were no visitors, she was unwise enough to listen to her maid's advice. She went down the steps and along the narrow path to the area below the Study Terrace, where she found that the ornamental rocks, bamboos, and trees did indeed make for a quiet and pleasant scene. She and her maid skirted the ornamental rocks and went up on the terrace, where there was a small shrine containing the statue of a god. To the left of the shrine was a brazier for burning paper offerings, and to the right a large stone tub for water lilies.

Having previously relieved herself, Lianfang walked over to the tub to wash her hands. She took one look and called out, "Miss, come and look at the water in this tub. It's crystal clear all the way to the bottom—perfectly clean. Why don't you come and wash your hands, too?"

"I don't need to. Mine are clean."

"But the water's so pure, it's nice to wash your hands in it."

Once more Ziying unwisely listened to her maid's suggestion and went over to the tub and washed her hands, after which Lianfang fished a white silk cloth from her sleeve and gave it to her mistress to dry her hands on. As they amused themselves washing their hands, they were completely unaware that Shuihe had climbed up on the terrace behind them and was studying them closely. But after drying her hands, Ziying turned around—and there in front of her stood a young man! In her shock, she immediately regretted what she had done. As a woman, I should never have listened to that maid and come up here. To Lianfang she murmured, "There's somebody here. Let's go."

They were about to leave when Lianfang noticed that Shuihe was blocking their way. Nothing if not astute, she said to her mistress, "Now that you've washed your hands, let's go and worship." With that, she led the way into the shrine. Ziying had no idea what kind of bodhisattva Dong Zhongshu might be, but she stuck a few joss sticks in at random and prostrated herself before leaving.

By this time Shuihe was beside himself with desire, but he couldn't think how to start a conversation. Then an idea came to him: I'll wash my hands, too, and burn some incense. He swirled his hands about in the tub, then unfolded the cuff on his sleeve to dry his hands on, displaying his crimson jacket as he did so. For days now, while strolling about the temple dreaming of encounters he had dressed in his most splendid style. On his head he wore a fashionable crepe-silk turban in the lotus-leaf design. Next to his skin he had on a white raw-silk shirt, and above it a jacket lined with crimson crepe silk, a white damask vest, and an outer coat of soft, pure white silk. He had prepared all these clothes at home before leaving on his journey, thinking that after his success in the examination he would be able to show off his youthful elegance before the chief examiner and his fellow graduates at the imperial banquet. After illness had prevented him from taking part, he wore the same clothes while flaunting himself in the Jade Flower Temple.

If at this moment Ziying had turned and left after finishing her devotions, Shuihe could only have taken visual advantage of her, which would hardly have mattered. But Master Si had always been a thrifty manager of his household—all food and clothing had to be uniformly simple, and any extravagance was frowned upon—and his daughter had picked up these attitudes from her father and was extremely frugal herself. Now, as she left the shrine, she looked up and saw Shuihe opening the cuff of his sleeve to dry his hands, and her frugal instincts asserted themselves. What a crime! she said to herself. Such new clothes, and he's going to wipe his hands on them! He can't have brought a cloth with him. Then, most unwisely, she turned to Lianfang and told her to lend him the white silk cloth to dry his hands on.

Shuihe leapt to the wrong conclusion, thinking she had an ulterior motive, and became even more delirious with joy. As he took the cloth and dried his hands on it, he said to Lianfang, "Please thank the young lady for her kindness in lending me this cloth." He produced an ingot of silver and handed it to her. "This is a token of my gratitude for her great generosity." Lianfang, who had her own ideas, refused to accept the money and turned to go, but Shuihe caught hold of her and stuffed it in her sleeve. Then he raced down from the terrace and barred the rear door of Zitong Hall.

When Lianfang fled back to her mistress and told her what he had said, Ziying turned on her. "Wretched girl! Why didn't you say that I'm the daughter of Master Si and don't give a fig for his money?" After this outburst, the maid hurried down from the terrace and told Shuihe what Ziying had said, at the same time handing him back the money.

But Shuihe would not take it back. "So you're Master Si's daughter and you don't give a fig for my money?[28] Well, I'll have you know that I'm a provincial graduate. When your mistress was so concerned as to lend me her cloth to dry my hands on, surely she didn't think these are the only clothes I possess?"

When she saw the conversation taking this unpleasant turn, Lianfang did not attempt to reply, but flung the money down and fled back up the terrace. "I threw the money back at him," she said. "He's not from around here. He claims to be a provincial graduate, but he's being *most* unreasonable. I didn't take any notice of him."

"Quite right, too. We've been here a long time, and I'm sure the men are looking for us outside. Let's go."

Lianfang helped her mistress as she walked over the pebbles and around the ornamental rocks—where they found Shuihe blocking their way. "Just a moment, miss," he said. "There's something else I have to say."

Ziying was so frightened that she fell back a few steps, then

28. Shuihe addresses Ziying directly in this part of his message.

turned and hid behind a rock, telling Lianfang to say, "Since you claim to be a graduate, you must have learned something about proper behavior. Why are you preventing us from going back? What possible reason could you have?"

When Lianfang relayed this message to Shuihe, he gave a broad grin. "I'm from Guangxi, a thousand miles away. I never expected to come upon your mistress here—it can only be a matter of destiny! I simply want her to allow me to greet her in person and exchange a few words, after which I'll let her go. That's my only reason."

When Lianfang reported the message, Ziying flared up and told her to reply in these words: "As a graduate from Guangxi, you should save your truly appalling behavior for your own province. Here in Yangzhou it's simply not acceptable. Kindly let us go back, and you'll hear no more about this. But if you persist in your unreasonable behavior, I'll have to call in our servants, which would be a terrible blow to your dignity. What's more, my father is not the sort of man you would want to cross, and if I tell him about it, he'll show you no mercy."

As Shuihe listened, another idea came to him. "What your mistress says would be fine for scaring off some country bumpkin, but no matter how fearsome your Master Si is, he can't do anything to a graduate like me from a long way off. The entrances here are all blocked, so even if you had some servants, they couldn't fly in, any more than your mistress could fly out. But there's another point, too. You surely don't imagine that after imploring her all this time, I'll let her go without getting something in return, do you? That would be just too boring. If she won't allow me to greet her and exchange a few words, she could still save face by giving me something as a sort of highway toll. Otherwise, she'll never get out, not even if she waits until next year."

When Ziying received this message from Lianfang, she became upset and began blaming her maid. "It's all your fault, you little wretch, for talking me into coming here. That's what got us into this trouble."

Lianfang was ready with her response. "Yes, I did mention it, and that really was my mistake. But miss, it was *your* idea to tell me to give him the cloth to dry his hands on."

This silenced Ziying. In any case, she thought, what's done cannot be undone. She was also afraid that he might use force, and what could she do then? Her thoughts were in a whirl and she was at her wits' end when, in another unwise move, she pulled a red silk handkerchief out of her sleeve and told Lianfang to deliver it to Shuihe with the following message: "As a cultivated gentleman, sir, you must surely understand the principles of moral behavior. You and I are neither relatives nor acquaintances, and so greeting each other is quite out of the question. A single handkerchief cannot be regarded as a present. Let's consider it as gate money instead."

Shuihe laughed as he took the handkerchief. "I'm not the gatekeeper of the Jade Flower Temple, so what would I want with gate money? The cloth was yours, and this handkerchief was yours too—and both things are tangible evidence. If your mistress will allow me to greet her, fine. If not, I shall just have to let Master Si know about this evidence. As to what people will make of it, I shall leave that for you and your mistress to consider."

Lianfang was a young maid and timid, and when she heard these words, her heart flew into her mouth, and she dashed back to her mistress. "It's going from bad to worse. He's behaving dreadfully. . . ."[29] Miss, if you don't let him exchange greetings, and he really does tell the Master, I'm sure to be dragged in, and I'll get beaten to death. Just give him some kind of greeting and beg him to let us go back."

Ziying knew she had meddled where she shouldn't have, and she regretted it now more than ever. She hesitated, but eventually she had to follow Lianfang's suggestion and come out from behind the rock. Lianfang beckoned to Shuihe. "My mistress has agreed to exchange greetings."

His face lit up with joy as he came forward and bowed deeply. For her part, Ziying turned her back on him as she curtsied. Straightening up from his bow, Shuihe folded his hands across his chest. "I am a new provincial graduate from Lingui county of Guilin prefecture of Guangxi, Mo Ke by name. I was

29. The Chinese uses a formula here to indicate that she is reporting the message.

on my way to the capital to take the metropolitan examination and was passing through your city when I heard of your peerless beauty. For that reason I decided not to go on to the capital, but to stay here in hopes of catching sight of you. To my great delight, Heaven granted my wish—our meeting today must surely have been foreordained. I am also indebted to you for the silk handkerchief, which I shall treasure for the rest of my life. But such a glorious occasion rarely comes twice—who knows when we will meet again? How can you possibly send me off like this?"

Ziying flushed scarlet, but for all her anger, she also felt like laughing. How could he *say* such things, she asked herself. She whispered to Lianfang, "Remind him that he promised to let us go after we had exchanged greetings. We've done that, so what more does he want?"

Lianfang gave him the message. He replied, "My one wish is that your mistress should make some suitable arrangement for me. If not, I'll keep her here even if it costs me my life!"

Ziying was trapped. Sighing, she said to herself, There's nothing else for it; the man is my enemy from some former existence.[30] She told Lianfang to whisper this message to him: "Services will be held on the anniversary of my mother's death, which is on the first of the third month. They will conclude on the third, and at dusk, when the bodhisattva is being sent off and the paper offerings burned, we can meet at the gate and talk."

Shuihe was as jubilant as if he had just received a special directive from the emperor. "Your mistress wouldn't be fibbing, would she?" he asked.

Ziying sent back the message: "If I break my word, you are free to tell my father."

Shuihe nodded, and gave another bow. "Your mistress's precious words are engraved upon my heart." So saying, he

30. The word *yuanjia*, meaning an enemy from a previous existence whose vendetta will be played out in this life, becomes adulterated in popular literature until it means little more than "lover." Here it retains some of its original meaning, but not as much as we find in the story's denouement.

hastily opened the rear door of Zitong Hall and vanished among the trees.

After seeing such a dashing young man, Ziying inevitably felt a certain degree of attraction. She was just a girl, however, and on suddenly undergoing such a baffling experience, she flushed and blanched in turn and her heart raced out of control as she and Lianfang hurried from the hall. The escorts and bearers did not know where they were and had been searching frantically for goodness knows how long. Not daring to delay a moment longer, Ziying stepped into the sedan chair and went straight home, but even when she was back in her own room, she still felt in a daze.

> Flames must come near for the fire to break out;
> Before grubs can breed, the tree must decay.
> Were blossoms not floating out from the spring,
> How could the fisherman's boat find its way? [31]

Despite Ziying's promise, Shuihe was plagued by doubts as to whether she really meant it. He found the waiting unbearable, as he checked off the days until the first of the month and then went over to the Si house. There he found that memorial services were indeed being held, and he exulted, She really did tell me the truth, so there's reason for hope. Then another thought occurred to him, and he walked from the front gate around to the back and then from east to west. He noted that the front gate opened onto a main street and the back gate onto an alley, while the east side of the property adjoined one of the city gates and the west side bordered the river.

Toward evening on the third, he dressed up surreptitiously in Laiyuan's black clothes and small cap, slipped out of the inn, and went straight to the Si house. By dusk there was still no sign of the bodhisattva being sent off, and he became anxious. Even

31. A reference to the legend of two young men, Liu Chen and Ruan Zhao, who wandered as far as a Peach Blossom Spring, where they met two female immortals. The legend appeared first in the *Youming lu* compiled by Liu Yiqing (403–444), but it later absorbed motifs from the famous Peach Blossom Spring described by the poet Tao Yuanming.

if there is such a ceremony, he thought, I can't be sure that she really will put in an appearance at it. He was on tenterhooks.

If Shuihe was agitated, Ziying was in a far worse state, as she discussed her dilemma with Lianfang. If she went out, it might lead to trouble, but if she stayed inside, and he did his worst and used the handkerchief as evidence against her, her reputation would be ruined. "So far as I can judge his behavior," said Lianfang, "he's dashing, yes, but he's also cunning and ruthless—you're quite right about that. On the whole I think it would be best if you went out while the bodhisattva is being sent off. Let him see you, then come straight in again. He'll know that you kept your word, and in plain view of all those other people he won't dare try to grab you." At this point Ziying had little choice but to take her maid's advice.

There was a full moon that night. The priests all had their assistants, and the relatives who were proceeding to the temple also had young servants attending on them. The clothes Shuihe wore made him look just like one of these assistants or servants; in fact each group thought he belonged to the other, and so no one paid any particular attention to him. Before it grew dark, the priests were seeing off the bodhisattva and came out to burn the paper offerings. Ziying suddenly appeared beside the door and sneaked a look around her. From his position in the crowd, Shuihe had his eyes riveted on the door, and as soon as he saw her standing there, he turned around, raced up the steps—and came face to face with her. Now that the two had seen each other, Lianfang tugged at Ziying, who turned and went in. By this time the priests had finished chanting the lauds, and the drums and cymbals were striking up. The people in the crowd had eyes only for the priests. In less time than it takes to say the words, Shuihe seized his chance and darted in after the girl as she turned and re-entered her house. His action must have been ordained by fate, for no one noticed him, and he followed close behind her all the way to her room. If anyone had come upon him during that time, he would have been taken for a rapist or a burglar breaking into the house at night and summarily dispatched. By following Ziying inside like this he was defying a mortal danger, a case of risking his life for the sake of sex. If it meant sudden death, so be it.

When Ziying saw Shuihe coming into her room, her heart flew into her mouth—she was terrified of what might happen if he were seen. Casting aside all thought of feminine modesty, she tried her utmost with Lianfang's help to push him out again. But he was a man, and the two girls' combined efforts could not budge him. "Miss, don't be so impatient! Don't be so hasty!" he protested. "There's something I want to say."

Lianfang clamped her hand over his mouth. "This is not the place for you to say *anything*," she said.

"Then let me say just this one word. I'm a provincial graduate from Guangxi who came through here on my way to the metropolitan examination. I admired your talent and beauty so much that I gave up my chance of success in order to stay on here. Then Heaven granted me a fortunate union—I was able to see you at the Dong Zhongshu Terrace, to receive your silk handkerchief as a keepsake, and to be invited to meet you tonight! That is why I risked a thousand deaths to come here. For the sake of love, I've given up any success in the examinations so how can you possibly refuse me?" He knelt down in front of her.

"Who asked you to kneel down? Or kowtow? Out you go, and be quick about it!"

"At this point, how *can* I go out? As I see it, if I go out I die, and if you go on refusing me I die, and I'd rather die inside your room than outside it." He pulled a stiletto from his stocking and made as if to stab himself in the throat. Ziying, scared out of her wits, tried to wrest the stiletto away from him, but Shuihe dropped the weapon and seized her around the waist. In no time at all he had one hand inside the crotch of her trousers, caressing her unopened flower bud. There was nothing she could do but let him fondle her. Lianfang stood guard outside the door to watch for anyone coming.

> One was a student from the examination hall,
> The other a maiden in her private chamber.
> He was as avid for sex
> As a thirsty dragon at sight of water.
> She was as timid and abashed
> As a nestling before a bird of prey.

She was ignorant of the facts of life,
Let alone of the sexual act.
He was adept at romantic affairs,
Well versed in the art of love.
And the outcome?
The flower bud breached, with drop after blood-red drop;
The jade stalk fallen, with a stream as white as snow.

That night the affair was consummated. Even though she had no experience of lovemaking, Ziying was ripe and ready for it. The following night Shuihe seduced Lianfang, who, since her mistress gave her consent, offered no resistance. From that time on, the three of them lived together as one, in complete harmony. In the daytime Shuihe hid behind the screen at the back of the bed, emerging only at night when everybody was asleep, and so no one was aware of his presence. However, the maids who brought food and drink to the room were a constant concern, and Ziying worried day and night that their secret might be revealed. Another concern was for Shuihe, with his wild, uninhibited nature, who had become bored and restless after a dozen nights behind the bed screen. After talking it over together, they decided to flee to his home in Guilin. They gathered their valuables and packed up, and with Ziying and Lianfang dressed like Shuihe, they left during the night by the garden gate and went along the little alley. Shuihe knew the way well, but in his haste he lost one of his shoes. Once out of the gate, it was an easy carriage ride to the customs house, where they hired a boat and went directly to Guangxi. There was no time even to contact his servant Laiyuan. A poem runs:

Illicit love indeed is cause for shame;
For her, elopement was her wedding day.
But silk, once blackened, will never come white,
And when has a river run the other way?

When Master Si discovered that his daughter and her personal maid had disappeared, he knew well enough that it was because of some love affair, but for fear of the furor it would cause he kept their disappearance secret. His only worry was that Subprefect Hu's family would want to set a date for the wedding and he would not be able to respond. It so happened that a maid of his named Lanxiang had come down with a fever. She was quite pretty, which gave Master Si the idea of administering a dose of poison to her and finishing her off. He made out that it was his daughter who had died of an illness, and duly informed Subprefect Hu, who sent women servants over to offer condolences. Since the servants had never seen Ziying, they did not realize that the deceased was someone else. Master Si staged a lavish funeral and wept broken-heartedly for his daughter. Seven times at seven-day intervals the priests read sutras for her, at great expense. Friends and relatives came to offer their condolences. Subprefect Hu's grandson, although he had not actually married Ziying, came in mourning clothes to offer sacrifices. Even the subprefect paid a visit. The whole sordid business arose from using a scapegoat to cover up an elopement.

> One person drinks, another pays the price—
> A maid was poisoned for a daughter's sake.
> From Yellow Springs,[32] with no one to blame,
> She should point to our world and curse the rake.[33]

On the third of the third month, when Shuihe suddenly left the inn and stayed away overnight, Laiyuan assumed that his master had wearied of the lonely life and gone off again to seek his pleasure in the brothels. After breakfast the next morning, when he was getting ready to go out and search, he noticed that his own clothes were missing. How very odd, he thought; surely his master hadn't been wearing them when he went out? He looked for him everywhere without success, but after five or six days he grew tired of searching and decided to let matters take their course. Another day passed, and then when he got up early in the morning to go to the privy, he noticed a yellow cloth

32. The world of the dead.
33. I.e., Mo Shuihe.

wrapper on the floor. Picking it up, he saw the words "Ever Prosperous Company" stitched on it. I'm in luck, he thought. What a fine big wrapper! It'll do for wrapping up clothes or food, or even as a bed sheet cover. In high spirits, he took it back with him to his room.

When another twenty or more days had passed without any sign of Shuihe, Laiyuan's supply of rice and fuel was running out and he had no money left. The master's off enjoying himself somewhere, he thought, while I'm left behind to suffer. I don't even have any rice left, but I'm certainly not going to let myself starve! I'll pawn some of his clothes and buy food and fuel and eat some meat and fish before deciding what to do. He took out two silk jackets, wrapped them in the yellow cloth lest they get soiled in the pawnshop, then locked his room and left the inn.

Which pawnshop shall I go to, he wondered. Then it occurred to him that "If you have the goods, you can sell them anywhere." He had the articles and any pawnshop would take them, so it didn't matter which one he went to. But he was destined for misfortune. With no particular shop in mind, he let his feet carry him where they would, and as bad luck would have it, he ended up at the Si house. In the alley at the back he noticed a yellow pebble-dash wall, a small gatehouse with the name tablet "Renounce Ambition" above it, and a half-opened gate. Realizing it was a private garden, he slipped inside to take a look. It was the end of the third month, and the foliage was a dense green, the plums were thick on the boughs, the orioles practiced their cadences in the weeping willows, and the tree peonies were in full bloom beside the stone balustrade. At this time of the year in our Lingui garden the willows would also be green and the orioles singing, he thought. The only pity is that I can't get home. While musing about such things, he spotted a pink shoe beside a cypress hedge and, on picking it up, recognized it as one of his master's. But how had it got here? He stood rooted to the spot, pondering this question and muttering to himself with a growing sense of alarm.

Although Master Si had deceived the public about his lost daughter by giving out that she died of illness, he found himself in a constant state of depression, as well as bored and angry.

He was trying to revive his spirits by taking a walk in the garden when suddenly he saw Laiyuan pick up a shoe and stand there lost in thought. "Who do you think you are, barging in here?" he shouted. "Trying to rob us, are you?" He told his servants to seize the man, and no sooner had he issued the order than several villagers rushed out and, without giving Laiyuan a chance to explain, grabbed him by the hair and began kicking and pummeling him.

"Stop it! Stop hitting me!" yelled Laiyuan. "I'm the steward of a provincial graduate!" At these words, they ceased their assault.

"We have several provincial graduates in Yangzhou," said the Master. "Which one is your master?"

"He's not from around here. His name's Mo Shuihe, from Lingui county in Guilin, Guangxi."

"Since he comes from elsewhere, I have no way of checking up on what you're saying. But tell me, just what are you doing in here?"

"My master came to Yangzhou last winter on his way to the capital to take the examinations. On the third of this month he left the inn we are staying at and hasn't been back since, although almost a month has gone by. I am running short of necessities and need to pawn some of his clothes for ready cash so that I can go on looking for him—wherever he's enjoying himself. I came by here, saw it was a garden, and dropped in to take a look. Then I happened to pick up this shoe beside the hedge and recognized it as one of my master's. I was just puzzling over it."

The Master looked at the shoe. If he wears this sort of thing, he must be a rake, he thought. "Since your master is a provincial graduate, why didn't he attend the metropolitan examinations?" he demanded.

"He fell ill on the way and stayed behind to recover. He missed the examinations."

"How old is he? And how does he like to spend his time?"

"He's nineteen. He's tall and pale, a very dashing figure. He's skilled in all the arts and a thoroughgoing romantic."

When he heard this, Master Si thought, The fellow's a reprobate. But how did his shoe get left in my garden? Could he be the one who abducted my daughter? But she never left her chamber! There was no way he could have seen her. Then another thought struck him: On the nineteenth of last month she did pay a visit to Jade Flower Temple to donate those pennants. The two of them must have met secretly that day and arranged the whole thing. It looks highly suspicious, but I've been deceiving everybody about her disappearance, and anyway, family scandals shouldn't be aired in public, so there's no point in bringing it up. To Laiyuan he said, "Since you're not a thief, off you go. There's no need for any more of this palaver."

Laiyuan picked up the bundle as well as the shoe, and after leaving the garden called in at a pawnshop next door that was run by a man named Cheng from Huizhou. The manager opened the bundle, noticed the words "Ever Prosperous Company" and shouted to his assistants, "Hurrah! We've found that stuff we lost!" The assistants came running up to see.

"That's it, all right," they said, fetching a chain and fastening it around Laiyuan's neck. He tried to explain, but all he received in return were a couple of slaps and a volley of curses. "You robber, you! Caught red-handed, and you still deny it!" In fact, in the early morning hours of the nineteenth of that month, robbers had broken into the pawnshop and stolen a quantity of gold and silver but left behind the jewels and the clothes. The wrapper had also been taken, but for some reason the robbers had discarded it. Laiyuan, who had found it and brought it here full of clothes to pawn, had walked straight into a trap.

Without giving him a chance to explain, they trussed him up and delivered him to the constables, who took him before the Jiangdu magistrate for interrogation. Laiyuan testified that he was the servant of provincial graduate Mo and that the wrapper was something he had found on the morning of the twentieth. The magistrate reasoned that if Laiyuan had robbed the shop, he would hardly have tried to pawn the stolen goods at the same place, so he could not possibly be the real culprit. He held him in custody while he sent his constables out to catch the robbers. However, the arrest came to the ears of Master Si, who believed that his daughter had gone off with a robber, and having no other outlet for his anger, he wrote to the magistrate charging that Laiyuan had sneaked into his garden that very morning to spy out the land—he must surely be one of the robbers. The magistrate took note of the charge and had Laiyuan brought out for further questioning.

When Laiyuan testified that he was the servant of provincial graduate Mo, the magistrate asked, "And where is the graduate now?"

"He went out on the third of the third month, and to this day I don't know where he went," Laiyuan answered truthfully.

The magistrate laughed. "When has anyone ever gone out and stayed away such a long time without his servant knowing where he is? That's absurd on the face of it." After ordering the finger press applied, he questioned Laiyuan again under torture.

Unable to bear the pain, Laiyuan had to confess to joining a gang that carried out the robbery and then divided up the stolen goods before going their separate ways. The magistrate reflected that the case involved only a single wrapper, after all, and it would be hard to convict anyone on that basis alone, so he sent Laiyuan back to prison and set a strict deadline for the arrest of the other robbers. He would dispose of the case as soon as they were caught.

Since Laiyuan had not been convicted of a crime, he received no share of prisoner rations, and without any relatives to bring him food, he concluded that he had very little chance of surviving. Fortunately the innkeeper, Zhu Xiaoqiao, knew him as Mo Shuihe's steward, an honest, prudent fellow who had never stayed away from the inn for so much as a night and who had suffered this misfortune through no fault of his own. Zhu cared for him as if he had been a relative, visiting him in prison and consoling him. "Your master left many more cases of clothes and bedding, which can be sold off, if necessary. When he comes back, he's bound to understand." Laiyuan thanked him through his tears and resigned himself to life in prison. He took good care of his health, while waiting anxiously for his master to come back and rescue him.

If you can't cook the tortoise meat tender,
You mustn't put the blame on the mulberry wood.[34]

Let me turn back to Mo Shuihe. After bringing Ziying and Lianfang back to Lingui, he let it be known that he had failed in the examination but taken a wife and acquired a maid in Yangzhou on the return journey. None of his friends or relatives ever learned the true story.

It has always been the case that illicit passion is much more ardent than conjugal love, and after a few months at home Ziying gave birth to a son, followed the next year by a second son. Although Lianfang had been the recipient of some surplus attentions from Shuihe, she did not conceive, either because she suffered from a cold womb or because the embryo failed to develop. Amusingly enough, after obtaining Ziying, Shuihe reined in his promiscuous behavior and sought his sexual pleasures with his own women in his own home. He was twenty-one when it came time for the next metropolitan examinations, and in the tenth month of that year he prepared to set off for the capital. As he was about to leave, Ziying said to him with a smile, "On your way to the capital, you're bound to pass through Yangzhou, but this time see that you don't spend your time in the Jade Flower Temple."

"There's no reason you shouldn't spend time in the temple," put in Lianfang, "so long as you don't go washing your hands in that stone tub on Dong Zhongshu Terrace."

Although both women were joking, their jokes served to remind Shuihe of his shameless behavior two years before. He broke into a cold sweat and was at a loss for words. After hesitating for some time, he finally came out with, "If my journey takes me through Yangzhou, all I shall want to do is to find out where Laiyuan is. I've lost all interest in romantic affairs; you needn't worry your heads on that account." He took his leave and set off for the capital.

After enduring the usual rigors of travel, he arrived in the capital and proceeded to triumph in the examination, graduat-

34. A variation of the common proverb "If you can't cook the old tortoise tender, place the blame on the withered mulberry wood."

ing in the top group. After three months' observation of government,[35] he was selected as magistrate of Yizhen county[36] and, once he had received his credentials, he left to take up office, traveling by way of Yangzhou, which was in the next county. While there, he made a private visit in plain clothes to the inn where he had previously stayed. Despite the passage of three years, it still looked practically the same. The innkeeper, Zhu Xiaoqiao, seized hold of him the moment he saw him. "Master Mo, where have you *been* all this time? You've brought great harm to that servant of yours. He was falsely accused of robbery by Cheng's pawnshop and has suffered terribly." He gave a detailed account of all that had happened.

"Keep your voice down. I know what I'll do. The last time I was here, I felt so frustrated at missing the exam that I went off somewhere else to try and get over it. I never intended to be gone three years or do him any harm. I've now managed to qualify as a metropolitan graduate and been selected as magistrate of Yizhen. As soon as I take up office, I'll see to his case." When Zhu Xiaoqiao heard he was the magistrate of Yizhen, he knelt down and kowtowed, but Shuihe pulled him to his feet, protesting, "Let's have none of that! We used to live together, remember." He went on, "I need to take up office at once, so I can't linger. Don't tell anyone about this, not even Laiyuan. If he gets out of prison, he'll certainly seek you out. Bring him over to Yizhen without letting anyone else know, and I'll reward you handsomely." He boarded his boat again and sailed on to Yizhen.

After a few days, he sent a man down to Guangxi, to bring Ziying and Lianfang up to Yizhen. That year the newly appointed inspector-general made his tour of inspection. He had been chief examiner in the year Shuihe graduated, and mentor and student had formed a close bond. Shuihe now presented him with the facts of the false accusation. When the inspector-general traveled to Yangzhou that autumn, Jiangdu county sent its cases over to him for re-examination, and on coming to the

35. Newly minted graduates were often seconded to a ministry in the capital before receiving a posting in the provinces.
36. Its name was changed to Yizheng in the Qing dynasty.

Laiyuan file, he found the evidence insufficient and attached this comment to it:

> The robbers stole the gold and silver but threw away the wrapper, and Laiyuan picked up something that had already been discarded. This is a case of a man taking what someone else has thrown away, not a case of the King of Chu's bow.[37] Since none of the robbers has been apprehended, Laiyuan is seen as a prize catch, which is unjust.
>
> I hereby order Jiangdu county to retry the case with a view to exonerating him.

When the documents were received in the Jiangdu county offices, the magistrate had Laiyuan brought out for re-examination. By this time Cheng the pawnbroker no longer had a shop in Yangzhou. The magistrate set Laiyuan free, declaring, "It's a pity the owner of the stolen goods isn't present. He ought to be punished for bringing a false accusation."

Laiyuan returned to his lodgings and thanked Zhu Xiaoqiao. He was under the impression that he was benefiting from a general amnesty and had no idea of the real reason for his release until Zhu told him. That night the two men set off for the Yizhen county offices. Zhu spent the night outside while Laiyuan presented himself to the magistrate. On seeing his master, he knelt down and kowtowed before him, then told again and again of the torture and other sufferings he had endured because of the false accusation. He sobbed as he spoke, shedding rivers of tears.

"It's true that your master abandoned you," said Shuihe, "but you must admit that this was also due to your own bad luck." Laiyuan ceased sobbing and bowed in greeting to Ziying.

When he heard her accent, he said, "So you're from Yangzhou, ma'am? When did you get married?"

Still troubled by his conscience, Shuihe flushed and would say only, "Oh, we've been married a long time." That day, after a

---

37. The King of Chu lost his bow, which was retrieved by someone else in Chu. The king said that it was no loss, because the bow would still be in the possession of a fellow countryman. The anecdote occurs in a number of early texts.

royal celebration, Shuihe sent thirty taels of silver to Zhu Xiao-qiao for services rendered. From that time on, he completely reformed his behavior and took a principled approach to his official duties, while totally ignoring the courtesan scene.

One day he said to Ziying, "Laiyuan really does deserve our sympathy—it was because of me that he was forced to spend three years in jail. He's getting on in years but still doesn't have a wife, while Lianfang, although she's been attending on me, has fortunately never had a child. I'd like to suggest that we marry her to Laiyuan and send them both back home to manage our property. He'll be able to enjoy himself there in a free, relaxed way instead of being cooped up in an office as he is here." At first Lianfang affected reluctance, but in fact she had a lively nature and was more than willing to take a husband of her own. It fell to Ziying to do her a second favor, as that night she arranged the marriage to Laiyuan. The couple knelt in the ceremonial hall, sat on the edge of the bed, and drank from the wedding cup. Their names may not have been inscribed on any honor roll, but theirs was a night of wedded bliss. They celebrated for the first month after the wedding and were then sent back to Guangxi. It may not have been a triumphal return, but it was certainly an honorable homecoming.

> Without a blast of bone-chilling cold,
> How would we get the plum blossom's scent?

When Ziying had been living for a year in Yizhen, she remarked to her husband, "Ever since we had our affair and managed to pass ourselves off as husband and wife, I've not been able to see my parents. My mother died a long time ago, but I believe my father is still alive. Jiangdu can't be more than forty miles from here. I wish you would find some way for me to meet him." She wept silently, in sorrow and shame.

"Just so long as you're not too impatient, my dear. I'll need time to arrange it."

A few days later, when he was in Yangzhou on official business, he took the opportunity to call at Master Si's house and send in his visiting card. Noticing that the card read "Your junior, Mo Ke, bows his head in deference," the Master assumed that the visitor had come to see him as magistrate of a neighboring county; he had no idea that the man was his son-in-law. Shuihe stayed a long time, so long that Master Si had to offer him refreshments. As they ate and drank, he suddenly asked, "Are you doubly blessed, sir?" Now, examination graduates use the term "doubly blessed" to mean that both their parents are still alive. If only their father or mother survives, the terms they use are "serving the pater" or "serving the mater." And if both their parents are dead, they refer to themselves as "ever grieving."

Shuihe shed some tears. "Mine is an ill fate, I'm afraid. Both my parents passed away long ago. To this day I regret that I can no longer take care of them."

"We are both grieving, you because you have lost your parents, I because I have no children," said the Master, shedding tears. On this sad note the meal came to an end.

As he left the house, Shuihe said, "I don't know when we shall meet in the future, but if you don't reject me because of my lack of cultivation, I should like to wait on you again."

"My family's tombs are at the foot of Mt. Qixia. Whenever I go there to perform the spring rites, my route takes me through your county. From now on I shall certainly call on you." With that, they parted.

In the third month of the following year, the Master did pay a visit. As soon as Shuihe learned of it, he told his wife, "Your father will be here today. Would you like to see him?"

"When I think of his kindness in giving me birth and raising me, I have no choice but to put aside my shame and go and see him."

Shuihe ordered wine to be prepared and invited Master Si into his private quarters. In the middle of their drinking, Shuihe said, "There is something highly irregular that I would like to ask of you."

"What is it you wish me to do?"

"As a new relative, I ought from now on to perform the ritual duties of a son-in-law. And my wife also wishes to come out and greet you."

"But how could I presume . . . ?" Before Master Si could finish the sentence, Ziying had come out, fallen to her knees, and begun kowtowing. The Master was elderly and had poor eyesight, and he, too, dropped to his knees. But when he stood up and looked at her, he began roaring, "*Why? Why? How could you?* No wonder they said that pink shoe in the garden belonged to a graduate named Mo! *Now* I understand!" On and on he stormed. After the loss of his daughter several years ago, it was a display, not of joy at blessings dropping down from above, but of anger welling up from below. Finally, he heaved a sigh and said, "Well, if our daughters turn out badly, we have nobody to blame but ourselves."

He turned to Shuihe. "That unworthy daughter of mine lost her integrity and her decency. She had no backbone, and she's gone to hell. That day when a real robber abducted her, I had to make out that she had died, and I deceived Subprefect Hu and his family. If the facts are ever revealed, I will be disgraced and so will you. We must never meet again as long as we live." Straightening his gown, he swept out of the room.

His tirade left the impetuous Shuihe speechless and abashed as he saw Master Si out the door. Ziying retired to her room and for three months suffered from an illness that she could not name.

By spring of the following year, Shuihe had completed his three-year term and was promoted to the lieutenant governorship of Fujian. He kept castigating himself for the wildness of his youth, for ruining his own conduct and destroying a girl's virtue, and he gave strict instructions to his own sons that they were never to compromise their moral standards in the slightest degree. The elder son was named Woru, the younger Wosi.[38] Both succeeded in their studies, graduating together in the same metropolitan examination and going on to serve as officials in the capital.

And now the time of Shuihe's death was drawing near. He fell ill in his Fujian offices of some strange malady. It was not a disorder of the emotions or the senses, nor did it consist of fevers or chills or internal or external disease. He was alternately comatose and frenetic, from time to time roaring with laughter and singing wildly, beating his chest and falling over

38. Both names mean "like me."

backwards, seizing a dagger or a sword and gouging flesh from his arms, all the while shouting, "Ghosts! Thieves! Spies!" Ziying attended on him from morning to night—she was afraid to leave him on his own.

One day he was asleep in bed when all of a sudden he sat up and declared, "I am none other than the guardian god of the Jade Flower Temple. In Ziying's former existence, she was a rich man from Jiangdu, while Mo Shuihe was a courtesan in Guilin.[39] The rich man promised to buy her out and marry her, but he broke his word and went back to Yangzhou. In her bitterness and frustration, the courtesan took her own life. That is why the man was reborn as a woman and the woman as a man, and why events in this life have unfolded in the way they have. The fact that this time Mo Shuihe is rich and distinguished and his two sons successful is a reward for all the good works he did as a courtesan in his earlier existence. The malignant disease that overwhelms him now before his death is retribution for gratuitously forcing Ziying to submit to him, thus corrupting her good intentions. The reward comes in the next life; the retribution in this. I urge all men and women to start doing good without delay." He fell back on his bed and reverted to his original self as Mo Shuihe. Sadly, a moment later he began vomiting quantities of blood and died.

Full of apprehension over the god's manifestation, Ziying had Shuihe's body laid in a coffin and taken back to Guangxi, where Laiyuan and his wife welcomed her. Lianfang was greatly saddened by the news of Shuihe's death, recalling the affection that had existed between them. Shuihe's two sons rushed home for their father's funeral.

Just as the three years of mourning were coming to an end, Ziying herself fell ill. Calling her sons to her bedside, she instructed them in these words: "Your father was born in Lingui; your mother in Jiangdu. Each dreaming soul has its ultimate resting place. Because of our fated attraction, we happened to be born together in this life. These are my final words." So saying, she drew her last breath. Her sons, who could make no

39. The strange events are explained as a case of karmic reward and retribution.

sense of what she said, assumed that *in extremis* her mind was disturbed and did not pursue the matter. In fact, Ziying's mind was perfectly clear right up until the moment of her death, and these were more words of enlightenment from the guardian god. In later times someone wrote a poem that makes the point:

> Every fated attraction has its reason—
> A past love present in the love you share.
> And should you fail to clear the old love's debts,
> Your next life may be more than you can bear.

7
The Lovers' Tombs

Red leaves, red thread[1]—it's destiny, they say;
In the flower of youth it's manifest.
Fond, foolish love, it seems, is karmic fate.
Two towns were roiled by one with sex obsessed;
The other, unprepared for noxious weeds,[2]
Was in the past as "Pan An Junior"[3] blessed.
To libertines it's a romantic tale,
But to all the others a cause for jest.

*E*ver since Heaven and Earth came into existence, the forces of yin and yang have acted in complementary fashion, and the bond between husband and wife has been the starting point of the Five Relationships. This is the correct principle, as we scarcely need to be reminded. Even concubinage is referred to in the ancient rites; in any case it is a common practice. As for the libertines who frequent houses of ill fame and pay for their pleasures, or the reprobates who hold secret assignations and engage in illicit affairs, although their behavior may amount to lechery, in the final analysis it still arises from heterosexual desire and is hardly to be wondered at. The one ridiculous case is that of those men who are addicted to the pleasures of the

---

The full title is "Pan Wenzi Is Matched with Another in the Lovers' Tombs."

1. Red leaves: In a Tang story, Lu Wo picked up a red leaf with a poem on it in the palace moat. When later the emperor allowed his palace women to marry, Lu Wo happened to choose the one who had written the poem. Similar stories are told of others; see particularly "Liu hong ji" in the Song collection of tales *Qing suo gao yi*. Red thread: In Chinese mythology, the Old Man Beneath the Moon (Yuexia Laoren) tied with red thread the feet of people who were destined to marry.

2. An allusion to slander with reference to Zhuge Ying of the sixth century. See his biography in the *Sui History, juan* 76.

3. Pan An (Pan Yue) was an icon of male beauty.

rear courtyard,[4] who treat males as females and enjoy the same lustful delights as other men, transported into a similar state of ecstasy. Is that not the strangest thing?

It may well be so, but the fact remains that homosexual activity has always been with us. Educated people have a single name for it, Academicians' Love, but the local dialects show a wide variety of terms. The northerners call it Frying Roots,[5] the southerners Hitting the Mat; in Huizhou it is known as Collapsing Toufu, in Jiangxi as Melting the Firebox, and in Ningbo as What You Will. The people of Longyou call it Playing the Bitter Scallion, the people of Ciqi Frog Play, and the people of Suzhou Drain the Teacher. In the *Ming Law Code,* it is defined as "the insertion of the penis into the anus of another person for the purpose of lustful pleasure."[6] But widely as the terms may differ, the reality behind them is the same. For example, there are places in Fujian province where, if the common people have a good-looking son, they will accept a betrothal settlement for the lad when he is no more than eleven or twelve. Fully ninety percent of the cases brought before the court in Zhangzhou have to do with buggery. What a colossal joke!

As a prologue to my story, let me tell of two leaders in the field of homosexual love. A certain King Gong of Chu was a passionate devotee.[7] His particular favorite was one Lord Anling who, for all his physical beauty, was getting on in years and beginning to worry that the king's love for him might fade. He sought the advice of Jiang Yi, who put the following question to him: "Are you familiar, by any chance, with the expression 'The odalisque does not let her bed grow old, nor the ganymede his carriage?'"[8] The elegant language of the expression was quite beyond the comprehension of Lord Anling, and so Jiang Yi explained it to him as follows: "'Odalisque' means the same as

4. A euphemism for sodomy.
5. The translation of these expressions is rank guesswork.
6. *Da Ming lü,* of which the standard revision appeared in 1397.
7. The anecdote first appears in the *Zhanguo ce* (Intrigues of the warring states), *Chu ce* (Intrigues of Chu) 1. Here it is reduced and given a different emphasis; Lord Anling, instead of appealing to the king's sympathy, merely resorts to new methods. Jiang Yi was a trusted adviser to the king.
8. See *Zhanguo ce, Chu ce* 1 ("Jiang Yi shui yu Anling Jun"). The end of the anecdote has been changed.

palace woman, and well before the bed on which she sleeps is worn out, the emperor will have ceased to take any pleasure in her. 'Ganymede' refers to someone like you, and before the carriage that the emperor gave you has broken down, you will be out of favor. It makes the point that you have no time to lose."

From that day forward Lord Anling began to employ every kind of unseemly and ingratiating practice, as a result of which the king grew fonder of him than ever. The favorite never did lose favor with the king, not even in his old age.

There was also a certain Lord Longyang of Wei, whose beauty was fully the equal of Lord Anling's.[9] The King of Wei was also particularly devoted to homosexual pleasures; none of his palace women was favored to anything like the same degree as Lord Longyang. One day the king and his favorite were amusing themselves in a small boat, the *Wild Duck*, on a lake in the palace grounds when they noticed some goldfish in the water below them, goldfish fiery red and jade white. Lord Longyang asked for a fishing pole and, after attaching a succulent piece of bait, cast his line into the water. With every cast he hooked a fish, until he had more than a dozen. Finally he caught a big one—and promptly burst into tears. Astonished, the king asked him why.

"The moment I caught this big fish," said Lord Longyang, "I felt like throwing all the little ones back. One day Your Majesty is going to find someone better than I am, and then of course I shall be discarded. That fish set me thinking of myself, and I couldn't help crying."

The king laughed. "So long as you keep your looks, you needn't worry about anyone taking your place."

> For long-term favor, he could stop at nothing;
> Fearing rejection, he wept over a fish.

From this we can see that Lords Anling and Longyang were champions in the homosexual ranks and the kings of Chu and Wei were captains of the homosexual legions. But the two kings did, after all, appoint their favorites to official rank as para-

9. See *Zhanguo ce, Wei ce* (Intrigues of Wei) 4. The end has been changed.

mour officials,[10] and that was a far cry from the behavior of a man who rejected his fiancée in favor of a concubine with unshaven eyebrows, unbound feet, unpierced ears—and a male organ. This concubine, who wore a scholar's cap and gown, allowed the base of the alimentary canal, that narrow outlet through which the body breaks its wind, to substitute for that other passageway that is meant for purging and impregnation. At the time the affair occurred, it was described as romantic, but later on it was generally regarded as a joke.

Who was this person? His surname was Pan, his personal name Zhang, and his style Wenzi, and he hailed from Jinling. After his father, Pan Du, lost his wife, he took a concubine named Huiniang, an attractive girl who was just eighteen at the time. He married her in his old age, primarily to have a child, and within a year she became pregnant and gave birth to Wenzi. In looks the child took after his mother far more than his father; his beauty was something he brought with him from the womb.

The people in the neighborhood were struck by the child's looks. "If old Pan had managed to have a daughter who looked like this, she'd have qualified not just as some palace woman or favorite, but as the empress herself," they declared. "The imperial astronomer would surely have observed some sign in the heavens!"

When Wenzi was four or five, he started school, and by the time he was eleven or twelve he had a complete grasp of the texts, after which he proceeded to excel at writing essays. By the age of sixteen, he was recognized as one of the most outstanding students in all of Jinling. In addition to his talent, he had a pink and white complexion of the softest, most delicate texture. His mother delighted in his scholarly achievements but she also dressed him up exquisitely and pomaded his hair until it was too glossy for even a fly to settle on. His gown was the color of blue lotus flowers, and he wore it over a pale rose jacket and a white damask vest. His trousers were crimson, his shoes were of crimson crepe silk in the latest fashion, and his stockings were of sheer white satin. Out walking in the

10. *Nongchen.* The term was first used (of Deng Tong) by the Han emperor Wen.

street, he looked simply charming—he could have passed for the reincarnation of Sudhana or for Golden Lad sent down to earth.[11] As soon as the local scholars, who were pederasts to a man, set eyes on this beautiful youth, their eyes flashed fire as they inhaled the fragrance he gave off. The older ones wanted him as a protégé, the middle-aged wanted to drag him off to join their study societies, and the rich wanted to bankroll him. There were also middle-aged women with daughters who were eager to have him as a son-in-law, and young unmarried girls who were just as eager to have him as a husband. In addition to all of these, there were Buddhist and Daoist priests anxious to take him on as a disciple, as well as professional spongers who wanted to entice him into paying court to rich and powerful men of homoerotic tastes. Everybody exclaimed over his good looks. A born-again Pan An, they said, and gave him the nickname of Pan An Junior. Someone even made up a "Hanging Branch" song in his praise:

> A lad of tender years.
> His value? A thousand in gold wouldn't come near.
> Such charming looks—
> Pan is the fitting surname here.
> "Pan An Junior"—a name to revere.
> But the crimson trousers once removed,
> You'll find a white expanse appear,
> And though he's not laid down in front,
> We'll gladly mind the rear.

Despite his beauty and charm, however, Pan Wenzi held to the straight and narrow. He never entered into any casual relationships, and much as his admirers doted on him, they found his friendship far from easy to win. On hearing this song he was furious, and resolved to triumph in his studies in order to wipe out the disgrace. That was why, when his parents wanted him to marry, he firmly opposed the idea.

11. Sudhana (Shancai) is the young hero of the *Huayan Sutra*. Golden Lad (Jintong) was an attendant at the court of the Queen Mother of the West. He fell in love with Jade Girl (Yunü) and was sent down to earth with her.

Let me explain. While he was still a child, his father had betrothed him to one of his cousins. His uncle, the cousin's father, had since died without having a son, and his aunt, his father's sister, with no one to care for her, turned to his father for support and urged that a date be set for the wedding. In her opinion, both families would benefit.

But Wenzi refused. Again and again his mother tried to persuade him to agree to a wedding date. "When boys and girls grow up, they have to marry, you know; that's been the practice from time immemorial. Just consider your father's situation. He had no son, and only after praying to goodness knows how many gods, worshipping countless buddhas, swearing innumerable vows, and accumulating a vast amount of merit,[12] did he finally manage to produce you, my dear. And now you're sixteen, and it's high time you married and had children of your own to continue the family line. If you're so stubborn as to refuse, not only will you be cutting off the family line, but if anything should happen to your father, all the work that he put into building up his fortune will have been in vain. And with no wife, you'll definitely be laying yourself open to public ridicule."

"The ancients used to marry at thirty," countered Wenzi, after listening to his mother, "and I'm only sixteen. Having a wife would distract me from my studies. What's more, my education is far from complete; this is no time to be setting up a family. Not long ago I heard that Master Longqiu had established an academy at Southside Temple in Hangzhou that has attracted two or three hundred students. I would like to go there, too, and study under him. Mother, would you *please* have a word with Father and ask him for travel money and expenses so that I can study in Hangzhou for a year or two? When I have acquired enough education and, with any luck, passed the provincial examination, it will still not be too late for me to come back and marry. At this point I definitely don't want to hear any more about it."

Because her husband had had his son late in life and had cosseted him from birth, letting him have his way in everything,

12. An age-old belief that by good deeds one accumulates unseen moral credit, which then influences one's own and one's family's fortunes.

Huiniang knew that she would have to put the marriage question aside. She spoke to her husband about Wenzi's desire to travel for the purpose of further study.

Pan Du was reluctant to part with his son, but faced with Wenzi's desperate, tearful pleas, he had to relent, and offered fifty taels for travel and living expenses. Wenzi thought the allowance was too small and won an increase to one hundred and twenty taels plus a quantity of gifts.

Huiniang prepared a wardrobe for all the seasons, as well as her son's bedclothes and book boxes. She detailed a young servant, Diligent, to accompany him, and reserved passage on a boat bound for Hangzhou. The frivolous young rakes of the town, resenting the fact that Wenzi had rebuffed their advances, began smearing him by saying, "He's not going to study with any master. Most likely, he's looking for a patron to Drain the Teacher with." They also made up another "Hanging Branch" song:

> Pan An Junior,
> So it's to Hangzhou you're about to head?
> Remember now, don't be a Mizi Xia;[13]
> Rather be a Dong Xian[14] instead.
> The hammer and last you'll come to dread;
> It's real pain you'll have to bear,
> Pounded mercilessly in bed,
> On and on till ultimate collapse,
> When it's a Mr.Chen that you'll need to spread.

Gentle readers, do you know what a "Mr. Chen" is? Well, when women are having sex with men, the cloth they use to wipe up the secretions is known as a "Mrs. Chen." Now, if two men having sex together use a cloth, shouldn't it be called a "Mr. Chen"? Of course, this was just a joke. But although the

13. Paramour official of Duke Ling of Wei. Anecdotes about him are found in the *Zuo zhuan* and other early texts.
14. Paramour official of Emperor Ai of the Han dynasty. See his biography in the *Han History* 93. He attained senior civil and military rank before committing suicide during the Wang Mang usurpation.

rakes poked fun at Pan Wenzi, he continued to ignore them and embarked for Hangzhou.

In less than five days the boat had arrived in the city and moored by Pine Needle Square. Wenzi sent the boatman for a sedan chair and told two porters to carry his bags, then went straight to the West Lake and found his way to Southside Temple. Master Longqiu had established his academy in quarters at the western end of the Buddha Hall that were spacious and surrounded by trees. Above the door was a tablet with blue lettering against a white background bearing the words "Nest of Clouds." Wenzi handed in the disciple's visiting card that he had prepared and was ushered into the Master's presence. He asked the Master to take the place of honor while he bowed low four times before him, then offered the presents he had brought. He was invited to a light supper, and after spending the night in the Master's quarters went out next morning to find himself a place in the monks' cells.

He wrote out visiting cards for all of his fellow students. To those who were considerably older than he was, he referred to himself as "your humble younger brother"; to those of about the same age, he wrote "your younger brother"; and to those who were just a few years older, he wrote "your younger brother who aspires to learn from you." Master Longqiu had a large number of students who were scattered throughout dozens of monks' cells, and with Diligent carrying the cards for him, Wenzi called on each one.

The next day a swarm of new friends returned the compliment. One by one they came, until Wenzi's room was so crammed they could hardly breathe—someone had to leave before anyone else could come in.[15] The new friends were all young students away from home who had long been deprived of sex. Some were merely nominal students, their sole aim being to beguile youngsters into dubious activities, and at the sight of Wenzi's beauty, their tongues began to wag, they shot glances back and forth, and they muttered to one another. "Could this

15. The original edition has a comparison with "Prince Guan's grain" *(Guan wang liang),* which presumably refers to an anecdote about Guan Yu.

be Sudhana appearing in front of us?" said one. "Could it be Lord Zitong[16] come down to earth?" said another. "It's probably the bodhisattva Guanyin in human form," said a third. "Long ago Zhu Yingtai[17] dressed up as a boy and came to Hangzhou to study. Could it be her, I wonder?" said a fourth. A fifth declared, "If right here and now I could go to bed with a friend like that, it wouldn't be just to satisfy a momentary need. I'd be willing to do without a wife for good!"

Although the greetings these students offered Wenzi were perfectly proper, each of them cherished the desire to swear an oath of brotherhood with him. A variety of questions were put. "Brother Pan, what classic are you working on?" "Which part of the country do you hail from?" "Are you married?" "Are your honorable parents still alive?" "How many brothers do you have?" "Where do you come in seniority?" "Please tell us your honorable style and studio name, so that next time we meet I can address you properly." There were some who folded their hands together and bowed before declaring, "It's an honor to make your acquaintance!" And there were others who, exuding false solicitude, exclaimed, "We're so *fortunate* to have you studying with us!"

The stream of welcoming remarks soon exhausted Wenzi's patience. Even Diligent, who was serving the visitors tea, found himself as busy as a waiter in a wine shop, unable to keep up with demand. Meanwhile, comically enough, these new friends kept staring, goggle-eyed, at Wenzi's face. Eventually, after taking up a great deal of his time, they departed.

In his studies Wenzi kept to the schedule laid down by the Master. Of every ten-day period, the third, sixth, and ninth days were for writing essays, while the second, fifth, and eighth were for explicating the classics. Each evening he worked until midnight before going to bed.

> In the morning he pored over the *Statutes* of Yao and Shun,
> In the evening he worked through the *Plans* of Yu and Tang,

---

16. I.e., Wen Chang, god of literature.
17. In the well-known romance, Zhu Yingtai dressed as a boy and traveled to Hangzhou for the purpose of study. She met her lover Liang Shanbo there.

But the teachings of Yao and Shun, Yu and Tang, as well as
   Kings Wen and Wu do not exceed a single section of the
   Classic of Documents;[18]
Ceremonies, sacrifices, rituals are all set down in the
   hundred-chapter *Record of Rites;*
Rebels and traitors are set forth in the *Spring and Autumn
   Annals* from the beginning.
Brilliant youths and beautiful girls are recorded in the
   Zheng and Wei songs of the *Poetry Classic.*
In the *Classic of Changes* are the hexagrams, arranged under
   the Four Virtues;
In the *Classic of Music* are the sounds, with all the notes
   clearly distinguished.
At length you realize that you must read all these books in
   order to profit;
You no longer believe that idleness is the same as study.

But let me put aside the subject of Pan Wenzi's studies
in the academy and tell of a licentiate named Wang Zhongxian who lived in Xiangtan county of Changsha prefecture. His
father, Wang Shanwen, was a local landowner with two sons.
The elder, Boyuan, had been managing his father's land ever
since his marriage. Zhongxian, the younger, had fine, clear-cut
features and a quick intelligence, and from childhood on had
shown an aptitude for study. In discussing the latter's future
with his wife, Mistress Song, Wang Shanwen remarked, "We've
made our elder boy our manager, but the younger one is a
handsome lad with all the intelligence needed to go further in
his studies. We've been farmers for generations, but we've also
been a charitable family with many good deeds to our credit.
If Zhongxian could succeed in his studies, it would raise our
social standing and bring honor to the whole clan, demonstrat-
ing that our ancestors' good works were not in vain. It would
also show the people of this county that a farming family can
produce an official. We'd be an example to others in educating
good men!"

18. This is a description of the Six Classics, the basis of formal higher education.

"If the elder son farms and the younger one studies, we'll be a farmer-scholar family!" exclaimed Mistress Song.

Wang Shanwen was now determined that his second son should become a scholar. Although the son in question was engaged to the daughter of Zhang Sanlao in the next village, Shanwen was unwilling to let the wedding take place. He wanted the boy to succeed in the metropolitan examination and secure an appointment before returning to claim his bride. As a result Zhongxian was still unmarried at the age of eighteen.

His father also thought there would be too many distractions at home, so he found a quiet place up in the hills for his son to use as a study, and Zhongxian did indeed work tirelessly there at preparing himself.

Now, once scholars have finished their proper work, they devote their spare time to copying calligraphy, learning how to paint a few withered trees or rocks flanked by bamboo, or practicing their poetry. The least intelligent ones among them also tend to read idle literature and plays.

One day Zhongxian was reading the *Liqingji*[19] when he came upon these lines:

> How many are they, the River Qis and the Shanggongs?
> Far fewer than the shared peaches and the cut sleeves!

River Qi and Shanggong refer to illicit affairs between men and women, as in the expression "in the mulberry orchard above the River Pu."[20] The shared peach and the cut sleeve, on the other hand, refer to homoerotic affairs. There was once a ruler who was addicted to such pleasures, and one day, when his favorite was eating a peach, he snatched the half-eaten peach

---

19. There are two works called *Liqingji*, one by Zhang Junfang (early eleventh century), the other by Yang Shen (1488–1559). Both are compilations of anecdotes, comments, and notes. This poem does not appear in the available versions of either, but both versions are extremely short and have no doubt been abridged.

20. These lines originate in Shen Yue's (441–513) confessional piece "Chan hui wen" (Repentance and remorse). The expressions "River Qi" and "Shanggong" both occur in a *Poetry Classic* poem about an illicit rendezvous (Mao 48, "Sang zhong"). "In the mulberry orchard above the River Pu" is a reference to an illicit rendezvous drawn from the *Li ji (Yue ji)*.

from the man's hand and ate it himself.[21] Not even the peaches served at the Queen Mother's feast on Jasper Pond[22] tasted quite as good as that peach. This is where the expression "shared peach" comes from.

On another occasion the same pair, after indulging in their lewd pleasures in broad daylight, lay down and went to sleep side by side.[23] The ruler was the first to awaken. He wanted to get up, but one sleeve of his gown was pinned beneath his favorite's body. Fearing to awaken him, he whispered to a servant to bring him a pair of scissors and then cut the sleeve right off. Soon afterward the favorite awoke and was so moved by his master's love that he kept the sleeve as a memento. This is where the expression "cut sleeve" comes from.

When Zhongxian came upon these lines, he felt a wave of sexual excitement surging through him. River Qi and Shanggong, he thought, refer to a poem about an illicit affair between a man and a woman. But adultery leads to a drastic loss of moral merit, whereas the shared peach and the cut sleeve do not violate the Principle of Heaven. Moreover, I'm eighteen now, and I've never had sex. Father wants me to succeed in the examinations before he will let me marry, but the future is impossible to predict. How long will I have to wait before I succeed and can marry? I'm afraid adultery would result in a loss of merit, and as for visiting prostitutes, the nearest town is a long way off, and even if I were to spend a night or two there, I wouldn't get any pleasure from it. The best thing would be to find myself a young friend whom I love and seal a pact of brotherhood with him. We could live together over the long term, and I could escape the loneliness I feel. On the other hand, how would I ever have the luck to find a good-looking young fellow who would be my soul mate? Preoccupied with these thoughts, he ceased to apply himself to his studies, and at the annual examination in Xiangtan, he spent the time toiling in vain; he failed. Heaving a sigh, he quoted the lines:

21. The anecdote is told of Mizi Xia.
22. The Queen Mother of the West was a goddess whose peaches conferred immortality on those who ate them.
23. The anecdote is actually told of Dong Xian, not Mizi Xia.

Don't hope your writing pleases the world;
Just hope it pleases the examiner.

He was at home brooding over his failure when Zhang San-lao paid a call on his father. Zhongxian came face to face with his visitor; there was no chance to escape. He had to receive him and bow low, partly because Mr. Zhang was his fiancée's father, and partly because of apprehension over his failure. As Zhang Sanlao repeated his greeting, Zhangxian flushed a deep red and began to stammer, unable to get the words out.

He was still struggling to reply when his father came out and greeted Mr. Zhang. "Well, kinsman," said Mr. Wang with a smile, "are you here to see me, or to ask my son about his examination?"

"There's something I'd like to talk to you about," said Zhang. "Xiangtan county may be part of the city of Changsha, but the province as a whole has always suffered from poor teaching. You were adamant that your son should continue his studies, insisting that he succeed before you would allow him to marry. But although success is undeniably important, marriage is no small matter either. My daughter is seventeen now, a grown woman. If we delayed the wedding before for the sake of examination success, I'm afraid that now we may delay the success for the sake of the wedding. What do you suggest?"

Wang Shanwen thought for a moment. "I grew up as a farmer and have no book learning myself, but as things are now, my son's knowledge is certainly not good enough. It would be best if he gave up his studies, got married, and saved you from any further worries about your daughter."

"But scholarship is the highest vocation of all! How could he possibly give it up? What a poor return that would be for the great kindness you've shown! I should like to suggest a plan that would meet both needs. I understand that Master Longqiu has established an academy at Southside Temple in Hangzhou and that students are flocking there from all parts of the country. When his pupils come to take the examinations, you can be sure that some of them will do well; based on past experience, the prospects are good. The best plan would be to give your son an allowance and send him off to Hangzhou to study with the

Master. When he has completed his education he should take the examination just once, no matter what the circumstances are. If he succeeds, even my daughter, needless to say, will share in the glory. But if the result is as disappointing as the last time, you should give up your aspirations for your son and complete the marriage. That way, neither study nor marriage would be unduly delayed."

Wang Shanwen was delighted with this suggestion. After saying goodbye to Zhang Sanlao, he arranged an allowance, saw to the packing, and ordered Oxboy, a young servant, to accompany his son to Hangzhou for the purpose of further study. From this same suggestion, however, certain consequences flowed:

> A youth in Nest of Clouds paired with a male lovebird;
> A girl on Mt. Luofu joined a female phoenix.

With Oxboy as his page, Zhongxian traveled downstream from Changsha to Runzhou, where he changed boats. On arriving at Southside Temple in Hangzhou, he prepared his gifts as Pan Wenzi had done, wrote out a visiting card, and called on Master Longqiu. He then went the rounds of his fellow students in search of a place to stay. Because of the Master's vast reputation, students had flocked to the academy from all parts of the country. There were not a great number of monks' cells to begin with, and rents had soared; as a result each cell now held three or four occupants. Pan Wenzi was the sole exception; he declined to share with anyone else and had a cell all to himself. By the time Zhongxian arrived, there were no vacancies, and because Wenzi had a room of his own, but also because of his peculiar demeanor, the other students made a point of showing Zhongxian to his door. "All the other rooms are full," they told Zhongxian. "There are no vacancies anywhere, but Pan has a room all to himself and could certainly share with you. In fact, he could hardly refuse." Although they offered this advice, they felt quite sure that Wenzi would in fact refuse.

To their surprise, it was as if the two youths had been destined to meet. To Wenzi, Zhongxian seemed like an old friend, and he received him with pleasure. "All men are brothers within the four seas," he declared. "Why don't we share? You'll find that all the everyday necessities have been taken care of. You won't need to buy anything except a bed."

From the moment Zhongxian set eyes on Wenzi he was enthralled, and a shameful thought entered his mind. His only fear was that he might not be accepted, but now that Wenzi had generously invited him to share, he was beside himself with joy. He folded his hands in greeting. "I'm most grateful to you, dear brother, for being so noble and gracious. I only hope that I won't disturb you too much." He had Oxboy bring in his bags.

Their classmates, who had never expected Wenzi to accept Zhongxian so readily, now resented him more than ever. Which only goes to show that you can push an ox's head down, but you cannot make him eat.[24]

> With a bond, you are sure to meet though far apart,
> Without a bond, you'll never join though face to face.

Wang and Pan spent their days sitting side by side but their nights in separate beds. They got along famously, just as if they had been real brothers.

But a young gentleman scholar has a certain air of dignity about him, after all. Although Zhongxian had every intention of seducing his roommate, the latter's genteel refinement and scrupulous way of expressing himself left him without an opening, and unable to give voice to his passion, he had to confine it to the imagination. Outwardly, he affected the same piety as before, as he discoursed on subjects ancient and modern. After six months of living together, the two youths were on terms of the greatest courtesy and respect, but Zhongxian had still found no chance to broach the matter that was uppermost in his mind.

One day they were attending a seminar on the "Duke Ai Inquired about Government" chapter of the *Doctrine of the Mean*,[25] and at the end of the discussion the Master told his students, "This is the only chapter of the *Doctrine of the Mean* that refers to the Three Universal Virtues and the Five Universal

---

24. Cf. "You can lead a horse to water, but you cannot make him drink."
25. Chapter 20.

Obligations,[26] which form the basis of moral cultivation. You must study it with the greatest care." The other students then filed out, all except Zhongxian and Wenzi, who stayed behind to ask their teacher about some points that they found puzzling.

By the time they returned to their room, it was getting dark. They lit the lamp and read for a while before retiring, but they had not been in bed long before Zhongxian called out, "Pan, are you asleep?"

"No, I'm still thinking about the principles behind that passage in the *Doctrine of the Mean*."

"Exactly what I was doing." In fact Zhongxian's thoughts had been far removed from textual interpretation, but since Wenzi had mentioned the subject, he was quick to take it up. "Those references to 'husband and wife' and 'the intercourse of friends'—do they mean one thing or two?" he asked.

"'Husband and wife' refers to harmonious relations between the married couple. 'The intercourse of friends' refers to two friends improving each other's characters through mutual discussion. They're two quite different things!"

"In that case, you still haven't grasped the full meaning," said Zhongxian with a smile. "In the final analysis, they're one and the same."

"But husband and wife are entirely different from friends! How can you possibly lump them together?"

"If a husband and wife correct and encourage each other, they're acting as good friends, and if friends are on the most intimate terms with one another, they're acting as good husbands and wives. Of course, they're one thing!"

At this point Wenzi realized that Zhongxian was trying to provoke him. "In our studies we have to understand what the sages meant," he declared in a righteous tone of voice. "How can you come out with such heretical talk?"

"Oh, it was just a wild idea that came to me. Please don't take offense." But although Zhongxian said this, he was actually

26. The obligations are "those between sovereign and minister, between father and son, between husband and wife, between elder brother and younger brother, and those belonging to the intercourse of friends." See James Legge, *The Chinese Classics* (rpt., Hong Kong: Hong Kong University Press, 1960), v. 1.1, pp. 406–407.

consumed by a feverish desire, and he continued to fantasize for several hours before falling asleep.

On another occasion, in late fall, Zhongxian found himself unable to get to sleep because his bed was too cold. He sighed.

"Why the heavy sigh? There must be a reason," said Wenzi.

"Well, to be frank with you, I was engaged for years, but my father was determined that I should get through the exams before I married. He was against the Changsha area because it had no tradition of classics teaching, so he sent me down to Hangzhou to study. But here, although I benefit from the Master's teaching as well as from your gracious help, I feel restless and unsettled. I've been neglecting my studies, and I don't suppose I shall ever succeed. If I don't pass, I'll have kept my fiancée waiting to no purpose whatsoever. That's why I sighed."

"I've never asked you about yourself, and I didn't realize you weren't married. Well, in that case we're both in the same position."

"You're not married either? Does that mean that you're not engaged, or simply that you're engaged but not married?"

"I do have a fiancée, but in my case I was the one who was unwilling to marry. I was afraid that once I had a wife I wouldn't be able to concentrate on my studies. With you, it was your father's idea, and I can well understand why you gave such an unhappy sigh."

"I'm no match for you where ambition's concerned, but anyway, in my opinion the most important thing in life is not ambition, but pleasure. Why do we have to succeed in the examinations in order to be happy? As the ancients said, 'We are the ones most affected by passion.'[27] In our youth, when by rights we should be enjoying ourselves, we're held back by these rotten examinations. If we never have any luck, won't we have wasted our own lives as well as those of our fiancées? And even if we do meet with success, it may come in our old age, which means we'll have lost our chance of happiness in the whole first half of our lives—a dreadful pity! On this interminable autumn night, if I were lucky enough to have you beside me to talk to,

27. A quotation from *Shishuo xinyu* (A new account of tales of the world), chap. 17.

it might take my mind off these things. But if I have to sleep on my own in a cold bed, the sheer misery and loneliness of it all will be more than I can bear!"

Wenzi laughed. "And all this time I thought you were suffering from the autumn blues! It turns out it's spring passion, after all! Well then, why don't you go straight home and get married! You'll be able to enjoy yourself to your heart's content all this winter."

"'You can't put out a fire with water from miles away.' I need a lover right now to relieve this craving."

"If you need someone right now, the only thing is to go to a brothel for temporary relief."

"I've honored the word 'love' all my life, and prostitutes are the most false-hearted of creatures. Anyway, I don't care for them."

"*Of course* prostitutes are false in matters of love. But even between husband and wife, it's still only a feeling of gratitude — you can hardly call it love. Love is a far more difficult proposition."

Zhongxian heaved another sigh. "What a profound knowledge of love you have!" Lapsing into silence, he lay back again in his bed.

Next morning he devised a scheme. "What you said last night made me feel quite homesick — I really must go back," he said. "But we've been living together for several months now, as close as two brothers, and I can't bear to leave you with only a casual goodbye. Moreover, given your determination to succeed, you'll obviously do brilliantly in your career, and I'm afraid that one day we'll belong to different social worlds and can hardly be the friends we are now. What I would like to do is swear an oath of brotherhood with you, to stand by each other through thick and thin. Would you be willing to do that?"

"Why, it's my dearest wish!" exclaimed Wenzi with delight. "Of course I'm willing. Ever since I came here, you're the one person out of all our classmates that I've felt closest to. I was hoping to go on benefiting from your teaching. I never expected that you'd suddenly leave like this, and it's hard to bear."

"I'm only leaving for a few months. After that I'll be back again."

Each man then performed the eight bows of brotherhood. By virtue of his age, Zhongxian became the senior brother. He produced some money and bought wine and sweetmeats, and they sat opposite each other drinking until late at night, by which time they were both a little intoxicated. Zhongxian had bought an extra supply of wine for their pages, who had got themselves drunk and were now sound asleep.

"We've always slept in separate beds, never shared one," said Zhongxian. "Why don't we try it tonight?"

Wenzi was so drunk that without thinking he replied, "All right."

They undressed and got into bed. Wenzi wanted his own bedclothes, but Zhongxian said, "What's the point of having your own bedclothes when we're sharing the same bed?"

Wenzi agreed and joined him under his bedding. He lay on the inside, his back to the wall, and no sooner had his head touched the pillow than he fell asleep and began to snore. Zhongxian, who was far from ready for sleep, watched him intently, then stretched out his hand and began stroking Wenzi's leg. He had worked his way up to the midriff before Wenzi awoke with a start. "Why don't you go to sleep instead of bothering me like this?" he said.

Zhongxian smiled. "When I saw how soft and smooth your skin was, I began to feel it—purely as a gesture of affection, of course."

"Look, cut the nonsense and go to sleep!"

"There's also something very important that I need to talk to you about."

"It can wait till morning."

"What I have to say can't wait."

"Well, what is it that's so important, then?"

"To be frank, ever since we first met, I've adored your looks every minute of the day and night. I've longed for an intimate relationship with you, but I was always afraid of giving offense, so I didn't dare open my mouth. But that's what I had in mind that time when I started talking about close friends being the same as husband and wife. I'm hoping you'll take pity on me for my love and admiration and see your way to accepting me." He sat up and threw his arms around Wenzi.

Wenzi pushed him away and sat up himself.

"You and I have a friendship that's based on moral principle—how can you even *think* of such an evil thing? Our boys and the priests would find out about it and tattle, to say nothing of our friends, who'd gossip behind our backs. It's out of the question!"

But Zhongxian's passions were on fire, and he persisted. "We've been close friends all this time. Everyone knows that, and they'll never suspect us of anything like this. And even if they do talk, you'd just have to pretend you hadn't heard them." As he spoke, he made a wild lunge, but Wenzi evaded him, jumped down from the bed, and quickly dressed himself.

"I may lack ability, but I still hope to have a career," he said. "If I do such a disgraceful thing with you now and then one day I have a little success and think back on it, I'll die of shame!"

Zhongxian also got down from the bed. "What old fuddy-duddies you scholars are!" he said with a laugh. "In ancient times Mizi Xia was loved by Duke Ling of Wei, and Dong Xian was the special favorite of Emperor Ai of the Han dynasty. Both men were officials, and yet they didn't think it in the least disgraceful, so why should you, when you haven't even passed the exams? At the age of fifteen or sixteen it's considered nothing more than youthful fun and games—what's so shameful about it? If you still won't accept me, I'll just have to kowtow and beg you to." He dropped to his knees and rattled off an endless series of kowtows.

Wenzi was torn between anger and amusement. "Don't be so daft! You must be really drunk. Do get up!"

"If you won't agree, I'll go on kowtowing until next year."

"If you leave for home now and get married, you'll have your wedded bliss. You don't need to destroy *my* character!"

"If you'll accept me, I'm willing to go through life without ever marrying."

"That sort of thing might fool a two-year-old, but what makes you think it'll fool me?"

"If you don't believe me, I'll swear an oath right here and now." Throwing open the window, he knelt down and kowtowed twice to Heaven, then swore this oath: "O Heaven above, if I should take a wife after Pan Wenzi and I have sealed a pact of friendship, let me be devoured by tigers in the mountains or by fish in the sea. Let me be obliterated once and for all and never reborn. Or in warfare, let me be hacked into a thousand pieces. And if Pan Wenzi continues to reject me after I have sworn this oath, let me suffer those same afflictions anyway."

"Get on with you!" exclaimed Wenzi. "What do I have to do with your oath? Why drag me in?"

Zhongxian jumped up and caught hold of him. "Look, I've just sworn that oath. Do you mean to say you're still going to reject me?"

The hardest thing in the world to resist is endless importuning. Even the singularly high-minded Pan Wenzi was affected by Zhongxian's persistent pleading and unseemly antics, and his heart, once as hard as iron, now turned as soft as cotton floss. "Nobody is made of brass or stone," he said. "Since you're willing to renounce marriage for my sake, it would hardly be the act of a friend to keep on refusing you. But 'take care how ye end and how ye begin.'[28] Before we can seal our union, we'll need to choose an auspicious day and prepare a little wine and food as a wedding feast."

Zhongxian laughed. "Don't worry, I chose today with that in mind. The sun and moon are in the right conjunction for meetings[29] and weddings. We've exchanged our eight bows, and everything is set for a perfect union. There's no better day than today for meetings and weddings. The wine we drank just now was our wedding feast and the day after tomorrow will be our 'third day.'"

Wenzi smiled. "How *devious* of you! You planned this whole thing! And how stupid I was! I fell right into your trap."

"I come from Hubei, you come from Jiangsu, and we meet in Zhejiang. That's a sign of Heaven's will, not the result of any human scheme!"

As he spoke, he began removing Wenzi's clothes, then took him in his arms and laid him down on the bed. Wenzi, still affecting a coy embarrassment, put up only a half-hearted re-

---

28. A saying drawn originally from the *Shu jing* (Classic of documents; "Cai Zhong zhi ming").
29. I.e., the meeting between the heads of families before the wedding.

sistance in Zhongxian's tight embrace. Their two bodies came together, and Zhongxian breached his friend's defenses. Wenzi, virgin land beneath the plow, knitted his brows against the pain, the very picture of tender vulnerability, as Zhongxian gave free rein to his now violent passions and thrust with complete abandon.

> He took the scholar's erotic aperture
> In preference to the goddess's zone of love.[30]

In the course of their lewd pleasures, not only was Zhongxian carried away with delight, even Pan Wenzi was transported into a state of ecstasy—which surprised him, because he had never realized that such rapture existed. Women must obviously enjoy these pleasures, too, he thought to himself.

From this time on he made a bonfire of his scholarly ambitions and instead spent every day and night beside his friend, a far cry from their previous relationship. But unbeknownst to them, other people had already noted the tell-tale signs of their affair. Their classmates, jealous to a man, made up a "Hanging Branch" song, which they sang as follows:

> Wang Zhongxian,
> You lucky devil, you!
> Our young friend's as lovely as a flower,
> Yet somehow you wore him down.
> All night long he's with you;
> And you show him no mercy in the daytime too.
> A fine infertile couple you make!
> It's hard to tell the false from the true.

When first they heard the song, Wang Zhongxian and Pan Wenzi felt hurt but retained their composure and pretended they had no idea what it referred to. Later, however, their classmates took to taunting them and pulling faces at them, and

---

30. A reference to the "Gaotang Rhapsody" of Song Yu. It tells of King Xiang's dream of his meeting with the goddess of Mt. Wu. The "Rhapsody" supplies much of Chinese erotic imagery.

even their own pages could no longer stand the sight of their gross behavior and began talking behind their backs and saying how undignified it all was—talk that served only to inflame the monks in their part of the temple and made them drool with desire. The two youths soon realized that they could not go on living there.

At that point the song came to the ears of the Master himself. He asked the other students if it was true, and they related the whole story to him in great detail. Furious, he called the two students in and launched into a tirade about their dishonorable behavior, before expelling them both. They were not to hide out in the temple, lest they bring it into disrepute.

Wang Zhongxian accepted the decision, but Pan Wenzi was so ashamed that he would have liked to conceal himself somewhere. His face was as raw and red as if it had been flayed. Had a hole opened up in front of him, he would have thrown himself into it.

> You could scoop up the entire Qiantang River
> And still not wash all the shame from that face.

Deeply humiliated, Wenzi took leave of the Master and returned with Zhongxian to their room. Their classmates, knowing well enough that the pair had been expelled, made a point of coming to visit them, but Wenzi told the monks to say they were out. Then, stamping his feet, he raged on and on. "It's all the fault of those gossiping tattletales who provoked the Master into humiliating us like this! What on earth are we going to do now?"

"We certainly can't stay here. It occurs to me that your home isn't so far away. It might be best to go there and find some quiet place where we can help each other with our studies. That's one idea, anyhow."

"Impossible! Our pages know what happened, and when they get home they're bound to tell Father. They might even broadcast it outside the family, in which case I wouldn't be able to show my face anywhere. I now believe that success, fame, wealth, and honor are all ephemeral things; in any case, you can never count on them. Since for my sake you're never going to marry, and since I'm too ashamed to go home, we ought to find some remote place in the mountains where we can get away from all this bedlam and live free of social restraints. If we run short of food, we'll take our own lives and bring a perfect friendship to a close. What do you say?"

"If we can do that," exclaimed a delighted Zhongxian, "I'll have achieved my lifelong desire! But where should we go?"

"Some time ago an elderly priest visited the temple from Mt. Luofu[31] and told me that the scenery of Yongjia was superb. Mt. Luofu is cut off by the East Oujiang river—it's a heavenly place, a paradise. I had a talk with the priest and told him that if someday I were to visit Yongjia, I'd call on him, and he extended a warm welcome to me, and said that if I came I should ask for the priest Apratihata of the Prajna Temple; everyone would know who he was. We were not being serious at the time, but now I come to think of it, it strikes me as an ideal retreat from the world. What's more, there's somebody there whom we know and can rely on for help."

Once they had made their decision, they sold all of the splendid clothes they had been accustomed to wear, as well as their bedding and other belongings, and bought two suits of plain cotton and two bedrolls of coarse cloth. After that, they sent their pages home with letters severing relations with their parents and instructing their fiancées to marry other men. Then they packed up and took leave of the abbot, crossed the Qiantang River, and headed for Fuyang and Yongkang. They went first to Chuzhou and then to Yongjia, which they left through the Double Gate. Taking the ferry at Riverheart Temple, they went directly to Mt. Luofu and asked where they could find the priest Apratihata of the Prajna Temple. They learned then that he had died two months before, but his disciple Wuzhang, on hearing them say they were friends of the priest's, invited them to stay in the temple.

When Wenzi asked him to find them a place to live, Wuzhang said he happened to own a cottage himself at the foot of the mountain with a couple of acres under cultivation as well

31. Mt. Luofu, the storied retreat of Daoist and other masters, is actually far to the south, in Guangdong province.

as a good deal of hill country, and he wanted to sell both properties together. Wenzi and Zhongxian talked it over. The fields could supply them with food, and the hill country would serve two purposes: they could build tombs for themselves on part of it and gather firewood from the rest. So they bought both cottage and land for fifty taels. The central room of the cottage served as a sitting room, the room on the left as a bedroom, and the one on the right as a kitchen. They did not hire any servants, but did the cooking themselves. Their days were spent in leisurely artistic pursuits, in spontaneously expressing their feelings in poetry, and in playing the game of love. They also began building tombs, one for each of them, and appointed their tenant farmer as grave keeper. Within two months the tombs were finished. What a pity that for love of the rear courtyard, two young men should abandon their parents, reject their fiancées, and come to this remote hillside to make these final preparations! Were they not the greatest sinners between Heaven and Earth? Was this not one of the greatest oddities of human history? One of the greatest jokes of all time? As the poem says,

> Male and female, yes, but when did two males
> Ever take their vows as a lifelong pair,
> Cut all their bonds, and go live in the wilds,
> As their parents wait for the son and heir?

Let me turn to the two pages, Diligent and Oxboy, who had been told to take letters home. Oxboy, a dull-witted village boy, boarded a boat and set off. Diligent, who was smart and shrewd, understood the reason for the expulsion but was not inclined to return at once. Instead, he sold off his clothes and replaced them with plain cotton garments, as if he were about to set off on a long journey. He did not know where to go, and he hesitated before deciding to trail the two masters and see where they settled down before he returned home. He informed the monks in confidence as to what he planned to do and, after he had said goodbye to Oxboy, hid out in the temple. It occurred to him that although he had managed to skim off some of his master's travel expenses, it would not be enough for travel there and back, so he sold a few items of clothing to the temple assistants. After Wenzi and Zhongxian had set off and crossed the river, he began to follow them at a safe distance. He took a different ferry, then trailed them by land and water all the way to Mt. Luofu. Only when he learned that the two men had bought a place to live did he turn for home, traveling by day and night.

Unfortunately, some two weeks before his arrival Pan Du and the mother of Wenzi's fiancée had both died in an epidemic. Since the fiancée was a grown woman and alone in the world with no family to support her, Huiniang, Wenzi's mother, promptly took the girl into her own household and sent a servant to Hangzhou to call Wenzi home. She wanted him to see to his father's funeral and then marry the girl, despite the fact that the wedding would take place during the mourning period. After a dozen or more days the servant returned and reported that Wenzi had left the school a month before with a fellow student named Wang from Xiangyang. The present whereabouts of the pair were unknown. This news sent Huiniang into a deep depression, and she wept and wailed constantly. When Diligent arrived, she was at her wits' end and leapt to the conclusion that he brought good news. But when she tore open the letter, she found that it spoke of breaking off relations with his parents, renouncing any family of his own in order to study the Dao, and instructing his fiancée to find someone else to marry. In her bitterness and anger she first cried out to high Heaven, and then began asking questions.

In front of his mistress, Diligent could not bring himself to describe the many unseemly things the young master had done. He confined himself to saying that in the first few months Wenzi had worked really hard at his studies, but that later he had been corrupted by that scoundrel Wang and condemned by the Master, after which he decided to go and live at Mt. Luofu. Diligent also told her in great detail how he had trailed them and noted where they settled down. Huiniang ground her teeth in fury and began to curse Wang Zhongxian, calling down on him the most horrible of fates.

In her predicament, she invited a few relatives over to discuss how to get Wenzi home again. "What a worthless creature he is!" she exclaimed. "If we did as he said and had his fiancée marry someone else, I'd cut off my hair, go into a nunnery, and be done with it all!"

A man with some worldly experience commented, "There's no sense in being so hasty. Students have no idea what it's like to go hungry and so they rush off and study the Dao or whatever, but after a while, when their money runs out and they have nothing left to eat, they come scurrying home quick enough. Just now he's full of enthusiasm, and if you try to bring him back, he may not agree, and you'll have wasted all your travel money."

Huiniang saw the point and settled down to await her son's return.

Let me turn now to Oxboy. After braving the rigors of the journey, he arrived many days later in Xiangtan and handed the letter to his master, who asked him before opening it, "Has the young master been all right?"

"Not only has he been all right, but someone else has really been enjoying himself, too."

"What do you mean?"

At inordinate length Oxboy told him the full story of Wenzi's seduction. Wang Shanwen sighed. "This comes of Zhang Sanlao's sending the boy away," he said. He tore the letter open and read it.

Your son Zhongxian bows before you a hundred times. Since I took leave of you both and went to Hangzhou, due to my own natural stupidity I have made no progress in my studies. I have now sworn a pact of brotherhood with my roommate, Pan Wenzi. We are traveling about, visiting famous mountains and scenic places in order to study the Dao and learn to be immortals. You are both elderly, but you have my brother to attend on you, and I, your unworthy son, draw comfort from that fact. You need have no concerns about me. Please allow my fiancée, Miss Zhang, to marry someone else as soon as possible, lest she waste all her youth. The attached letter is for Zhang Sanlao. Kindly see that he receives it.

Your son Zhongxian, student of the Dao, bows before you a hundred times.

Shanwen stamped his feet and cried aloud in anguish, alarming his wife who, when she heard the news, fell sobbing to the floor. "He was perfectly all right while he was at home," she said. "It's all Zhang Sanlao's talk about Master Longqiu, or whatever his name is, that caused this scandal. And we don't even know where in the world he's gone! In any event, that spineless creature of ours is lost to us forever!"

Shanwen sent Oxboy to invite Zhang Sanlao over and showed him the letter. After he had read it, the room was filled with mutual recrimination as well as weeping and sobbing. No one had the least idea what to do. Then the Wangs' eldest son, Boyuan, came in and urged his father to calm down. "It's all my brother's fault for being such a worthless wretch. You mustn't put the blame on Zhang Sanlao. If his daughter is willing to marry someone else, there's nothing more to be said. But if she's determined not to marry, you'll just have to accompany Mr. Zhang and his daughter to the Pans' and put the onus on them to find your son and return him to you. At that point, you should deliver his fiancée to him and see where he decides to go."

Zhang Sanlao was quick to endorse the plan. He returned home and informed his daughter, then asked her in so many words if she would be willing to marry someone other than her fiancé. The girl was so overcome with embarrassment that she turned away and said nothing. "This will affect you for the rest of your life," he said to her. "Are you willing to or not? Come on, give me a clear answer—don't be tongue-tied. You're holding up both families."

Finally she gave way, murmuring, "As a woman, I know nothing about what they call higher principle, but I have heard that a loyal official doesn't serve a second ruler nor a virtuous woman take a second husband, and I shall hold to that. I don't wish to hear about anything else."

"In that case, nothing more needs to be said. I'll go over to the Wangs' tomorrow and talk to them about going to find the young master."

"If he doesn't come back, I'm quite prepared to spend the rest of my life alone. But if you're thinking of taking a long journey in hopes of finding him, that's out of the question! If the news ever got out, I'm afraid we'd be laughed to scorn."

"Look, whether you marry or not is up to you, but when it comes to searching for young Wang, that's my decision. If he doesn't come back, neither your parents nor your in-laws will be able to support you for the rest of your life. Tell me, what would you do in that case? And if people do laugh at us, well, it can't be helped."

She wept, not daring to say another word.

Next morning Zhang Sanlao went over and told Wang Shanwen of the girl's decision. At once they began making preparations for the journey. They had the people at the dock choose a boat for them and reserve suitable berths. Zhang Sanlao told his daughter to pack up and board the boat, and she had no choice but to comply.

Wang arrived with Oxboy. On board the boat he met his prospective daughter-in-law for the first time—a remarkable event in itself.

Setting off from Xiangyang, they sailed downstream and in less than twenty days reached Jingkou, where they changed boats. One more day brought them to Jinling. After Shanwen and Oxboy had gone ashore and asked the way to Pan Wenzi's house, the whole party headed there with their baggage.

Huiniang was suddenly confronted with the sight of three strange men and a girl coming into her house. She had no idea why they had come and was startled out of her wits. When she asked them, she found that she couldn't understand a word of their Xiangyang dialect. Fortunately Diligent came in at that moment and recognized Oxboy, and Huiniang finally realized that they were Zhongxian's father, prospective father-in-law, and fiancée, and that they had come for Zhongxian. The room soon filled with raucous quarreling.

Wenzi's fiancée heard and rushed out to see what was happening. After exchanging greetings with Zhang Sanlao's daughter, she asked, "Where are you from? And why all this commotion?"

Zhang Sanlao stepped forward, bowed, and explained in Mandarin the many reasons for their coming.

"It's purely by chance that we're meeting here," said Huiniang to Wang Shanwen. "There's never been the slightest connection between us. Your son and mine, that unworthy wretch, have exiled themselves somewhere or other. Come to think of it, your son is the older one, and so he's obviously to blame for seducing my boy. You can count yourself lucky that I'm not accusing you. What right do you have to come in here and demand your son from me? He's living in some place called Mt. Luofu in Yongjia. Why don't you go there and look for him? If you can bring back my wretch as well, I'll gladly go down on my knees to you."

Zhang Sanlao was nodding his head as she spoke. "You're quite right. Now that we know where they are, we can easily settle this." He added, "Mistress Pan, who might this young lady be?"

"She's my son's fiancée."

"So your son's not married either? In my humble opinion, since your son and my prospective son-in-law are both at Mt. Luofu, and since you have no other boy, we ought to take this young woman with us when we go. One way or another, we'll deliver their fiancées to them and complete our responsibilities as parents. They won't be able to stay on there—of course they'll have to come home. What do you say to that idea?"

"It sounds reasonable to me," she said.

She insisted that they stay there the night. Wang Shanwen and Zhang Sanlao slept in the outer rooms, while Zhang's daughter stayed in the inner quarters. The two fiancées, who were of similar age and caught in the same predicament, struck up a warm friendship. They shared a bedroom and spent the whole night in talk, the only drawback being that their accents differed so widely that they couldn't fully understand each other.

The next morning Huiniang began packing in preparation for the journey. She asked her brother and his wife to come over and look after the house while she was gone. In addition to her son's fiancée and Diligent, she also took a woman servant with her. Two boats were ordered, one for the men, the other for the women, and they went directly to Hangzhou, where they crossed the river and continued on their arduous journey by land and water until they arrived after many days at Mt. Luofu.

For Wang Zhongxian and Pan Wenzi, meanwhile, "joy at its height had given way to sorrow." From the moment they completed their tombs, both came down with a strange affliction that caused them to sing, chant, laugh, or cry. There were times when they climbed the hill and started howling madly. At other times, they went to the Prajna Temple and discussed the Buddhist law or the doctrine of cause and effect[32] with the priest Wuzhang. They seemed almost out of their minds. After fasting for a dozen days, they suddenly summoned Wuzhang and proceeded to donate their land and cottage to the temple. They also gave their clothes and money to the priest, and asked him to see to their funeral and burial. He assumed that the bequests arose out of delirium and consented just to humor them, little realizing that they were about to die that very night.

> They cared not that they weren't born in the same hour, day,
>   month, year;
> They cared only that they should die in the same hour, day,
>   month, year.

When the priest visited them next morning, he found them both dead—although their faces gave the impression they were still alive. He had his assistant buy joss sticks, paper money, and vegetarian food, and then go to the other Buddhist temples and invite a number of priests to come and participate. The following day was set aside for chanting sutras and laying the bodies in their coffins. Then, just as the final preparations were being made, in walked Diligent, followed by Huiniang, Wang Shanwen, and the rest of the party.

The visitors found the cottage full of priests and the lanterns ablaze. When they heard that the two youths had died the night before, Wang Shanwen fell sobbing to the floor while Hui-

---

32. The text specifies the doctrine of Matanga, an Indian monk who came to China during the Han dynasty. He is said to have translated the first sutra into Chinese.

niang gave way to heart-rending moans. Zhang Sanlao, standing beside them, wept for his prospective son-in-law. The dead men's fiancées, however, turned away and shed their tears in private.

Soon after the bodies had been laid in their coffins, the burial service was held.

Meanwhile, Zhang's daughter was thinking to herself, My father forced me into coming here to look for my fiancé, which was not the right thing to do. If I had been able to go back with him, well and good, but all this babble is enough to make one die laughing. What's more, I have many years ahead of me, and as my father said, he and my mother won't be able to support me, any more than my prospective in-laws will. My life is not due for a proper ending. Far better to die now and be done with it—and save myself all the public criticism." Her mind made up, she waited until the middle of the night when everybody was asleep, then quietly got up and hanged herself from one of the rafters.

It was daybreak before her body was discovered. Zhang Sanlao broke into heart-rending sobs, bitterly regretting his warning, which had resulted in his daughter's death. Wang Shanwen and Huiniang felt for him and consoled him as best they could. They arranged to buy a coffin and prepared for the funeral.

Strangely enough, Wenzi's fiancée had been struck by a similar idea. I came here to look for my fiancé, just as she did, she thought. She has shown her courage and determination, and I'm perfectly willing to follow her to the grave. If I were shameless enough to try and eke out a dishonorable existence while she lies there dead, just think how I'd be criticized! "A pretty face spells a sorry fate"—that's been the rule through the ages, and I'd rather die a noble death than live an ignoble life! She waited until midnight and then sought out a piece of rope and hanged herself.

When Huiniang noticed her body, she scrambled up and tried to resuscitate her, but it was too late; her breathing had ceased. This time Huiniang's grief was even more intense, and it moved Zhang Sanlao and Wang Shanwen to mourn with her.

They mourned for their children and those to whom their children had been betrothed, mourned fit to shake the heavens, mourned for one and all, indiscriminately. Their mourning startled the people in the surrounding villages and the priests in the local temples, who came flocking there to see what was amiss. All of them marveled at the extraordinary event. Another coffin was bought, and a laying-in ceremony was held for both girls.

Their parents asked Wuzhang to conduct a service for the souls of the dead, after which the girls were buried alongside the graves of Wang Zhongxian and Pan Wenzi. The parents also donated several dozen taels to Wuzhang to build up the soil there and plant trees. When all this had been done, they packed their belongings, lamented broken-heartedly one last time before the graves, and then said goodbye and left for home.

৵৯

In later times people noticed that whereas the pines on the women's graves stood straight and tall, the two huge trees on Zhongxian's and Wenzi's graves had interlocking branches, so that they appeared to be clasped in each other's arms. Lovebirds often nested in the treetops and sang to each other, and their songs went like this:

> Of the lovebird pair,
> Each had a wife,
> A wife he did not even know.
> Around the tombs the grasses thickly grow.

> Of the lovebird pair,
> Each had parents,
> Parents for whom they could not care.
> Around the tombs the grasses are trodden bare.

> Of the lovebird pair,
> Each had a home,
> A home they never again saw.
> Around the tombs the grasses grow forever more.

To this day legend has it that on Mt. Luofu there are lovers' tombs as well as lovebirds, and the reference is to this story of Wang Zhongxian and Pan Wenzi.

There is a poem that runs:

> A male lovebird pair? Intolerable!
> Day and night they make the west wind cry.
> Two virtuous women proved no match for men
> Who now together in joint graves lie.

Appendix

Two Sources

The two short classical tales translated below are both by Ming dynasty authors. "Zhang Jin" is the source of "The Rainbow Slippers," and "The Provincial Graduate" is the source of "The Reckless Scholar." For details, see "Notes on Texts."

Zhang Jin

Zhang Jin, who came from a wealthy family, was accustomed to spending his days among the courtesans. He chanced to see an extremely beautiful girl upstairs in a house on the street and directed amorous glances at her. Unable to express his feelings, he went constantly back and forth flirting with her, and she responded to his advances.

One evening of bright moonlight she was at her window gazing off into the distance when he wrapped up a billet-doux in his sash and threw it up to her. She responded with a red slipper. Although both had passionate feelings, they were always apart, she upstairs in her house and he on the street below, and there was no way they could meet. He asked everywhere if there were someone who knew her family well, and found Mrs. Lu, who sold flowers and face powder. He told her of his heartache and handed her a substantial bribe, and she consented to take the girl a message. She tucked the slipper in her breast pocket and made her way to the girl's house, where she dropped a hint about what she knew. The girl flushed, but denied it. Then Mrs. Lu told her in detail how strong Zhang's yearning was for her, and produced the slipper. The girl could no longer hide her secret and begged Mrs. Lu to think of a plan. Mrs. Lu told her to tie several cloths together, making them long enough to reach the ground. When Zhang came, he would give a cough as a signal, at which point she should open the window and let down the cloths so that he could climb up. She proposed a meeting that very night, and the girl agreed.

Mrs. Lu then went to see Zhang to report on her mission, but he happened to be out. She returned to her own house, where she found her son, a butcher, with a knife in his hand—he wanted to slaughter a pig and called out to his mother to help him tie it up. As she turned around, the slipper dropped out of her sleeve and fell to the floor. He asked her why she had it, and she was unable to keep her secret.

"So that's it! You must on no account do this. If it gets out, we'll be in terrible trouble."

"But I've already arranged it for tonight."

He flew into a rage. "If you don't do as I say, I'll have to inform the authorities lest I be implicated myself." He took the slipper away from her and hid it. There was nothing she could do.

Just then someone arrived from Zhang to ask for information. Since she didn't have the slipper any longer, there was nothing she could use for her plan, so she put him off, telling him to think of the future. At this news, Zhang's interest dwindled.

The butcher sneaked over to the girl's house under cover of darkness. As he expected, the upper-story window was half open and the girl was leaning out and gazing down as if waiting for someone. The butcher gave a slight cough, and she let down the cloths for him to climb up on. In the dark she thought he was Zhang and led him to the bed, where he took out the slipper and gave it to her, and then expressed his love. She felt even more certain that he was Zhang. Before dawn, she let down the cloths and he left the way he had come.

For half a year they enjoyed a passionate relationship, until her parents realized something was amiss and harshly interrogated her, threatening to give her a beating. She became afraid, and that night when the butcher came she told him, "My parents have been attacking me very severely. Please don't come again for the time being. Wait until they get over their worries before arranging another meeting."

The butcher agreed, but inwardly he was fuming with anger. He waited until she was fast asleep, then sneaked downstairs, picked up a kitchen knife, and killed both of her parents. He waited until dawn and then fled. She was completely unaware of what had happened.

When the sun was high in the sky and the front door still bolted, the neighbors shouted out but got no response. Timorously, the girl went downstairs and found both her parents beheaded. Panic-stricken, she opened the door. The neighbors then took her with them to the magistrate. He interrogated her under torture, and she confessed. At once he ordered Zhang brought to court. Zhang declared that he knew nothing about it, but the girl angrily denounced him and gave a detailed account of all that had happened. The magistrate hastily applied the torture instruments. Eventually, under extreme pain he made a false confession. Both he and the girl were sentenced to execution and in the meantime were held in prison.

"I really didn't kill anyone," Zhang protested to the jailers. "I never had relations with that girl. Now all of a sudden I'm going to be executed. It's my fate, that's all. But the girl had so much to say for herself that there must be something behind it. I would like to offer you ten taels to take me to her so that I can ask her the details. If I can do that, I'll die content." The jailers, eager for the bribe, agreed.

When the girl saw Zhang, she spoke in great bitterness and distress. "I was deceived by you and lost my innocence. How could you betray me like this, killing my parents and destroying my life?"

"I did propose the affair, but Mrs. Lu said it wasn't feasible, so I gave up hope. I *never* climbed up to your room!"

"She suggested that I tie some cloths together to form a ladder, and you came that night and gave me back the slipper as a token of good faith. After that you came every night. Why do you deny it?"

"Some scoundrel must have got hold of that slipper and deceived you. If I was really the one visiting you for half a year, you must be very familiar with my figure and my voice. Now take a good, hard look at me—am I the one or not?"

She hesitated, gazing at him for a long time as if in some doubt. When he asked her again, she said, "Your voice *is* rather different, and you're slimmer too. We were always in the dark, so I never had a chance to examine you closely. All I remember is that you had a scar at your waist the size of a copper coin. We can check to see if you have it. That should settle the matter."

Zhang undressed, and the jailers brought out candles and examined him. No scar was found. They realized then that he had been framed and declared that an injustice had occurred.

At dawn next day Zhang set out the evidence and appealed to the magistrate, declaring that he had given the slipper to Mrs. Lu. When she had been brought in and interrogated under torture, she repeated what her son had said to her. The son was arrested and, when his clothes were removed, the scar was found. He was dealt with according to the law, while Zhang was set free.

The Provincial Graduate

Mo, a provincial graduate from Guangxi, was passing through Jiangdu on his way to the metropolitan examinations in Beijing. An official in Jiangdu had a daughter fourteen years old who went to worship in a temple, and Mo happened to be strolling about. Before offering the incense, the girl washed her hands, and her maid passed her a cloth to dry them on. Mo then went to the water himself and washed his hands and then began wiping them on the formal clothes he was wearing. The girl gave her maid a look to indicate that she should hand Mo the cloth. He considered this a romantic encounter. Waiting until the maid came out, he took some money from his pocket and gave it to her and asked her to convey his thanks to the girl.

This made the girl angry, and she ordered the maid to take the money back. "I want you to thank your mistress for me," Mo said. "The money is of no significance." The maid reported this to her mistress, who was afraid other people might learn about the incident. She ordered the maid to tell him to leave at once, lest it give rise to gossip.

"But I want to see her," said Mo. "Unless I do, I'm not leaving this place—even if I have to stay here forever!"

There was nothing she could do. She took one of her hairpins and a handkerchief and told her maid to give them to him in thanks, saying, "My mistress appreciates your kind intention, sir, but it would be improper for her to meet you. These gifts are her response to you. She hopes you will now give up your idea and leave."

"The fact that she gives me these things means that she is hoping for a meeting," he said to the maid.

On hearing this, the girl regretted ever giving him the items, but the deed was done. After a great deal of hesitation, she said, "On such-and-such a day, a religious service will be held at our house, and at dusk the god will be ceremonially sent off from our doorway. This man can see me once at the door, but that is all." When the maid reported this to him, Mo was delighted.

On the evening of that day, the girl did appear and, after giving a bow, turned and went in again. Mo took advantage of the general confusion to suddenly follow her in. When she arrived at her room, it was getting dark, and she pressed him to leave. "Now that I'm here, I can't leave," he said. "My hopes of a career are at an end. By giving me a hairpin and a handkerchief, you invited me here, and if we cannot be together now, death is the only course for me." He drew a dagger from his stocking and went to cut his throat.

She was horrified, and kept him with her, remaining in her room and pretending to be ill. Anticipating that news of the affair would eventually get out, they absconded one night, taking the maid with them.

Her family was aghast at losing their daughter. Since she was already engaged to the son of another official, they were afraid that the news would leak out and lead to a lawsuit. At that time one of their maids was sick, and so they poisoned her to death and made out that it was their daughter who had died. They had the body buried with the ceremony due a daughter.

Mo took the girl home, where she bore him two sons. A few years later, he succeeded in the metropolitan examinations and was appointed magistrate of a county next to Jiangdu. He brought his wife to his place of office and also visited her father.

After a long time, having established a close relationship with her father, Mo invited him to his official residence, where he had arranged a feast. They drank until nightfall, when he called on his wife to come out and pay her respects. The former maid was also present.

Her father was thunderstruck. "So *this* is where you've been! It all comes of your disgraceful behavior; it's not your husband's fault. But when I lost my daughter, I was afraid her fiancé's family would learn of it, and I gave out that she had died of an illness. From now on we must keep this absolutely secret. I won't dare visit you frequently. When you've finished your term and have been transferred elsewhere, naturally I'll come and see you." With that, he took his leave.

Mo was later appointed to a high position, and both of his sons served as officials.

What business was it of hers that he was drying his hands on his own clothes? The look she directed at her maid to offer him the cloth inevitably showed that she had feelings for him. Her gift of the hairpin and handkerchief was even more likely to give rise to gossip. And as for her appearance in the doorway—how can that be justified? Her heart must have been overflowing with loving thoughts—the only problem being that she was a novice and lacked the expertise of an old hand. She won this reprobate of a scholar, who behaved more and more outrageously, and eventually they came to share a close and harmonious relationship. But supposing he had already been married to a jealous wife, what would have become of this girl then? What a risk she took! Why didn't she think of that?[1]

1. This paragraph was appended to the tale by the commentator in the *Qing shi leilüe*.

Notes on Texts

The first edition of *Xing shi hengyan* (Constant words to awaken the world) was published in 1627 by Ye Jingchi of Suzhou. The compilation is attributed to Keyi Jushi (The Keyi Recluse) and the editing to Molang Zhuren (Master of the Ink-Wild Studio). Keyi Jushi was presumably Feng Menglong, and Molang Zhuren may have been the pseudonym of the writer responsible for many of the stories. Keyi Jushi's preface is dated the equivalent of 1627. There are occasional notes in the upper margins as well as wood-block illustrations for almost all of the forty stories. A facsimile edition is available in the *Guben xiaoshuo congkan* series published by the Zhonghua shuju in Beijing in 1991. The translated stories with their positions in the collection are "Shengxian" (14), "The Oil Seller" (3), "Marriage Destinies Rearranged" (8), "The Rainbow Slippers" (16), and "Wu Yan" (28).

The first edition of *Shi dian tou* (The rocks nod their heads) was published by the same Ye Jingchi of Suzhou, who also published a historical novel by Feng Menglong. The author of *Shi dian tou* is given as Tianran Chisou (Foolish Old Man of Nature). Feng Menglong contributed the preface, which refers to the author as "Langxian" (Free-Spirited Immortal). Feng also wrote the occasional notes. There is one wood-block illustration for each of the fourteen stories. A facsimile edition was published by the Dalian chubanshe in Dalian in 2000 (series title *Dalian tushuguan guxiben Ming Qing xiaoshuo congkan*). "The Reckless Scholar" is no. 5; "The Lovers' Tombs" is no. 14.

The translation "Zhang Jin" is from the *Qing shi leilüe, juan* 18, 1:546–548. For an earlier version of the tale, which is practically identical, see Sun Kaidi, *Xiaoshuo pangzheng*, pp. 168–169. (The version is from the *Jing lin xuji* by the sixteenth-century author Zhou Xuanwei.) The *Qing shi leilüe* places it in the category of "The Impediments of Passion," subcategory "False Charges." The translation "The Provincial Graduate" is from "Mo Juren," *Qing shi leilüe, juan* 3, pp. 82–83. "Mo Juren" is in the "Clandestine Liaisons" category, subcategory "Clandestine Liaisons Resulting in Marriage." This version is a reprint of a Ming tale. The seventeenth-century compendium *Yuexi congzai* contains (in *juan* 17) the almost identical text (without the comment) and gives the source as *Tan lin* (Forest of tales). The *Tan lin*, which is no longer extant, is listed in the library catalog of Zhao Yongxian (1535–1596). See his *Zhao Dingyu shumu* (Shanghai: Gudian wenxue chubanshe, 1957), p. 146. It is impossible to know for certain, in this case as in that of "Zhang Jin," whether the author of this vernacular story relied on the earlier version or on the reprint.

About the Translator

PATRICK HANAN is Victor S. Thomas Professor of Chinese Literature, Emeritus, at Harvard University. He is the author of *The Chinese Vernacular Story*, a history of the genre, and the translator of many works of Chinese traditional fiction, including *The Carnal Prayer Mat* and *The Sea of Regret*.

Production Notes for Hanan/*Falling in Love*

Cover design by Santos Barbasa Jr.

Text design by University of Hawai'i Press production staff with text in New Aster and display in Aristoteles Script

Text composition by Tseng Information Systems, Inc.

Printing and binding by Versa Press

Printed on 60 lb. Glatfelter Writers Book, 360 ppi